Always Love You More

Lauren Monica

Copyright © 2026 by Lauren Monica

All rights reserved.

No part of this publication may be reproduced, distributed, or transmitted in any form or by any means, including photocopying, recording, or other electronic or mechanical methods, without the prior written permission of the publisher, except as permitted by U.S. copyright law. For permission requests, email contact@laurenmonicawrites.com.

The story, all names, characters, and incidents portrayed in this production are fictitious. No identification with actual persons (living or deceased) is intended or should be inferred.

All brand names and product names used in this book are trademarks, registered trademarks, or trade names of their respective holders. The author is not associated with any product or vendor in this book.

Book Cover Illustration: Kate Lozovska

Book Cover Design: Angelee Van Allman

Copy Edit: Kristin Campbell

ISBN 979-8-9887867-5-7

ISBN (ebook) 979-8-9887867-6-4

Visit the author's website at laurenmonicawrites.com

Author's Note

Always Love You More is a prequel to *A Yes or No Question*, following Sam and Jameson's story. It can be read before or after reading *A Yes or No Question*.

This story deals strongly with grief. It is my hope that I handled the topic with care, but please keep this in mind when going into the book.

This book also contains heavy topics, such as abuse, violence, mental health challenges, and substance/alcohol abuse.

These characters are incredibly close to my heart, and I hope you enjoy reading their story as much as I enjoyed writing it.

To those who have been made to feel like you're too much or not enough, may you find someone who always loves you more.

Part 1: The Summer We Met

Chapter 1

Jameson - 16 Years Old

I'm jolted awake when I feel the cool barrel of a gun pressed against my temple.

I don't move.

I barely even breathe.

A familiar voice grates against my skin. "Get out of it."

I know I have to be quick—that's part of the game—so I take in everything I can from the position I'm in.

He's crouched over the mattress. Obviously, one of his hands is on the gun, but where's the other one?

My gaze is fixed on the ceiling. I blink a few times, adjusting to the bright overhead light as I think. I can't turn to look at him without pressing the gun further into my head. I could roll to the left and off the other side of the mattress, but that leaves me exposed, so he could easily get on top of me. And he'll see that as running away.

His words echo through my mind—*If you can't walk away on top, don't bother walking away at all.*

I feel him shift. He's running out of patience.

I reach out for his other hand, finding it on the floor, where I hoped it would be. He's using it to keep himself upright as he leans over me.

He wobbles as I knock him off balance, and the gun lowers for just long enough that I can get up and push him to the floor. I drop my heel down over his hand, and his fingers loosen around the gun from the force of it. I grab the gun and, using my legs to pin his arms, I straddle his chest and point it at him.

A smile spreads across his face. "Good."

Inside, I sag in relief, but I keep my posture rigid, my face unreadable.

He looks at me expectantly. "Get up."

I stand, allowing him to follow.

"And give me back my gun," he says, holding out his hand.

I drop it into his open palm, waiting as he tucks it into the back of his jeans.

"Jameson."

"Yes, sir," I answer, the response immediate.

"What did I tell you about overthinking things?"

"It gets you killed."

He points to the mattress. "If I wasn't your old man, you would have been dead before you even made a move." He pauses. "Trust your gut. I know the first thing you thought about is where my other hand was. Getting me off balance."

I nod.

He keeps his stare trained on me, and I push down the unease that always comes when he gives me these looks. He's waiting for me to break, and he can always tell the second I do.

I've gotten better at faking it. And now, with years of practice, I can completely lock the fear away.

Finally, he turns to leave. "Don't hesitate again," he says, shutting the door behind him.

I wait until I hear his footsteps fade before letting go of the breath I've been holding since he woke me up. Pacing in front of my bed, I try to calm down, but I'm too amped up, asking for a fight.

Grabbing my pillow, I press it against my face and scream into it until it feels like I can't breathe. Then, slamming it against the bed, I drop to my knees and pound my fists against the mattress, swinging until I'm panting.

Slowly, I get up, walk over to the light switch, and turn it off. The glow of my alarm clock burns through the darkness, showing that it's just past three in the morning.

I hate it when he does this in the middle of the night. It's always so hard to get back to sleep.

Dropping down onto the mattress, I prop my pillow up and lean back, fighting the urge to remove it and slam my head against the wall. Instead, I grab the DVD player from the floor beside me and pull the attached headphones over my ears.

As I wait for it to power up, I run my hand along the side of the mattress until it catches on my knife, sliding my thumb along the side of it enough times until I believe it's there. Satisfied, I settle back, pulling the sheet up over my bare chest as the movie starts.

LOYALTY

My eyes snap open at the sound of my alarm, surprised I'd fallen asleep. After untangling the headphones that are wrapped around me, I drag a hand down my face and wish I could be anywhere but inside my own body. My head is killing me, and my ribs are aching from yesterday, as I stumble to the bathroom.

I'm grateful to find it empty and take a quick shower. It doesn't do much to wake me up, but I know I don't have a lot of time, so I move through the motions of getting ready before heading to the kitchen.

As I round the corner, I'm met with the smell of coffee and the sound of oil popping. My mother is bent over the stove, her light pink robe hanging loosely around her. She turns as she hears me walk in. "Mornin', baby."

"Mornin', Ma," I answer, stepping around her to grab a mug.

"I'm doing eggs," she says. "You want yours fried?"

I nod, reaching for the pot of coffee and pouring myself a cup.

Leaning against the counter, I look over at the kitchen table and note all the things laid across it. There's no room for me to sit, but I don't move anything.

I learned that lesson the hard way.

I'm almost done with my coffee when I hear heavy boots thumping down the hall. I can already tell what mood he's in by the way he's dragging his feet.

My father turns the corner, and his eyes go right to the table before he slides them over to me. "There a reason you're lounging back, looking at this mess, instead of doing something about it?"

"Last time you told me—"

The look on his face shuts me up.

This is what he does. Why I can't ever win with him.

He makes situations where, either way you're wrong, 'cause that way he's always right.

That's another thing I learned young—he's *always* right. If he tells you two plus two is five, you nod your head and accept it as a fact. So, that's what I do. I move to the table and start to clear it off.

He watches me as I grab the empty beer cans and toss them into the trash. Next, I go for the motor oil, toothbrush, and .45, trying not to think about the one I had pressed against my head last night.

I look up at him, asking where he wants me to put everything.

I know where it goes, but I never assume.

"Garage," he says.

Nodding, I step around him and yank open the side door. The wooden stairs creak under my boots as I head for the safe.

After punching in the code, I spin the handle and pull the door open. Setting the gun beside the others, my eyes catch on a tray of watches.

Those weren't here last week.

I want to pull the tray out and look at them, but I don't. Instead, I lock away my questions, shut the safe, and head back inside.

The second I walk into the kitchen, my father's eyes meet mine. He's waiting to see if I'll ask about them.

I play through all the scenarios, trying to decide if I should. *If he wants me to.*

He knew I'd see them when he sent me out there, but I can't tell if this is a test in keeping quiet or in speaking up.

I take in his posture.

It's relaxed. He's leaning back in his chair, arms crossed over his chest. His mouth is set in a thin line, like he's purposely trying to hide any tell, but he still has one. His right brow is arched, as if he's daring me to say something.

Quiet then. He wants me to be quiet.

I drop into my seat, and he shifts, bringing his elbows to the table.

"Any trouble?"

"All good," I answer.

"Good," he says, and with that word, I know I guessed right.

My mother sets down a mug of coffee in front of him then moves back to the stove, returning a minute later with his plate of food.

She brings mine next before finally sitting down with her cup of coffee. She never eats breakfast. Instead, she lights a cigarette and picks at her long red nails.

My father's fork scrapes against the plate as he cuts into his eggs, the yolk running into his toast. I wait until he's taken his first bite before cutting into my own.

He looks up from his food, glancing around the table. "Orange juice?"

My mother follows, looking around like, at any moment, it'll just appear.

"I've got it," I say, pushing my chair back, but I only get so far before it stops, blocked by my father's leg.

"I didn't ask you," he grits out.

I picture what it would feel like to lean forward and grab him by the collar of his shirt. To slam my fist against his face and see his eyes go wide with shock.

But I keep still, my attention shifting to my mother as she stands and mumbles an apology, coming back a minute later with a glass of orange juice.

I scooch my chair in and start eating again, if only to give my hands something to do.

I'm halfway through my plate when she finishes her cigarette. Stubbing it out, she says, "We need groceries, and I don't have enough."

My father cuts his eyes to her. "I just gave you money a few days ago."

"We needed things for the house. Cleaning stuff," she rambles on.

"Uh-huh," he grunts, pulling a clip of money from his back pocket. He sets down three twenties on the table. "I want to see the receipt when you get home."

She blows out a breath. "Come on, Levi. Seriously?"

He tips his head to the side and slips his voice into that tone you never want to hear. "Yes, seriously." He leans forward. "Do you really want to have this conversation right now?"

Her eyes drop as she shakes her head. "No."

"That's what I thought."

She snatches the money from the table without meeting his eyes. Then, starting to stand, she murmurs, "I've gotta go get dressed."

He grabs her wrist. "I'm not done eating yet."

Slowly, she lowers herself back into her seat, while my father picks his fork back up and turns toward me.

"Now, you—"

A loud pounding interrupts him, and if I could, I'd flinch.

He drags his eyes from me to the door and tips his head in its direction. I follow his silent command and go to answer it.

I keep myself hidden and slide back the small curtain that covers the top of the door just enough to see who's there.

Marcus.

Pulling it open, I squint from the morning sun. Raising a hand to block out the brightness, I find him staring at me with that unhinged smile he always has, making the scar that runs from his eye to the bottom of his lip crinkle.

He pushes past me, always in a rush, and I follow behind him, sliding back into my seat.

He stops in front of the table and gets right to the point, not even bothering with a hello. "Got a new kid I want you to meet."

Marcus is always trying to do anything he can to impress my father. He's been around since before I can remember, climbing his way up to be my father's second years ago.

"We don't need any more strays," my father answers.

Marcus shifts with excited energy. "Just wait till you see what this kid can do, though."

"Who's his old man?"

"Some deadbeat drunk. He wants to make some quick cash. Seems real motivated."

My father sets down his coffee cup. "All right, fine. When do you have him coming in?"

"This afternoon," he answers.

A horn sounds from outside, and I look at the clock.

Right on time.

"I've gotta get to school," I say, waiting to be excused.

My father waves a hand. "Go."

I stand, starting for the door, when he calls my name and I turn back to look at him.

"Come to the garage right after school. You've got errands today."

Fuck.

"Yes, sir," I answer.

Chapter 2

Jameson

I slam the car door shut after getting in, and Billy snaps his head in my direction. "You good?"

I nod, sinking back into my seat.

Luke catches my eyes in the rearview mirror, and I blink them closed, reminding myself that he isn't my old man.

They look just like each other.

"You sure?" Billy asks again.

"I'm fine," I mumble, rolling my shoulders and dropping my bag onto the floor.

Luke looks at the house then back to me with that same face he always gets, the one that makes me feel like my skin is too tight for my body.

We've been down this road before, and it's never gotten me anywhere but worse off.

Still, I hate the pity on his face.

I hate the curl to his lips.

And the tick of his jaw.

But most of all, I hate the guilt in his eyes.

Because none of this is his fault.

He may be my uncle, but there's nothing he can do.

I lean down, unzipping my bag, and feel the car jerk forward. "Do you have the ...?" I start before hearing a paper being waved in front of my face. I grab it, seeing Billy's finished algebra homework. "Thanks," I tell him, smoothing out my own balled-up paper.

I spend the rest of the car ride scribbling down his answers, listening to him and Luke talk, trying not to hate myself for how jealous I feel at the ease of their conversation.

We pull up in front of the school, and Luke slows to a stop. Billy holds out his hand, and I give him his homework, just as his attention catches on a blonde girl walking by. He basically throws himself out of the car to catch up with her.

Luke lets out a shallow laugh. "This one's new."

I hum back a non-response because we both know he'll likely be on to someone else by next week.

After shoving my paper back into my bag, I reach for the door handle just as Luke says, "Jameson."

"Yeah," I mutter, glancing over at him. He gives me that fucking look again, and I instantly turn back to the door.

He waits for a minute, and I give it to him before finally he says, "Have a good day."

His words hit me harder than words as simple as that should, and I tuck them away into that place inside myself.

"You, too," I answer before pushing the door open and stepping out of the car.

I walk past Billy, and he trails after me with what's-her-name tucked under his arm. Kids move out of the way, stepping to the side when they see us coming.

I don't know when people started reacting to me like this, though it's not much of a surprise. I have a short temper and a last name that a lot of people know stories about.

Me and Billy get a lot of cling-ons—people who like the idea of us. Who want to play pretend or try us on. Like what's-her-name, who's now giggling in that obnoxious way girls do. The kind where you know that's not really their laugh and they don't think what you just said was all that funny. But Billy just soaks it in. He always does. I don't even think he cares that it's fake.

"I tried calling you this weekend," she says, looking up at him.

Before he can answer, I tip my chin, letting him know I'm out. I've heard this back and forth before and don't feel like listening to it again.

He nods in response then quickly turns his attention back to the blonde.

Breaking away from them, I push up the sleeves of my flannel and pull my sunglasses out of the front pocket. I throw them on as I make my way over to the wall. It's out by the side of the school, an old storage shed that they half tore down. It's sort of become our place.

Mason yells out to me as he sees me walking up, kicking his feet back and forth as they dangle over the cement. A few other heads look in my direction, faces that I guess I'd call friends.

Other than Billy, there's nobody I really like to spend time with. I hang around 'cause it's what you do, and it's better than being at home, but I could take it or leave it.

I've known Mason forever. He lives on the street behind mine. He's pretty chill, but he's kind of a leech—always wants something from you.

"We're all going to the park after school. You wanna come?"

"Can't," I answer.

He jumps down from the wall, landing in front of me. "Why not?"

"I've got stuff to do."

His eyes light up like he's in on a secret, as if everyone doesn't already know. "What about after?"

"Don't think so," I say, my voice harder this time.

He kicks the rocks at his feet, and I know what's coming.

"We were just hoping you might bring some weed."

And there it is.

I roll my neck. "You got money?"

"Oh, come on, man; we're friends," he says, throwing his hands out in front of him.

"The shit's not free."

"But, I mean, we just heard—"

The glare on my face has him swallowing the end of the sentence.

His eyes drift over my head, and I follow them, finding Billy coming up behind me.

"Hey," he says with that easy smirk he always has plastered on his face.

He must have ditched the blonde.

Mason's shoulders relax as he turns his efforts toward Billy. "Been seeing you around with Madison Sanders. She's hot, man." When Billy doesn't answer, he keeps going. "We're all going to the park tonight. You should come. Ask Madison if she wants to come, too."

Billy turns to me, and the look I give him lets him know I'm not going.

"Maybe," he answers.

"Cool, cool." Mason nods just as Dylan jumps down next to him.

Out of everyone, Dylan's probably who I get along with the best. He doesn't talk much, and when he does, it isn't annoying.

"I finally got the garage cleaned out," he tells Billy, "so we can start using it after school."

"Hell yeah," Billy shoots back.

They've been wanting to get a band together for months.

"I talked to Rowan, he's in." Dylan tips his head toward Mason, "He's in, too, so I think we're good." Glancing over at me, he asks, "Sure you don't wanna join?"

"Yeah, no, thanks. I can't play anything for shit."

His lips twitch, trying to keep a straight face. "We could put you on triangle. Something easy like that."

Billy bursts out laughing. "Imagine him holding a triangle and hitting it with the little stick, looking like he wants to murder the thing."

I shove his arm. "Fuck off."

"Aw ... don't worry; you can come watch us practice." Billy grins. "Be our groupie."

I take a step toward him. "You want me to beat your ass?"

"Oh, like you could," he answers as everyone's eyes ping pong between us.

I raise an eyebrow, and he stares back at me, squaring up and bouncing on his feet. He throws an uppercut, making a swooshing noise, and says, "Come and get me."

Licking back a smile, I shake my head. "You're such an idiot."

He barrels toward me, throwing his arm around my neck and ruffling my hair. "You love me."

If anyone else did that to me, they'd be flat on their back right now, with my fist in their face. But he's right; I do love him, and he's the only one who gets away with messing with me like this.

We grew up more like brothers than cousins, since we're so close in age. I'm only two months older, so we've been in the same grade all through school. We even had the same kindergarten class.

I push him off me as he looks toward the school.

"Gotta get to class," he says. "We have that lab today."

I have science first period, and the only good thing about the class is that Billy has it, too. Although, it doesn't really matter since he isn't my lab partner anymore.

The teacher gave us assigned seats at the beginning of the year, putting us all in alphabetical order, meaning me and Billy were paired up next to each other.

We were partners for the first few weeks until we got a little carried away with the Bunsen burner and were moved to opposite sides of the room.

Now, I'm paired with a girl who's a bit of a goody-goody. She's all right, but I catch her watching me a lot. I don't know if it's 'cause she's scared or she has a crush. Either way, it's been working out fine for me since she makes it real easy to copy off her tests, and she does most of the work on the labs.

After walking into the classroom, I slide into my chair, letting my head come down to rest against my arm while I wait for the rest of the kids to show up.

A few minutes later, I hear shuffling next to me and squint my eyes open to see the girl settle in beside me. She flashes a small smile, and I let my eyes close again.

I stiffen when I feel a hand tap my arm before I bolt upright and snatch it, blinking the room into focus. Realizing it's just my lab partner, I drop her wrist, blowing out a breath.

"S-sorry," the girl stutters. "You fell asleep, and I didn't want Mrs. Campbell to give you another detention."

I try to soften my face and nod. "Thanks."

She quickly turns back to the worksheet in front of her then slides it over to me. "I'm on step three."

The rest of the class drags by as we work through the lab. By the time the bell rings, I'm already ready for this day to be over.

I manage to make it to my last class without falling asleep again, but the teacher could be speaking another language for all I know. I haven't heard one thing that's come out of his mouth since I sat down here an hour ago. My body is all locked up, thinking about going to the garage this afternoon.

What's he gonna have for me today?

"What about you, Jameson?"

"Huh?"

Mr. Roberts purses his lips. "What did you think the ending of the book symbolized?"

I look up at the copy of *Lord of the Flies* in his hand. "I don't—"

"Did you finish the book?" he interrupts.

When I don't answer, he lets out a sigh. "How far did you get?"

I haven't even opened the thing.

He watches me like I'm not worth the effort, and after a minute of waiting for me to respond, he moves on to someone else.

The final bell cuts off their answer, and I move to slip out of the room as Mr. Roberts says something about a test next week.

He calls out to me that he isn't finished yet, but I ignore him.

I can't be late.

Chapter 3

Sam - 15 Years Old

I grab the girl pinned beneath me by her ponytail and pull. She lets out a shriek and swings her leg, trying to roll out from under me, but misses.

"Say it again," I warn.

She throws her elbow back, connecting with my stomach, and I slump forward as the air leaves my lungs. Rolling on top of me, she switches our positions. "You're a slut."

"I'm gonna—"

My words are cut off when a sharp pain slices down my face.

"Break it up," someone yells just before she's hauled off of me by a teacher.

I run my hand over my face and find my fingers red.

The bitch scratched me.

Jumping to my feet, I lunge for her.

"Whoa, whoa, whoa," someone bellows as I feel a pair of hands grab my wrists and pull them behind my back.

"Don't fucking touch me!" I shout, trying to break out of their hold.

"Principal's office—now," the person behind me cracks, and I look over my shoulder, finding another teacher.

"I have to catch my bus," I say, my gaze falling to the line of buses in front of the school and the waiting kids who are all watching us.

He tightens his grip on my wrists. "Yeah, that's not happening."

The other teacher is already leading the girl inside, and I realize I'm not getting out of this.

"Fine," I relent, yanking my arms forward. "But get your hands off me."

I'm surprised when he lets go, not having expected him to actually listen. I turn toward him, and he winces when he sees my face.

"I'll take you to the nurses office first."

"I'm fine," I mutter, watching the buses pull away.

Shit.

He shakes his head. "I'd really feel better if you got that looked at."

Reluctantly, I follow him to the nurses office. She cleans out the scratch, bandages it, and sends us on our way.

I trail after him in silence to the principal's office, and he pulls open the door, ushering me inside. Dropping into the open chair, I look from the girl to Principal Hansley.

"Miss Barlowe," he greets me. "How nice to see you again."

I scoff, and his eyes narrow.

Principal Hansley is ancient. He was all of my siblings' principal, too, and he's judged me based on them since the first time he met me.

He shifts his attention to the girl next to me, and his face softens. "Sophia told me you attacked her while you were waiting for your buses."

I turn toward her. "She looks fine to me."

"She pulled my hair and threw me onto the ground," the girl whines.

I bring my hand up to my face. "She got me back, so seems like we're even."

Principal Hansley leans forward, resting his elbows on the desk. "Self-defense is not the same thing as initiating a fight."

"It's not like I did it for no reason. I don't even know who she is."

He levels me with a hard stare. "So, why did you do it then? What happened that made you think it was okay to assault someone?"

I wave my hand in her direction. "Come on; you're calling *that* assault?"

He raises a brow. "Well?"

"Well, what?"

He lets out a long breath and turns to the girl, "Did you do something to get a reaction from Samantha?"

"I told her—"

"Sam," I snap, cutting her off.

Principal Hansley tilts his head. "Excuse me?"

"Sam. My name is Sam. You know that. I tell you every time."

He brings his focus back to the girl like I didn't even say anything. "Continue," he tells her.

She shifts in her seat and mutters, "I called her a slut."

I watch for his reaction, but there's nothing. No disgust. No shock. He just stares back at her like he isn't surprised at all by what she just confessed.

He opens a drawer in his desk and says, "I see." After writing something across the sheet, he hands it to me. "Two weeks of detention."

"*Two weeks*? That's basically the rest of the year."

He pulls out another sheet of paper. "You're lucky it's not a suspension. End up here another time before the summer, and your luck will run out." He slides the other piece of paper to the girl but doesn't say anything.

"How long does she get?"

"That's none of your business."

"That's bullshit. I bet you let her off with nothing."

He snatches back my sheet and crosses something out. "You just earned yourself another week with that language."

"Seriously?"

Jerking his head up, he points at the girl but keeps his eyes on me. "You might want to take a page from her book and learn to be quiet. You're not doing yourself any favors." He doesn't give me any time to respond before he asks her, "Who am I calling to give you a ride home?"

After he calls her mother, Principal Hansley dials my home number. I wish he wouldn't. I don't want my father to pick up, but he pulls it from the system without asking.

We all sit awkwardly as it rings with no answer.

"Do you have anyone else I can call?" Principal Hansley asks with a smug look on his face. "What about Carson? He must have only just left."

My brother Carson is a grade above me and the school's star quarterback. He's also a complete asshole, so I give him my oldest brother Johnny's number instead.

It picks up on the second ring, and I sit back as he tells my brother what happened. After setting the phone down, Principal Hansley says, "Well, he didn't sound very happy."

I don't respond, and silence stretches between us before he finally waves his hand toward the door, signaling that we can go. "Make better choices, Miss Barlowe. I don't want to see you in here again."

LOYALTY

After waiting in the library for thirty minutes, I figure my brother is probably here by now, so I pack up my bag and head for the front of the school.

Pushing open the door, I squint against the sun and wince as the fresh cut on my face pulls with the movement.

My brother takes a step forward from his place leaning against the car door, a cigarette perched between his fingers. "You okay?"

"Fine," I answer.

He looks from my bandage, to the school, then back to my face again.

"Really, Johnny, I'm fine." My attention catches on his hand. "Can I get one of those?"

"No, you can't."

"Why not?" I groan.

"Because you're in trouble. What did I tell you about fighting?"

"It wasn't my fault," I huff.

"It never is," he says, stomping the cigarette out with his boot and rounding the car. "Come on, or I'm gonna be late."

"Late for what?"

He throws the door open. "A job thing."

"What kind of job thing?" I ask, sliding into my seat.

"The kind that pays money."

I roll my eyes.

"So what happened with this fight?"

"Nothing."

"Nothing?"

"I don't want to talk about it."

He eyes me wearily. "You can tell me anything."

"I know."

He arches a brow, and I realize he's not going to let this go.

"She said something to me."

"Something you couldn't have just walked away from?"

I snort. "Would you actually have wanted me to?"

"What'd she say?"

My shoulders drop. "I really don't want to talk about it."

We pull up to a light, and he turns toward me, scanning my face like he's looking for a clue. "All right, but if you change your mind, I'm here."

I dip my chin. "Thanks."

He leans over and messes with my hair. "You're a good kid. Okay?"

I swat his hand away. "Okay, *Dad*."

"Fuck you." He laughs. "I'm trying to be nice." He throws the pack of cigarettes at me. "Here, I'll balance it out with some corruption."

A laugh slips from my lips as I flip up the center console to look for a lighter. Finding one, I glance up just as we pull through an open gate.

My stomach sinks and my head whips toward him. "The job is here?"

Chapter 4

Jameson

The front door opens, and I glance up as it chimes. A rough-looking kid walks in, probably the age where he just finished school. He strides up to the desk, with a determined look on his face.

"I'm here to see Marcus."

Luke gives him a once-over before pushing his chair back. "I'll go get him," he sighs out.

I watch from my place on the couch while the new guy waits. He's completely still, not even the slightest tick. It's impressive considering who he's about to meet.

Billy shifts beside me, his attention on the homework spread out before him.

It's not long until Marcus's footsteps echo through the room. "Good, you're here," he says to the kid. "Follow me."

Luke takes his seat at the desk, always trying to distance himself from what goes on in the back.

"Who was that?" Billy asks.

"Some new kid Marcus is trying to bring in."

"You think he'll go for it?"

"Don't know," I tell him. It's been a while since they've brought in someone new.

He turns back to the worksheet in front of him, and I try to focus on the open history book sitting on my lap. I only get through a couple pages before I hear my name being called.

Marcus tilts his head toward the back room, and I stand to follow. Luke catches my eye, but I turn away before I have to see the look on his face.

I trail behind Marcus in silence as he leads us to a familiar closed door. He pushes it open, and my father's gaze locks on me.

After I enter the room, he turns to the new guy and explains, "This is Johnny. He's gonna be helping out with some things."

I tip my chin up.

My old man waves a hand in my direction. "My son."

Johnny tips his chin back at me in greeting.

"Johnny here is gonna do your pickup from Sid today," my father says to me.

I raise an eyebrow, surprised he would trust the new kid with something like that so soon. "Do you want me to—"

The back of his hand connects with the side of my face, his ring catching my lip. I run my tongue across my bottom teeth, tasting blood.

"Don't interrupt me," he spits.

Before I can say anything, he turns to Marcus. "You're with the kid."

Marcus grunts his understanding, and my father shifts to Johnny. The kid stares back at him with a blank look on his face, seemingly unfazed by the whole situation, but then I notice his hand balled in a fist at his side.

My father crosses his arms over his chest. "You do good today, and we'll see."

"I will," Johnny answers coolly.

Marcus exchanges a silent conversation with my old man before he heads for the door. "Let's go."

Johnny follows him out, his gaze briefly catching on my lip.

The door clicks shut again, and I stand in place, waiting.

I keep my chin raised as my father takes two fast steps toward me. "Don't you ever fucking question me in front of others again."

I don't respond. I know he doesn't want me to.

"You're useless, Jameson." He leans forward. "Say it."

I keep my eyes trained forward. "I'm useless."

"Without me, you're nothing. Isn't that right?"

"Yes, sir," I answer. "That's right."

He walks around his desk, speaking more to himself than to me. "But I'm gonna make you into a man." He looks back at me. "Everything I do is for your own good." He's watching me like he expects an answer.

I keep my voice even, burying the anger beneath the words. "I know."

Nodding, he crouches down in front of the safe behind his desk. He punches in the code then grabs a wrapped brown paper bag. "I've got somewhere I gotta be," he tells me. "I want the rest of this rolled by the time I get back tonight."

I take it from him and nod, already knowing what's inside.

He turns back to the safe. "Get out of here."

I pull the door shut behind me and head right to the bathroom. The dim light flickers on above me as I twist the lock shut. Dropping the toilet lid, I set the bag on top of it before bracing my arms on either side of the sink. Finally, I let myself breathe, the air coming in as gulps, making it feel like I'm drowning inside my own body.

Slowly, I raise my head and run my tongue over my split lip. The faucet whines, and the water rushes out too quickly as I cup my hands and splash it over my face. I rub until the caked blood washes away then dry it off with a paper towel.

Closing my eyes, I count to three, letting each number bring me back to myself. My eyes blink open, and the mask slips back into place.

I don't give myself time to think before I leave the bathroom and start toward the front of the garage.

Billy looks up, and his pen stops when he sees my lip. His face hardens as I drop down beside him, shoving the brown paper bag into my backpack.

"I'm fine," I tell him before he can start in on me.

"He shouldn't be able to—"

"I said, I'm fine, Billy. Drop it."

He blows out a breath, scrubbing a hand down his face. "You want a soda?" He starts to stand. "I'll go get you a soda."

I sling my bag over my shoulder. "I'll go with you. I want some air."

He watches me, looking for a sign he knows I'm not going to give him before he turns toward the door.

I grab his arm and mutter, "Thanks."

"Always," he answers.

LOYALTY

I press the can of Coke against my lip before cracking it open. A cool breeze cuts through the heat as I take a sip.

Billy slides down the side of the building, and I do the same, coming to sit beside him.

"There's a girl in that car over there," he says.

I follow his gaze to the beater parked right up front. "So?"

He chokes out a laugh. "I don't know. We could go say hi. She's just sitting there."

I can't make out much of what she looks like. Her head is bent down, causing her hair to fall over her face. "Go over if you want," I tell him. "I'm not in the mood to talk."

He tips his head back, resting it against the wall. "Nah. I'll hang here."

A tapping noise fills the silence as he drums his fingers on the side of his Coke can and I let my eyes close, the hot sun beating down on my face.

I don't get much of a rest before I feel his elbow dig into my side.

"What?" I grunt.

"Marcus," he mutters.

I blink my eyes open, adjusting to the sudden brightness. Pushing up to my feet, I turn just as Marcus approaches. He looks from me to Billy.

"Your dad needs you for something."

Billy hesitates until I give him a subtle nod.

Once he's gone, Marcus says, "I'm taking the new guy out."

I already know this, so why is he telling me?

"He's got his kid sister with him. We don't have time to drop her at home, so I told him she could stay here till we get back. I want you to keep an eye on her."

I pull my head back. "You want me to *babysit*?"

"She's fifteen, not five."

I flick my eyes over to the girl in the car. That must be his sister.

"Yeah, okay," I tell him.

"Good," he says, patting me on the chest.

Johnny comes up behind him, and Marcus mumbles, "Be back out in a minute."

He stalks off inside, and Johnny takes his place in front of me, leveling me with a hard stare. "Hear you're watching out for Sam while I'm gone."

I nod.

His hand comes down on my shoulder, and my eyes narrow. "If anything happens to her—"

I shake his hand off. "It won't."

He keeps his gaze trained on me, and I don't back down until finally he nods. "Good."

Brushing past me, he starts toward the car. After opening the passenger door, he bends over, probably explaining the situation. He's blocking my view of the girl, and they're speaking too low for me to hear what they're saying, but it isn't long until he steps away.

Tan legs swing out of the car before a pair of dirty Converse hit the ground. She stands, and my eyes rake up her body until they settle on her face.

I've never seen a girl who looks like her before.

Not even close.

She catches me watching, and her eyes brighten with curiosity.

My heart begins to race as she walks toward me, never letting her gaze stray from mine. She stops right in front of me, pushing her nearly black hair away from her face. I follow the movement, frowning when I see a butterfly bandage covering an angry red scratch by her hairline.

"What happened to your face?" I blurt out.

"What happened to yours?"

I bite back a smile. I'm not used to people talking to me like this, especially not girls. They usually just tell me what I want to hear or don't say anything at all.

"I fell."

She snorts, and I again fight back the urge to smile. The sound couldn't be more different than the obnoxious giggle that came from Billy's cling-on earlier.

"Sure, let's go with that," she says. "I fell, too."

"If somebody—"

"So, are you Jameson?" she questions, cutting me off.

I want to keep asking her about the cut on her face, if somebody's hurting her ...

"Well?" she presses. "Are you? My brother said I'm supposed to—"

"Yeah." I clear my throat. "I am. And you're Sam, right?"

She stiffens like she just remembered where she is and why she's here. "Right."

"Do you want to go in?" I ask, motioning to the side door.

She turns to look over her shoulder. "Do you know where my brother is?"

"He might have already left," I tell her, and she nervously bites her lip. "But I can find out for you."

She nods, and I lead her inside.

"Want a drink?" I ask as we pass by the break room. The question seems to relax her.

"Sure," she answers, walking in behind me.

"Grab anything you want from the fridge."

She opens the door, and her eyes widen at all the choices. She takes her time scanning each of them before settling on a can of Coke. After shutting the door, she wraps her long hair around her hand, pulling it up and placing the cold can against her neck. "Thanks," she sighs.

I nod toward the table in the middle of the room. "You can wait in here if you want."

"Are you gonna be in here?"

Does she want me to be?

"I have to go check on a couple of things."

"Like my brother?"

I run a hand through my hair. "Yeah, like your brother."

"And then?"

"And then I've got some work to do."

"I'm guessing it's not homework," she deadpans.

I actually laugh, and she lowers into a chair with a satisfied smile.

"No," I tell her. "It's not."

She watches me with newfound interest. "Well," she says, relaxing back into her seat, "I'll be here."

Chapter 5

Sam

Jameson leaves without another word, and once again, I'm alone.

I was starting to get worried earlier when Johnny was taking so long inside. Levi Baxston has a reputation, and so does his son. I've heard stories about Jameson but never met him before. Our school is huge, and he's a grade above me, so our paths have never crossed.

Until now.

All the girls talk about him, and after meeting him, I can see why. I've heard he's an underground fighter, and he definitely looks like one—tall and muscular—but it's the energy he gives off more than anything else. He's the kind of guy you know you shouldn't want, but it only makes you want him more.

Except, the boy I just met doesn't exactly match all the stories. He's different than I thought he'd be. I've heard he's mean and violent. That he never talks. There are lots of rumors about the things he's done. I wonder if any of them are true.

He's definitely ... intense, but there's something about him that makes me feel almost comfortable. I've been around enough bad people that I feel like I'm pretty good at picking them out, and Jameson doesn't seem bad to me. He's intimidating, for sure. I mean, you'd be stupid not to see that. But ... I don't know, there's just something about him. Something that makes me want to keep being around him.

I push back from the table and pace around the small break room, needing to do something other than just sit here. After glancing over at the door Jameson closed when he left, I look through all the cabinets and drawers. I find an ashtray and set it on the table, wishing I'd found some food hidden away, too. Going over to the fridge, I open the door and lean into the coolness. Johnny's AC is out, and it doesn't seem like this place has any either.

I grab a couple more cans of soda, reorganizing them so you can't tell, and put them in my bag for later.

When I've finished snooping through everything, I open the small corner window then slide back into my chair. At this point, I'm not so sure if Jameson is actually coming back, so I decide to get comfortable.

Taking a sip of Coke, I rifle through my bag and pull out my copy of *Jane Eyre*. I grab the pack of cigarettes Johnny gave me earlier and a lighter. Shuffling the bag around, I find a half-eaten pack of M&Ms and set that in front of me, too. Then I drop my bag down by my feet, pop an M&M into my mouth, and crack open my book.

I startle when the door pushes open. Looking up, I see Jameson standing in the doorway with his eyes trained on me. They drift over everything I have spread out on the table then back to my face.

"I see you've made yourself right at home," he quips, settling into the seat across from me.

I flip over my book, setting it on the table to save my place. "That a problem?"

He huffs out an amused breath. "No." He lifts his hand to his hair, and I trace the movement as he brushes it through the dark strands a few times then runs it down his face, flinching when it passes over his bruised lip.

I take him in and notice another faded scar that runs through his eyebrow, right above his hooded brown eyes.

He looks exhausted.

"You gonna share?" he asks, and I realize I've been staring.

"Huh?"

He tips his chin toward everything laid out in front of me.

I tilt my head. "M&Ms or cigarette?"

He holds out a hand. "M&Ms."

I pour some into his open palm. "Did you find out if my brother is still here?"

He absentmindedly sorts the colors. "Yeah, he left already."

"Where'd he go?"

His eyes flick up to meet mine.

"It's not like I'm gonna rat on my own brother."

He hesitates before saying, "A pickup ..."

I nod.

"And ..." he starts.

"And?" I ask, trying to hide my fear.

"Never mind."

I fold my arms over my chest. "No, tell me."

He sighs. "Your brother any good with cars?"

Waving my hand around, I make a face that says, *Duh, we're sitting in a mechanic shop.*

He gives me a face back that says, *You know that's not what I mean.*

I drop my hand, tilting my head. "Yeah, really good."

"Then they're probably going scouting."

Realization dawns on me, and I notice Jameson is watching to see how I'm going to react.

"Oh," I mutter, pulling a cigarette out of the pack. I light it. "Do you know when they'll be back?"

He shakes his head.

I wait to see if he'll give anything else away, but he doesn't, so I pick my book back up, needing to give my mind a place to escape to. I don't want to think about what my brother is doing right now and what would happen if he got caught.

Jameson shifts in his seat, and I hear the zipper of his backpack sliding open. A brown paper bag crinkles and glass clanks together as he sets it on the table. I glance up from my book to see what's inside, and my eyes widen when he takes out three jars filled with weed.

After pulling the rest of the things out—a Ziplock half-filled with joints, rolling papers, and something circular I don't recognize—he gets up and rummages around the kitchen, returning with a tray and another Ziplock bag.

I flick the ash off my cigarette and follow his movements as he lines everything up. Once he seems content with the placement, he twists the lid off one of the jars and a pungent smell fills the room.

He blows out a breath and looks up at me. "You're staring."

"What do you expect?" I sweep a hand out. "This isn't exactly normal."

A laugh that sounds more like a push of air leaves his lips. "No, I guess it isn't."

"*You guess?*"

He runs a hand through his hair, which I'm starting to notice seems to be his tick. "Guess I'm just used to it."

I set my book back down, giving him my full attention.

"Do you read a lot?" he asks.

"You're changing the subject."

"So?"

I stub out my cigarette as he starts the process of rolling a joint. "Yeah, I do."

"What kind of books do you like?"

"Whatever I can find."

"But what's your favorite?"

I motion to my book. "I like classics."

He hums in agreement.

"Do you read?"

He scoffs.

"What—too cool?"

"No," he says, shaking his head.

"So, what then?"

"Just don't think I've ever read a book."

I pull my head back. "Ever?"

"I mean, probably at some point. A picture book maybe when I was a kid."

"You're missing out."

He looks up at me. "Then lend me your favorite, and I'll read it."

"Really?"

He watches me for a minute, but it doesn't give me that skin crawling feeling I get when other boys stare. He looks at me like I'm a person, instead of just a pretty face he wants by his side. And I realize I like his eyes on me. That I want to keep them there.

Finally, he nods, the motion pulling me from my thoughts.

"Why?" I ask.

"You seem like you have good taste," he answers. "And I want to see what your favorite is."

I roll my lips to hide a smile. "Well, I'll lend it to you when I get a copy."

"You don't have a copy of your favorite book?"

"I did," I start. "It ... um ... it got lost."

"Lost, huh?"

I nod.

"So what is it?"

"What?"

"Your favorite book?"

"Oh, it's *The Picture of Dorian Gray*."

He watches me like those words mean nothing to him.

"What about you?"

He runs his tongue across the rolling paper before sealing it. "What about me?"

"What do you like to do?"

His brows furrow.

"Like, for fun?"

"I hang out with my cousin Billy." He twists up the end of the joint. "You'll probably meet him. His dad owns this place."

"Oh, I thought your dad did."

"They both do," he mutters.

"So, you don't have anything you're into then?"

"Movies." He clears his throat. "I like movies."

"What're your favorite kind?"

He smirks. "Classics."

"Jameson," someone calls out from the hallway.

Jameson goes rigid, and I watch as the light from his eyes fades. His chair drags across the floor as he quickly pushes away from the table like he doesn't want to keep whoever just called his name waiting.

"I'll be right back," he says. "Stay—"

Before he can finish, a man fills the doorway and drags his gaze between me and Jameson. "What's going on in here?"

Chapter 6

Sam

The man looks just like Jameson, only older. His dark hair is slicked back, showcasing his cold eyes and an expression that makes me wish I could make myself smaller.

It's obvious who the man is.

Levi Baxston. Jameson's father.

Jameson rounds the table, putting himself between me and his father. He sounds completely disinterested when he shrugs and says, "Marcus told me to watch her. She's the new kid's sister."

Levi folds his tattooed arms across his chest as he leans against the doorframe. His gaze lingers on me before he brings it back to Jameson and teases, "Bet you were happy to be given that job."

Jameson doesn't respond.

His father assesses him, the seconds stretching until it feels like the tension is about to snap. Finally, he says, "I need you to help me load something into the car."

"Sure," Jameson answers, seemingly unaffected, and follows his father without sparing me even a glance.

I release a long breath as soon as they leave the room, letting my shoulders fall. I'm grateful they're gone. Well, that Levi is, anyway.

Leaning back in my chair, I look over at Jameson's empty seat, realizing just how much I liked talking to him. It was easy. Something I almost never find conversation to be.

Grabbing my book, I pick up where I left off, trying to distract myself. I get through another chapter before my eyes drift over to the closed door. It's taking Jameson a while to come back. Definitely longer than you would need to load something into a car.

I wonder what they're really doing.

Reaching across the table, I snag a couple of joints from the bag Jameson rolled. There's enough in there that I'm sure he won't notice. After stashing them inside the pocket of my bag, I turn back to my book.

I've just finished another cigarette when the door pushes open. "Time for you to go."

I jump at the voice, having expected Jameson. Turning, I see an unfamiliar man around Levi's age, with a long scar down the side of his face.

"I'm Marcus," he says, just as my brother comes up behind him.

"Sam," I answer quietly.

He takes a step forward and extends his hand. "Nice to meet you, sweetheart."

I find my brother over Marcus's shoulder. He's watching us carefully, a hard look on his face. He inclines his head slightly, and I stand, taking Marcus's hand.

He towers over me, tall and overly skinny. His clammy hand closes over mine, and I'm hit with the smell of weed mixed with engine oil.

"Nice to meet you, too," I tell him.

He hums under his breath, dropping my hand. As he walks out of the room, he pats Johnny on the chest and says, "See you later, yeah?"

Johnny nods. "Yeah."

Marcus hovers just outside the door, clearly waiting for me to leave, so I quickly shove my things into my bag. Keys rattle as I step into the hall, and he locks the door behind me.

Where's Jameson?

"This way," my brother says, leading me down the hall.

I follow him outside and into the car. Once we're settled, I look him over. "Everything go okay?"

He starts the engine. "Yup."

"That's it?" I ask, irritated. "Not gonna give me anything else?"

He shrugs. "Nothing else to tell."

"So, you're working here now then?"

"Uh-huh."

"Officially or unofficially?"

"Both," he answers quickly, like he doesn't want me to think about what that means.

Sighing, I slump back in my seat, annoyed by how secretive he's being.

"I don't wanna hear it," Johnny says, his tone final.

"I didn't say anything."

"We need the money." He glances over at me. "You think this is what I want to do?"

"I'll get a job," I interject.

"Your job is school."

I throw out a hand. "It shouldn't all be on you."

"But it is, and you're going to let me handle it, okay?"

"I don't—"

"Bug," he interrupts, and the childhood nickname softens me. "I've got this, really. I don't want you to worry about it."

"I just don't want anything to happen to you."

"It won't," he answers firmly.

I really want to believe him.

"So, Jameson treat you okay?" he asks, changing the subject.

I want to keep asking him about the job, about what he'll be doing, but I know he'll only brush me off. So, I give him the out he's looking for.

"He was fine," I answer.

"Then why do you sound pissed?"

I cross my arms over my chest. "I'm not."

Well, maybe I am. And not just about my brother starting this job, but maybe a little bit about Jameson, too.

Johnny scoffs. "Yeah, all right." When I don't say anything, his voice hardens. "Seriously, do I need to have a talk with him?"

"No." I fidget. "He just …"

Johnny goes still. "He just what?"

"He didn't hurt me, okay?" I drop my hands. "I'm fine. You don't have to go all overprotective." I shake my head. "It's stupid."

"Tell me."

I turn to look out the window, embarrassed that this even bothers me at all.

"Sam?" he prompts.

"I don't know …" I hesitate. "I thought maybe he liked me … or liked talking to me. He was nice, actually. I mean, after the stuff I've heard about him, I didn't think he would be. But then his dad came in, and he changed. He acted like I was barely there, and then he just left. I thought he would come back, but he never did."

Johnny visibly relaxes. His words come out tentative, like he's not quite sure how to deal with the side of me that has emotions. "Jameson's dad—"

"I know."

"No, let me finish," he says. "You need to be careful around him. I saw how he treated Jameson, and if what I saw is how he treats him in front of a stranger, I don't want to know what he does behind closed doors."

I tense.

"The guy uses mind games. Always has to be the one in power." He looks over at me. "Don't think how Jameson acted in front of him has anything to do with you."

I nod, but it must not be convincing.

"What?" my brother asks.

I pick at my fingernail. "It was just nice to hang out with someone. I don't really have any ..." I clear my throat, not liking how vulnerable I sound. I've never had an easy time making friends.

"I know," Johnny says as we pull into the driveway. "Maybe I can bring you along with me sometimes. Would that ...? Would that help?"

Surveying the house, I notice our father's car then the light on in the living room and go rigid. Distractedly, I answer, "Yeah, thanks."

Johnny watches me. "You're okay." It's a statement rather than a question.

"Yeah, I'm good," I answer, anyway, forcing a smile onto my face.

He already does so much for me, carries so many burdens that aren't his own. The least I can do is give him this lie.

LOYALTY

Johnny pushes open the front door, and I follow in behind him.

Our father keeps his eyes on the TV when he asks, "Where've you been?"

Johnny steps farther into the living room. "I got a—"

"See? That's what I'm talking about." Our father turns, cutting Johnny off. He points to the game on the TV. "You're spending way too long in the pocket."

Carson shifts next to him. "I wouldn't have to if—"

"Excuses don't win games," our father barks, pausing the tape they're reviewing of one of Carson's games.

It's off-season, but football never stops in our house. Our father played all through high school. He was good, but never good enough to get recruited.

Johnny played up until his sophomore year. It was a big deal when he quit. I think he finally hit a breaking point with our father's obsession around the game, around winning. I don't know exactly what pushed him over the edge, but one day, he just quit. Our father didn't speak to him for weeks.

After that, Carson became the golden boy. Not only did he keep playing, but he's really good. Our father is convinced he'll go all the way, that Carson is gonna be the one who gets us out of this neighborhood.

He turns from Carson to Johnny. "What'd you say?"

"I got a new job."

Our father sits up straighter. "Where?"

"Baxston & Sons."

"Money must be good."

Johnny's jaw ticks. "It is."

Our father's gaze cuts to me. "Stop hiding behind him."

I step around my brother and mumble, "I'm not."

"And where have you been?"

"I—"

"What happened to your face?" Carson asks before I can respond.

"I picked her up from school," Johnny answers for me. "The nurse called. She tripped on the stairs and cut her face. Made her miss the bus."

I keep still, not wanting to give away the fact that Johnny just lied to cover for me.

The last time I got in a fight at school, our father had been the one to pick me up. He was about to go run drills with Carson and was pissed I interrupted him. I'm honestly surprised he didn't just leave me there. I got a whole lecture on the way to the field about reining in my temper.

Where does he think I learned it from?

He watches me and Johnny like he knows we're lying, but I don't think he cares enough to give it the energy. "You missed dinner," he says to me, unpausing the tape.

I take that as my cue to leave, starting for the kitchen.

"Make something quick," he calls after me. "It's late. I'm hungry."

I let his words roll off me because if I don't, they'll only make me angry.

Opening the fridge, I search for something fast I can make, but the shelves are nearly empty. Well, except the door that's fully stocked with beer.

I move on to the cabinets, pulling out some tuna and bread. I also find a half-eaten package of cheese in the fridge, so I decide on tuna melts. There are a few potatoes left that aren't too bad, so I start to heat some oil, cut off the sprouted parts, then chop the rest.

The hot oil begins to pop below me and beads of sweat run down my back. I push open the window above the sink, wishing we had AC.

I just get the last of the fried potatoes out when I hear my name being called.

Shutting off the burner, I move into the living room, where our father holds his beer out, not bothering to stop what he's saying to Carson. I take it from him and bring back a cold one.

"You almost done?" he asks.

"Five more minutes."

I hurry back into the kitchen and finish mixing the tuna salad. I throw the sandwiches under the broiler and then plate everything up, bringing two of them into the living room.

I hand one to our father and one to Carson before collecting the empty beer bottles from the coffee table.

"Thanks," our father offers, just as Carson grunts in agreement.

I nod and turn back to the kitchen.

The beer bottles clank against each other as I drop them into the bin. I grab one from the fridge for myself and finally sink into a seat at the table with my dinner.

I'm about to take a bite when the house phone rings.

Just like always, there's a moment when I think it might be her. I don't know when I'm going to get over the delusion that my mother will just randomly call one day.

It's been over ten years since she left.

"Will you pick up the goddamn phone already!" our father hollers, his voice springing me into action.

I push my chair back and grab the phone, twisting the cord around my hand. "Hello."

"Hey," my sister says, and a part of me deflates.

Of course it's not her, I tell myself. *Don't be stupid.*

"Sam?"

"Hmm?" I answer. "Sorry, what's up?"

"Just calling to check in," she says.

Cathleen's more of a mother than a sister to me. She's the oldest of all of us and stepped up, practically raising us, after our mother left. She moved out last year to go live with her boyfriend. Now she's miles away, and I hardly ever see her. I know it was hard for her to leave, but she deserves it after all the shit she had to put up with.

"How's school been?" she asks.

"Good," I tell her, not mentioning the fight today. I already got a lecture from Johnny, so I don't need another one from her.

"And things at home?"

"You know," I respond vaguely.

"Anything I need to know about?"

"No, everything's fine."

"You sure?"

"Yeah," I mutter. "How about you?"

"The same," she says, though her voice sounds off.

"Things with Adam okay?" Her boyfriend's a bit of a prick, and they're always having issues.

"Yeah," she murmurs. "He's actually about to get home, so I should probably go."

"Me, too," I add. "I was about to eat dinner."

"All right," she says. "Don't be a stranger, yeah?"

I hum my agreement.

"Love you," she breathes.

"Love you, too."

I hang up and move for the kitchen table, but just as I sit, Johnny walks in, his hair wet from a shower.

"I made you a plate," I tell him, starting to stand again.

"Thanks, Bug." He smiles. "But I've gotta go."

"Where?" I ask.

He shakes his head.

And so it starts.

"I'll wrap a sandwich for you. You can bring it with you."

"Sit," he says. "I've got it."

I lower back in my chair while he moves around the kitchen. He catches me watching him and tips up his chin. "Eat."

I sink my teeth into the sandwich, and he turns away, satisfied, then tosses one into a brown paper bag, adding some fried potatoes in with it. Once he's done, he comes over to the table and throws down a few bills. "For groceries."

I eye the money, knowing where it likely came from, but we're really not in a position to be picky, so I grab it and tuck it into my bag. "Thanks."

He kisses the top of my head. "See you later."

I want to ask him where he's going, what he's doing, but I keep the questions tucked away.

He walks to the back door.

"Johnny," I call out as he opens it.

"Yeah."

"Please be safe."

He nods then turns, shutting the door behind him.

I don't sleep that night until I hear him get home.

CHAPTER 7

JAMESON

When the credits of the movie roll, I push out of my seat. Billy follows as the theater lights come on.

I know a guy who works here, and he lets me in for free, so I come by a lot. Probably more than I should. There's something about being in a theater. No windows. No clocks. No talking. Nothing but the movie in front of you. You can just disappear. Escape.

If I don't feel like being alone, I'll bring Billy along with me, like I did tonight. He's always so restless when he's watching a movie, though, so I have to be in the mood to invite him.

He holds open the door for a couple of girls behind us, letting them step out into the night before we do. They both blush, leaning into each other and whispering something before peeking up at him.

"That one was good," he says, waiting for the road to clear so we can cross the intersection.

I grunt in agreement.

"You've seen it before," he says rather than asks.

"A few times," I mutter.

The cars finally stop, and we quickly make it to the other side of the road. It's a Thursday night, so it's quiet, only a few places still open. The glow of streetlamps light our way as we take our time getting back to the garage.

We get a few blocks before Billy nudges me. "I've been waiting all night for you to bring her up."

"Who?" I ask, playing dumb.

He rolls his eyes. "Don't give me that bullshit. When I left last night, Marcus said you were stuck in the back room with the new kid's sister."

"I don't know what you want me to say?"

"What's she like?"

Interesting.

Beautiful.

Sad.

I shrug. "She's cool."

He raises an eyebrow. "Really?"

"Yeah, why?" I ask defensively. "She can't be cool?"

"Is she hot?"

My jaw ticks, and he smiles.

Why the fuck is he smiling?

"What?" I snap.

His smile turns smug. "You like her."

"I just met her."

"But you like her. Don't you?" He shakes his head. "You don't like anyone." He pauses, looking over at me with a smirk. "Well, except for me, obviously."

"Obviously," I snort.

The humor leaves his voice. "Seriously, though."

My shoulders drop. Billy is the only person in my life I talk to. I mean *actually* talk to.

"There's something about her. I don't know …"

"I'm excited to meet her."

I scowl at him, and he laughs.

"Not like that." Elbowing me, he adds. "You've clearly already called dibs."

We round the corner that the garage is on, hearing music pour out into the street. The doors are open, and the lot is full.

Another one of my old man's parties.

Billy slows next to me. "You good?"

I lock myself away, becoming what I need to be, and jerk my head in a nod.

"I hate what he makes you into," Billy says so quietly I barely hear him over the music.

I push his words down, burying them, and walk forward.

My father isn't hard to find. He's always at the center of these things.

I step inside and see him sprawled out on the couch, my mother draped over him. She's wearing what I guess you could call a dress. The tight red fabric looks like a second skin, and it's so short all you can see are bare legs. My father's hand covers her thigh, like he wants to remind everyone she's his.

She sees me coming up to them and turns toward me, dazed. I spot the drink in her hand, knowing she's already drunk.

I wish I could bring her home. Get her away from here.

She leans into my father, and I quickly take in the people lounging by the couch, recognizing a few guys who always hang around, along with Luke, Marcus, and Sam's brother, Johnny.

Before I can think better of it, a flash of excitement runs through me, thinking Sam might be here, too. I look around the room for her, coming up empty.

Good. She shouldn't be here. It's selfish of me to want her to be.

"There he is," my father booms. "Fucking finally."

Everyone turns to me, only Luke's eyes finding Billy behind me. He gets up, and we trade places, putting me next to my father and him standing in front of Billy.

"Get my boy a drink," my father says to some young guy I don't know.

A minute later, a Solo cup is being pushed into my hand.

I throw it back before setting the cup down on the table in front of me.

My father watches me, eyes bright. "How're you doing? You doing good?"

I force myself to keep my attention on him and not let it drift to my mother. "Good. Yeah, I'm good."

He smiles, and my guard goes up.

What's he so happy about?

His attention flits to Johnny, and I understand.

"Yesterday go good then?" I ask.

"Real good," he says. "Great even. Big things are coming."

I don't ask, knowing this isn't the place. I'm sure I'll be filled in later.

My father tips his cup in Johnny's direction. "Got ourselves a real one here."

Johnny takes a step forward, coming up next to my chair. "Appreciate the chance."

"I'm feeling generous," my father says before looking over at me. "We got any party favors?"

I nod.

He slaps a hand on the couch. "Well, go get 'em. It's a fucking party, isn't it?"

I start to stand, but then I still when Luke warns, "Levi."

My father looks up at him and snaps, "What?"

"It's a school night."

My father laughs. "*It's a school night?* The fuck do I care?"

Luke glances at me, and my father follows his gaze.

"I can take him home," Luke offers.

Yes, I wanna go home, but I know better than to think I'll be able to.

"He is home," my father says through gritted teeth. "I'm his home, and he's with me. Isn't he?"

Luke shakes his head. "He's a kid, Levi—"

"That's right," my father interrupts, losing his patience. "He's *my* kid, Luke, not yours."

Luke looks over at me, and I can feel my father's eyes on me, too. I'm standing between them, literally caught in the middle.

"If you wanna go home, Jameson, I'll bring you home," Luke tells me.

"What did I just fucking say?" my father growls.

I take a step away from Luke. "I'm fine here."

"See?" my father sneers. "He's fine. It's a party. It's fun. You don't always have to be so fucking uptight."

"We're leaving," Luke says, his voice strained. He nods toward the door. "Billy."

Luke glances over his shoulder at me, and Billy mutters a goodbye.

I dip my chin but don't say anything. Instead, I head for the back room to get what my father asked for.

When I return, the music has been turned up even louder, and my father's head is pulled back in a laugh, Marcus sitting in the seat next to him.

I drop the stuff on the table, and Marcus leans forward greedily. He pours out some coke, cuts it into lines, and then rolls up a bill and snorts it. He gives a turn to whoever wants it, and I notice Johnny passes. My father notices, too.

I've never liked the idea of doing drugs. I've seen firsthand what it can do to people. How desperate it makes them. I'd never want something to have control over me like that. The idea scares the shit out of me. So, I keep my distance from it. But sometimes, when everyone's watching like they are now, image has to win over fear.

The only thing worse than being weak is looking weak.

Taking the dollar bill, I drop to my knees and bend forward. I don't have to look up to know my father is watching me. I snort the line, scrunching my nose at the burn, and run my fingers across it.

Marcus slaps my back, hooting and hollering about something. He glances over at Johnny. "You sure you don't want some? It's good quality shit."

"It's not my thing," Johnny answers.

My father leans in, his hand sliding down my mother's leg. She reaches forward. "I'll have some."

Marcus looks to my father, who shakes his head. "She's done."

"But I—"

A glare from my father cuts her off.

She glances over at me.

"Don't look at him," my father snaps. "The answer is no."

She pushes back into the couch with a pout.

My father turns his attention to Johnny. "It's rude not to accept a gift," he tells him.

My attention shifts between the two of them as I lick my lips, my mouth suddenly dry.

Johnny takes a sip of his beer, and I grab my empty cup, standing to go in search of some water.

"Don't mean any disrespect." he answers.

My father assesses him, but Johnny doesn't waver.

"You've got balls, kid," he says. "I'll give you that." He points at him, but turns to Marcus. "I like this one."

I wonder if I would have gotten the same reaction if I refused.

I doubt it.

Slipping away, I finally find a drink and linger around the party, trying to avoid anyone's attention. I'm jittery as fuck, and the music and people are only making it worse.

My father's voice filters through the noise, and I eventually make my way back over to him. I've already been gone for at least an hour, and if I keep to myself much longer, he'll just come looking for me.

"Where's Big Jim?" he asks Marcus as I sit down beside him. "I thought I told you to tell him to come tonight."

Marcus looks around, fidgeting. "I did."

My father stares at him, waiting. When Marcus just stands there, he says, "Well, go find him." He looks over at me. "I think it's time Jameson here gets his first tattoo."

Marcus returns not even five minutes later with Big Jim in tow. My father stands and grabs his hand, smacking him on the back. "Thanks for coming."

"Of course," Big Jim answers, his voice labored. He got the nickname for a reason, and it isn't his height. He's completely covered in tattoos, even his face. The guy looks scary as hell, but I've known him since I was a little kid. He's actually really chill.

"Left my shit out in the car," Big Jim says, starting for the door. My father has been getting his tattoos done by him forever. He owns a tattoo place downtown, but he usually comes to us.

A hand to his chest stops him. "Jameson will get it," my father insists.

I take a step forward, and Big Jim smiles. "No shit, look at you. All grown and everything."

"It hasn't been that long," I mutter.

"Ain't seen you since before you really started fighting. You're not a scrawny little kid anymore, are you?" He eyes me. "Heard you're real good, too."

"Course he is," my father cuts in. "I'm training him myself. I'll let you know when the next one is. You've gotta come out."

Big Jim nods. "I'll be there." He tosses me his keys. "It's the black pickup right out front. Stuff's on the passenger seat."

"Got it," I answer, catching the keys.

I pass Johnny on my way to the door, and we silently acknowledge each other.

I want to ask him about Sam.

Where she is tonight.

If he's gonna bring her back here.

If she's said anything about me.

Instead, I keep walking.

She has no place in a life like mine.

Nobody does.

I grab the bags from Big Jim's truck and carry them inside.

Setting them down, he tells me, "Your old man said you're up first. You know what you want already?"

Growing up, I always knew I'd get tattoos. I've never asked my father for any, though. I guess I just figured he'd take me to get one someday. Apparently, that day is today.

I haven't put a lot of thought into what I'd get, so I shake my head.

"I've got a book," he says, opening one of the bags and handing it to me.

I flip through all the designs, looking for something that stands out while he gets ready. I find one I like and glance up, finding Marcus talking to my father, who has his arm around my mother, her body pulled into his side.

My father catches my eye and motions for me to join them. "You pick something?" he asks.

I nod, turning the book to show him the skull. "Gonna get it on my shoulder."

Marcus whistles. "That's tough."

My father's hand comes down on my back. "I like it."

I turn toward my mother, waiting for her to say something.

She smiles, her eyes a bit more clear. "Very cool."

"First tattoo," my father says, pride in the words. He nods to where Big Jim is setting up. "Go on. I'll come over with you in a minute."

I take the book and turn to leave.

"Hold on," my father calls out. "Give the book to Johnny."

He walks over, and I hand it to him.

"You got any ink?" my father asks.

Johnny nods. "A couple."

"Well, get another one."

"I don't—"

My father holds up a hand, silencing him. "You don't gotta pay. It's a perk of the job."

"All right, thanks," Johnny says, closing the book and starting from the front.

Big Jim comes over and says he's all set up. I tell him what I want and wait as he draws it. Then I drop into the chair and let him prep my arm.

My father pulls up a seat, and my mother slides onto his lap, Marcus and Johnny coming to stand beside me.

Soon, the tattoo gun buzzes to life. It presses into my skin and, after a couple minutes, I relax into the pain. I close my eyes, and a sense of calm washes over me. I listen to everyone talk around me, my heartrate finally beginning to slow.

"Okay, kid, you're done," Big Jim says.

I blink my eyes open. *How is he already finished?*

"That was quick."

He snorts. "Been over an hour."

Really?

My father looms over me. "Let me see."

I turn toward him.

His lips pull up. "That's a good first piece." Then motions toward the bathroom. "Go check it out."

When I walk back into the room after seeing the tattoo for myself, Big Jim laughs. "I know that look," he says. "You already want another one, don't know."

"That obvious, huh?"

He starts to wrap my shoulder. "Been doing this a long time," he mutters. "And people who sit like you do," He shakes his head. "They never stop coming back."

Chapter 8

Sam

I'M STARTING TO GO crazy. School got out almost three weeks ago, and I've barely left the house.

Johnny's been gone during the day, and I'm usually already in bed before he gets home.

It sucks that he's never around. But it also means that if I want to go anywhere, I have to ask either Carson or my father to take me. The few times I've been desperate enough to ask either of them for a ride, they always say no. So, I'm left stranded at home with nothing to do and nobody to talk to.

The sun set a few hours ago, and I'm holed up in my room. I spent the day cleaning the house, cooking and reading in-between. I've been trying to go to the library, but it's too far to walk and, according to my father, I'm not allowed to *wander around the streets alone*. So, I've just been reading the few books I own over and over again. Hopefully, Johnny can take me soon.

I'm sitting on my bed, reading *Jane Eyre* for probably the dozenth time, and the words are starting to bleed together.

I slam the book shut. Then, pushing off my bed, I begin to pace, feeling like I'm starting to lose it. I open the door to the hall, debating if I should go downstairs. I hear the sound of the TV and peer over the banister. Carson is on the couch next to our father, and there are enough beer bottles spread over the coffee table that I know better than to go down there.

Sighing, I head back for my room and lock the door. Shuffling through my purse, I find one of the joints I've been saving since the day I stole a couple from Jameson.

I open the window and climb out onto the garage roof. The lighter sparks, and I watch the flame cut through the darkness. Inhaling, I close my eyes as the smoke hits the back of my throat.

Cars pass on the street below, and I wonder where the people inside are going. What their lives are like.

I bring the joint back to my lips and think about Jameson. I haven't been back to the garage since that day I met him. I've been waiting for Johnny to bring me along, but he hasn't, and I haven't wanted to burden him by asking.

Still, in the few weeks that have passed, my mind keeps drifting back to Jameson. I want to know more about him, to learn who he is when he isn't being someone else.

I hate that I can't just go see him. That I can't go see anyone or do anything. I have to rely on someone to bring me places. I have to ask my father's permission. It feels like my whole life is dictated by other people, and I'm sick of it.

I feel so restless, so trapped inside myself, like there's this overwhelming need to escape.

Without thinking, I stub out the joint, slip back inside, and save the other half of it for later. Then I slide on my shoes and climb back out through the window, moving to the edge of the roof and making my way down the side of the house. My heart drops when I nearly slip, but I use the nearby tree to steady myself.

I don't usually sneak out like this. The risk of getting caught never feels worth it, and walking around alone at night in my neighborhood isn't exactly smart. But tonight, I don't care about the risks. I need to get out of here. I just need to fucking breathe.

My feet hit the grass, and I duck below the living room window, crawling until I'm out of view. I start down the street, glancing over my shoulder to make sure I haven't been caught.

I'm not even sure where I'm going. It doesn't matter, really. I just need to move. To breathe. To have nothing holding me in place.

I'm not sure how long I walk for. The sounds of night fold around me, my footsteps creating a steady rhythm. My mind empties out until I feel nothing but numb. My head has gone fuzzy, my body a weightless thing.

I look up at the streetlights, wondering if they've always burned this brightly. Blinking up at them, I feel tears streak down my face. I don't bother to wipe them away. Instead, all I think about are my moving feet. On getting farther and farther away.

Left.

Right.

Left.

Right.

I turn down a street that's gone quiet. The signs are all dark and parking lots abandoned. It must be really late now, but I have no way of knowing the time.

You should go home, a voice in my head says.

Shh, I tell it.

My legs are beginning to ache. A warmth spreads through them, making it feel like they're vibrating. I don't mind the sensation—it gives me something to focus on.

I keep walking.

Left.

Right.

Left.

Right.

The trees around me rustle as a breeze drifts across my face. I close my eyes and let my head fall back. When I open them again, I notice the space around me is suddenly brighter.

I turn to look over my shoulder and see headlights break through the darkness. The car is the only one on the road, causing a chill to run down my spine as it approaches.

Reality comes crashing down on me when I notice just how alone I am out here. How stupid I've been to walk this far on my own. I have nothing with me that I could use as a weapon. I don't even own a phone. *What was I thinking?*

I glance around for an answer, like someone will magically tell me what to do. But there's nobody out here. Just me and the car closing in behind me.

Do I run? Find somewhere to hide?

I shake my head. *It's just the weed*, I tell myself. It's making me paranoid. They'll probably drive past, and I'll have worried for nothing.

But when I chance another glance over my shoulder, I notice the car is definitely driving way too slowly.

Fuck.

They're close enough that they can see me now.

There's no time to run. No time to hide.

I begin to shake and pray to a god I don't believe in that if they save me right now, I promise I won't ever do anything this stupid again.

The lights become brighter as the car approaches. It slows to a roll, and my heart begins to violently pound.

I'm just about to take off into a sprint, at least try to give myself a fighting chance, when I hear a familiar voice.

I freeze when they call out my name.

Chapter 9

Sam

I deflate. "Johnny?" I ask, his name coming out shaky. "You scared the shit out of me. What are you doing here?"

"What am *I* doing here? I was coming home from work." He gestures to me. "What the fuck are you doing out here?"

My relief is quickly replaced with worry.

"It's two o'clock in the fucking morning," he spits.

"I—"

How do I explain this?

"Are you okay?" He looks around. "Are you alone?"

I stare back at him, fidgeting with my hands.

"Did someone hurt you?"

I shake my head.

Concern flashes across his face, and he leans over to open the passenger door. "Just come on. Get off the street."

I take a step forward but hesitate, glancing at the open door.

"Jesus, Sam," he sighs. "Get in the car."

"You're mad," I whisper.

"Of course I'm mad," he snaps. "I just found you walking down the street alone in the middle of the night. If someone else found you out here ..." He grinds his teeth. "What were you thinking?"

"I wasn't," I mutter.

"Clearly." He motions to the passenger seat. "I'm not going to ask you again. Get in the car."

I drop my gaze to the ground and slide into the seat.

He turns toward me, taking me in. "You're shaking," he says, his tone softer now.

"When I saw the headlights ..." I wrap my arms around myself. "I thought ... I didn't ..."

"Did something happen tonight?" he asks.

I shake my head.

"I don't understand." He blows out a breath. "You gotta start making this make sense."

"I'm sorry," I mumble.

"It's okay," he pushes out. "But you need to tell me what's going on."

"I just couldn't ..." My voice cracks.

"You just couldn't what?"

"Take it. I couldn't take it anymore. Being in that house. Being alone. I'm always fucking alone." I grip my hands, trying to make them stop shaking. "Johnny? Do you have a cigarette?"

He tears his pained eyes from me and grabs a pack from the center console, handing me one. I place it between my lips, and he lights it.

I inhale, letting it calm me. "Sometimes, I just feel so trapped, you know?"

He nods.

"Dad's been … well, you know how he is." I exhale a cloud of smoke. "I can't go anywhere. Do anything. He's always keeping tabs on me. Carson is, too."

Johnny's expression darkens at the mention of Carson. They've never gotten along.

"What can I do?" he asks. "How can I make it better?"

"You're always gone," I say before quickly adding, "And I'm grateful for all you do for us, really. It's just—"

"I get it," he interrupts. Leaning into his seat, he tilts his head back, thinking. "Maybe I could bring you to the garage with me during the day."

"I thought—"

"Would that be better?" he cuts in again, silencing my protest. "If you could come with me?"

I exhale a cloud of smoke. "Yeah, but I don't want to make trouble for you."

"You won't."

"What about Dad?"

"What about him?"

"You think he'll let me go?"

He's quiet for a minute. "I'll say you're helping out, working the front desk. He won't care what you do if you're getting paid."

My eyes widen. "You think they'll actually give me a job?"

"I don't know, but I'll ask. Even if they don't, it's not like he's gonna show up there."

"But then I won't be making any money."

We both know if I say I'm bringing money home, our father will want to see it. Will likely *take* it.

"I'll give you some if I have to." He levels me with a serious look. "We'll sort out the details. The only thing that matters is that you don't feel"—I watch his eyes flit to the street—"like this anymore. That you don't put yourself in a situation like this again."

I dip my chin. "I won't."

"Why didn't you just come to me if you were this upset?"

"I didn't want to be another thing you had to deal with."

He pulls his head back. "You're not *something I have to deal with*," he says, like the idea is ridiculous. "You're my sister. I'll always be here for you."

I clear my throat. "I know."

He stares back at me. "No, I don't think you do." He leans forward. "You're not a burden. You're not something I have to deal with. And you sure as fuck are not alone. You understand me?"

"Yes," I answer, my voice just above a whisper.

"Good." Pointing to the street, he adds, "And don't you ever let me find you out here at night again."

"You won't."

He nods then throws the car into drive and peels away from the curb.

"Thank you," I tell him, pulling my knees up to my chest. "For picking me up and … and for everything you said."

"Of course," he answers. "Tomorrow will be better."

He says it with such certainty that I actually believe him.

Chapter 10

Jameson

"Can I talk to you about something?" Johnny asks.

"Course," Luke answers, sliding out from underneath the Camry we're working on.

Johnny leans against the doorframe, crossing one foot over the other. "My sister ... you remember her from a few weeks ago?"

My head jerks up as Luke nods.

"I was wondering if you had any work for her here? Cleaning or working the front desk? Anything really."

"I don't—"

"You wouldn't even have to pay her, if you can't swing it," Johnny cuts in. "I just want to get her out of the house. Give her something to do."

"How old is she?"

"Fifteen."

Luke wipes the grease from his hands. "I guess I can set her up at the front desk." He pauses, thinking to himself. "It'll free me up to get more repairs done."

Sam ... working here?

Johnny lets out a breath. "Thanks, Luke. I really appreciate it."

"I'm not letting her work for free, though."

"You don't—"

"Five dollars an hour is the best I can do."

"Fine," Johnny says. "That's more than fine. Seriously, thank you."

Luke waves a hand. "Don't thank me. I'm the one getting a good deal."

My father stalks through the door. "What deal are you getting?"

Luke grabs a wrench from the pile of tools next to him. "Johnny's kid sister is gonna start working the front desk."

My father cuts his eyes to me, but I keep my face blank.

"No," he snaps.

Luke looks up at him. "Excuse me?"

"I said no. I don't want her working here."

Johnny shifts uncomfortably.

"Didn't ask you," Luke says. "It's my garage, and I decide who gets hired."

My father scoffs.

"I don't get involved in your business." Luke gives him a hard stare. "Don't get involved in mine."

Johnny takes a step forward. "I don't want to—"

"You're not," Luke dismisses him.

But Luke's opinion isn't what matters to Johnny. He's not his boss, not really.

Johnny turns and looks at my father. "If this is gonna create a problem—"

My father stares back at him, the seconds dragging by before finally he grunts. "It's fine."

"You sure?" Johnny asks, and I internally cringe.

Slowly, my father tilts his head to the side. "Didn't I just say it was?"

"Yeah," Johnny answers, clearing his throat. "Just checking."

"Well, don't."

Johnny nods.

My father's attention shifts to me. He gives a pointed look toward the door, and I get up to follow him.

Once we're in the back room, he grabs a piece of paper from his desk and hands it to me. I look down, seeing five names written messily, and my stomach sinks. Next to each one is a number.

He leans against the desk. "I want you with Marcus on this."

I tuck the paper into my back pocket. "Got it."

"If they don't have the money today, let them know this is their final warning." He watches me carefully. "Make sure they're motivated to pay, yeah?"

"Yeah," I answer.

"Good. Marcus is waiting by the car."

I turn to leave and make my way outside, silently hoping those five names have the money.

I know the kind of *motivation* I'll have to help deliver if they don't. And since Marcus is coming with me, there's no getting out of it. He'll report back to my father if I don't follow through.

When I slide into the passenger seat of Marcus's car, he looks over at me. "You ready?"

"Yes," I lie.

LOYALTY

Yesterday was a shitshow.

Only one of the five names had the money they owed.

I hate who I have to become in those situations. What I have to be when my father or Marcus is watching. How easily it comes.

Pushing through the front door of the garage, all those thoughts leave my mind when my eyes land on Billy. He has a wide smile on his face as he leans his elbows on the reception desk.

I stop when I see who he's talking to.

Sam.

I knew she would probably be here today. I haven't stopped thinking about it since Johnny asked Luke yesterday.

It's already past noon, so she's likely been here for a while. I was training this morning with my old man for the fight I have in a few weeks. It was hard to keep my head in it, thinking about seeing her again.

I've never met a girl who's stayed in my mind like she has. I keep telling myself that I must be holding onto an idea of her, that I can't possibly feel this strongly about someone I've only met once. But as I come up to the desk, her eyes flick up to mine and I know it's more than just an idea.

When she looks at me, I feel something. I don't know what it is or why I feel anything at all. I just know I do.

"Hey," she says.

I tip my chin up at her. "Hey." Looking between her and Billy, I ask, "How's it going?"

"Good," he says. "My dad trained her on the basics this morning, but it's been slow, so we've just been hanging out and talking."

Talking? What have they been talking about?

"I see what you mean," Billy tells me.

Sam glances between us. "What are you talking about?"

"Jameson said you were cool."

"He did?"

"Mmhmm." Billy nods. "And he doesn't think anyone's cool."

She leans back in her chair and puts her feet up on the desk. "Well, I'm honored."

I snort, and Billy snaps his head in my direction.

"So," Sam starts, "Billy says he's working here this summer. Are you?"

I run a hand through my hair. "I'll be around."

Her lips purse before she evens out her expression. "You don't work on the cars?"

"Sometimes I do."

How I spend the rest of my time sits between us.

"There's a hangout tonight at the park," Billy says, redirecting the conversation toward something lighter. "You wanna go?"

Sam shifts in her seat, twisting a ring on her finger. "Are you asking me?"

"I'm asking both of you."

I'm about to say no when Sam answers, "Sure. I'll just have to ask my brother."

Billy knows he has me. "Jameson?" he prompts.

"Yeah, I'll go."

He slaps me on the back. "Sweet!"

The side door creaks open, and my father walks through with Luke behind him. Sam immediately drops her feet from the desk before Luke stops in front of it.

My father strides past us without a word.

I turn toward Luke for an explanation, but he subtly shakes his head. He pastes a smile on his face and says, "I'm ordering pizza to celebrate Sam's first day."

"Oh, you don't have to do that," she tells him.

"I want to," he answers. "Now, I know you boys want pepperoni." He looks over at Sam. "What toppings do you like?"

"Just cheese is fine," she says. "Or I can have pepperoni. I'm not picky."

Luke watches her like he doesn't believe her answer, but he doesn't push it. "What about your brother?"

"Johnny will eat anything."

"Okay, pepperoni it is then."

"Thank you," she breathes.

"No, thank you." He motions toward the computer. "You're a fast learner. I can already tell having you here is going to help out a lot."

She fidgets under his compliment, like she isn't used to receiving them.

How can someone like her not be used to getting compliments?

Luke calls in the order then looks between me and Billy. "Can you boys come give me a hand in the garage?"

We both nod and start to follow him out. Once I reach the door, I quickly look over my shoulder at Sam and find her already watching me. Instead of dropping her eyes, she keeps them fixed on mine.

God, she's beautiful.

I hear Billy call my name and reluctantly turn away from her.

Chapter 11

Jameson

We're all gathered around the table in the break room with open pizza boxes laid out in front of us. Sam is next to her brother, and I'm between Marcus and my father, with Luke and Billy across from me. Luke and my father won't even look at each other. I'm not sure what's going on there, and I honestly don't want to know. It's not uncommon for them to act this way. They always get over it sooner or later.

It's hard to believe they're brothers, that they were raised in a house with the same parents. How can two people who grew up together turn out so differently?

Sam sits back as everyone fights for a slice. Once all of us have taken a piece, she grabs one for herself.

The first few minutes are filled with silence, and not the comfortable kind. Eventually, Luke speaks up, trying to cut through the tensions like he always does. "Noticed you were reading," he says to Sam.

She bounces her eyes from Luke to her brother then back to Luke again. "Oh, I'm sorry," she pushes out.

Luke waves a hand. "Don't be. It can get boring sitting out there alone. Trust me, I know."

She watches him wearily, like his words are a trap.

"I'm a big reader myself," he says.

My father gives a condescending laugh, but Luke ignores him.

"You are?" Sam asks.

"Oh, yeah," Luke answers. "Ask Billy."

Billy nods. "If he doesn't have a wrench in his hand, it's a book."

"Explains your lack of living in reality," my father mumbles.

"What was that?" Luke grits out.

My father looks right at him. "You live in a fantasy world. Always have."

Luke starts to respond, but my father cuts him off before he can get a word out.

"You have no idea the shit I do for you." He pushes his plate away. "For this family."

"Oh, give me a fucking break," Luke snaps. "Keep telling yourself this is all for us. You know you only do what's best for you." Luke points to me. "You can't even see what you're doing to your own son."

My father is up from his chair in an instant. "Don't bring him into this."

Sam's attention slows on me, but I lower my eyes to the table, wanting nothing to do with this conversation. It's not like they haven't had it before.

"Outside," my father demands.

Luke slides his chair back. "Gladly."

They both storm out, and Marcus gets up to follow them. "Stay here," he says to no one in particular, but I know he's talking to me. The door slams shut behind him.

"You know what that was about?" Billy asks me.

I shake my head.

Johnny shifts in his seat. "They like this a lot?"

Billy sighs. "All the time."

Johnny catches my eye, and there's pity in his expression. I don't forget how he saw my father hit me that first day he came in.

I turn from him to Sam, but there's no pity on her face. Instead, she looks sad, like she understands, and that only makes me feel worse.

She clears her throat and turns to Johnny. "There's a thing at the park tonight." She motions to me and Billy. "Can I go with them?"

Johnny looks between us. "What kind of thing?"

"Just a few of us hanging out," Billy says. "We go all the time."

"What park?" he asks.

"The one off of Cromwell. We can walk."

Johnny grabs another slice of pizza. "You'll look out for her?"

"Of course," Billy answers.

Johnny glances at me, and I nod.

"All right, sure. I'll swing by after to pick you up."

Sam smiles. "Thanks."

He gives her a warning stare. "I'm trusting you."

His words hold a story. *Has she given him a reason not to trust her before?*

"I'll be fine," she assures him.

Something passes between them before finally he nods. "We should get back," he says, shifting his attention to me. "You think we're good to go out there. Marcus said—"

I stand. "I'll go look."

Pushing open the door, I can hear Marcus talking to my father. I quietly take a few steps until I'm sure their voices are coming from the back room. I check the garage next and find Luke underneath a car.

Returning to the break room, I hover in the doorway. "We're all good."

LOYALTY

I spend the rest of the day helping Billy and Luke in the garage, my muscles aching from the hours I put in earlier at the gym. I'm not sure where Johnny went off to, but I'm relieved I haven't been called in by Marcus or my old man. I really don't want to deal with him when he's in a mood like this.

Luke has been pleasant, but he always is. I can tell by his short responses and the strain in his eyes that he's still upset, though.

It's just past six when he tells me and Billy that we can be done for the day. Billy lets him know that we're heading out, and I stop by my father's office to let him know, too. I brace myself for him to tell me that he needs me to stay back and help him with something, but he just waves me off.

When I get back to the front, Billy is already standing by Sam, who's packing up her bag excitedly, throwing in all the things she has spread across the desk. She tosses it over her shoulder then ties up her hair and secures it with a clip she was holding in her mouth.

She has such a hectic energy to her, so different from how controlled I am. She kind of reminds me of Billy in that way.

I pull my sunglasses from where they're tucked into the front of my shirt and slide them on. "You ready?"

She nods, coming around the desk.

When we step outside, she shuffles through her purse and grabs her own pair of sunglasses. They're huge, covering half her face.

Billy laughs. "You look like a movie star."

She smiles, but instead of answering, she digs through her purse again, pulling out a pack of cigarettes and a lighter. She waves the pack between us. "Either of you want one?"

Neither of us really smoke, so we both shake our heads.

She lights one, and I watch as she brings it to her lips.

Exhaling, she asks, "So, who's gonna be there tonight?"

"Just a few of our friends," Billy says. "They're chill. You'll like 'em."

She nods, but looks unsure.

"A few of us are in a band together," Billy adds.

"Really?" She looks up at me. "Are you in the band, too?"

I shake my head.

"Do you play any instruments?" Billy asks her.

She lets out a short laugh. "No."

"What about sing?"

She takes another drag. "Absolutely not."

"Well, you can be a groupie then."

I quickly shoot him a glare. The last thing I want is all of those guys drooling over her.

Billy smirks. "Jameson's a groupie, too."

"I'm not a fucking groupie."

"Do you come watch us practice?"

I stay silent.

"Did you come to our first show?"

I scowl at him.

"Are you gonna come to our show in a couple weeks?" He throws out his hand. "I don't know what to tell you, man, but you're definitely a groupie."

"I'm not a groupie. I'm your cousin."

Sam laughs.

"I'm just hanging out."

"You can be in denial all you want," Billy teases.

Sam turns toward him. "What kind of music do you guys play?"

"Rock."

She shifts the bag on her shoulder. "All right, cool."

"Do you want me to carry that for you?" I ask.

"What?"

"Your bag," I say. "Do you want me to carry it for you? You keep fidgeting with it."

"Oh, um, you don't have to do that."

I hold out my hand. "It's no problem."

I can't tell because those ridiculous sunglasses cover so much of her face, but I think she blushes.

The bag slides down her shoulder, and then she passes it to me. "Thanks," she murmurs.

"Jesus. What do you have in here?"

"You really don't have to carry it," she says.

I switch the bag to my other hand. "There's no way I'm having you carry this now that I know how heavy it is."

She rubs at her neck. "I like to have a lot of stuff with me. You never know where you're gonna end up."

I think about how her brother brought her with him that first day I met her. How she had to stay at the garage for hours.

I nod. "Makes sense."

When we come up to the park, the guys start hollering at us. Billy races over to them, but I stay next to Sam.

Everyone is gathered around a picnic table. Some of them are sitting on top of it, while a few groups stand around. They all watch Billy approach, but one of the girls breaks away and starts toward him. It's Madison, the blonde he was hanging around with at school.

"Is that Billy's girlfriend?" Sam asks, watching the girl stop in front of him.

I shake my head. "Billy doesn't do girlfriends."

She glances over at me with a look that says, *Do you?*

I keep talking, just to fill the space, suddenly feeling restless. "She's turned into a real cling-on."

"A cling-on?"

"Girls know what they're getting with him. He never promises them anything." I look over at where they're standing. "Some of them can't take a hint."

I expect her to think that's harsh, but she only nods. "I've heard some girls talk about him," she admits.

Has she heard people talk about me?

She seems to know that's what I'm thinking because she continues on quickly. "They act like he's a thing."

I tilt my head. "What do you mean, *a thing*?"

"Like he's not even a person." She watches Billy with Madison. "But maybe that's what he wants."

We reach the table, and the conversation stops. Everyone glances from me to Sam, their eyes lingering on her. The way some of the guys are staring makes me tense, but I have no claim over her. Still, I take a step closer to her side.

As much as it pisses me off, I'm not surprised by their reactions. Sam's the kind of pretty that you can't help but notice. It's not just on the surface, either; she's got this way about her, this confidence, that you just ... I don't know ... get pulled in by.

"Who's this?" Mason asks.

"I'm Sam." She pauses. Then, like she needs to offer more of an explanation, she adds, "I work at their garage."

"Do you go to Lincoln? I've never seen you before."

I watch his eyes trail her body, and I have to fight to stand still.

"I'd definitely remember if I had."

"Yeah," she answers. "I'll be a sophomore this year."

He watches her with interest. "Well, hope I see you around."

Did he not see me coming over with her? Carrying her bag? Standing right by her fucking side?

I move even closer and lean down so just she can hear me. "Want a drink?"

"Sure," she says.

I lead her over to a cooler. There are a few sodas and a couple cans of beer floating around in melted ice. She reads the question on my face and answers, "I'll take a beer."

I hand her one and grab a soda for myself. She cracks it open, the can hissing before she takes a sip.

"We can stay over here if you'd rather," I tell her.

She peers over at the table. "No, it's fine."

I hold out my hand, and she looks up at me before taking it. Her hand is so much smaller than mine, so much softer.

I've never held a girl's hand before. I never saw the point. But I want it to be clear as we walk back over to the table that even though she technically isn't mine, she can't be anyone else's, either.

I climb up onto the table, above the spot I left her purse, and she sinks down on the bench below me, sitting between my legs.

I know everyone saw us come over. Saw her hand in mine. The way she's sitting with me.

Good.

Mason doesn't try anything with her after that.

We sit as everyone talks around us, sipping our drinks. Eventually, Billy comes over with Madison, his arm slung over her shoulders.

I guess he's gone back to her tonight.

He was just complaining to me a few days ago that she wouldn't leave him alone, that she keeps calling his house. I've told him that he's confusing as fuck. He tells girls he's done then goes back so many times that they never believe him when he says it.

She leans into him and looks at Sam. "Hi, I'm Madison," she says, her voice pitched high.

Sam's attention shifts from her to Billy, and I wish I could see the look on her face. I want to know if she finds this girl as ridiculous as I do. From the way she deadpans, "Hi, I'm Sam," I'm pretty sure she does.

"Billy told me you work at the garage."

Sam nods.

"That must be fun." Madison beams. "Maybe I can come hang out, too."

"Don't think so," I mutter.

She puffs out her bottom lip and turns to Billy, who throws me a dirty look.

"What he means is we're working," Billy tells her. "We can't just have people hanging around."

"I know," she whines, and I seriously don't understand how Billy can stand her grating voice. "But you're always working. I never get to see you."

Billy rolls his neck. "You're seeing me right now."

She deflates. "You're right." Forcing her face into a smile, she adds, "Sorry. I just miss you."

He pulls her in tighter but doesn't answer.

She turns her attention back to Sam. "Billy said you're going to be a sophomore this year at Lincoln. We can all hang out."

"Sure," Sam mumbles halfheartedly.

"Do you play any sports?" Madison asks. "Or are you in any clubs?"

"No."

"Oh," Madison says. "Well, I'm on the cheerleading squad. You should try out next year."

Sam looks down at herself then back up to Madison. "Not really my thing."

Madison is in a little pink sundress and sandals, while Sam has on cutoff denim shorts, a tight black T-shirt that hits her belly button, and her dirty black Converse. They couldn't look any more different if they tried.

Sam drains the rest of her beer and crushes the can under her foot. Madison jumps at the noise, and I have to keep myself from smiling.

Dylan comes up just as Sam is leaning back and starts talking to Billy about the upcoming show they're playing. They managed to get a daytime slot at this restaurant and bar called Rosette's. Madison keeps trying to insert herself into the conversation. After the third time, Sam glances up at me and mouths, "*What the fuck?*"

I shake my head and try to cover the laugh that slips from my lips.

Sam stays by my side the whole night. She's mostly quiet, but it seems like she's having fun.

Eventually, headlights cut through the darkness, and we both know it's her brother.

I don't want her to leave, but I feel better when she says, "See you tomorrow, yeah?"

"Yeah," I answer.

She tips her head toward the car. "Well, I've gotta go."

I nod before she turns, watching her walk away.

Billy's elbow nudges me. "I get it now," he whispers.

Chapter 12

Sam

I'm happier than I've been in a long time, or maybe ever.

I've been working at the garage for a few weeks now and, for the most part, it's been great. I get to see my brother all the time. Luke has been so kind. Billy makes me laugh more than I think anyone ever has. And Jameson ... I don't know what to think about Jameson. It seems like that's all I really do now, though ... think about him.

The way he towers over me, glancing down with that almost smile he seems to reserve for just me.

The way I catch him watching me when he thinks I'm not looking.

The way he stops by the front desk to see me any chance he gets.

I can't get him out of my mind.

And I don't think I want to.

I hang out with him and Billy during breaks and after the shop has closed. Sometimes, Jameson's father calls him away, or he's gone training for his next fight, but he stays at the shop with us more times than not.

We talk or listen to music, although our favorite thing to do together is play gin. None of us have much money, so we bet whatever we can find. It's fun.

The only part of it that isn't great is Jameson's father and knowing what goes on behind closed doors. The guy, Marcus, who's always with him, gives me the creeps, too.

When I have to stay past closing, it's because Johnny has to do things for the "unofficial" part of his job. It still scares me when I think about what he's out there doing.

Hanging out with Billy and Jameson helps distract me, but sometimes that life even bleeds into those moments. It happens when Jameson gets called away. When I can see the weight of what he's carrying in his eyes. When he comes in with a new bruise or cut. When he turns into a shell of himself the minute his father steps into the room. Or when I hear the way his father speaks to him.

I wish there was something I could do. I know Billy feels the same way. Luke, too. But it's almost like this unspoken thing that hangs in the air. We all know it's going on, but nobody feels like they can stop it.

It's the same way with the illegal shit we know they're doing. It's a clear divide with me, Billy, and Luke on one side and the rest of them on the other.

The strain between Levi and Luke is obvious, and it's not getting any better. I think we're all waiting for them to explode.

But even with all of that, I'm happy. With Jameson and Billy, it feels like I have a place where I fit in. Like I have *actual* friends.

Staring back at myself in the mirror, I finish touching up my eyeliner.

I got home from the shop about an hour ago, but Johnny and I are getting ready to head out again to go to Jameson's fight. It took a lot of convincing for my brother to let me go. I had to promise to stay right by his side the whole time.

Jameson wasn't at the shop today, and Luke won't let Billy go, so I'm gonna surprise him. I thought it would be nice for Jameson to have at least one of us there.

I don't know what to expect, though Billy told me he's really good. He seems like he would be. But I'm not sure if I'll be able to watch him take a hit.

Still, I want to be there.

A knock sounds at my door. "You ready?" Johnny asks.

I step back, glancing at myself in the mirror and running my fingers through my hair, shaking it out.

"Sam," my brother calls.

"Coming!"

We walk through the empty living room. My father left for the bar a couple of hours ago and Carson wasn't here when we got home.

Once we're in the car, Johnny turns to me. "You sure you want to go?"

"Yeah, I'm sure."

He stares out the windshield. After a minute, he says, "I don't know."

"You can't baby me, Johnny. You have to let me do things. I'm not some helpless little girl."

"I got you the job," he says. "That's doing something."

"I know, and I'm grateful, really." I set my bag down by my feet. "I just ... I like Jameson. I want to be there for him."

He softens. "All right, fine." Throwing the car in drive, he shakes his head. "God knows that kid could use someone in his corner." He pauses. "But you stay where I can see you, understood?"

"You've said that like five times already," I say just to give him shit. "I already promised, didn't I?"

He rolls his eyes. "Don't get smart."

I lean forward and switch on the radio before sinking back into my seat. We ride the rest of the way with the windows down and music blasting.

LOYALTY

My eyes widen when we pull up to what looks like an abandoned warehouse. "Have you been here before?" I ask.

Johnny parks next to a line of cars. "Couple times."

"But you didn't ..."

"No, I didn't fight," he clarifies. "Just bet."

"Bet?"

He waves his hand. "Why do you think these people are all here?"

I look at the long row of cars and shrug.

"It's not just for the show."

He steps out of the car, and I push my door open to follow him.

The parking lot, if you can even call it that, has weeds growing through the cracked asphalt. There are broken beer bottles and abandoned cigarette butts. The place is a dump.

Loud voices and cheers filter from inside as we make our way closer to the entrance.

As we move inside, I realize a fight is already going on—people are gathered in a wide circle, outlining a makeshift ring. My heart races as I step onto my tiptoes to try to see if one of the guys is Jameson.

Johnny leans down so I can hear him over the noise. "His fight isn't until later."

I relax a bit, knowing he's not out there, but then I tense again when the crowd erupts.

Someone starts counting, and then the crowd goes wild again.

As the winner walks away, the people around me shift, and a window opens, allowing me to see the ring. My eyes catch on the guy who lost, and I feel like I'm gonna be sick.

His body is beaten and bruised. He's bleeding, but I can't even tell where the blood is coming from.

Is that going to be Jameson?

Someone helps him up, and he's able to walk away on his own, but he looks awful.

Johnny shifts closer to me. "You all right?"

I nod.

The next fight is over quickly. The one after that takes a bit longer. We're close enough now that I can just barely see, and the initial shock is starting to wear off a bit. It's still brutal and, at times, I have to look away, but I'm starting to get into it, calling out like the people around me. Johnny watches it like a sport, which I guess it is.

As another fight ends, he pulls money out of his pocket, handing it to someone and yelling a name over the noise—Jameson.

He turns back to me and finds me watching him. "He's next."

A voice announces Jameson, and I stand on my tiptoes again, scanning the room for him.

Across from me, there's a break in the circle, and I see him walk through. He's in jeans ... just jeans.

My face heats at the sight of him.

His chest is tanned, and as he brings a hand up to push the dark hair out his face, the muscles in his arm flex. I notice a tattoo on his shoulder that I didn't know he had. It looks like maybe a skull.

His father walks behind him, and once they stop at the edge of the circle, he leans over to say something into Jameson's ear. I watch as Jameson stares back at him and nods.

His father steps back, and then I jump when his hand comes down against Jameson's cheek. He shouts something I can't hear, and Jameson shouts something back. They do it again and again until Jameson is clearly fired up.

The guy he'll be fighting is announced, someone named Kayden. I drag my eyes away from Jameson and see his opponent walk into the circle. He's about fifty pounds heavier and maybe ten years older, but I'd still put money on Jameson. The guy's big, but he doesn't look like he spends nearly as much time training. He bounces from foot to foot then paces from side to side like he can't get his energy out fast enough.

I look back at Jameson. Where Kayden is chaos, Jameson is pure control.

His father has faded back into the crowd, while Jameson stands still, watching his opponent.

A voice yells fight, and Kayden instantly moves forward. He throws a punch, but Jameson dodges it easily, like he saw it coming.

He circles Kayden, who tries to land another punch, but before he can right himself, Jameson's fist connects with his cheek.

I suck in a breath.

Kayden stumbles back, shakes his head, and then charges Jameson. He goes for Jameson's face but, when he misses, quickly switches to his stomach. He connects, and Jameson hunches over, the wind knocked out of him.

Fuck.

He recovers quickly, moving out of Kayden's reach before he can land another hit.

Kayden takes two quick steps and is suddenly in front of Jameson again, but Jameson swings out a leg, and Kayden trips back, allowing him to get in another hit.

People start cheering, and I hear myself joining in.

"Finish him," my brother yells.

Jameson's fist connects with Kayden's jaw then stomach, making him stagger back.

"Yes!" I yell.

He's gonna win. He's gonna be fine.

Kayden slows, and Jameson stands in place. It's a stand-off, both of them waiting for the other to make a move.

I'm not surprised when it's Kayden who moves forward, and neither is Jameson. He ducks when Kayden throws his arm out, going for another hit to Kayden's stomach. He gets the hit in, but Kayden swipes his foot out, throwing Jameson off balance and forcing him to his back.

The crowd goes crazy as Kayden pins Jameson to the ground, and panic courses through me.

"I can't see him!" I yell to my brother. "I can't see Jameson!"

There's fear in Johnny's eyes, but there's nothing he can do.

I can see Kayden moving over him, but I can't see what's happening to Jameson. All I know is he isn't getting up.

I search the crowd for his father. There's anger on his face, and he's screaming something I can't hear.

Time slows down.

I keep waiting for Jameson to get up, but he doesn't.

It starts to feel like I can't breathe.

Is he okay?

Why isn't anyone doing anything?

"Tap out," I hear my brother say.

I shift, desperately trying to see him. Finally, he manages to roll out from under Kayden.

The crowd gets so loud I have to bring my hands up to my ears to cover them. I didn't realize until now that I'm shaking.

Jameson pushes himself up, and I close my eyes when I see him, hoping that when I open them, he won't have blood dripping down his chest anymore.

Obviously, that doesn't work.

I blink my eyes open and fully take him in. There's a cut dripping blood above his eye. He's slightly hunched like he can't quite hold the weight of his body. And he starts to go fucking crazy.

The control he started the fight with is gone.

He launches at Kayden, cracking him so hard with his fist that Kayden drops to his knees. Jameson kicks him so he's flat on his back and stands over him. He waits a few seconds then rears back to kick him again but stops before his foot connects when Kayden begins hitting his hand against the ground.

"Winner," a voice yells.

I exhale, my shoulders slumping forward.

He won.

Jameson won.

Chapter 13

Jameson

Everywhere hurts.

Each breath I take stings, and my legs are screaming at me to just let myself collapse.

People are shouting my name, but their voices sound muffled. I shake my head to try to clear the fog.

My mouth still tastes like coppery blood mixed with sweat, and before Ryan can grab my hand, I turn to spit.

He pulls my arm up above my head, and I fight back a wince. The crowd grows even louder from the show of victory.

I struggle to keep my head high. All I want to do is go find a quiet corner. To sit down. To be alone.

Ryan leans into me. "That was one hell of a show, kid. I didn't think you were gonna get up this time."

I lean away from him, and he takes the hint, dropping my hand.

"You have my money?"

He gives me a quick nod and jerks his head to follow him.

I look around for Marcus or my old man but don't see them, which is weird because they usually hover around me during fights.

When I went down, I saw my father's face and heard him yelling, but when I glanced back at where he'd been standing, he wasn't there.

I push the thought away and follow Ryan. He's quick to pull the money together, and once he hands it over, I shove the bills into my front pocket.

"Gotta go," he tells me. "Next fight starts in five."

I try to make a lap around the room, but it's too crowded to get far and I don't know how much longer I can hold myself up.

After making it outside, I find an overturned crate and slowly lower myself onto it.

Just a minute. I'll just sit for a minute.

I let my eyes close and focus on breathing. It hurts so bad I think that asshole might've cracked a rib.

"Jameson?"

My eyes snap open at the familiar voice.

Sam drops to her knees in front of me. "Oh my God, Jameson. Are you okay?"

I start to stand, but she puts her hand on my knee, and I freeze.

"Don't try to get up."

"Why are you …?" I shake my head. "How are you …?" I look down at her hand that's still on my knee. "You shouldn't be here."

She rakes her eyes over me, lingering on the places I feel the most pain. "You—"

Her brother calling her name cuts her off.

I didn't even notice he was here. But it makes sense. How else would she have gotten here?

His gaze is hard, attention focused on something behind me. I know what he's looking at before I even hear my father's voice.

"Go to your brother," I force out.

Her face is pleading, almost desperate, but she stands and takes a few steps back.

A minute later, my father is in front of me, Marcus just behind him. I turn, expecting to see Big Jim walking up, too—he was here at the start of the fight—but the space behind me is empty.

My father doesn't acknowledge Sam or Johnny before closing the distance between us. I pull my head back to look up at him and wish I didn't when I see what's staring back at me.

I need to get off this crate.

I need to put space between us.

"What was that?" he asks. His voice is quiet, too quiet.

I stay silent.

"I swear to fucking God, Jameson." He shakes his head, the rage barely contained. "What was that?"

"I don't know."

I regret the answer right as the words leave my lips. My mind isn't working right. It's hard to focus on anything but the pain.

"You don't know?" He draws out the question, mocking me.

I clear my throat, the motion making it feel like my insides are on fire. "No, I do know."

He laughs, and the sound makes me want to curl in on myself. I need to get away from him.

"Which is it?"

"He just got me off balance." I look down at the ground. "I didn't see it."

Fingers grip my face, forcing me to look up. "You look at me when I'm talking to you," my father sneers. Then he lets go roughly, pushing me back. The crate stumbles, and I throw out a hand to keep from falling.

"Get up." His voice cracks.

I push myself up, and pain slices down my side. I cough, clutching my rib.

Fuck, that hurts.

My father's lip curls. "Pathetic."

The word hits me the way he knew it would.

I look past him just long enough to meet Sam's and Johnny's stares. Just long enough to beg them with my eyes to leave.

They both stand firm, Sam giving me a slight shake of her head.

My father's hand is on my face again, his fingers digging into my skin. "What did I tell you boy, hmm?" When my eyes meet his, he mutters, "You need to learn to listen."

I keep my focus on him, not letting myself move an inch.

"You were an embarrassment in there."

I don't move.

"How do you think it makes me look when I tell people I train you?" He takes a step closer. "How it makes me look when my son is lying on the ground, letting someone beat on him?"

I keep still.

"How many times have we gone over how to get out of a hold like the one he had you in?" When I don't say anything, he snaps, "That was a fucking question!"

"A lot," I answer. "We've gone over it a lot."

"Then why'd you just lay there, huh? You were down for over a minute, Jameson. A whole fucking minute!" He leans closer, his body crowding mine. "Did you give up?"

"No," I respond immediately.

"No?" he questions. "What was it then? Are you just that much of a shit fighter?"

I shake my head.

He motions to the dried blood on my chest I didn't even notice was there. "It looks like you are."

"I'm not."

He clicks his tongue. "Prove it."

"What?"

"Fight me." He pushes at my chest.

"I don't—"

"I said, *fight me*!"

"I think he's—"

"Shut up," my father bites out, cutting Marcus off.

"You just gonna stand there? I thought you said you could fight."

"I won."

He scoffs. "That win was nothing to be proud of."

"Can we just go home?" I ask, hating how quiet my voice comes out. How broken.

"After you show me you can fight."

"I—"

He pushes at my chest again. "Show me how you fight."

"Please—"

"Show me how you fight," he says again, his tone turning manic.

That pressure I hate starts to build inside me, begging to get out. It needs to escape.

I need to escape.

"Show me how you fight," he repeats.

The words won't stop coming.

They're circling around me.

Closing in on me.

I can't fucking breathe.

"Show me how you fight."

"Show me how you fight."

"Show me how you fight."

My fist flies out, and he catches it before it can connect with his face.

A laugh pours from his lips. "There he is."

I twist my hand from his hold, and just when I think it might be over, I have to drop down to avoid his fist that's now coming at my face. My whole body burns, my legs shaking as I push myself back up to standing.

He circles around me, and as I turn to follow his movement, my eyes slip past Sam.

I don't want her to—

My knees connect with the hard ground, and I throw out my hands to catch myself. My stomach heaves from the impact of the hit.

I want to fucking kill him.

I hear Sam yell for him to stop.

I really wish she wasn't here.

I glance up and see Johnny inch forward, just as my father asks, "You done already? That all it takes?"

I suck in a breath, letting the burn that comes with it center me. Slowly, I get up off the ground.

My father smiles, and all I can think about is wiping that fucking look off his face.

I accept the pain.

Let it consume me.

Until I can barely feel it anymore.

Until it becomes a pulse in the background.

The force that drives me forward.

I know I'm moving, but it's like my mind has emptied out. My fist connects with my father's jaw, and I only faintly feel the pain that runs through my knuckles.

He comes back at me, but his hit never lands. Someone pulls him back, pinning his arms behind his back.

I lunge for him but am stopped when someone grabs me from behind. I try to break out of their hold, wanting to get to my father, to sink my fist into his face again.

"Stop," the voice behind me shouts. "Jameson, calm down."

I don't listen.

I don't want to stop.

I don't want to calm down.

I want to fucking kill him.

All the pain.

All the humiliation.

All the shit he makes me do.

All the ways he's ruined my mother.

It would all be so much better if he was just gone.

I flail, trying to get free, and watch as my father does the same. The fight isn't finished. Nobody won.

"Stop it," the voice yells.

"Let me—"

My words are cut off when I see Sam push herself between me and my father.

The person behind me goes still. "I told you to wait over there."

Johnny, I realize. The voice behind me is Johnny's.

She lets her attention drift over me briefly before spinning and facing my father.

He's still moving, attempting to get out of Marcus's hold. His eyes are blazing with determination. With rage.

"Get her out of here," I force out. "Please."

"She won't leave unless you do," Johnny mutters.

"Okay." I nod. "Okay."

He lets go of me, and I try to take a step forward but stumble.

"Jesus," he hisses, throwing out a hand to steady me.

Sam turns, the fire in her eyes blinking into worry.

"Lean on me," Johnny instructs.

I do as he says, and Sam comes over to my other side.

Johnny looks over at Marcus, who's still fighting to restrain my father. "I'm taking him home with me," Johnny tells them. He starts to drag me along, not waiting for a response.

"No, you aren't," my father yells after us, pulling forward. "You get back here, Jameson."

I fight to keep my head up. "I need to—"

"No, you don't," Johnny says firmly.

He turns back toward them. "Things got heated," he says to my father. "You both just need to cool down, all right?"

"Don't you tell me—"

"Levi," Marcus cuts in. "Look at him."

My father's gaze shifts to me, and it's like he's just now realized what I look like. From the way his face shifts, I must look pretty fucking bad.

Marcus releases him, and my father pushes out his chest, raising his chin. "Why don't you go get cleaned up," he says as if it was his idea. "Get some rest."

I nod, or at least I try to.

"You can stay the night at Johnny's," he offers, like I should be thankful. "But I want you back at the garage in the morning." He watches me, waiting for a response.

My head is spinning. I just want to lay down. I'm so fucking tired.

"Jameson?"

"Yeah, thank you," I push out, and Johnny goes rigid beside me. "I'll be there tomorrow."

Satisfied, my father turns and stalks off.

Marcus watches me for a minute before my father calls his name and he quickly follows after him.

Johnny and Sam silently lead me to the car. She opens the door to the back seat, and Johnny asks me if I need help getting in. I probably do, but I shake my head.

I don't even know what to say, how to thank them. I hover in the open door and look between them. "Thank—"

"Don't," Johnny says, his tone telling me there's more to their story than I know. "That never should have ... Just get in the car. There's no need for a thank you."

I drop my chin in a silent thank you, anyway, then attempt to fold my body into the back seat. It takes twice as long as it should, but I'm finally in.

Johnny goes to the driver's seat, and I expect Sam to open the passenger door, but she slides in next to me. I don't look over at her, keeping my eyes forward, my body locked up.

We pull out of the lot, and I feel her slide closer to me. Gently, she lowers her hand over mine. Her thumb begins to slide back and forth, so lightly I can just barely feel it. I let my head fall back, my muscles unclench.

She leans into me, coming so close that our bodies almost touch. "You're going to be okay," she whispers.

Chapter 14

Sam

After pulling into our driveway, Johnny turns back and says, "Wait here."

Jameson sits up straight, softly groaning with the effort. He watches Johnny slip into the house. "I don't want to cause any trouble for you. Are your parents—"

"It's fine," I assure him.

"Why did he have to go inside then?"

I'm quiet for a minute, thinking about how to answer his question. Before I can give him a reason, Johnny is already making his way back to the car.

He opens my door and crouches down, so he's at eye level. "They're both asleep."

"Good," I answer, relieved. That'll make things easier.

"It's just our brother and old man inside," Johnny says, looking past me to Jameson. "Neither of them can know you were here."

"I'm really fine," Jameson mutters. "I don't want to create a problem for you guys. You can take me home."

Johnny shakes his head. "We've got you. I'm just gonna need you to be real quiet until we get you into Sam's room."

Jameson freezes beside me. "*Sam's room?*"

"There's an empty bed in there. I share a bedroom with my brother, so you can't stay in my room. Sam used to share with our sister Cathleen, but she moved out." Johnny glances between us, settling his eyes on Jameson. "I'm trusting you."

"I would never—"

"I know," Johnny cuts him off. "Like I said—I trust you."

Jameson nods, a look on his face that makes it clear how much my brother's show of faith means to him.

"Okay, good," Johnny says. "Now, a few things before we go in. Our old man is asleep on the couch. It usually takes a lot to wake him, but we still need to be careful." He pauses, thinking. "And we'll need to be out by seven tomorrow morning; that should give us enough time before they wake up. And if, for some reason, they're already awake by then, we'll use the window."

I expect Jameson to ask questions, but he just responds, "Got it."

"Oh," Johnny adds, "and obviously lock the door." He turns to me. "You need anything, you come get me. Okay?"

"Okay," I answer.

Johnny stands and starts to round the car. Before I can slide out of my seat, he's already opening Jameson's door and helping him out.

I move to Jameson's other side, and we slowly make our way up the lawn.

Pushing the front door open, I cringe at the way the hinges creak before we step into the dimly lit living room. All the lights are off, but the glow of the streetlamps and brightness of the TV illuminates the space enough to see our path.

I watch Jameson scan the space, his eyes lingering on my father and the beer cans spread out on the table in front of him.

When we start up the stairs, I hear Jameson suck in a couple of sharp breaths, but he manages them without complaint.

We make it into the hallway, which is nearly too dark to see. Luckily, Johnny and I can navigate our little house blindfolded. We guide Jameson between us until we make it to the end of the hall where my room is.

I turn the knob and flick on a light. Johnny helps lower Jameson onto my sister's abandoned bed, and once he's settled, he looks around.

There's not much to take in. Cathleen's side is practically empty. I have a couple posters taped to the wall above my bed and my small stack of books, but that's about it.

Johnny hovers over Jameson as I come to stand next to him. I thought Jameson looked bad before, but now that I can see him in the light, I'm starting to worry he needs more help than we can give him.

My eyes trail from his face down to his bare chest, noting all the places he's bruised or bleeding.

"I'll go get you something to ice that," Johnny says, his gaze fixed on Jameson's bruised side. "And a shirt."

He starts to leave, but I grab his arm. "Maybe we should …" I turn my attention from him to Jameson. "Maybe we should take him to the hospital."

"No," Jameson mutters. "No doctors."

Johnny doesn't seem surprised by his response, but I shake my head. "You haven't seen yourself. You look—"

"I'm fine."

"You don't look fine," I respond quietly.

"I just need to get cleaned up. Rest." He glances at Johnny, and something passes between them. "I'll be fine in the morning. Trust me."

I hesitate. "But—"

"I would know if it was that bad." He sits up straighter, like that'll prove his point. "And it isn't."

It occurs to me that the only way he'd know what it would feel like to need a doctor is because he's experienced it. Because, at one point, he *did* need one.

The realization must be written all over my face because he softens. "Do you have a first-aid kit?" he asks. "That would help."

He's giving me something. A way to feel useful. Some semblance of control.

I nod.

"You get that," Johnny says. "And I'll go get the ice."

I hesitate until Jameson says gently, "I'll be fine."

"Okay, yeah." I breathe out. "Okay."

Johnny leads the way out of the room. Once we're in the hall, he whispers, "You good?"

"Yeah," I answer quietly.

He moves toward the kitchen, and I duck into the bathroom. I find the first-aid kit under the sink and wet two washcloths before returning to my room.

Johnny comes in right behind me. He sets down a frozen bag of peas and a T-shirt on the bed beside Jameson.

I put the first-aid kit on the desk, and Johnny motions toward it. "You need help?" he asks. "I can stay."

I shake my head. "I can do it."

He looks between the two of us. It seems like he's about to say something, but then he just nods. "Seven a.m. tomorrow," he reminds us.

We both mumble in agreement.

He's still for a moment before eventually starting toward the door. "Lock it behind me."

"I will."

I follow him and wait as he closes the door then lock me and Jameson inside.

Chapter 15

Jameson

Sam turns away from the door, her eyes meeting mine. She looks almost ... shy.

I watch her walk over to me, her gaze moving from my face to the floor. It's surreal to be here with her. To be in her room. In her space, the two of us alone.

She stops in front of the desk that's shoved between the two beds. It's old, with lots of drawers that I wish I could go through.

Her room is so empty it makes me wonder where she keeps all her things. I expected her space to be chaotic, overflowing with the pieces of her life. The bag she always carries around seems to hold an endless amount of stuff. But the only way you can even tell the room is hers is the small stack of books that's balanced on her side of the desk.

She has some posters up on the wall of bands I've never heard her talk about. Other than that, the room is lifeless, sterile even.

I move the frozen bag of peas from my face to my side. They aren't very cold anymore, but I don't want her to leave again, so I don't say anything.

She looks over her shoulder when she hears me move, her hands hovering above the first-aid kit. After setting something down, she spins the desk chair around so it's facing me, lowering herself into it.

Her face is level with mine as she twists to grab a wet washcloth off the desk. "I'm gonna start with your face. Is that all right?"

I nod.

She leans forward, and I spread my legs to accommodate hers. Her attention quickly drops down before she settles it back on my face. Gently, she presses the washcloth to my eyebrow and rubs at the dried blood. She watches me for a reaction, but I keep still. "Does that hurt?"

"No," I lie.

She pulls the washcloth away, folds it over, then runs it down my cheeks and above my lip.

I close my eyes and drop my shoulders.

"You okay?"

"Yeah, it feels nice." I sigh. "I've never had someone do this for me before. I always do it myself."

Her hand slows, but she doesn't say anything. She just keeps dragging the washcloth along my face. Eventually, she pulls away, and I hear a wrapper being ripped open.

I open my eyes as she says, "This is gonna hurt."

She pours hydrogen peroxide on a gauze pad then presses it against my eyebrow. I hiss at the sting, and she winces from the sound.

"Sorry," she whispers.

I lick my lip. "I'm fine."

She peels open a butterfly bandage, and it reminds me of the time I first saw her.

"What actually happened that first day you came to the garage?"

"What?"

"With your face."

She smooths the bandage over my eyebrow.

"You had a cut on your face."

"Oh, that."

"You said you fell, but"—I shake my head—"you didn't."

She busies herself, shuffling through the kit. "I got into a fight."

I tense. "With who?"

She shrugs. "Some girl." Turning back, she has a fresh washcloth in her hand.

"What'd you—"

"I'm going to—" she says at the same time.

I let out a short laugh. "Sorry, go ahead."

She grazes her teeth over her bottom lip. "I'm going to do your chest now." She begins to wipe away at the blood that's caked onto my chest, her brows furrowed.

"Most of it isn't mine," I tell her.

I wait for her judgment, but it doesn't come.

"So, why'd you and this girl get into a fight?"

"It was stupid."

"Doesn't matter. I've been in plenty of stupid fights."

She hesitates.

"You don't have to tell me."

"It's just ..." She trails off. "It's embarrassing."

I gesture toward myself. "Can't get any more vulnerable than this."

She drops her eyes to her lowered hands and sighs. "She called me a slut." Before I can say anything, she continues quickly, "I didn't even know who she was. She and her friend came up to me, accusing me of trying to get with her boyfriend." She shakes her head. "I asked her who her boyfriend was and that only made her more mad. When she told me, I realized I have English with him, but we've never done anything." She raises the washcloth back to my chest.

"That's not a stupid reason to get into a fight," I tell her.

"I just get sick of it," she mumbles.

"Sick of what?"

"The rumors."

I suck in a breath when she skates the washcloth over my rib.

She yanks her hand back. "Shit, sorry."

"It's okay," I groan, fighting back a cough. "What rumors?"

"I'm surprised you haven't heard them."

"It's a really big school."

She bites her lip, folding the washcloth in her lap.

"Sam," I push, and she looks back up at me. "What rumors?"

"Guys..." She drops the washcloth onto the desk so she has an excuse to look away from me again. "Guys sometimes say they've been with me when they haven't."

I grind my teeth. "What?"

"It's not—"

"Who?"

"Hmm?"

"Who started the rumors?"

"Oh, I don't ..." She turns back to me. "It's okay."

"That's not okay, Sam."

"When I hear something, I deal with it," she says defensively. "Like that girl." Leaning back in her chair, she adds, "I can handle myself."

"But you shouldn't have to."

Her eyes go to the bruise on my side. "We both deal with things we shouldn't have to."

"If you hear a rumor like that again, you tell me, okay?"

She watches me for a moment before she finally whispers, "Okay."

"I mean it," I tell her.

She dips her chin, and I watch as she moves to neaten the supplies on the desk, putting everything in its place, then reaches for the frozen bag of peas. "I'll go get you another bag."

"You don't have to—"

"I'm not asking," she cuts me off. "You need to keep icing"—she waves her hand—"everywhere."

She starts to stand, and I grab her wrist. "Thank you, seriously."

She looks at me, like *really* looks at me, and it makes me feel like maybe ... I don't know ... like maybe she sees me as something better. *Someone* better than I really am.

"Of course," she breathes. "Be right back."

She's only gone a couple minutes before she's silently easing through the door. It's obvious from the way she moves that she's used to quietly slipping through the house.

She hands me another bag of peas, and I press it against my side.

She slowly rakes her eyes down my chest. "Isn't that cold?"

I tilt my head. "Thought that was the point."

She laughs. "Don't be a smartass."

"And why do you have so many bags of peas?"

She pulls her lip between her teeth, trying to stifle another laugh. "They were on sale."

I pull the bag away from my side because it really is cold.

She nods toward the shirt Johnny brought for me. "Do you wanna put that on?"

I eye it wearily before setting down the peas and grabbing the shirt. She stands over me as I attempt to pull it over my head, but I grimace when I raise my arm.

She takes a step toward me. "I can help you ..." She pauses. "I mean, if you want me to."

"Yeah," I choke out through the pain.

Slowly, she helps me thread my arms through the sleeves, her hands gently brushing against my skin. I've never had someone treat me like this before, be this soft with me, this careful.

I try to move, but she tells me to keep still and slides the shirt over me.

She picks up the peas and hands them to me. "When'd you get that tattoo?"

"What?"

"The skull."

"Oh, yeah, that." I shift in place, my mind all scattered from how close she is, from the way her hands felt on me and how I wish I could have them on me again. "Not too long ago."

"Does it mean anything?"

"No, just thought it looked cool."

"Do you want more?" she asks, lowering herself back into her chair.

I nod. "I'll probably end up with a bunch." I press the peas back to my side. "What about you?"

"I don't know," she says. "I think I'd get one if it meant something." She's quiet for a minute before she asks, "Why'd you go to that fight?"

"What do you mean?"

"Like, did you want to do it? Do you like fighting?"

"It's complicated."

"I told you my stuff," she says.

I blow out a breath. "I like to fight, but ..."

"But what?"

"I don't like who I am when I do. I don't like that I like it."

She nods like she understands.

I wonder if she really does.

"And it's a lot of pressure." I move the peas up to my face. "I always have to win. With my old man, there's not really any room for error."

"Yeah," she says, her voice dropping, "I saw."

"I ..." I run a hand through my hair out of habit and flinch from the pain that shoots up my side. "I wish you didn't see that."

"I wish it didn't happen," she tells me. "But I'm not sorry that I saw it, that I was there."

She stands from her chair, opens the window that's over the desk, then rummages through a drawer. I lean forward, waiting to see what she's looking for.

She pulls out a small tin and a lighter. Hoisting herself onto the desk, she settles in and takes out a half-smoked joint. I don't ask her where she got it from, but part of me wonders if she stole it from one of the few times she's sat with me while I rolled them.

She lights it, takes a hit, then offers it to me.

Normally, I would pass, never wanting to give up control, but with the amount of pain I'm in right now, I take it from her.

"How long have you been fighting?"

"Actual fights like that"—I pass her back the joint—"about a year."

"Have you ever lost?"

"Once," I answer, my hand instinctively dropping to my side.

She traces the movement, her eyes darkening. "Bet that didn't go over well."

I shake my head. "Once was more than enough, that's for fucking sure. Never let myself lose after that."

"What did he ...?" She pauses. "Never mind, sorry ..."

"It's all right," I tell her as she brings the joint up to her lips, as if to silence herself. "It's ... uh ..."

She watches me. "It's what?"

"Nice that you care."

"Why wouldn't I?" she asks, tilting her head to the side.

I shrug. "It's easier to look the other way. Most people do."

"Yeah, well, that's shitty."

"Doesn't make it any less true, though."

She shifts on the desk. "It scared the shit out of me when you went down," she admits. "I couldn't see you with everyone in front of me. I didn't think you were gonna get up."

"Me, neither," I answer, remembering the feeling of being pinned to the ground, my body beaten, my father screaming at me.

"Johnny bet on you," she says, her words pulling me from my thoughts.

"He did?"

"If I had money, I would have bet on you, too."

"Next time," I tell her, but she frowns.

"I didn't ..." She twists a ring on her hand, something I've noticed her do before. "It was hard for me to watch you get hurt like that."

My stomach tightens. "It was?"

She nods.

"When I saw you there, I was upset," I say, and she ducks her head. "But only because I didn't want you to be in a place like that and ... and also because I was happy you were there, and I felt like I shouldn't be."

Slowly, she raises her head, her eyes brighter than they've been all night.

"You've seen what my life is like. Being around me isn't a good place to be. It's ..." I wrap a hand around my middle. "It's selfish for me to want you there."

"But I like being there," she says quietly. "I like being with you."

"You do?"

"Yeah." She blushes. "A lot."

I blink as she stubs out the joint.

"I like being with you, too," I murmur.

She brings her knees up to her chest. "Really?"

I nod then repeat her words. "A lot."

She smiles, and it's the best thing I've ever seen.

Catching me watching her, she asks, "What?"

"Your smile," I tell her. "I like it when you smile."

She runs her fingers over her lips before she slides off the desk and steps over to a chest of drawers. "Are you tired?"

Exhausted.

"A little," I answer.

"I'm going to change. I'll um …" She bends down to grab her sleep clothes. "I'll be right back."

"I can step out."

"No, it's okay." The drawer squeaks as she closes it. "Do you need anything?"

"I'm all right."

"Water?"

"That's okay."

She nods before leaving, the door softly closing behind her.

It's not long until she's back, wearing a T-shirt that swallows her whole. I drop my eyes to the floor so I won't stare as I hear her walk over to her bed.

I look up when the springs creak, finding her sitting across from me, her body mirroring mine.

"I'll let you get some sleep," I mutter, turning to stack the pillows behind me, but before I can get far, Sam comes up beside me.

"Let me," she says.

I drop my hand and look up at her.

She arranges the pillows, and I attempt to move my body back.

"Whoa, easy," she warns. She holds out her arm for me to grab onto, helping me lower myself down. Once I'm settled, she asks, "That feel all right?"

I nod.

The bottom of the bed dips as she sits by my feet. She reaches for my boots, and her eyes move up to mine, asking permission. I dip my chin, and she begins to untie them.

She places both boots on the floor beside the bed, sets an alarm, and then turns off the light. The room falls into darkness, and I hear her climb into bed.

Enough time passes that I think she's fallen asleep, but then her small voice breaks through the quiet. "Jameson, are you still awake?"

I turn my head toward her. "Yes."

Chapter 16

Sam

I roll to my side. "I can't sleep."

"Me neither," he says.

"Can I ...?" I start, my voice just above a whisper. "Can I come lay with you?"

He looks over at me, his face illuminated by the light of the moon, and watches me for a minute before he softly murmurs, "Yeah."

Slipping out of bed, I take my blanket with me and climb in next to him, moving over until we're side-by-side, keeping still so I won't hurt him.

"You won't break me," he mutters.

You're already broken, I want to say.

"Come here," he breathes. He pulls his arm back and shifts.

Gently, I lower my head down to his chest and fit into the curve of his body. He wraps his arms around me, pulling me into him.

"Am I hurting you?" I ask.

"No, you're fine."

"Are you sure?"

He shushes me, bringing his hand down to my hair. He lightly strokes it and says, "You don't have to worry about me."

"But I do," I tell him. "Worry about you."

His hand stills.

"Whenever you get pulled away at the garage, I wonder where you are. If you come in late, I wonder if you're okay. When I see another bruise or cut on your face, I wonder how you got it." I swallow. "And today, when you went down ... I was worried you weren't gonna get up."

"This is why I'm no good for you," he says. "I don't want you to always be worried."

"I can't help it."

He begins to pull away from me, but I grab his arm and place it back around my waist. "Don't," I whisper.

"You don't want this," he states. "I'm not an easy person—"

"Neither am I," I cut in before he can finish.

"No, you're not like me." He shakes his head. "This world isn't for you. I mean, look at me."

I tilt my head back and glance up at him. "You're not gonna scare me away." I lay my head against his chest again. "And how do you know I'm not like you? You don't know what my life has been like."

He goes still beneath me. "What does that mean?"

"My life has been hard, too," I answer. "There's lots of things about me that aren't easy, that're fucked up."

"You're not fucked up," he says like it's a fact.

"No, but I am." I sigh. "I've never really had friends ... or anything more." I feel his thumb brush lightly against my waist. "But I like you. You make me feel like I'm not fucked up. Like I fit." I peer over at him. "I don't know if that even makes sense."

"It does."

"Really?"

"I've been trying to fight it, telling myself I'm no good for you ... but you make me feel that way, too." He pauses. "When I'm around you, I feel like myself."

"Jameson?" I murmur.

"Yeah."

"You can stop fighting it now."

"What do you—"

I shift in his hold, rolling onto my side so our faces are just inches apart, giving him a clear invitation.

He lets out a soft breath, his eyes fixed on mine before they drop down to my lips. Slowly, like he's giving me time to back away, he leans in and presses his lips against mine.

LOYALTY

The sound of my alarm going off makes me flinch. I turn to look over at the clock, not believing it's already six thirty.

Me and Jameson talked all night, and I shared things with him that I've never told anyone before. Details about my family that I keep locked away, the struggles I try to hide and the things I secretly wish for. Jameson listened to everything, never judging, and it felt good, foreign, to be seen in the way that he sees me.

He shared just as much—the moments of his life that he keeps hidden behind the mask he wears so well. I knew things were hard for him, but I hadn't realized quite how bad they really are.

As he spoke, I could tell these were things he's rarely ever talked about, or maybe things he's *never* talked about. And even though I was tearing down my walls for him, there was a part of me that couldn't believe he was doing the same for me. That not only did I trust him with my secrets, but he trusted me with his.

The kiss he gave me was short, more gentle than I would have imagined, but things felt different after. Like we both stopped fighting the obvious and accepted what we clearly are to each other.

The alarm continues to blare, and I slide out from under Jameson's arm, hitting the top of it. The room goes quiet as I switch on the bedside lamp then turn back to him, a gasp falling from my lips.

"That bad, huh?"

"Do you want something for the pain?" I stammer, my attention slowing on his bruised cheek and eye that's nearly swollen shut. "I should have asked you last night. I wasn't thinking."

He shrugs as if it's nothing. "I'm fine."

"No," I tell him, "you're not, so stop saying that." Before he can give me an excuse, I'm already starting for the door, stopping to grab a change of clothes on the way. "Be right back," I call over my shoulder.

Tiptoeing out of my bedroom, I get dressed in the bathroom then move down the dark hallway, relieved when I see my father still passed out on the couch.

After grabbing the few things I'm looking for, I quickly head back for my room. When I open the door, I find Jameson standing, with the bed made and his shoes on.

"How did you ...?" I shake my head. "I would have helped you."

He doesn't say anything. Instead, he watches me walk to the desk and drop all the things I've collected.

"You running away or something?"

I roll my eyes. "Someone has to take care of you." I pull out the desk chair. "Sit."

He drags his gaze from the desk to me, and I arch a brow. Finally, he lowers himself into the chair.

I hand him a banana and another frozen bag of peas.

He tilts his head.

"You need something in your stomach for the ibuprofen, and those bruises could use all the help they can get."

He's swallowing the pills when a knock quietly sounds from the door. I rush over to open it.

Johnny looks past me, his eyes finding Jameson. "We've gotta go."

"Is he—"

"Still asleep," Johnny answers.

I let out a breath. "Okay, good."

He lowers his voice so only I can hear him. "Everything go all right last night?"

I nod, a smile pulling at my lips.

Johnny studies me like he's searching for something. Then he moves his gaze past me, and I feel the heat of Jameson's body come up behind mine.

"We good to go?" he asks.

Johnny gives me a knowing look, and I turn away from him to grab my bag.

"Yeah," he answers. "Be quiet leaving."

Jameson nods before Johnny moves out into the hall. I throw a few things into my bag while Jameson waits for me by the door. He steps away as I approach, letting me go out first, and lightly places his hand on my lower back.

The house is lifeless as we make our way toward the front door, being extra careful when we slip through the living room.

The ride over to the garage is short and quiet. All of us seem to be processing what happened last night and anticipating what we'll be met with when we get to the garage.

I'm not sure how Jameson's father is going to react to the fact that I got between them. To that fact that me and Johnny witnessed a scene between him and Jameson that is normally kept behind closed doors. Whatever he does, however he reacts, I'll take it, because I don't regret what I did. Levi can throw whatever he wants at me, and it'll still be worth stepping in and protecting Jameson.

We pull in through the gates, and I immediately scan the parking lot, looking for one car in particular. I tense when I see it—the shiny black car Jameson's father drives, parked up front in his usual spot.

I know that Johnny and Jameson see it, too, but if Jameson is nervous to see his father, he doesn't show it.

The bell over the door chimes as we walk in, causing Billy and Luke to turn from where they were talking at the front desk.

Luke's face instantly drops into a scowl, and as we get closer, Billy mutters, "Jesus, Jameson."

Luke turns his attention from Jameson to me and my brother. "Why are you coming in with them?"

Jameson shakes his head, offering no explanation.

"Did something happen at the fight?" Luke pushes.

"I've gotta go check in," Jameson says, looking anywhere but at them.

"This has to stop," Luke mutters. "This fighting. I don't understand it."

"It's all good," Jameson tells him. "I won."

"I don't care if you won," he says, his voice ringing out through the empty space. "I care that you're hurt."

"He back there?" Jameson asks, ignoring the worry pressing in around him.

Luke's shoulders drop in defeat. "Yeah, he's back there."

Jameson starts toward the hallway, and Johnny takes a step behind him. "I'll go with you."

"I'm all set."

"I've gotta talk to him about something, anyway."

Jameson turns. "Later," he says, the word leaving no room for argument.

The minute he disappears into the hallway, Luke shifts to me and Johnny. "What was that about? What happened?"

"We were at the fight," Johnny answers. "We took him home."

"Why?"

"Levi ..." Johnny starts. "He needed some time to cool down."

"From what?"

Johnny rubs at the back of his neck. "You know I can't—"

Luke pushes away from the front desk. "For fuck's sake," he snaps, storming out into the garage.

"I've gotta ..." Johnny points toward the back room. "You good?"

"Yeah, fine," I tell him, trying to hide the lie. Really, I'm just overwhelmed. Nervous about what's coming. About all the different personalities. Who's upset with who. Who has power over who. The things I can't say. And the things I wish I could.

I round the desk and take my place behind it.

Billy lowers his elbows on the edge of it, his voice quiet. "Tell me what happened."

I shake my head.

"Come on; it's me," he presses.

"Ask Jameson."

He sighs. "You know how he is." He drums his hands nervously. "Just tell me he's okay."

I open my mouth, willing the words to come out, but when I look up at Billy, at the fear in his eyes, all I give him is silence. Because as much as I want to, I can't make myself lie to him.

Chapter 17

Jameson

The door to my father's office is half open, but I still knock.

"Come in," he grunts from behind his desk.

I brace myself for his reaction, not sure what I'll get.

He shuffles some papers in front of him, not bothering to look up at me. "I need you to go make a pickup." His voice is calm, giving nothing away. He finally glances up at me, his expression neutral, as if I don't look like I just got the shit kicked out of me.

"Sure," I tell him, noticing the bruise that's coloring his jaw from where I hit him. "Sid?"

He nods then goes back to the papers on his desk.

I stand in place, waiting to be dismissed. *Is he fucking with me? Putting me at ease before he snaps?*

I don't let my guard down. Then again, I never do.

The seconds tick by, and I keep myself from anxiously shifting my feet.

Finally, he breaks the silence. "So, Johnny's kid sister, huh?"

"What?"

"The girl," he says. "You seeing her?"

I think before I respond. I want to tell him that I don't know, but he hates when people give him anything less than a straight answer. "Yeah," I tell him. "I am."

"I would be, too, if I were your age," he says. "Hot little thing like that."

My hand flinches at my side, itching to form into a fist.

He leans back in his chair. "We're having a family dinner tonight."

A family dinner?

"Bring her," he adds.

"It's still new." My words rush out. "Real new."

He clicks his tongue. "That's not what it looked like from where I was standing. Seems like she's all up in your business. Put herself between us without a second thought, like she didn't care what happened to her."

"It's—"

He shifts forward, his elbows coming down on the desk. "Dinner tonight, Jameson. Don't fucking test me, or I'll take your little plaything away."

What the fuck does that mean? And she's not my plaything.

I roll my lips to keep the words inside. Instead of snapping back, I nod.

"Good," he says then waves his hand for me to leave.

I push the door open and find Johnny leaning against the wall beside it.

"You all right?" he asks quietly.

"Fine."

He scans the length of my body like he's looking for evidence that I'm lying.

I move past him, and he slips into the office.

Sam is sitting alone behind the desk, her head bent over a book. When she hears me approaching, her gaze pulls up, finding mine.

She sets down the book. "How'd it go?"

I run a hand through my hair and wince at the pain in my ribs.

"That bad?" she asks.

"Huh?"

"You only do that when you're upset." She motions to me. "Run your fingers through your hair."

I drop my hand. "You been watching me?"

A blush creeps up her neck.

"Billy wants to talk to you," she says, instead of answering my question.

"Figured he would."

"I didn't tell him anything ... 'cause I didn't know ..." She trails off.

"Thanks."

"Are you feeling okay?" she asks, running her eyes over me.

"Just a bit sore," I answer. "I'm all right, though."

She doesn't look convinced. "Let me know if you need anything."

"I will," I tell her then hesitate. "I need to, uh ... I need to talk to you about something."

She straightens. "Okay."

"My dad wants you to come over for dinner tonight."

Surprise quickly flashes across her face. "Why?"

"Because, you know, we're ..."

"We're what?"

I blow out a breath. "After what happened last night, what you did ..."

"What I did?"

"Stepping in between us."

"Oh," she says, as if it's an afterthought.

"I was pissed when you did it ..." I mutter, and she crosses her arms over her chest. "I didn't want you to get hurt."

"Well, it worked, didn't it?" she huffs.

"Yeah." I smirk. "It was also pretty badass."

She lifts her chin, a small smile coming to her lips.

"But, anyway, after what you did last night, he asked if we were together."

She blinks. "What'd you say?"

"I told him we are."

Her small smile turns into a full one. "Did you really?"

I take a step closer.

"So, what are you—my ...?" She shifts in her seat nervously. "Are you my boyfriend now?"

"Do you want me to be?"

She bites her lip and nods.

"Then, yeah," I tell her. "I'm your boyfriend now."

"And I'm your girlfriend," she says more to herself.

I place my elbows on the desk, and our eyes lock. She leans forward, erasing the distance between us, and I brush my lips over hers. Her breath hitches as I wrap a hand around the back of her head, pulling her into me. Her soft lips move over mine. I could do this all day, but I break the kiss with a sigh.

"I've gotta go."

She runs her tongue over her bottom lip, clearing her throat. "Where?"

"I've gotta pick something up," I answer vaguely.

Her face falls, but she doesn't say anything.

"So, dinner tonight?" I ask.

She plays with one of her rings. "I'll have to check with Johnny." She looks up at me. "Your dad asking me to come over for dinner ..."

"Yeah?"

"Is that a good thing or a bad thing?"

I start to raise my hand to run it through my hair, but stop when she tracks the motion. I lower it back to my side and shake my head. "I really don't know."

Chapter 18

Sam

Johnny was reluctant to let me go to dinner at Jameson's house, but I convinced him that I would be fine. He told me he'd come to pick me up at nine and to call if anything happened. I promised him I would. He also said he would cover for me if our dad asked where I was, although he probably wouldn't be home until late, anyway. Our father usually spends Friday nights in his favorite seat at Al's bar.

The question of me and Jameson lingered between us, the answer practically implied, but when Johnny came out and asked if we were together, I didn't deny it. He just told me to be careful, and I assured him that I would be.

When Jameson finally came back from *picking something up*, I watched as Johnny cornered him. His protectiveness is a lot sometimes, but I guess it's nice to have someone who's always looking out for me.

I honestly don't know what I'd do without Johnny here to have my back.

LOYALTY

The shop has been busy, and the day has gone by quickly. I haven't had much time to think about what dinner tonight will be like. I'm definitely nervous to go, but it feels like it can't be avoided. If I want to be with Jameson, which I do, I can't let him think I'm scared of his life.

The door to the garage pushes open, and Billy waltzes through.

"So"—he grins—"you and Jameson, huh?"

I look behind Billy as Jameson comes in after him.

They must have had their talk.

"I've been telling him he likes you, but the idiot kept denying it like it wasn't fucking obvious."

My eyes flit over to Jameson, and I fight to hide a smile. "You guys been talking about me?"

Billy stops in front of the desk, leaning against it. "Oh, he's liked you since—"

"Jameson!" a deep voice barks. "Let's go."

Billy's expression goes flat as Levi walks through the side door and comes up behind Jameson.

His father looks around him at me, his voice taking on a sickly-sweet tone as he asks, "You ready to go, honey?"

It takes all I have not to say something I shouldn't. I knew this dinner was going to be a test from the moment Jameson told me about it. His father is going to try to get a rise out of us. Yesterday can't go unpunished, and this seems to be how he plans on delivering it.

I stand and grab my purse from where it's sitting at my feet then round the desk. "Let me just go tell my brother I'm leaving."

"No need," Levi says. "I already told him."

Hit number one: Reminding me that my brother works for him. That my family's income relies on him.

I nod stiffly.

"Good," he says then starts for the door.

Jameson and I tell Billy goodbye and follow Levi to the car.

"Sorry about ..." Jameson slows. "You don't have to come."

I grab his hand. "I'm all right."

"I don't know what he's—"

"Jameson," I stop him. "I can handle it, really."

He jerks his head into a nod, but he doesn't look any less unsure.

Levi stops at the old classic black car I've come to recognize as his. Jameson opens the passenger door and lowers the front seat, motioning for me to climb into the back. He starts to follow in behind me when I hear Levi say over the roof of the car, "I'm not a goddamn taxi driver chauffeuring you around. Get up here."

Jameson's eyes briefly meet mine, an apology in them, before he rights the front seat. He sucks in a breath as he lowers himself into the car, trying to disguise the sound by clearing his throat.

Levi doesn't miss anything, though, and says, "Give me a number."

A number?

Jameson shifts in his seat. "Four."

"The real number, boy."

"Seven."

"Do you want something?"

"No," he answers. "I'm fine."

His pain, I realize. *He's asking Jameson to rate his pain.*

My stomach sinks at how he answered immediately, like he knew exactly what his father was asking.

Because this is common.

Because Jameson being in pain is *common*.

Levi takes him in, slowing at the bruising that colors his face, and shakes his head before starting up the car.

Anger courses through me at how wrong this is—at his father's lack of sympathy. But what can I do to stop it? What can anyone do, really?

We pull out onto the main road, the car silent. I wait for the questions to start, but they don't come. In fact, I've been waiting for Levi to ask me about the fight since we got to the shop this morning.

The silence pressurizes around us as we continue to drive, and I realize this is all part of his tactic. To put us on edge, to make us wonder why we're here and what's coming next.

Jameson finds my eyes in the rearview mirror, and I hold his stare.

The car pulls left off the main road, and we're soon pulling into a driveway. I look up at the house, surprised by how well it's taken care of. The lawn isn't cluttered with old junk, and the grass looks freshly cut. Its white paint seems new, barely even chipping.

The seat in front of me drops forward, and I realize I've been staring. I slide toward the door and climb out of the seat, pulling my bag out behind me.

"Your house is nice," I say quietly.

Jameson mutters a thanks, but the way he says it doesn't sound happy. He leads me behind his father up to the front door.

Levi pushes it open and hollers, "Aubrey!" into the quiet house.

"In the kitchen," a woman yells back.

Jameson takes my hand and positions himself in front of me as we move through the living room too quickly for me to take it in before we walk into the kitchen.

My eyes instantly land on his mother, and confusion sweeps through me. She has on skin-tight jeans, a little slinky black top, and stilettos. She's cooking dinner in *stilettos*.

Levi walks over to her and slides his hand down her back, sweeping it over her ass. "Smells good," he mutters.

She turns toward him, but her attention catches on Jameson. "Oh, your face!" she gasps, staring toward us. "Levi, his face."

It occurs to me that this is the first time she's seen Jameson since the fight.

She takes another step, her hand coming up to his cheek.

"I'm fine, Ma," he pushes out.

Moving back his hair, her gaze goes to the cut over his eyebrow.

"Don't coddle him," Levi says curtly. "He's fine." Then he motions to me. "Plus, we have company, remember?"

She peers around Jameson, her focus shifting to me. "God, you're gorgeous," she breathes before turning to Levi. "You didn't tell me she was gorgeous."

Just like that, Jameson is forgotten. Levi told her that he was fine, so I guess that means he's fine.

She moves around Jameson, assessing me. "I can see why my Jameson likes you." She trails her eyes down my body, her lips pursing when she gets to my dirty Converse. "Although your clothes could—"

"Ma," Jameson warns.

She moves her eyes back up my body until they meet mine. "A pretty girl like you would look so much better if—"

"Jesus, Ma," Jameson groans. "Seriously, enough."

"What?" she says, looking over at him. "I can take her shopping, get her fixed right up." She turns to me. "Do you want me to take you shopping?"

"Oh, I, um—"

"I always wished I had a daughter," she says more to herself before I can respond.

"Well, you're stuck with me," Jameson says.

"You want a drink?" he asks, glancing over at me.

"Sure," I answer, grateful for any reason to end this conversation.

His mother turns back to the stove while Levi takes a seat at the table. Jameson opens the fridge and gently pulls me into his side.

"I'm so sorry she said that," he whispers.

"It's okay," I tell him.

"No," he grits out, "it isn't." He grabs a can of Coke from the fridge and hands it to me before completely closing the space between us. "Don't let them get into your head."

I look up, my eyes meeting his. "I won't," I murmur, hoping it's the truth.

Chapter 19

Sam

Levi's knife scrapes loudly against his plate as he cuts into his piece of chicken. Jameson's mother watches me, waiting for me to follow suit.

I take a bite and smile at her, trying not to make a bad impression. "This is really good, thank you."

Her painted lips tip up as she pushes the peas around her plate. "I'm glad you like it." She reaches for the drink in front of her, a low glass with clear liquid and way too many olives. "So," she says, "how long have you and Jameson been together?" She looks over at him, her expression pinching. "Apparently, he never tells me anything."

I clear my throat. "It's new."

She hums in response.

"We've just been friends," Jameson cuts in. "Until today."

"You looked like a lot more than friends last night," Levi counters.

His mother looks between us, realizing she's missing something. "Last night?"

"At his fight," Levi clarifies.

"You were at his fight?" she asks me, and I nod.

Turning back to Levi, she says, "But you told me women aren't allowed to go."

Women aren't allowed to go? There were plenty of women there.

"It's no place for a woman," he answers dismissively before pinning me with a stare. "Just like it wasn't your place to get between me and my son."

I refuse to apologize, so I say nothing.

Jameson shifts in his seat beside me, and his mother catches the movement, noticing the tension in the air. Her gaze lingers on his face. "Did you lose?"

"No."

She looks between him and Levi. "Then what?"

Levi leans forward. "He—"

The sound of ringing cuts him off.

He slides a phone out of his pocket, placing it against his ear. He listens for a few seconds before snapping his fingers and pointing at the table. Jameson gets up, coming back a minute later with a piece of paper and a pen.

"Repeat that," Levi says. "Uh-huh," he mutters as he scribbles an address onto the paper. "Ten o'clock, sure." He nods to himself. "Yeah, see you then." After hanging up, he slides the phone back into his pocket.

"Everything good?" Jameson asks.

Levi digs into his mashed potatoes. "Great," he mutters, a warning in his tone.

His mother swirls her drink, moving her attention back to me and Jameson. "So, you two met at the shop then?"

I can't tell if she's ignoring Levi's growing irritation or trying to distract from it.

"Yeah," I answer. "I work the front desk."

"How'd you end up with that job?"

"My brother he—"

"Works for me," Levi interrupts.

"Oh," she breathes, as if it all just clicked. "Who's your brother?"

"The new kid," Levi says, answering for me again. "You met him at the last party."

Party?

Noting the confusion on my face, Levi clarifies, "An after hours thing."

Right, another thing on the side of the divide that I'm not a part of.

"I'm sure we'll catch you at the next one, though. Now that you're with my boy and all."

I watch as he slides his empty plate back and fishes for a pack of cigarettes, pulling one out and tucking it between his lips. He turns, tilting the pack toward Jameson's mother before offering it to me.

I wave him off. "I'm okay, thank you."

"What is it with you and your brother, hmm? Don't you know it's rude not to accept things that people offer you?"

What's that supposed to mean? What kind of things is he offering Johnny?

He extends the pack of cigarettes. "Come on; I know you smoke."

Hit number two: Making it clear that he keeps tabs on me.

I tuck my chin and pull a cigarette from the pack.

"Good," he says before lighting his wife's, his own, and then handing the lighter to me.

"Thanks," I mutter.

"You know," he starts, exhaling a cloud of smoke, "lying's not a great way to make a good impression."

Anxiety coils through me as I bring the cigarette to my lips. "What?"

"A girl like you would never turn down a free smoke," he answers matter-of-factly. "You don't think I haven't noticed the bag of joints Jameson rolls for me has been light since you've started hanging around?"

Shit.

"You think I don't have cameras in that room?"

Jameson goes still beside me. He clearly wasn't aware of the cameras, either.

"But you're the kind of girl who will take anything you can get, isn't that right?"

"I—"

"Are you using my son, or just stealing from him?"

I begin to respond but Levi continues on.

"You know who I am. What I do. Yes?"

I swallow. "Yes."

"And yet, you steal from me? You insert yourself in my business? Come between me and my son?"

Jameson leans forward. "She—"

"I'm not talking to you," Levi snaps before turning his attention back to me, dismissing Jameson altogether.

Fuck this. I'm sick of his games, the way he manipulates everyone around him, the way he speaks to people. The way he treats Jameson.

"I was helping him," I spit. "In case you haven't seen what he looks like, he didn't need you to use him as your personal punching bag last night." I lower my voice. "Who picks a fight with someone who can barely stand?"

Jameson's mother fidgets uncomfortably as Levi cocks his head. Jameson shifts closer to me, his arm brushing against mine.

"So you really do care about him, then?" Levi muses.

I blink. "Excuse me?"

"You're not weak"—he flicks his hand in Jameson's direction—"and you've clearly proven that you'll stand by him."

I nod tentatively.

"I had to make sure you weren't just using him."

"I'm not."

He settles back in his seat, and with that one movement, the room relaxes. "I know that now."

"What—so I pass your little test?"

He smirks. "Yeah, you pass."

Turning to Jameson, he says, "I like this one. Reminds me of her brother."

He points at me, his cigarette dangling between his fingers. "But don't get between us again."

"Then don't make me have to."

He laughs. "Jesus, girl. You don't hold back, do you?"

When I keep quiet, he shifts to Jameson. "You better keep an eye on this one."

Jameson nods, his hand coming down to rest on my leg.

Levi pushes his chair back and stands. "All right, then I think we're done here."

He starts to walk into the living room, Jameson's mother reaching over the table to begin clearing the dishes.

"Oh, and one last thing," Levi mutters, turning back to us.

"Yeah?" Jameson says, his voice even.

"If I ever find out you're dipping into the product again ..." He trails off, the undelivered threat hanging in the air.

"I'm—"

Jameson squeezes my thigh, and I go silent.

"Consider this first mishap a gift, yeah?" Levi slides his eyes over, meeting mine. "But next time, I won't be so generous."

"There won't be a next time," Jameson assures him.

Levi grunts. "Remember what I told you—about testing me." He motions between us. "I'd hate for this to have to end."

Jameson's fingers tighten around my leg.

"Do you understand what I'm saying?"

Jameson is quiet before he clears his throat. "Yes, sir, I understand."

His father nods, his gaze still locked with mine, before he turns and stalks out of the room.

Once they're gone, Jameson lets out a breath, his shoulders dropping, and I realize that Levi just dealt the final blow.

Hit number three: The only reason Jameson and I are together is because Levi is allowing us to be. And he's just found another thing he can hold over Jameson's head.

Me.

Chapter 20

Jameson

"I'm sorry about the joints," Sam whispers. "I—"

"Don't," I tell her. "It's fine."

"Is he gonna give you shit?"

I shake my head. "That was probably it," I answer, although I'm not sure if that's the truth.

"I didn't know there were cameras. I should have thought ... I just ... I didn't think anyone would notice."

"It's all right, really."

She nods, but still looks nervous.

"Do you wanna go to my room?" I ask, wanting to get her out of here in case my old man comes back.

"Sure," she says, some of the tension leaving her.

I stand and take her hand, leading her down the hall.

The door to my room clicks shut behind me as I watch Sam's eyes roam around the space.

She looks back at me before taking a step forward and walking over to the desk I have crammed between my dresser and bed. She trails her hand over the surface before picking up a picture that's leaning against the wall. She turns to me, a smile pulling at her lips. "You and Billy?"

I nod.

"How old were you guys?"

I shrug. "I don't know, maybe five."

She sets the photo down, and I come up behind her, peering over her shoulder.

"You were cute," she murmurs.

I snort.

She leans into me, tilting her head up so her eyes meet mine. "What?"

"Just don't think anyone's ever called me *cute* before."

"Well, you were." She moves to the stack of DVDs I have balanced on the corner of the desk. "Who uses DVDs anymore?" she teases.

"It helps me sleep."

She glances around, looking for a TV.

"I, uh ... I have a DVD player that I use."

She doesn't say anything; instead, she starts sorting through the pile. "I haven't seen any of these."

"We could watch one," I offer hesitantly. Why am I so fucking nervous? This whole night has just put me on edge.

"Like, right now?" she asks.

"Only if you want to."

She seems wary, and it only makes me more nervous.

I asked her if she was all right when we left the table, and she said she was, but maybe she was only saying that to make me feel better. Maybe she just feels sorry for me. For my fucked-up life. Maybe it's all too much for her. Maybe *I'm* too much for her.

"I get it if you don't want to," I say, my voice coming out colder than I meant it to.

Her body goes stiff against mine before she turns. "What was that?"

"What?"

"That *fuck you* voice."

"I didn't use a *fuck you* voice."

Maybe I did.

"Uh, yeah, you did." She folds her arms over her chest. "You know you did."

"You just don't have to do me any favors, that's all."

"*Favors?*"

"Yeah, favors." I take a step back, needing the space. "You don't have to stick around 'cause you ..."

She leans forward. "'Cause I what?"

"Pity me."

"You think I'm here because I *pity* you?"

God, everything in my head right now is all fucked up. I've never brought a girl home. I've never brought *anyone* except Billy home.

"I don't—"

"Why would you think that?"

I run a hand through my hair like it'll erase her question. Erase the skin-crawling feeling I'm getting talking about this.

"I don't know." I blow out a breath. "It's just ... I would understand if you wanna leave after that dinner."

"None of that was your fault," she says. "If anything, it made me want to stay even more."

I throw out a hand. "Because you feel bad for me."

"No, Jameson." She takes a step forward. "Because even after that shit, after all he puts you through, you're still you."

"What does that mean?"

"You're not him," she says, and her words cut through me. "You'll never be him."

"You don't know that."

"Yes, I do."

"His shit has a way of bleeding into people," I say. "You don't know the stuff I've done."

"It doesn't matter." She takes another step forward, and I take one back. "I know you."

"But you don't," I tell her. "Not really."

"Then tell me."

"What?"

"Tell me who you are." She takes another step forward, closing the distance I put between us. "You're not gonna scare me away."

"You don't know that."

"Stop telling me what I do and don't know," she demands. "And stop telling me what I should want."

"I'm not trying to—"

"If I don't want to be with you, I won't." She takes another step forward, forcing me back. "If I want to leave, I will." My back hits the wall. "But until I tell you I want out, stop trying to push me away."

I stare down at her, my jaw working. "Okay."

She pulls her head back. "Okay?"

"Yeah," I say, leaning in, closing the inch that separates us. "I hear you."

"Well"—she straightens—"good, then."

I bring my hands to her waist. "You're bossy, you know that?" I tighten my grip on her, spinning us so now it's her back that's against the wall. "I kinda like it when you get mean."

"Then do something about it," she whispers.

I bring my hand up to her neck, angling her head to give me access to her lips, hovering over them until I feel her squirm.

"I never told you," she breathes against my mouth. "Last night ... with you ..."

"Hmm?" I prompt, sliding my other hand up her body.

"That was my first kiss."

I stare back at her. "You've never kissed anyone before?"

She shakes her head. "That surprises you?" Her eyes cloud with something I don't like. "It's not like I'm a sl—"

"Don't finish that sentence," I growl. "That's not what I was thinking." I make my voice softer. "That was never what I was thinking."

She doesn't look convinced, and I want to find anyone who's ever called her that and teach them what'll happen if they call her that again. "I just can't believe I'm the first person who you've let kiss you."

She bites her lower lip. "I've wanted you to kiss me for a while."

"Oh yeah?"

She nods.

"Well," I tell her, "I've never kissed anyone before you, either."

"Really?" she blurts out.

I smirk. "See? You're surprised, too."

"It's just that you're"—she waves a hand—"you're ..."

"I'm what?"

"You."

"What's that supposed to mean?"

"Oh, come on," she huffs. "Don't pretend you don't know how girls talk about you."

"So?"

"So ..." She arches back. "You could probably have any girl you want at school."

"And you could probably have any guy," I counter. "I'm sure there's not one guy at school who wouldn't want to kiss you."

"That doesn't mean I want to kiss them."

"And just because girls want me, doesn't mean I want them back. In case you haven't noticed, I don't really like other people."

"But you like me?"

I laugh. "I think that's pretty fucking clear."

"Then do it again?"

"Hmm?"

"Kiss me," she says. "Stop teasing and kiss me again."

She doesn't have to ask me twice. I bring my lips to hers, not nearly as gentle as I was the first time. She lifts her hands to my hair and pulls as I press her up against the wall.

Lost.

I'm completely fucking lost in this girl.

The room around me disappears, but I'm quickly jolted back to reality by three loud knocks on the door. "Johnny's here," my father shouts. "Get out here."

"He's early." Sam's wide eyes find mine. "Why's he early?"

"I don't know, but I really fucking wish he wasn't."

"Me, too," she says. "I wish I could stay and watch that movie with you"—she looks over at the door—"but I should really get out there."

Reluctantly, I nod.

She steps back, but I grab her wrist.

"Hold on."

"My brother ..." she starts.

"I have something for you." I go to my closet and reach for the brown paper bag I put there a few days ago. "Here," I say, holding it out to her.

She glances at me skeptically as she takes it and pulls a cell phone out. Her eyes flick up to meet mine. "You got me a phone?"

"Well, you don't have one, and"—I watch as she turns it over in her hands—"I wanted a way to be able to talk to you and a way for you to reach out if you ever need me. Or your brother," I tack on. "You can always call your brother with it."

"I don't ..." She shakes her head. "This is too much."

"There are some cards in the bag with minutes," I tell her, moving right past what she said. "Just let me know when they run out, and I'll get you more."

"You don't have to ..." She puts the phone back in the bag. "You don't have to buy me things. I'm not with you because—"

"I know."

"So, then why—"

"It's more for me than it is for you, anyway."

Her brows furrow. "How's that?"

"Now I can talk to you whenever I want."

I watch as a smile lights up her face.

"And I won't have to worry about you as much."

She tilts her head. "You worry about me?"

I rub the back of my neck. "Yeah, all the time." *If she only knew.*

"Well, thank you." She folds the top of the bag, tucking it under her arm. "Really."

"Anything," I say, the word falling easily from my lips.

"Hmm?"

"Anything for you."

Her face shifts, and she stares back at me with this look. Like I matter. Like I mean something to her.

I rush on, suddenly feeling overwhelmed. "My number's on a piece of paper in the bag."

She glances down at it.

"I put Billy's in there, too."

She opens her mouth to respond then snaps it shut when my father yells from down the hall, "I'm not telling you again, boy!"

I stride past Sam so I can walk out first, turning to make sure she's following me, and when I push open the door, I'm relieved to find the hallway empty.

Voices filter into the space as I grab Sam's hand and guide her back into the kitchen. We round the corner, and her brother's gaze immediately finds hers. He looks from her to me then back to her again, his attention briefly catching on our intertwined hands. Johnny doesn't say anything. Instead, he tilts his head to the side, and Sam quickly nods in response.

My father watches them curiously before turning to Johnny. "Thirty minutes," he states.

"Just gotta drop her home and grab the bag."

My father looks over at me. "You're with us."

Sam tenses beside me, her grip on my hand growing tighter.

My old man tracks the movement. "Sweetheart," he condescends, "you've gotta let him go."

She doesn't.

He takes a step forward, and the second he does, so does Johnny.

"Sam," her brother says, the word a warning.

Her hand drops from mine before she goes to her brother.

Johnny shifts so he's between her and my father. "Thanks for having her," he offers. He holds out his hand, and my father takes it, shaking it roughly.

Johnny gives Sam a look that has her stepping forward, glancing from my father to my mother. "Thank you for dinner," she mutters.

"Anytime," my mother answers before pulling Sam into a hug.

Sam goes still, her arms slack at her sides.

"All right," Johnny interrupts. "We should go."

My mother backs up. "Let me know about shopping."

Johnny takes in the two of them, confusion etched into his face.

"I'll walk them out," I offer, looking to my father for permission, which I get in the form of a grunt.

Sam and Johnny come up beside me, and I lead them out through the living room to the front door. When we get to the porch, Sam stops, and because she does, so does Johnny.

He looks down at her. "What?"

"Can you ... you know?" She waves a hand. "Leave us alone for a minute?"

"Why?"

She groans. "I want to say goodbye and don't want my brother standing over my shoulder."

"Fine," Johnny relents. "But I'll be right over there." He points at me before leaving. "You remember what I told you, right?"

"Don't think I could forget a threat like that," I mutter.

"What threat?" Sam asks.

"Nothing," Johnny and I say at the same time.

She puts her hands on her hips. "What threat, Johnny?"

"Just reminded him what the consequences would be if anything happens to you," Johnny responds. "What would happen if he hurt you."

"He won't," Sam says firmly.

Johnny ruffles her hair. "Relax, Bug. I'm just doing my job."

She swats his hand away, smoothing down the strands he just messed up. "Which is?"

"Making sure you're taken care of." Before she can respond, he turns and starts down the front lawn. "Say *goodbye* quick," he throws over his shoulder. "I've gotta get back."

Sam turns, looking up at me. "What'd he say to you?"

I start to answer *nothing*, but she cuts me off.

"And don't say nothing."

I let out a short laugh.

"What's so funny?"

"It's weird how well you know me."

"I thought you said I didn't know you," she replies, throwing my words back at me. "*Not really.*"

I hesitate. "You know what I meant."

"I can't know that part of you if you don't let me."

I take a step closer to her, wrapping my arms around her waist. "I'm trying."

"Well," she says, "you can start by telling me what my brother said to you."

I shake my head, grinning. "Fine."

She softens in my hold.

"He said that he doesn't care who my old man is, if anything happens to you, death will look good compared to what he'll do to me."

"Fuck."

"Yeah," I say. "Your brother's a scary dude."

She glances at him, where he's parked in the driveway. "I should go." Her teeth graze her bottom lip. "I'll call you."

She takes a step back, but I reach out and take her hand, pulling her into me. She tilts her head up, and I bring my lips to hers. I only mean for it to be a quick kiss, but I can't seem to pull away.

The sound of a horn blaring makes my head jerk away from hers. She turns with a laugh, throwing her middle finger in her brother's directions.

"Okay, I've really gotta go now," she says, stepping up onto her tiptoes. She sweeps her lips over mine so fast I barely register it and whispers, "See ya, Jamie."

Part 2: The Night Everything Changed

Chapter 21

Sam

It's the first day of school, and I'm actually excited, which I don't think has ever happened before.

Usually, I take the bus, but Jameson insisted that Luke would pick me up, so I have a few extra minutes to get ready.

Ever since I went to his house for dinner a few weeks ago, we've been inseparable. If we're not together, we're on the phone, and the only time we're really apart is when he's with his father.

My phone chimes with a text, and I look down, grabbing it from the top of my dresser and see that they'll be here in ten minutes.

I slide the phone into my back pocket and take one last look in the mirror. My eyes are lined in black, like they always are, and my dark hair spills down my back. My jeans are tight and flare at the bottom, just covering my black Converse. I have on a gray faded band tee that was Johnny's. I cut off the bottom and stretched out the top so it falls off my shoulder and shows off my layered necklaces.

Satisfied, I grab the book I'm in the middle of from my bed and shove it into my purse before heading for the door.

Once I'm in the hallway, I hear rustling coming from the kitchen and figure it's Carson. I peek my head into my brothers' room and see Johnny passed out in bed. He's still dressed in his clothes from yesterday. He even has his boots on still.

I sigh, thinking about how late he must have gotten home last night.

Walking silently into the room, I drape a blanket over him.

His eyes flit open, and he croaks, "Bug?"

"Yeah, it's just me." I move to his side. "Sorry, didn't mean to wake you."

He shakes his head against the pillow. "I wanted to be up for your first day." He turns. "My alarm ..."

"It's okay, really."

"You heading out now?"

I nod. "Luke will be here in a few minutes."

"All right," he says. "Well, have a good day."

"You, too," I answer. "Try to get some sleep."

He's already shutting his eyes before I turn to leave.

I start down the stairs and see my father still asleep on the couch. I'm relieved I won't have to deal with him this morning, but that quickly fades when I spot Carson sitting at the kitchen table.

His head is bent over his phone, a protein shake on the table beside him. I skirt past him, into the kitchen, and start a pot of coffee.

It just begins brewing when he asks, "That what you're wearing?"

I glance down at myself but don't respond.

The sound of his chair dragging against the floor fills the room. "I asked you a question."

"Obviously, it's what I'm wearing if I have it on," I snap back.

"You're asking for it, you know that?" He stands, leaning against the counter. "It's a good thing you have that boyfriend now, 'cause I'm sure as shit not stepping in anymore."

I set the coffee pot down and face him. "What are you talking about?"

"You think I don't hear what people say about you at school?" He crosses his arms over his chest. "I'm your brother; I can't let people say that shit in front of me and not correct them."

"I never asked—"

"How do you think it would make me look if I didn't step in, hmm?

"It's not my fault people say that stuff."

He laughs. "Yeah, it is." Waving a hand, he adds, "Look at you."

A knock sounds at the door, and my head jerks up. I twist the lid on my travel mug and move to leave the kitchen, but when I start to pass by the counter, Carson steps in front of me.

"I've gotta go," I mutter. He still doesn't move, forcing me to look up at him. "Carson, come on. He's waiting for me." I move to sidestep him, and he mirrors me, continuing to block my way. "Move."

He tsks. "Aw ... that's not very polite of you. Come on, sis; say please."

I try to move around him again, but he shifts with me.

"Seriously, fuck off."

He snatches my arm so tightly I wince. "Say please, Samantha."

I look down at my arm and whisper, "You're hurting me."

"Say it."

I blink my eyes closed. "*Please*, Carson, let me past."

There's another knock at the door, and he drops my arm. "There, that wasn't so hard, was it?"

I storm past him, flitting my eyes over my father's curled-up body. I swear a bomb could drop on this house and he still wouldn't wake up.

I get to the door, but before throwing it open, Carson sarcastically calls across the room, "Have a good first day of school."

Shutting out his comment, I push open the door and find Jameson leaning against the side of the house. The second I'm outside, he drags his gaze over me, slowing on my face. "What's wrong?" he asks, looking past me and into the house. "Did something happen? I was giving you another minute before I came in there."

"I'm fine. Just my asshole brother."

His eyes darken. "Johnny?"

"Carson."

"What'd he do to you?" Jameson questions, already starting to step around me.

I grab his hand. "Nothing."

"Don't lie to me."

"I just want to go to school," I tell him, pulling on his hand. "He's just a dick. It's not gonna change."

Jameson scoffs. "Oh, I'll make him change."

"Jamie, please." My voice drops. "I don't want you to make things worse."

"I won't—"

"Can we please just go?"

He turns, looking over at me. "Fine, but you'll tell me if he needs to be put in his place. Yeah?"

"Yeah," I murmur.

He pulls me into him, kissing the top of my head, and throws his arm around my shoulders. We walk like that together over to the car that's idling at the top of my driveway.

Jameson opens the door to the back of Luke's truck, and I slide into the far seat, allowing him to come in after me.

Luke turns, glancing from me to Jameson. "Everything good?"

Jameson gives him a quick nod.

Luke brings his attention back to me, a smile pulling at his lips. "Then let's go. Don't want you three to be late on the first day."

The truck jerks forward as Billy says, "Did you guys look at your schedules yet? I hope we have the same lunch."

I pull the paper from my purse and turn to Jameson. "Do you have yours?" I ask. "They sent them in the mail."

He shakes his head. "Never got it."

I shift my eyes from him to the floor of the truck and realize he has nothing with him. No bag, no papers, not even a pencil.

I smooth the paper out on my lap. "I'm sure they can print you one at guidance."

He grunts before I tell Billy, "I have A lunch on day one and C lunch on day two."

"Sweet!" Billy answers. "I've got the same." He pauses for a minute. "What teachers and classes do you have? I'll give you the dirt on them if I had them last year."

I rattle off my schedule before Billy says, "*Those* are the classes you're taking?"

"What's wrong with her classes?" Jameson snaps.

Billy holds up his hands. "Whoa, easy. I didn't mean any offense." He shifts to me. "Just didn't realize you were some sort of genius or something."

"I'm not a genius," I say quietly.

"You're taking AP Chemistry, Advanced English, and AP American History, aren't you?" When I don't say anything, he turns in his seat. "Who knew you were secretly a nerd this whole time?"

I roll my eyes. "I'm not a nerd."

"What's your GPA?"

"I don't know."

"Come on," he teases. "I bet you do."

I peer over at Jameson and find him smiling at me. "What?"

"Nothing." He shrugs. "Just didn't realize I was dating a genius."

"Would you guys stop?"

Luke chuckles as Billy pushes, "Come on; what is it?"

"Fine," I relent. "My weighted is a four point three."

"Jesus," Billy mutters as Jameson asks, "Doesn't it only go to four?"

"Well, yeah, the unweighted does, but AP classes can push it over a four."

"So, you're better than perfect?" Billy asks.

Jameson lets out a short laugh. "Not surprised."

My face heats. "Really, it's not a big deal."

"It is," Luke cuts in. "That's something you should be proud of."

He pulls to a stop in front of the school as I mutter a shy thanks.

I drift my gaze over to the building and the students passing by, excited that this year I'll have someone to walk in with.

As if he can read my thoughts, Jameson's hand comes down over mine.

"All right," Luke says. "Have a good first day."

We all mumble our replies as we climb out of the truck. Billy jumps out first, opening my door for me. I slide out, and Jameson steps out behind me.

They each position themselves on either side of me, and a warmth spreads through me.

For the first time, I'm starting a new school year and I don't feel completely alone.

Chapter 22

Jameson

As we make our way down the hall, we get the same reactions that me and Billy have grown used to—people move out of the way, their gazes linger, and whispers follow behind us. But it's different this time. They watch us with newfound interest, their attention focusing on Sam. I reach out, sliding my hand along the small of her back, making it clear who she is to me.

I pull open the door to the office, following in behind Sam. The small brunette at the front desk is a student, and I vaguely recognize her as one of the girls who's hung around Billy.

I lean against the counter of the desk, Sam pressed into my side. After clearing my throat, the brunette's head jerks up and her eyes widen when she sees me. "Oh, sorry. I didn't hear you come in," she breathes. Her gaze moves from me to Sam and her brows pinch. "Can I help you with something?"

"Yeah—"

Her attention moves from me, and a blush colors her cheeks.

Billy comes up behind me. "Lilliana." He nods.

She wets her lips. "Hi, Billy."

"I need my schedule," I cut in.

Her eyes stay locked on Billy's, like she's lost in them.

I tap on the counter. "You think you can get it for me?"

The sound brings her out of her haze, and she clears her throat. "Yeah, just give me a second." She types in my name without me giving it to her.

"What lunches do I have?"

"Hmm?"

I wave my hand toward the computer. "On my schedule. What are my lunches."

"Oh … um … looks like you have B and then C." She blinks up at me. "Why?"

"Gonna need you to change the first one," I tell her. "I need it to be A."

"W-we …" She shakes her head. "We're not supposed to do that. And anyway, I'd have to move around other classes to make it work."

I look around the space. "Nobody's here."

"So?"

"So, nobody would know."

"I don't—"

"Come on, Liliana," Billy says, his voice taking on that tone that always makes girls fold. "Can't you just do it this once? Like a favor." He takes a step closer and drops his voice. "I'd owe you big time."

She looks up at him through her lashes. "You would?"

He nods.

She rolls her lips before peering over her shoulder. "Okay, fine."

"Aw ... you're the best," Billy tells her. "We really appreciate it." He raises an eyebrow at me. "Right?"

"Yeah, thanks."

She glances up at me and nods but doesn't say anything.

A few minutes later, the sound of the printer cuts through the room and she hands me my new schedule. "This work?"

I look it over and grunt.

"That means yes," Billy clarifies. "And thanks again," he adds with a wink.

We turn to leave, but before we get to the door, the girl blurts out, "So, I'll see you around then?"

Billy looks over his shoulder. "For sure."

The door shuts behind us, and he stops, turning to me.

"What?" I ask.

"You're welcome."

"I would have gotten it changed either way."

He laughs. "Yeah, but my way was so much easier." He tilts his head to the side. "Well ... I'm waiting."

"Fine, thank you." I blow out a breath. "You happy now?"

"So happy," he says teasingly.

I snort. "You're such a dumbass."

"Let me see it," Billy says, holding out his hand. I pass him my schedule and let him look it over. "We have first period together."

I glance over at Sam. "What do you have first? We'll walk you."

She unfolds the paper in her hand. "English with Mrs. Brown. It's room 402."

"All right," I say, grabbing hold of her hand and starting to lead us that way. Billy moves to the other side of her and follows.

It's a short walk to the classroom, and I find myself lingering in the doorway, looking down at Sam.

I don't want to leave her.

Billy breaks off from us, talking to this kid Jeremy who hangs around sometimes.

I lean in so only she can hear me. "Text me if you need anything or if anyone—"

"I will," she cuts in.

I nod quickly as people move around us, filtering into the classroom. A girl rushes past, nearly running into Sam, and I snake an arm around her waist to steady her.

"Jamie," she breathes.

"Yeah, baby?"

"I've gotta ..." Her eyes drift toward the room behind us.

"Oh, yeah, right."

She leans up, slipping a hand behind my neck, and brushes her lips over mine. "See ya."

I watch her walk into the classroom and find her seat before turning and walking over to Billy.

"You good?" he asks.

"Yup, let's go."

The hallways are almost completely empty now, and everyone is already in their seats by the time we get to class. The teacher's back is to the room as he writes something on the board. There aren't two seats next to each other, so Billy takes one closer to the front and I drop into a seat at the back.

I glance around the room, trying to figure out what subject this is. I never actually looked at my schedule. I just followed Billy after he said we had the same class.

There are maps hanging on the walls and a globe sitting on the table at the front of the room, so I'm guessing it's history or geography.

The teacher turns and moves his eyes across the room. "Welcome to World History," he says. "I'm Mr. Collins. When I call your name, please come to the front of the room to collect your textbook and class syllabus."

He moves down the list, and as I'm grabbing my book, I feel my phone vibrate in my back pocket. I tense, worried that something happened with Sam.

Sliding back into my seat, I pull my phone out under the desk. Relief washes over me when I see the message isn't from her, but my stomach sinks when I read the text.

> Dad: Call me.

Fuck.

I glance up and find Mr. Collins still moving down his list, sorting through the books in front of him, when my phone buzzes again.

> Dad: Now.

I stand and head for the door. Billy catches my eye, but I subtly shake my head.

Keeping my head down, I make it a few more steps before I hear, "Young man."

I don't stop.

He snaps his fingers and asks, "What's his name?"

Nobody answers him.

I take another step as he calls out, his voice closer this time, "Excuse me, young man. Where do you think you're going?"

I turn slowly. "Just going to the bathroom."

He points to a table pushed up against the wall. "You need to sign out first."

My phone buzzes again.

I don't have time for this bullshit.

"I've really gotta go," I tell him.

He watches me for a drawn-out second. "Fine, go, but sign in when you get back."

I nod before stepping out into the hall.

Not wanting to get caught with my phone out and skipping class, I start for the bathroom. It usually doesn't go well when I get detention. I can't work if I'm stuck at school.

There's a scrawny kid washing his hands when I step in. "Out," I bark.

He jumps and stares back at me, wide-eyed. "W-what?"

I sweep my hand toward the door. "Get out. Now."

"Yeah, okay, sure," he mumbles, rushing past me.

The door swings shut as I turn off the water he left running and pull my phone from my back pocket.

> Dad: Jameson.

I quickly hit his contact and press the phone against my ear. It only rings once before he picks up.

"What part of now don't you understand, boy?"

"Had to get out of class," I answer. "What's going on?"

"I have a job tonight I want you on."

I let out a breath, realizing he just didn't want to send the details over text.

He runs through the plan, telling me who's involved and where we'll meet. Apparently, there's some safe in the back of a pawn shop that one of our guys knows about. It's supposed to be full of cash and some old shit that's worth a lot.

"Need you ready at seven," he says. Before I can respond, he tells me, "Hold on," and shouts something at someone I can't make out. "We're gonna be gone for the day, but I'll have Johnny come by and grab you from the garage," he tells me.

"Got it."

"I've gotta go." He sighs. "I swear these idiots can't do shit without me having to spell it out for them." He shouts something else then mutters, "See you tonight."

He hangs up, and my shoulders drop. That wasn't nearly as bad as I thought it was going to be.

Shoving my phone into my pocket, I push through the bathroom door and head back to class.

When I slip inside, Mr. Collins is droning on about the syllabus, but when he sees me, he motions to the sign-out sheet. I crouch over it and scribble down my name before making my way back to my seat.

Billy catches my eye on the way there, and I give him a nod, letting him know I'm fine.

The rest of the class passes by slowly, and I try to make myself listen to the teacher, but my thoughts are all over the place. Instead, I watch the clock tick by until, finally, the bell rings.

Billy intercepts me at the door. "What was that about?"

"Nothing," I tell him.

He catches my arm. "Come on; don't bullshit me."

I lower my eyes to his hand, and he drops it, taking a step back.

"Just details for a job tonight."

His expression turns hard. "Oh."

"It's fine," I reassure him. "Should be easy."

"Uh-huh," he says skeptically.

"We should get to class," I mutter, wanting to change the subject.

"What have you got next?"

"Uh ..." I uncrumple my schedule. "Communication and Public Speaking."

He snickers.

"What?"

"Nothing, just think you'll learn a lot in that one."

I roll my eyes.

"You know, like how to communicate in ways other than just grunts and one syllable words."

When I only stare back at him, he laughs and says, "See you at lunch."

I'm slumped back at my desk, listening to everyone talk around me as I wait for class to start.

There's a kid sitting next to me, laughing loudly. The guy in front of him is turned around in his seat with a grin on his face.

The one who's laughing carries on, "Coach is gonna lose it after that stunt this morning, but it might be worth it. Did you see ...?" He trails off as he looks toward the door. "Jesus Christ, man. *She's* in this class?"

The guy in front of him turns, and I follow his gaze, my eyes landing on Sam as he says, "This year just got a whole lot better."

She doesn't notice me yet, but when she scans the room, looking for a seat, her attention catches on me. Her whole face lights up, and it just about kills me.

She starts down the row, her hips swaying in that way they always do.

"Dude, she's coming this way," the guy next to me whispers.

They glance around for the empty seat she's heading toward, but all the desks around us are full.

Her focus is on me, but the guys don't seem to notice.

"Hey—"

"Get up," I cut him off.

Shifting in my direction, he doesn't seem to recognize me. "What? No, I'm not getting up."

"She needs somewhere to sit."

He makes a show of looking around. "Seems like all the seats back here are full." He glances from her to his lap. "But I've got a place for her right here."

Sam stops in front of us.

"What do you think, sweetheart? I know how much you—"

I push my chair back, the metal dragging against the tiled floor. "I'm gonna say this one more time," I tell him slowly. "Get the fuck up so my girlfriend can sit."

He darts his eyes from me to Sam then back to me again. "Your *girlfriend*?" He turns back to her. "Your brother know about this?"

Instead of answering his question, she says, "I'd really get up if I were you."

When he continues to sit there, I push my chair back farther and start to stand.

He whips his head in my direction and raises his hands. "Fine, whatever, we'll move."

Him and his friend stand, starting for the front of the room, as Sam drops into the spot he just vacated. "Thanks for saving me a seat," she jokes.

"I actually would have, if I knew you were gonna be in this class."

"That was so much better, though." She beams. "I loved watching Miles squirm. He's such an asshole."

I frown. "You know that kid?"

"He's on the football team and friends with Carson."

"Your brother keeps shitty company."

"My brother *is* shitty company."

I'm about to respond when a bright voice filters through the room. "Welcome everyone!" I turn away from Sam and find a young blonde woman smiling at us. "I'm Ms. Morris, and I'm so excited to have you all with me this year."

She's clearly new to this—her tone is much too cheery, far too hopeful.

"This is my first year, so be patient with me."

Yup.

"But," she continues, "I'm sure we'll learn a lot together this year." She claps her hands. "Okay, let's start class with a get-to-know-you activity."

I internally groan as she explains, "We'll all go around and share our names and one fun thing we did this summer."

She moves through the room, and everyone introduces themselves. When she gets to Sam, she mutters her name and says she hung out with her friends this summer.

"Nice," Ms. Morris says. "What did you all do?"

Sam quickly glances at me. "I don't know," she answers. "Played cards and stuff."

Ms. Morris nods kindly and moves on to the next person.

I smirk, leaning into Sam. "And stuff?"

She rolls her eyes. "Shut up."

"I had fun this summer doing *stuff* with you, too."

"You know that's not what I meant."

"Sure," I whisper.

"How about you?" Ms. Morris asks.

I look up, realizing it's my turn. "I'm Jameson," I start. "And I—"

"Your last name?" she interrupts.

"Baxston."

She motions for me to continue.

"I hung out with my friends this summer."

"Wonderful," she answers. "And what did you all do?"

I shrug. "Played cards and stuff."

She looks between me and Sam. I wait for her to tell me to give an original answer or to sigh in disappointment as she writes me off, but she does neither. Instead, she says, "Seems like a great summer."

I look over at Sam. "It was."

The introductions take most of the class, so by the time we're done, Ms. Morris moves quickly through the syllabus. The bell rings right before she can finish, and she tells us that she trusts us to read the rest ourselves.

I wait for Sam as she grabs her bag and follow close behind as she walks to the front of the room.

We move past the two assholes from earlier, and I don't miss the way they watch us as we stride past them, but they're both smart enough to keep their mouths shut.

I come to Sam's side as we step into the crowded hallway, weaving around people as we head for the cafeteria.

She follows me into the food line, and I grab a tray, handing it to her. "I brought a sandwich," she murmurs, eyeing the food in front of us.

"Milk?" the lunch lady asks.

I nod, and she hands one over.

"Can I get a chocolate, too?"

She passes it to me, and we push through the line. I pay for my lunch and give the chocolate milk to Sam.

Smiling, she takes it and says, "You didn't have to."

"Baxston!" someone yells.

I scan the room until my eyes land on a table in the far corner and find Mason waving me over.

"You good to sit over there?" I ask Sam. Before she can answer, I add, "Or we can sit wherever you usually do."

She shakes her head. "I don't have a table."

I look down at her, reading the truth those words cover—*I don't have friends.*

"Well, you do now," I tell her.

Stopping in front of the table, all the attention turns to us.

"Hello again." Mason says, eyeing Sam.

She hasn't been around the guys since that time she came with me and Billy to the park.

"Hey," Sam answers, sliding into an empty chair.

Glancing from her to me, Mason questions, "So, is this"—he waves his hand—"like a thing?"

I cock my head. "*A thing*?"

"'Cause, if not ..."

Rowan shakes his head and mutters, "You're an idiot."

Billy comes up behind him and drops into the seat next to Sam. "Hey!" he says, looking between us all. "What's up?"

"Mason's looking to get his ass beat," Rowan answers.

Billy gives him a questioning look, and Rowan juts his chin forward, motioning to me and Sam. "Just asked Jameson if they're a thing."

Billy barks out a laugh.

"What?" Mason asks defensively.

"You got eyes?" Billy asks.

Mason grumbles. "Yeah."

Billy pushes the food around on his tray. "So use 'em." He points his fork at us. "They're clearly *a thing*."

"Well, how am I supposed to know?" he says. "It's Jameson we're talking about."

I turn toward him. "What's that supposed to mean?"

"Nothing, man. You're just …"

Rowan snorts.

"I'm what?"

Dylan comes up to the table, his focus instantly going to Sam.

"Jesus," I mutter. "You're all acting like you've never seen a girl before."

Rowan laughs. "Oh, we've seen girls before, just never one with you."

I quickly flit my gaze to Sam and see her eyeing me curiously, but then her attention shifts to Madison, who walks up to the table and slides into the chair next to Billy.

"I thought you said you were gonna wait for me after class," she whines.

He takes a bite of his burger. "Sorry, got caught up."

I give him a look that says, *I thought you were done with this.*

And he gives me one that says, *Fuck off.*

"Well," Rowen says, leaning forward to talk to Sam, "welcome to the group."

Chapter 23

Sam

The bell rings, signaling the end of the day. I swing my purse over my shoulder, heading for the door.

Today has been weird, a good kind of weird, but still ... weird. I'm not used to having a group. Having people to sit with at lunch. Someone to talk to in class. A boyfriend.

Jameson only left my side when our class schedule separated us. Other than that, he's been a constant throughout the day.

It's been nice to not be alone.

Last year, I'd bring my lunch to the library and read, wanting to avoid the cafeteria altogether. So, having a table to sit at, a group that seemed to immediately accept me, was something I didn't even know I wanted. Something I didn't even realize I *needed*.

My phone buzzes in my back pocket, and I pull it out, finding a text from Jameson telling me to meet him out front.

I push through the crowded hallway and out the doors of the school, a smile coming to my face when I see Jameson leaning against a column, Billy's head thrown back in laughter.

"Hey," I mutter, coming up beside them.

Jameson's eyes brighten, and I don't think I'll ever get over how his face goes from dark to light when he sees me.

"Hey, baby." He swings an arm around me, pulling me into him and bringing his lips to the top of my head. "You ready?"

I nod against him as we start for the garage.

It's just a few blocks away from school, so it doesn't take long for us to get there. Billy rambles on about his day, me and Jameson barely getting a word in, which is usually how conversations with the three of us go.

When we turn the corner and walk into the big lot in front of the garage, Billy's words fall away. I glance at him and find his eyes trained on a white car parked right in front of the entrance.

"What's she doing here?" he says to himself.

"Who?" I ask.

"My mother."

Billy rarely ever talks about his mom, which is kind of odd considering how close he seems to be with his dad. Luke is so great that I just assumed his mom is, too. I know she works as a hairdresser on Broadway, but that's pretty much it.

We walk past her car, and I'm surprised by how new it looks. I'm guessing Billy's family has decent money from the shop, but not *new car* kind of money.

Billy throws open the front door, and we follow in behind him.

Glancing around, I see the space is empty and drop my bag on the desk when I hear voices coming from the garage.

Voices that are *shouting* at each other.

"I don't know what you want me to say," a woman yells.

"Anything is better than fucking nothing," Luke shouts back.

Billy goes still beside me, his attention fixed on the door that leads out to the garage.

I turn to Jameson for an explanation, and the look he gives me tells me that this isn't anything new.

His mother's voice drifts into the room. "I'm chained to this fucking life."

Billy stands frozen, the casual look he always wears gone. In its place is an expression I've never seen on him before. A sadness I didn't know he carried.

Suddenly, all I can think about is getting him away from this. Taking that pained look away.

I grab my bag. "I need a smoke. You wanna come?"

He doesn't answer. It's like all he can hear is the conversation in the other room.

"I just need a break," his mother snaps. "Can't you just give me a break?"

"Billy?" I prompt again.

When he still doesn't answer, I walk up to him and grab his hand. "Let's go outside, yeah?"

He blinks, jerking his head into a nod.

I lead him outside, his parents' voices fading with each step we take.

Jameson moves in front of us, opening the door that leads to the side of the building. It slams shut behind us, acting as a barrier to Billy's problems inside.

Digging through my purse, I pull out a pack of cigarettes and my lighter. I place one between my lips and light it.

"Can I get one of those?" Billy asks.

I'm not expecting him to ask, having only seen him smoke a few times, but I hand one over without question.

He lights it, takes a long drag, and says, "Thanks," on an exhale.

"Of course," I answer tentatively. "You okay?"

"Just the same shit."

I'm quiet, waiting to see if he'll give any more than that away.

He flicks the ash off his cigarette. "It's been getting worse."

"Their fighting?"

He nods. "Don't know what happened to make her show up here, though."

It is unusual that I've never seen his mother around the garage, considering her husband owns it.

"I'm sure they'll get over it," Jameson offers. "They always do."

"Sometimes, I wish they wouldn't."

The side door opens with a groan, and a woman pushes through, a phone pressed to her ear. The second she sees us, she says, "I'll call you back."

It's instantly obvious that the woman is Billy's mother. They have the same dark hair, full lips, and high cheekbones. I'm taken aback by how young she looks, how untouched by life she seems.

Billy drops his cigarette, grinding it into the asphalt under the sole of his boot.

I bring mine up to my lips and take a drag. *She's not my mother.*

"Oh, Billy. Hi, honey," she pushes out.

"Hey, Mom," he murmurs.

She forces a smile to her face. "Jameson ... hi, sweetie. How are you?"

"I'm good," he answers. "You?"

Her voice is light, airy even. "Oh, I'm great." She shifts her attention back to Billy. "Was just stopping by to see your dad." She pauses before tacking on like she just remembered, "And to see how your first day was."

"It was fine," Billy answers.

She nods, not asking for any details, then passes her gaze over me, her expression pinching. "Hello," she says. "I don't think we've met."

"I'm Sam," I offer, my voice flat.

I can already tell that I don't like this woman. Her little nice mother act isn't fooling me.

She looks to Billy for an explanation, but it's Jameson who says, "My girlfriend."

"Your girlfriend?" she repeats, surprised, then sticks out her hand. "It's nice to meet you. I'm Evelyn, Billy's mom."

I look at her outstretched hand for a few seconds before taking it. "Nice to meet you, too."

She eyes the cigarette in my other hand. "Aren't you a little young to be smoking?"

"Probably," I answer, bringing it back up to my lips.

She watches me for a minute, and I see a small crack in her mask before she turns back to Billy. "Well, I've gotta go. I have an appointment." She leans in to give him a quick hug. "See you at home."

Billy stares after her until her car pulls out of the lot.

"Are you—"

"I don't wanna talk about it," he mutters. "We should get inside. Get to work."

I toss my cigarette as Billy reaches for the door. "All right." I grab his arm. "But if you change your mind …"

He stills.

"We've got you," Jameson says from beside me. "Always, you know that."

"Yeah," Billy answers. "Yeah, I know."

LOYALTY

It's just turned six when the front door chimes. Billy and Jameson have been out with Luke in the garage while I've been at my spot behind the front desk.

Luke has come by a few times, and I expected him to seem upset, but he's been his regular self. I would have never known he just had a shouting match with his wife, if I hadn't heard it.

I glance up from the textbook in front of me and smile when I see Johnny, but it quickly falls when I notice the look on his face.

"What's wrong?"

"Nothing."

I cross my arms over my chest defiantly. "You know I can always tell when you're lying."

"Just been a busy day."

"Johnny."

"Leave it," he spits, and I flinch at the harness of his words. "Shit, sorry, Bug ... I just ... I can't do this right now, all right?"

I nod. "Yeah, all right."

"We've gotta get going," he says. "I need to get back."

"Okay," I answer, shutting my textbook with a *thud* and packing up the rest of my things.

"Jameson in the garage?" he questions.

"Yeah."

"Can you go grab him for me?"

I start to ask him why, but he looks like he's one question away from snapping, so I just mumble, "Sure."

"Be quick about it."

What's his problem today?

I walk into the garage and find Jameson hunched over the engine of a car. "My brother asked me to come get you," I tell him. "Seems urgent."

"What time is it?"

"Just past six."

"Shit," he says under his breath before he yells out, "Gotta go, Luke."

"Okay, kid. See ya tomorrow," Luke shouts back.

"What's wrong?"

"Nothing," Jameson answers.

"Seriously? You, too?"

"What?"

"My brother said the same thing."

"That's 'cause there's nothing wrong." He pauses. "Nothing you need to worry about."

"But there's something *you* need to worry about."

He looks over at me as he starts for the door. "I didn't say that."

"You didn't have to."

The door swings shut behind us as Johnny calls out, "Come on; we're gonna be late."

The three of us step out into the night and round Johnny's car. "Late for what?"

Neither of them answer.

"Late for what?" I repeat. "And why is Jameson coming with us?"

"Get in the car; come on."

"No, I'm not getting in until you tell me what's going on."

"I don't have time for this," Johnny says. "Get in the car."

I stand my ground until he sighs.

"A job. We're gonna be late for a job, okay?"

I look between them. "What job?"

"Get in the car," Johnny presses.

"If I get in, will you tell me?"

"Fuck, fine." He waves a hand. "Just get in. I need to drop you at home first."

I slide into the passenger seat, shutting the door roughly as they both get in. "Well?"

"We're hitting a safe," Jameson answers simply.

"Like at a bank?" My gaze bounces between them. "You're gonna rob a bank?"

"No," Johnny clarifies. "It's just a pawn shop."

"*Just* a pawn shop?"

"It's fine," he says, starting the car.

"You using guns?"

"I said it's fine," he repeats in that tone he reserves for the times he takes on the role of a parent.

But fuck that.

"No."

"Excuse me?" my brother shoots back, his tone growing more defensive.

"I said no. I don't want you to go."

He scoffs, and Jameson grits out his name in warning.

"Don't start making me feel guilty for how I take care of this family."

I shake my head. "I'm not."

"You are."

"I'm just—"

"You think this is what I want to do?" he interrupts. "You think this is the life I want?" He runs a hand across his mouth like he didn't mean for those words to slip out, like maybe he can shove them back inside. His eyes flash to Jameson in the rearview mirror. "I didn't ..." He shakes his head. "Don't ..."

"I know, man," Jameson mutters.

The car falls silent.

"I just don't want anything to happen to you," I finally whisper. "Either of you."

"Nothing's gonna happen, baby," Jameson says, just before Johnny adds, "We're careful."

The car is quiet as we turn onto our street. Johnny slows in front of our house, and a heaviness fills the space as he parks.

I sit, wringing my hands in my lap.

"Bug," Johnny says gently. "We're gonna be fine, okay?"

"Mmhmm," I force out. "Yeah, okay."

"But we really need to go."

Jameson gets out and opens my door. "Come on; I'll walk you in."

I turn to Johnny. "Please, be careful."

"I always am."

I take Jameson's hands and let him lead me up to the front door.

"Text me as soon as you get home," I tell him.

"I will," he promises, leaning down to kiss me.

He tips his chin toward the door, and I turn, unlocking it, then watch from the window as he jogs toward Johnny's car and they pull away.

"What're you looking at?" My father's voice comes from behind me.

I spin around. "Nothing."

He grunts, and I start for the kitchen but pause when he surprises me by asking, "How was school?"

"It was good." I shrug. "I really—"

"Found it," Carson says, jogging down the stairs.

My father's attention shifts to him, and just like that, our conversation is completely forgotten.

"Well, put it on," he orders, motioning to the TV.

Carson crowds my space, muttering, "Move, you're in my way."

I take a step back and head for the kitchen, grabbing a glass and filling it from the sink, groaning when I see the pile of dirty dishes.

The sound of a football game comes from the living room as I grab the ingredients for dinner.

After frying up some chicken and making a quick side of mac and cheese, I take two plates to the living room. I get a grumbled thanks from Carson and our father before I go back into the kitchen.

I make myself a plate and settle in at the table, opening up my history textbook. My phone is sitting right beside me, and I can't stop myself from continually glancing over at it, as if that'll magically make a text come through from Jameson. I know it's probably too early for them to be done, but I can't help myself.

How long does it take to rob a pawn shop, anyway?

I push the anxiety away and tell myself that they'll be fine, trying to focus on what I'm reading instead.

I finish all of my homework and then scrub the kitchen until it's spotless, trying to give my mind anything that'll distract it.

I glance over at the clock.

8:45.

I push down the fear that something went wrong and grab my bag before going upstairs.

After dropping my stuff off in my room, I head for the bathroom and strip out of my clothes from the day, setting my phone on the sink so I can hear it if it goes off.

I take a longer shower than I normally would, hoping to kill more time. When I get out, I check the time again.

9:07.

I scrape my nails against my palm.

It doesn't mean anything, I tell myself. *I'm sure they're fine.*

But maybe I should text just to make sure. What if something happened? What if they need my help?

Reaching for my phone, I pull up my text thread with Jameson, begin to type, and then delete it. What if I distract him and mess things up, or what if his phone isn't on silent and it gives them away?

I drop my phone back onto the counter.

They're fine. I'm sure they're fine.

I get ready for bed then tidy my room even though it doesn't need to be tidied. When I realize I've started pacing, I crack open the window and light a cigarette. It's raining heavily, the sound of raindrops hitting the roof creating a steady rhythm in the background.

Grabbing *Great Expectations* from the pile of books on my desk, I open it and start reading. The words I've read countless times start to bleed together, and I look over at the clock.

10:04.

I light another cigarette.

It doesn't mean anything, I remind myself. *They're fine.*

I open the book and start reading again.

I'm starting to lose it when a ring echoes through my quiet room.

I scramble for my phone. "Jamie?"

"Yeah, it's me," he says. "I'm home."

"Johnny?" I ask.

"He's fine. Should be home soon."

"Fuck." I blow out a breath. "You scared me. Was it supposed to take that long? It seems like that took too long?"

"Whoa, baby, I'm fine. We're both fine," he assures me. "We just ran into a problem, but—"

"A problem?" I interrupt.

"Their security rotation was different than it was supposed to be, so we had to wait a bit longer."

"Oh," I murmur. "Okay."

"I would have texted you, but I couldn't have my phone with me where I was and—"

"It's okay, really," I tell him. "I'm just glad you're all right."

"You sure?" he asks nervously. "You don't seem—"

A muffled sound comes from the other line.

"Shit," he mumbles. "Hold on, sorry."

I wait a few seconds as he clearly pulls the phone away from his ear, so I only catch the tail end of his response. "—right there." He clears his throat, his voice closer this time. "You still there?"

"Yeah, I'm here," I answer quietly.

"Talk to me."

"What do you want me to tell you?" I exhale, stubbing my cigarette out. "There's nothing I can say. It is what it is."

He's quiet for so long that the only way I know the call didn't disconnect is the sound of him breathing.

"Jamie?"

"This is what I was talking about. You shouldn't have to ... I don't know. You just shouldn't have to ..."

"But I will," I tell him. "I'm not going anywhere, but I'm also not gonna to lie to you and pretend this is easy."

"No," he says. "You never have to pretend with me."

"Neither do you."

"I don't—"

"Yes, you do," I cut in. "You tell me you're fine when you're clearly not."

"I just ..." He pauses. "I've never ..."

"I know," I answer. "But you can't keep it all in, and if this is gonna work, you can't keep me out."

There's a long stretch of silence before he finally says, "Then you can't either."

"I can't what?"

"Keep me in the dark."

"I—"

"I know there are things you struggle with," he says softly. "If I give you my baggage, you have to give me yours, too, balance out the weight."

His words hit me. *Balance out the weight.*

"Okay," I breathe. "I will."

Another distant sound comes from his side of the line, and he curses under his breath. "I really have to go. You sure you're all right?"

"I wasn't," I respond, "but I'm better now." I press the phone to my ear, as if that'll somehow make me closer to him. "Are you?"

"No," he says and I think that might be the first time he's ever answered that question honestly. "But I'm better now, too. Talking to you makes me better."

"I'm always here."

"I know, baby, thanks," he says. "All right, talk to you later."

"Talk to you later," I answer before the line goes dead.

I set my phone down beside me but stay perched on my desk with the window cracked until bright headlights break through the darkness and pull into my driveway. A car door slams shut before I see my brother trudge up to the house.

After shutting the window, I slide off the desk and move into the hallway, peering over the ledge of the staircase.

My father left around an hour ago, and after a quick check, I confirm the door to my brothers' room is closed with loud music playing on the other side.

I take the stairs two at a time and only slow down once I've reached the living room.

Johnny has his back to me as he shuts the front door. He's dressed in all black, the clothes somehow looking even darker with the rain that's soaked them through. He has a black duffle bag dangling at his side, the straps gripped tightly in his hand.

He turns away from the door, his head bent. After stepping into the room, he looks up, pushing away the wet hair that's fallen into his eyes.

I rush toward him, wrapping my arms around his middle.

"Easy," he mutters. "I'm drenched."

"You're all right," I say into his chest.

He smooths his hand down my back. "Told you I'd be fine, didn't I?"

I step back. "Jameson told me you were ... but I don't know ... I just ... I was worried."

His face softens.

"Did you eat already? I ask. "I can make you something."

"Nah, you should get to bed."

"Johnny."

"What?"

"Did you eat?"

He shakes his head.

I motion toward the stairs. "Go get changed. I'll make you something."

He dips his chin. "Thanks, Bug."

I lower my gaze to the bag in his hand, and I know he senses me looking at it.

Without saying anything, he turns and starts up the stairs. "I'll be quick," he throws over his shoulder.

I head for the kitchen and try not to think about all the answers to the questions I'm too afraid to ask.

Everything's fine, I remind myself. *They're fine.*

Chapter 24

Jameson

Hot water beats down on me as I rub the sleep from my eyes. It felt like pulling teeth trying to drag myself out of bed this morning. The dream I was having felt far too real. Far too good.

I was down by the river with Sam. We were both floating on our backs, our bodies side by side, looking up at the sky. The sun was bright, but we could look right at it, its light wrapping around us.

I turned my head, and as I glanced over at her, she was already looking at me.

"You're glowing," she said.

I raised my hand above my face and realized she was right.

"You can see it, too?" she asked.

I nodded. "How long have I ...?" I couldn't believe I was even asking this. "How long have I been glowing?"

She glanced over at me, blinking. "You've always glowed." She turned back to look up at the sky, "Well, for me, anyway."

"Wait, what?"

"Nobody else can see it." She paused. "Even you couldn't see it, but I kept telling you, remember?"

I shook my head because, for some reason, I couldn't seem to remember anything but that moment.

"I told you one day you'd see it, too." She laughed lightly. "I must have told you a hundred times."

"Then why didn't you just give up?"

"Because—"

I never got to find out her answer because my alarm shattered the dream. I tried to hold onto it long enough to hear what she was going to say, but it was no use.

I wanted to go back to sleep, back to that river. Floating there, everything felt so ... easy. So right.

But I couldn't.

The water is starting to run cold, so I move through the rest of my shower quickly.

Stepping out, I stop in front of the sink and rub away the fogged-up mirror with the palm of my hand. My eyes instantly go to the new tattoo I got on my other shoulder—a clock that looks melted so you can't tell the time.

I got it a few weeks ago, the night after we hit that pawn shop. The score was more than we were expecting, and my old man was in a celebrating mood, so he invited Big Jim back to the garage and said anyone who wanted a new piece could get one.

I came up with the idea while I waited for Johnny to finish with his. Just thought it was a cool thing to think about—that time doesn't really exist. To not live your life by it.

After combing my hair back the way I like it, I slip into my room to get dressed before heading for the kitchen. I know what I'll find waiting for me before I even walk in.

Sitting on the table in front of my usual spot is a huge stack of pancakes with a collection of candles sticking out of the top.

My mother whirls around at the sound of my incoming steps. "There's my birthday boy." She beams.

She's always been big on birthdays. Ever since I was a little kid, she's made it a whole thing. No matter what else was going on, she found a way to make the moments special. To make it feel like we're a happy family. If only on those few days a year.

"Levi," she hollers. "It's time to sing."

I don't know when she started this tradition. I can't think of a time when we didn't do it. Every year, even if it's her own birthday, she makes pancakes, covers them with candles, and we sing "Happy Birthday."

I slide into my seat, and she comes over, standing behind me, then drops a kiss onto my head and says, "Happy birthday, honey."

"Thanks, Ma," I say, looking up at her.

My father walks in and tips his head up at me. "Happy birthday, boy."

I nod back in response. "Thanks."

Reaching into the pocket of her robe, my mother produces a lighter and begins lighting the candles. She claps once she's done and says, "You ready for your song?"

I nod, and she begins to sing, her light voice filling the room.

My father leans against the counter, his eyes on my mother. He never sings along, but he shows up every year.

The song finishes, and she places her hands on my shoulders. "Make a wish," she whispers.

For as long as I can remember, I've always wished for the same thing—to get out of this town, to leave this life. But this year, Sam pops into my mind and something becomes clear.

I don't want to leave, if it means leaving her.

"Jameson," my mother prompts, the word pulling me from my thoughts.

I focus on the candles in front of me, watching the wax begin to melt. Closing my eyes, I blow them out and silently make my wish.

My mother slides the plate away from me and starts to pluck out the candles.

"I've gotta head in early," my father says, pushing away from the counter. "See you at the garage tonight."

He's throwing a party to celebrate, something he started doing since I've gotten older. It's not how I'd choose to spend my birthday—around a bunch of people I don't know all that well. They usually get really rowdy, too. It's just not my thing. But, what am I gonna do? Not show up to my own party? So, I tip my chin. "See you tonight."

The front door slams closed behind him as I pour syrup over the plate of pancakes my mother sets back in front of me.

While I eat, she moves around the kitchen, cleaning as she hums to herself. I lean back in my chair, appreciating one of the few moments I feel at peace inside this house.

I mop up the remaining syrup with my last bite then bring the plate over to the sink. My mother takes it with a satisfied look. "That good, hmm?"

"Always," I tell her. "Thanks for making them."

Before she can answer, a horn sounds from outside.

"Gotta go," I mutter.

She nods. "See you at the party."

I push open the door and make my way out to Luke's waiting car.

Billy jumps out and pulls me into a one-armed hug, slapping his other hand against my back. "Happy birthday, old man."

The joke is worn out at this point. I'm only two months older than him, but he reminds me any chance he gets.

I move into the back seat, and Luke turns, wishing me a happy birthday, too.

"You coming to the party tonight?" I ask. It's rare that Luke ever hangs out at things after-hours and even more rare that he lets Billy, but in the past, my birthday has been an exception.

"Course we'll be there," Luke answers before pulling away from the curb.

"Sam coming?" Billy asks.

I've never brought her to a party at the garage before, but when she found out about the one tonight, she insisted on coming.

"She'll be there."

"Sweet!"

"Just keep an extra eye on her, yeah?" I say, noticing the way Luke tenses at the fact that I even have to ask. He lets out an angry breath but doesn't say anything, so I continue on. "Johnny will be there, too, but just in case, you know ..."

Billy's quiet for a second before he says, "Yeah, course I will."

We pull in front of her house, and I start up the lawn like I do every day then knock on the front door and wait.

A couple minutes go by before the door swings open and she walks out. For just a moment, she looks upset, but by the time she focuses on me, she's smoothed out her expression.

She inches into my space and glances up at me. "You look older," she murmurs.

"You saw me yesterday."

"Hmm," she breathes, slipping her arms around me. Her cold hands slide up the back of my shirt, dragging over my bare skin.

She called me last night at 12:01 a.m. to wish me a happy birthday; said she wanted to be the first one. Still, she smiles up at me and tells me again.

I pull her in closer and bring my lips to hers. "Thanks, baby."

"Get a room!" Billy yells at us from his open window.

I laugh against her mouth then take a step back, grabbing her hand. "Let's go."

LOYALTY

Me and Billy are in our usual spot after school. He's talking to Madison as I watch for Sam in the crowd of kids filtering out of the building.

Today was uneventful, boring even. But as much as the party tonight isn't how I'd like to spend my birthday, I'm excited I'll at least get to be with Sam and Billy.

The crowd begins to thin, and my attention catches on a flash of familiar dark hair. Her eyes are fixed on the ground, and my eyes are fixed on her.

They're always on her.

I take in her long legs and trail my gaze up to the short denim skirt she's wearing. I love that fucking skirt. I keep moving up, eyeing the black shirt she has on that hugs her small waist and drops off her shoulder. Finally, I reach her face and realize her eyes are no longer on the ground.

She's watching me, just as intently as I'm watching her.

Her lips tip up into a knowing smirk. Yeah, she knows exactly what she does to me and owns every bit of it.

"Hey," she says as she stops in front us.

I push off from the wall. "Hey."

Madison peeks around Billy and gives Sam a little wave.

Sam looks from her to Billy then to me with a question on her face.

I subtly shake my head, telling her that I'm just as confused as she is. Billy's been saying since the summer that he was gonna cut her loose, but he keeps going back.

It's clear Madison knows she's not the only girl he messes around with, but it doesn't seem to bother her. Or maybe she's just happy she seems to have his number one spot.

"So," Madison says, "what're you guys doing tonight?"

Billy glances at me. "Well, it's Jameson's birthday, so—"

"Wait," she interrupts. "How come you didn't say anything? I didn't know it was your birthday, Jamie."

"What'd you just call me?"

She stares back at me and stammers, "W-what do you mean?"

"Don't call me that," I snap.

"Dude," Billy cuts in. "Chill."

"Call you what? Jamie?" She looks over at Sam. "She calls you that all the time."

"Yeah, well, you're not her."

Madison holds up her hands. "Jeez, sorry, didn't realize it was a thing." She forces a smile. "Still, happy birthday."

When I don't say anything, Billy narrows his eyes.

"Thanks," I mumble.

"So, you doing anything fun to celebrate?"

Just as I answer, "No," Billy says, "We're having a party."

"It's a family thing," I butt in.

I don't want this girl anywhere near that party, and if I had my way, nowhere near Billy, either.

There's something about her that's always rubbed me the wrong way. Something about her that feels off. Maybe I just don't buy the nice girl cheerleader act. Plus, my old man doesn't do well with bringing outsiders around.

Noting the look on my face, Billy says, "Sorry, babe, it's just a small family thing."

She bites her lip. "I would never say anything about, you know—"

"Madison," Billy warns.

"No, let her finish. About what?"

She shifts nervously. "Just, um ... about what your dad does. I mean ..." She takes a breath before rushing on quickly, "Everybody already knows, but I wouldn't say anything. You can trust me."

"And why would I trust you? You've never given me any reason to."

"What about her?" she asks, motioning to Sam. "How come I have to prove myself and she just gets a free pass?"

"You wouldn't even be able to wrap your pretty little head around all the ways she's proven herself loyal," I respond coldly.

"All right, let's just calm down, huh?" Billy says, always trying to mediate the situation. "There's no need to—"

"No," Madison huffs. "He can't talk to me like that." Her face shifts, and for the first time, she drops the mask, glaring over at me. "You act like you can do and say whatever you want just because of who you are, like it's some sort of excuse to be an asshole."

Billy pulls his head back. "Whoa—"

"What'd you just call him?" Sam demands, taking a step forward.

"Just because I didn't grow up the way you guys did doesn't mean you can treat me like I don't matter."

"Pretty sure you're from the same shitty neighborhood," I mutter.

"Yeah, but my family is ..."

"Your family is what?"

"Nothing."

"No," I push. "Your family is *what*?"

"Respectable."

"Ah," I say. "And that what? Makes you better than me?" I wave my hand around. "Than us?" She starts to answer, but I cut her off. "This is why you can't come tonight, why I don't trust you, and why I don't fucking like you."

Her face drops before she turns to Billy. "Are you just gonna stand there and let him talk to me like this?"

"Why wouldn't I?"

"Because we're—"

"We're nothing," Billy tells her. "Not anymore."

"But—"

He backs away. "You should go find someone more *respectable*. You know, so my filth doesn't rub off on you."

"I wasn't talking about you," she sputters.

"Right," he says with a bitter laugh. "You realize Jameson *is* my family, right?"

"Yeah, but—"

"You should leave now."

"Billy," she pleads.

"Seriously, Madison, you should leave." He points at Sam. "I don't know how you got away with saying that shit about Jameson in front of her, but neither of us are gonna step in if she goes after you."

Her eyes widen. "Jesus, she's not gonna jump me."

Sam takes another step forward. "I'm not?"

Madison looks over at Sam and inches back. "Fine, I'm leaving. I don't need this shit, anyway."

Sam gives her a condescending wave, mirroring the one Madison gave her when she walked up.

Once she's gone, Sam mutters, "Bitch" under her breath.

I turn toward Billy. "You all right?"

"Yeah. Why wouldn't I be?" He shrugs, trying to appear unaffected. "Things were getting weird with her, anyway."

I start to answer, but he turns from me. "We should probably head to the garage; it's getting late."

I nod, giving him the out he clearly wants.

Sam must pick up on it, too, because after a couple minutes of walking, she changes the subject, asking, "So, when can I give you your presents?"

I slow. "You got me presents?"

"Of course I did," she answers. "It's your birthday."

"You didn't have to do that."

She smiles. "I know, but I wanted to."

"Oh, yeah," Billy says. "When are you gonna give it to him?" He motions to Sam. "We coordinated."

"You coordinated?"

"Yeah, on your gift," he clarifies. "What about now?"

"Now?"

"Can we give it to you now?" he asks, the question coming out in an excited rush.

I look between them. "You have it with you?"

They both nod.

"Okay, yeah, sure."

We move off to the side of the road, and Sam fishes around in her purse until she pulls out two packages.

She hands one to me and says, "This one is from Billy." Then hands me another and adds. "And this one is from me." She eyes them, shifting on her feet. "Well, they're really just both from us."

I look down at the packages. They're wrapped neatly in what looks to be a brown paper grocery bag.

Sam twists her lips. "Sorry, I didn't have any wrapping paper."

I shake my head. "It looks great."

Carefully, I begin to unwrap the first one. She holds out her hand, and I pass her the paper, watching as she crumples it up and tucks it into her purse.

Before unwrapping it, I could immediately tell it's a DVD, but when I flip it over, my eyes shoot up, glancing between the two of them. "You got me *Taxi Driver*?"

"Well, you said Scorsese was your favorite—"

"And I remember we saw it when they were doing that summer classics series last year at the drive-in and you said you liked it," Billy finishes.

Sam motions to the DVD. "You don't already have it, do you?"

"No. This is ... Thanks."

"All right, open the other one," Billy says.

I tear away the brown paper and find a box with headphones inside.

"When I was over, I noticed the cord on yours is all messed up," Sam explains. "Figured they must not work that well anymore."

"They don't," I answer. The sound cuts out unless I hold it at a certain angle.

I stare down at the gifts, feeling oddly emotional. They're so ... thoughtful.

With my free hand, I pull Sam into me and kiss her. "Thank you, baby."

"You're welcome," she breathes against me.

I look over at Billy, tipping my head up. "Thanks, man."

"Of course," he answers.

"Seriously," I say to the two of them. "These are … These are some of the best gifts I've ever gotten."

"Glad you like 'em." Billy grins, spinning and starting back down the road.

I keep Sam tucked under my arm as we follow behind him, needing to have her close.

Her and Billy are talking about something, but I'm not really listening. Instead, I'm watching her. I watch as she laughs, the sound pouring from her as her head drops back. I trace her lips with my gaze as they spread into a wide smile, and I realize how beautiful she looks when she's happy. That I'd do just about anything to keep her smiling like this.

I watch her, and it hits me.

I think I'm in love with this girl.

Chapter 25

Jameson

Once the sun sets, people start showing up for the party. Some of them I know. Most of them I don't. I've maybe seen them hanging around, but I couldn't tell you more than their name.

My father's always liked a lot of people around. I think it makes him feel important. These parties are always more for him than me, anyway. But this time, it's better because Sam hasn't left my side since it started.

I'm careful to watch the people who pass us, keeping extra close to her to make it clear she's not here alone. It's not that I don't trust her; it's that I don't trust anyone here.

We've each got a drink in hand when Billy comes up to us, a girl I don't recognize trailing closely behind him.

"Her lipstick is all over your mouth," I mutter, quiet enough that just Billy can hear me.

He smirks at me as he rubs it away, but the lightness doesn't reach his eyes. Instead, they look dead. Hollow.

I lean into him. "You all right?"

"Great. Why?"

I flick my eyes from him to the girl then back to him again.

"It's a party," he whispers, his voice defensive. "Just leave it."

The girl steps around Billy, and now that I get a better look at her, she seems familiar.

"Happy birthday," she tells me.

I tip my beer in her direction. "Thanks."

Her nose crinkles. "You don't remember me, do you?"

Sam presses into me, and the girl tracks the movement.

"Should I?"

"I'm Sasha," she says, like that should mean something to me. When I just stare back at her blankly, she adds, "Ivan's kid."

"Who?"

She fidgets, annoyed. "The Russian."

The pieces fall into place. I haven't seen her in years.

"You grew up."

She sweeps her gaze over me. "Yeah, you did, too."

Sam takes a step forward, subtly blocking my body with hers.

"Is this your ...?"

"Girlfriend," Sam answers.

Sasha tilts her head to the side. "Oh."

"What?" Sam snaps.

"Nothing." Sasha looks between us, letting her eyes rest on me. "You just never seemed like the girlfriend type."

"How would you know?" Sam asks. "He didn't even remember you."

"Exactly," Sasha says under her breath before forcing her face to brighten. "Well, it's nice to meet you."

Sam watches her for a second, like she's assessing if Sasha's a threat.

I snake my arm around her waist, running my finger under the hem of her shirt. I feel her uncoil before she finally says, "Yeah, you, too."

Billy drains the last of his beer then leans into Sasha, asking if she wants to go get a refill. She nods, looking thankful to get away from this conversation.

Once they're gone, Sam turns to me, and I bite back a smile.

She crosses her arms over her chest. "What?"

"You're a jealous little thing, aren't you?"

She narrows her eyes. "No."

"Yes, you are."

"Fine." She blows out a breath. "But so are you."

"Damn right I am."

That makes her smile.

I move forward until my lips graze her ear. "You're all mine."

Before she can respond, I pull back, grabbing her hand and guiding us over to the makeshift bar.

Billy and Sasha are nowhere to be found, but Johnny is hunched over the table, pouring himself a drink.

He turns, and a genuine smile lights his face. "Hey, Bug," he says to Sam before shifting to me. "Happy birthday."

I nod a thanks as Sam holds out her hand.

Johnny laughs and gives her the drink he just poured. "You behaving?"

She grins, bringing the Solo cup up to her lips. "Never."

I watch them as they talk about nothing in particular, just shooting the shit. She's different when she's around him, like he smooths out her edges.

She has another drink, and I watch as she becomes more loose.

"I want to go for a—"

Her words cut off when a hand comes down on Johnny's shoulder.

"Why're you all hiding in the corner?" my father asks. "It's a party."

His eyes lock with mine. "I have something for you."

"You do?"

"It's your birthday, isn't it?"

I nod.

My mother comes up beside him and asks excitedly, "Are you gonna give it to him now?"

"Everyone outside," my father yells.

I guess that's a yes.

We all follow him as he leads the way to the front lot.

I search for Billy, finding him next to Luke. We catch eyes, and he jogs over to me and Sam.

"You know about this?"

He shakes his head. "No idea."

I don't ask him where Sasha went. Instead, I just keep walking, Sam's hand in mine.

My father stops, and I look over at him, confused.

"Well?" he asks. "Do you like it?"

I glance around. I don't want to question him in front of everyone, but I have no idea what he's talking about.

"Like what?"

"Your new car."

I pull my head back. "My what?"

He sweeps his hand out, motioning to his black 1970 Dodge Challenger.

No, he's not saying ...

I look over at my mother, and she's nodding emphatically.

"It's yours," my father says.

Sam squeezes my hand, and Billy lets out a whoop of excitement. But I just stand there, frozen.

Waiting for him to take it back.

To start laughing and tell me he's just kidding.

But he doesn't.

He pulls the keys from his pocket and dangles them in front of me.

I let go of Sam's hand and step forward, reaching for them.

He drops the keys into my open palm and says, "One year late, but better than never. Happy seventeenth, kid."

I close my fist around them. "I don't …" I don't know what to say. "Thank you."

He smiles, and I know it's a real one because his eyes crinkle. Then, taking a step forward, he pulls me into a one-armed hug, using his other hand to slap my back affectionately. "I don't tell you this enough," he says to me quietly, "but I'm proud of you."

My chest tightens at his words, not knowing what to do with them.

He steps back, and my mother takes his place. She wraps her arms around me and says against my chest, "Love you, honey."

I don't know what to do with her words, either.

I must take longer than the standard time to say them back because she breaks the hug and looks up at me. "Jameson," she prompts.

I push the words out. "Love you, too."

"So," Billy cuts in, like he can sense my inner turmoil, "we gonna take her for a spin?"

I glance over at Sam. "You want to go for a ride, baby?"

"I want to go anywhere you're going," she answers, her words hitting me right in the chest.

"Wait," Luke says, stepping in front of me. "I've got something for you." He tilts his head. "It's in the office."

"Now?" I ask, and he nods. I search for my father and find him talking to Marcus. "All right, yeah," I tell Luke.

Leaning into Sam, I mutter, "You good here for a minute?"

She nods, glancing between Billy and her brother.

Knowing they're watching out for her, I follow Luke into the garage then wait as he pulls something from a drawer. His voice sounds almost nervous as he holds it out in front of me. "Wanted you to have this."

I look down, confused when I see denim. Taking it from him, I unfold the fabric and realize it's a jacket. The denim is worn and covered in patches. I jerk my head up, my eyes questioning.

"It was mine when I was your age," he explains.

I move my gaze over all the patches, realizing they're a collection of the stories he's told me about his life.

I push the jacket back toward him. "You can't give me this." I shake my head. "This is the kind of thing you give your son."

"I know," he says softly.

"Then why—"

"You know how I see you, Jameson." He rubs at his neck. "I know things haven't been easy for you, and I wish—"

"Don't," I cut him off, my voice strained. "You don't need to say whatever you're gonna say. You've done more than enough."

He nods, the motion rigid, then shoves the jacket back toward me. "Take it."

My eyes are on the floor when I mutter, "Thank you." I clear my throat. "For everything, really."

"I'm always here," he tells me. "No matter what. You need something, you can always come to me. You understand?"

"Yeah." I glance up. "I understand."

"Good," he grunts. "Now, try it on," he says with a smile.

I shift, attempting to pull my arm through the sleeve.

He laughs. "Figured this would happen."

I can barely pull the other sleeve on.

"I haven't shrunk with time," he says. "I was still this much shorter than you when I was your age."

I don't know how Billy managed to be a couple of inches taller than me because I've got about five inches on Luke.

"Plus," he adds, "even with the Army, I was always scrawnier than you." He grins. "You might not be able to wear it, but I still want you to have it."

I awkwardly pull it off and refold it.

"Come on," he says. "I'll walk back out with you."

We step outside, and I immediately seek out Sam. She's smoking a cigarette, talking with Billy and her brother. The sound of her laugh drifts toward me, pulling me in her direction.

I come up behind her, and she leans back into me, tilting her head up. "Hey," she breathes.

I brush my lips against the shell of her ear. "You look beautiful," I whisper. "Happy."

She flicks the ash off her cigarette. "I am happy."

I hum against her ear.

"You make me happy," she murmurs.

I watch as she brings the cigarette back up to her lips, taking another drag.

"You guys ready to go?" Billy asks, his words filled with anticipation. "How fast does she go, anyway?"

Johnny looks between Billy and me. "You're not gonna find out tonight." He points at Sam. "Not with her in the car." He raises a brow. "Are you?"

I shake my head as Billy mutters, "Buzzkill."

Johnny levels me with a hard stare. "Are you okay to drive?"

"Just had one drink," I assure him. "I'm good."

"Can you cover for me if you need to?" Sam asks. "We might be a while."

"Bug ..." Johnny starts.

"Come on," she pleads. "It's Jameson's birthday."

"I don't—"

"It's Friday," she pushes. "And I've been good. Come on."

"Fine."

"Wait, really?"

He nods. "Yeah, really. Just don't ... you know, do anything I wouldn't do."

"You mean, there are things you wouldn't do?" she teases.

Johnny rolls his eyes. "Smartass."

"So, can we go now?"

"Yeah, yeah," Johnny says. "Go ahead."

Billy walks off to tell Luke that we're leaving, and I go tell my old man before we meet Sam back at the car.

I drop the front seat for Billy, setting the jacket Luke gave me in the back. "Get in."

He folds himself into the back, and I right the seat, stepping away so Sam can sit.

She tilts her head. "Hmm."

"What?"

"Just didn't know you were such a gentleman."

"Oh, fuck off."

"Don't worry," she leans in conspiratorially, lowering her voice, "I won't tell anyone." She slides into her seat slowly, like she wants me to watch. So, I do.

I trace her legs all the way up to the tiny skirt she's wearing and suddenly wish Billy wasn't in the back seat.

She tsks. "That's not the way a gentleman is supposed to look at a lady."

"Then good thing you're not a lady," I say, my voice low.

She laughs. "And thank fuck you're not actually a gentleman."

Chapter 26

Sam

The windows are down, music blasting, and I can't take my eyes off of Jameson. I didn't think you could be attracted to the way someone drives a car, yet here we are.

The only time his hand isn't on my thigh is when he's shifting gears. He handles the car so smoothly I can barely tell how fast we're going.

We take a sharp turn, his grip on my thigh tightening, and I instinctively grab onto him, steadying myself.

"Goddamn, this car!" Billy yells from the back seat.

I close my eyes, letting the music wash over me and the wind hit my face, then turn to the window, cranking it down all the way. Shifting in my seat, I slide toward the door and lean my upper half out the window. Jameson keeps his hand on my leg, tethering me to both him and the car.

The world whips past me, my hair flying all over the place. I feel so fucking free. So alive.

I don't know how long I stay like this, probably not more than a couple of minutes, before I'm moving back into my seat.

Jameson looks over at me, his eyes bright. "You're crazy."

He shifts his attention back to the road, taking a turn that makes me squeal. The sound pulls his gaze back to me.

"You love it," he says. "Don't you?" He starts to move his hand on my thigh, slowly drifting back and forth. "Going fast."

"It's such a fucking rush," I shout over the music.

"If I didn't promise your brother, I'd show you how fast this thing can really go."

I catch his hand on my thigh, intertwining my fingers with his, and we keep driving until the back roads eventually lead us into town.

Jameson slows his speed as the signs of fast food restaurants light the street.

"You hungry?" he asks.

"I could eat."

He raises his voice so Billy can hear, repeating his question.

"Hell yeah," Billy answers, drumming his hands against the back of my seat. "I'm starving."

We pull into a McDonald's, and Jameson orders for us, already knowing what we like, then drives up to the window.

I reach for my purse but stop when he says, "Not a chance, baby. I've got ya."

Billy tries to push money into his hands, telling Jameson that he can't pay on his birthday, but Jameson only waves him off.

He shifts, grabbing his wallet from his back pocket, and I try not to think about what he's done to get the money. I push the thought down into the place I always bury it and accept the bag of food and drinks he hands me.

We find a spot in the nearly empty parking lot, the streetlamp above us flickering. Jameson cuts the engine and it's suddenly quiet.

I open the bag, handing out our food, before excitedly popping the top off my milkshake and dipping a fry in.

"I still don't believe that tastes good," Jameson tells me.

"You'll never know if you don't try," I respond, dipping another fry and holding it out to him.

"Yeah, that's still a no, baby."

The first time he saw me do this, he had the same reaction. Although he was a bit more dramatic that time. I told him to try it, and he refused.

Billy takes a bite of his burger. "Sorry," he says, "but I've gotta side with Jameson on this one."

"Whatever," I grumble. "You guys don't know what you're missing."

I pull my own burger from the bag, unwrap it, and stifle a yawn.

"You're tired," Jameson says.

"I'm fine," I answer, not wanting to be the reason the night ends, but my body betrays me, and I yawn again.

"Let me take you home," he says softly. "Let you get some sleep."

Reluctantly, I nod.

We start toward my neighborhood, but this time Jameson drives slowly, like he's dragging out our time together.

I relax back in the seat as the low rumble of the engine calms me. Letting my eyes close, I feel Jameson trace slow patterns on my leg, his callused finger gently skimming over my skin.

Eventually, the car slows, and I blink my eyes open. We're idling on the street, a few houses down from mine. When I look over at Jameson, he explains, "Figured you were sneaking in, and with the engine being so loud, I didn't want—"

I drop my hand on top of his. "Thank you."

He nods as I collect my purse from my feet, handing him the presents Billy and I got him.

"Was it a good birthday?" I ask.

"Best one I've had."

I smile at that.

"Text me when you get in, okay?"

"I will," I tell him before leaning in and sweeping my lips against his.

I push out of the car, and Billy swaps seats with me. "See ya later," he says through the open window.

I give them both a small wave then turn to walk home. When I get to my driveway, I look back and see the car still sitting in the same spot.

I climb up and through my bedroom window, but it isn't until I send Jameson a text that I finally hear his car drive past my house and down the street.

LOYALTY

By the time I wake up, it's already close to noon. I stretch my arms overhead and squint my eyes against the brightness filtering through my window.

I'm surprised nobody woke me.

I move through the motions of showering and getting ready before padding downstairs.

Everyone is in the living room, watching TV, and their eyes all flick up to me when I walk in.

My father looks me over. "What's wrong with you?" he asks. "Slept half the day away."

I quickly shift my gaze to Johnny, who subtly shakes his head. He hasn't told them anything, so there's no story for me to contradict.

"Sorry," I mutter. "I couldn't sleep." I clear my throat, trying to look embarrassed. "Woman troubles."

My father drops his eyes as Carson groans, "Jesus, we don't need to be hearing about that shit."

They make it so easy. All I have to do to get them to stop asking questions is bring up my period.

I move into the kitchen and start another pot of coffee. I've just poured myself some when Johnny walks in.

"You want a cup?"

"I'm good," he answers then lowers his voice. "Just wanted to check in; see how last night went."

"Oh." I bring the mug to my lips. "It was really fun."

"Good." He smiles. "You should be going out, having fun like that."

"So should you," I tell him. "You work too much."

He ignores my statement altogether and asks, "How's school going? How was that test you were studying for? What was it? Science?"

"History," I correct. "And it was good."

"Come on," he says. "I can tell you aced it by your face."

I roll my lips to hide a smile.

"Don't be modest; what'd you get?"

I take another sip of my coffee before telling him, "A ninety-eight."

"Couldn't get a hundred?" he teases.

I shake my head, the smile I tried to hide breaking through.

"Promise me you'll stick with it."

"With what?"

"School," he says. "You're too smart not to graduate."

Both him and my sister dropped out before they finished, and Johnny's always made it clear he didn't want that for me.

"You could even get a scholarship," he adds.

I snort. "College?"

"Why not?" He shrugs. "If anyone could get out of here, it's you."

He says the words like he really means them. He's always had more faith in me than I've had in myself.

I wonder what my life would be like if I didn't have at least one person rooting for me.

"I promise," I tell him. "I'll graduate."

"I'm gonna hold you to that."

I nod before turning in search of something to eat. "I'm making your favorite for dinner tonight," I say. "I thought we could—"

"Shit, Bug." He rubs at his jaw. "I've got work tonight. Probably gonna be a pretty late one."

"But it's Saturday, the shop closes ..." I catch the look on his face and realize how naïve I'm being. "Is Jameson going, too?"

He shakes his head.

"Do I need to be worried?"

"What have I told you, hmm?" He takes a step forward, "I'm always careful."

I nod, trying to believe him. "Okay," I say. "I'll save you a plate for when you get home."

He wraps his arm around me, dropping a kiss on my head. "Thanks, Bug."

Chapter 27

Jameson

I wake up to screaming.

It only takes me a few seconds to realize the sound is coming from my mother.

Jolting up, I push myself out of bed and quickly pull the gun from my nightstand. When I step into the hall, the sound only grows louder, making my heart race and my body move faster.

There's another low voice just below the sound of her wailing, and I realize why when I round the corner into the kitchen.

There are two cops standing in front of my mother, who's hunched over, sobbing.

Immediately, I know.

Pushing the gun into the back of my pants, I cover it with my shirt and step into the room. I go right for my mother, and the moment I'm beside her, she crumples in my arms.

I run my hand down her back, trying to calm her, but she won't stop crying. She's shaking so hard that I can barely keep her upright.

The cops look from her to me. "Is this your mother?"

I nod, looking between them, bracing myself for what they're about to tell me.

"I'm so sorry, son," the larger man says. "Your father has been killed."

So many emotions flood through me that it's like I don't feel any of them at all.

"Oh God," my mother wails. "Levi ..." She trails off as she continues to sob.

I push away the thoughts swirling around in my head, just needing to deal with what's in front of me.

I nod toward the kitchen table. "Can you ...?"

The cop pulls out a chair, and I gently set my mother into it. She slumps over the table, dropping her head into her hands.

I hold onto her shoulders to steady her and turn back to the cop. "What happened?"

His expression turns hard. "Your father was attempting to steal a car on Marshall Road. When officers arrived, he was armed. He was asked to drop his weapon but resisted, firing and injuring an officer. Shots were returned, and your father was killed on the scene."

He says it so prescriptively, like my father's life and death can be reduced to a few sentences.

"Was he alone?" I ask, already knowing the answer. If Johnny was able to flee, I don't want to give him away.

I tense when the officer says, "No."

Fuck.

They either have Johnny or he's ...

The officer looks down at the file that's opened in his hands. "It looks like a Jonathan Barlowe, age twenty, fled the scene ..." Hope ignites inside me, but then he continues, "Officers attempted to apprehend the suspect, but he lost control of the car, crashing into a tree." The man looks up at me. "He died on impact."

All I can think about is Sam.

I need to get to Sam.

I try to get the cops out of the house as quickly as possible, but they're hesitant to leave given the state of my mother.

"Do you have anyone you can call?" one of the officers asks.

"My uncle," I mutter, glancing at the clock and realizing it's already past one in the morning, dreading having to wake him up with this. But they insist that I call before they leave, telling me that they need to make sure someone is here with us.

"I left my cell in my room," I explain. "I need to go grab it."

He nods, and I try to step away from my mother, but she grabs my wrist, digging her long nails into my skin.

"I'm just gonna go grab my phone, all right?" I place my hand over hers until her grip on me loosens. "I'll be back in a minute."

She lets go, and I rush to my bedroom, grabbing my phone and calling Sam. It rings out, and fear ignites inside me.

I try again.

And again.

But still no answer.

The fear has turned into full-blown panic as I switch to Luke, needing him here with my mother so I can leave.

The phone rings a couple of times before his raspy voice comes over the line. "You all right?" he instantly asks.

"No," I answer without thinking. "My dad, he's ... he was killed. I need you to ..."

"We'll be right there," he says. "Are you—"

"I've gotta go," I cut him off, my words coming out quickly. "Johnny died in a car accident," I force out and hear him suck in a breath. "I need to—"

"Go," he says, and with that one word, I hang up.

I try Sam again, but still nothing.

My mind is racing as I start for the kitchen, trying to decide what to do. Should I leave now or wait until Luke gets here? I don't want to leave my mother alone with these cops, with nobody here she knows. Not like this. Luke only lives about five minutes away, so it's not like it'll take ...

I step into the kitchen, and the minute my eyes land on my mother, my decision is made. Her forehead is pressed against the table, arms wrapped around her head, and her body is shaking so badly with her sobs I can see it from here.

"Ma," I say gently as I close the distance between us, putting an arm around her and pulling her body into mine.

"Did you call?" one of the officers asks.

"Yeah," I answer distractedly. "My uncle will be here in a few minutes."

"Good," the officer states. "We'll wait."

The next few minutes drag by slowly. I keep glancing down at my phone as if that'll make it ring.

I'm about to try calling Sam again when I see Luke's truck barrel down the driveway.

He comes in without knocking, his gaze moving from me and my mother to the cops. Billy walks in behind him, his eyes going wide at the scene.

The cops talk to Luke in hushed voices for a couple of minutes, while Billy and I move my mother over to the couch before they finally leave.

"I need to get to Sam," I blurt out the second Luke walks into the room. It's the only thing I can think about. The only thing my mind will let me hold on to. I motion to my mother. "I need you to stay with her so I can—"

"Go," he cuts in, his voice broken, reminding me that he just lost his brother. I take a step toward him, but he shakes his head. "I've got it here. Go."

I hesitate for a second before I mutter a thanks and start for the door.

Billy follows after me. "I'm going with you."

I don't argue. I just grab my keys.

It's like I'm in a haze, some sort of fucked-up alternate reality where all I can think of is one thing ...

Getting to her.

Billy grabs my arm when we reach the car. "Give me the keys."

"What?" I startle, his touch pulling me from my thoughts. "No," I tell him. "I need to—"

"You shouldn't drive right now," he says, his face serious. Worried.

"I'm fine," I answer, but instead of sounding reassuring, it comes out like a warning.

"Jameson ..." he presses, my tone not even fazing him. Although, it never does.

Staring back at him, I can't imagine what I look like. I feel like a caged animal backed into a fucking corner.

"Let someone help you." He holds out his hand. "Let me help you."

I shake my head. "I don't need—"

"You just found out your dad's dead." His voice is soft, careful, his eyes boring into mine. "Give me the keys."

I close my fist over them. "I drive faster than you."

"We're wasting time," he argues. "I'm not letting you behind the wheel. Now give them to me."

Realizing he's not gonna let this go, I drop the keys into his hand, my mind still stuck on one thing.

Sam.

With a relieved sigh, Billy closes his fist around them and rounds the car as I slide into the passenger seat.

We drive to Sam's house in silence. Or maybe Billy tries talking to me. I don't know.

The world around me is blurry, distant. Like I'm just floating through the moment, trying to get to her.

To make sure she's okay.

I continue to call over and over again, but she never answers.

Minutes feel like hours as we fly down back roads, the streets dark and empty. My mind tries to grasp for something to hold on to, some way to make this better, something I can control. But there's nothing. I look around, and all I can see is darkness. That's all my life is—fucking darkness.

"You all right?" Billy asks, his voice slipping through the cracks.

I pull the phone away from my ear. "She still won't pick up. Why the fuck isn't she …? She always picks up."

"We're almost there," he says, but I don't miss the uncertainty in his voice.

The fear.

Finally, we pull into her driveway, and I'm out of the car before Billy even cuts the engine. I jog up to the front door and start to frantically knock on it.

Seconds drag by, and it only makes me pound harder.

Finally, it swings open, and Carson is standing in front of me. "Jesus, what're you—"

I push past him, darting my eyes around the space. The room is empty, the TV playing on a low volume, beer bottles scattered across the coffee table. "Where is she?"

He shuts the door, walking into the room and staring back at me, his gaze unfocused.

Where is she?" I repeat. "Come on."

"In her room," he says, his voice slow, like he's not all here.

"The cops," I ask. "They've been by already?"

He drops his eyes to the floor. "Yeah," he chokes out. "Yeah, they've been here."

"So she knows."

He nods.

Billy comes through the door, and Carson turns toward him.

I snap my fingers, bringing his attention back to me. "When?"

"What?"

"When did they come by?" I take a step forward. "How long has it been?"

"I don't know, maybe thirty minutes."

"Where's your old man?"

He clears his throat, looking past me. "He left after—"

"What do you mean he left?"

Carson shrugs, feigning indifference, but he looks gutted. "Probably went to get wasted."

I point toward the stairs. "So you're telling me she's been up there *alone* for thirty minutes?"

"Yeah, but—"

I don't listen to whatever else he says before I barrel up the stairs, searching for her room.

My mind is fuzzy as I try to remember the night her and Johnny led me through this dark hallway.

I push open the first door I see and find an empty bedroom. The next is a bathroom, and the door after that is just a closet. That only leaves one.

I hear my heart pounding in my ears as I reach for the door and realize my hand is shaking. My hands *never* fucking shake.

Pushing open the door, I search the room. It's dark inside and, at first, I don't think she's even in here, but then I see a shape on the floor and hear her muffled sobs.

A rush of air leaves me, and my heart fucking breaks.

I'm at her side in an instant, dropping down beside her on my knees.

She's curled up in a fetal position, her body shaking. I want to grab her and pull her to me, but it's like she doesn't even realize I'm here.

Gently, I brush the hair away from her face and whisper, "Sam?"

She blinks her eyes open, and then they widen when she sees me. "Jamie?"

"Yeah, baby, it's me."

"You know?" she asks, pushing herself up. "That's why you're here—you know."

I nod.

"H-he's really gone," she whispers, choking out the last word.

I can't tell if she's asking or telling me. So again, I just nod.

"What am I gonna do without him? Without him to take care of me? He was always there to … How am I gonna live without my brother?" she gasps, the questions coming one after another. "What am I gonna do? I don't know what I'm gonna …"

I wrap myself around her, tucking her into my chest. "Shh," I breathe. "I've got you."

It's like the contact rips her open, and now that there's someone to pick her up, she lets herself truly fall. A sob breaks from her lips, and I know it's a sound I'll never get out of my head. One I'll never fucking forget.

It's pure agony.

Pure heartbreak.

Movement from the other side of the room catches my eye, and I watch Billy slide down the doorway, his face painted with devastation.

I hold on to her tightly, stroking her hair, telling her it's going to be all right, that I've got her, that I'm not gonna let her go. And she continues to shatter in my arms. Her body shakes against mine as sobs rack through her, until she's crying so hard there's no air left for her to breathe.

"It hurts," she says, forcing the words out.

On instinct, I trail my eyes over her, looking for an injury, until I realize she's talking about inside.

That *inside* her hurts.

"My chest," she gasps. "I can't ..."

I pull away from her, giving her space.

"Jamie, I don't ..." She rubs at her chest before her hand moves up to her throat. "I ... can't ... breathe."

Fuck. Fuck. Fuck.

"Billy," I call out, and he rushes over to me. "Go to my house. There's a blue duffle bag in my closet. Top shelf. Grab it and bring it back here."

He nods, leaving without a word.

I turn back to Sam and keep my voice steady. "I need you to listen to me, okay? Can you do that?"

She stares back at me, eyes wide.

"You're having a panic attack. We just need to calm you down. Can you try to take a breath with me?" I grab her hand, bring it up to my chest, and breathe, hoping she'll follow.

She does, so I do it again.

"Good," I tell her, fighting to keep my voice calm. "Just like that. Can you give me another one?"

She sucks in another breath and exhales shakily. "That's it," I tell her. "You're okay."

We stay like this until her breathing becomes more steady.

I lean forward, wiping the tears from her face with the pad of my thumb, but they just keep falling.

"He was all I had," she whispers, her voice so low I can barely make out the words. "How am I supposed to live without—"

"You have me," I tell her. "As long as you want me, you'll always have me."

She gazes up at me, looking so fucking broken. "You promise?"

I pull her into my chest. "Yeah, baby, I promise."

"Thank you for coming," she says against me. "I was so alone ... and it was dark ... and I didn't know how I was gonna ... if I was ..."

"I'll always come when you need me, no matter what." I stroke her hair away from her face. "All I could think about when I found out was getting to you."

"Oh my God, Jamie!"

My heart drops at the alarm in her voice.

She pushes away from me, and all I want to do is pull her back in.

"What?"

"Your dad ..." She searches my eyes. "Are you okay?"

My shoulders drop, relieved. I thought something was wrong with her.

"I don't really know," I answer honestly. "I haven't gotten there yet."

I *can't* go there yet.

Not when she needs me.

"Gotten where?"

"In my head," I tell her. "It's ... a bit more complicated for me." *That's a fucking understatement.*

How do you even begin to grieve a person you've wished so many times was dead?

She nods, biting her lip, trying to hold back the sob that I know is crawling up her throat because it's not complicated for her. She and her brother loved each other unconditionally.

I take her hand. "You don't have to try to be strong for me now."

"But you lost ..." Her voice cracks. "You lost someone, too." Her lip trembles as she tries to hold it together.

I shake my head. "Not like you did."

"Jamie ..." The sob finally breaks free as she says my name.

"You just let me take care of you, okay?"

She stares back at me, a war going on behind her eyes. I squeeze her hand, and she finally murmurs, "Okay."

I let out a breath. "Let's get you off the floor." I move to pick her up and deposit her gently on the bed.

She curls up, making her body small, and I drape a blanket over her.

"I'm gonna go get you—"

She grabs my hand. "Don't go."

I still at the fear in her voice. "I was just gonna get you some water."

"No." Her grip on me tightens. "I don't wanna be alone. You ... Please don't leave me here alone."

"I won't." I drop down onto the bed beside her, and she immediately wraps herself around me. "I'm not going anywhere."

We sit like that for a few minutes, and I watch as she fidgets, like she can't stand to be inside her own body. I keep my hand in hers, running my thumb back and forth.

"A cigarette," she says, the words breaking through the quiet.

"Hmm?"

"I think ... I think a cigarette might help."

I stand from the bed and turn on a lamp. The only light before had been from the moon and streetlights. Now the space is blanketed in a warm glow.

Sam squints her eyes, rubbing at them, and when she pulls her hands away, her eyes are red, her face blotchy. There are tracks of black mascara running down her cheeks, and I realize she must have not even made it to bed before she found out.

I turn away from her, focusing on the task she gave me. Her purse is on the desk next to her bed. I sift through it until I find the familiar red and white pack and a lighter. I place two cigarettes in my mouth and light them both before handing one to her.

I don't usually smoke, but after tonight, I could fucking use one.

Sam takes the cigarette in her shaking hand and brings it up to her lips.

I push open the window, letting my eyes briefly close as a breeze touches my face.

How the fuck am I supposed to get through this?
Get her through this?

Opening my eyes, I grab the ashtray from her desk, settling back onto the bed and placing it between us.

A few minutes later, I hear footsteps coming up the stairs before Billy fills the doorway, the duffle bag I asked for in his hand.

I start to stand when Sam shifts nervously, reaching out for me.

"I'm just gonna go over there and talk to Billy."

She drops her hand, signaling that it's all right that I go, and takes another drag.

"My mother?" I ask once I'm in front of him.

"She's okay," Billy answers. "Think she exhausted herself. She was asleep when I left."

I rub the back of my neck. "Good." *At least there's that.*

He motions to Sam. "How is she?"

"I got her to calm down a bit, but I don't know..." I shake my head. "This is gonna destroy her."

"And you?" he asks.

"You know me." I shrug, bringing the cigarette to my lips.

"Yeah, I do," he says. "I know how you bury things. But this shit's too big to bury, Jameson."

"It's—"

He holds out a hand, stopping me. "Listen, I know how you work. You've gotta take care of everyone else before you take care of yourself. And I get it—I do." I watch his eyes flit past me, over to Sam. "I get that she needs you. That you've gotta be here for her. But this happened to you, too, and I'm not gonna let you deal with it alone."

"I won't," I tell him. "But I ..." I glance at Sam. "I can't now."

"I know," he says. "I'm just telling you that when you can't bury it anymore, I'm here."

I clap my hand on his shoulder and pull him into me, emotion clogging my throat. I don't say anything. I don't need to.

He hands me the duffle bag, and I bring it over to the empty bed.

Billy moves over to Sam and lowers himself in front of her. I watch as he wordlessly pulls her into a hug. "I'm so fucking sorry," he says, his voice strained with emotion.

She sags against him, breaking down in his hold. I turn my back to them and unzip the duffle, sorting through its contents before I find what I'm looking for.

I tuck my gun into the bag and stash it underneath the empty bed. Then I walk over to Sam and Billy. The lit cigarette in her hand is forgotten, burned almost to the butt now, ash drifting down onto her white comforter. I pull it from between her fingers and stub it out in the ashtray with mine.

"Here, baby," I say.

She separates from Billy, lowering her gaze to my outstretched hand. "What's that?" she asks, her eyes locked on the little blue pill in my palm.

"A Xanax," I tell her. "Thought it would help you calm down. Maybe you could get some sleep."

She sits up fully, leaning forward to take it from me. She doesn't ask any questions, just brings it to her mouth and swallows it dry.

"Should work pretty fast," I say, and she nods, reaching for another cigarette.

Footsteps sound from the stairs again, and Carson stops in front of the doorway. He moves his gaze over the three of us until it settles on Sam. He looks uncomfortable, nervous even. "You okay?"

She nods back at him. "You?"

He jerks his chin, mirroring the motion she gave him, but again, it doesn't look convincing.

"What about Dad? Is he ...?"

Carson tenses. "He ... uh ... he left."

Sam hums a nonresponse as she brings her cigarette up to take a drag. Exhaling a cloud of smoke, she asks, "Has anyone called Cathleen?'

He shakes his head. "I didn't know how to ..."

I look between them. "I can do it," I offer, glancing down at Sam. "Just give me your sister's number, and I can call for you."

"You don't have to do that," Carson cuts in, before she can respond. "And I don't know if it's a good idea for you to be here anymore."

"I'm not leaving," I say matter-of-factly.

He's quiet for a second then surprises me when he looks to Sam and asks, "You want them in here? You want them to stay?"

I turn toward her, pushing down the pain in my chest at how fragile she looks, how devastated.

"Yeah," she whispers. "I want them to stay."

"Okay." He nods tentatively. "But if Dad comes back, he might—"

"He left," Sam interrupts sharply. "He didn't even …" Her voice breaks. "He just left."

"Yeah," Carson says slowly. "Fuck that."

She nods. "Fuck that."

They watch each other for a moment, as if they've just come to some sort of unexpected understanding.

"I'll be downstairs," he finally says, turning to leave.

"Carson?" Sam calls out.

He stops and looks over at her.

She drops her gaze, grinding her cigarette out in the ashtray.

"What?" he asks.

They lock eyes, and she shrugs.

A sad smile comes to his lips, his eyes going glassy, before he turns and leaves the room.

I lower down beside her, and Billy takes a spot at the foot of the bed.

"You okay?" I ask. "I mean ... not that you're ..." I shake my head. "I don't know how to—"

She reaches for me. "You're fine. And I'm ..." She trails off. "I should, um ... I should call my sister."

I watch as she starts to move for her purse on the desk, but she stills when I hold out a hand.

"Like I said, I can call her for you."

"No." She shakes her head. "No, it should be me."

I glance at the alarm clock on her desk, seeing it's just past 2:30 a.m. "You could wait till morning."

She drops back on her heels. "You think?" Looking between me and Billy, she asks, "That's not bad? If I wait? I'm just so ..." She blows out a breath, shaking her head. "I don't even know."

"It's not bad," I tell her, knowing she's not in the space for anything else tonight. She just started to settle down, and I know this phone call will only tip her back over the edge.

"Not bad at all," Billy confirms.

"I don't know. Maybe I should ..."

I take her hand. "It's okay to give yourself some time. To not wake her up with this."

She bites her lip, thinking, before she finally nods.

"Do you think you can sleep?" I ask. "Or at least try to close your eyes for a bit?"

"Maybe, if you …" She lowers her eyes to the spot beside her.

"I'm not going anywhere."

She looks over at Billy.

"And I'll be right over there." He motions to the empty bed.

"Okay," she answers. "Yeah, okay, I can try."

I move the ashtray from the bed and slip off my boots before climbing in next to her, pulling the blankets over us.

Billy flicks off the light, and I hear him settle into the bed on the other side of the room.

Wrapping my arm around Sam, I pull her against me, lightly brushing my hand over her skin.

"Jamie?" she whispers.

"What, baby?"

"Thank you for taking care of me," she breathes. "I don't know what I would have …"

I lean into her, kissing her shoulder. "Always."

Chapter 28

Sam

I blink my eyes open, and for a few precious seconds, I forget.

I live in a place where my brother isn't gone.

Where last night didn't happen.

Where a piece of my world isn't missing.

But then, all at once, I remember.

I suck in a breath, tensing, and the arm that's draped over my middle draws me in closer.

Jameson rouses behind me, his voice coming out low against my ear. "I'm here," he tells me. "You're okay."

I shift, and he loosens his hold on me enough that I can turn to face him. I don't say anything, just stare back at him, until I eventually bury my face in his chest. He brings his hand to the back of my head, lightly running his fingers through my hair.

The room is bright enough that it must be nearly midday by now. I don't think we got to sleep until it was already early morning. "I should really call my sister," I say quietly.

Jameson's hand slows, and I pull back, moving to sit. I reach over him and grab my purse as he pushes up to lean against the headboard. The old wood creaks loudly beneath him, the noise making Billy stir.

"What's happening?" he asks, jerking upright and dragging his hands down his face, rubbing the sleep from his eyes. "Everything all right?"

"Everything's fine," I answer. "Sorry we woke you up. I was just about to call my sister."

He looks between me and Jameson. "Can I ...? Uh ... can I do anything?"

"Maybe call and check in at home," Jameson says.

"Okay, yeah, sure," Billy responds. "I can do that." He stands, stretching his arms overhead, before moving into the hall.

I pull my phone from my purse and hold it, making no move to dial my sister's number.

"Are you sure you don't want me to call for you?" Jameson asks.

I nod. "I can do it. I'm just ..." My shoulders drop. "I don't know ... preparing."

His hand comes down on my leg, silently reassuring me that he's here.

Like ripping off a Band-Aid, I dial the number and bring the phone up to my ear. It rings so many times that I think it might go to voicemail. I cling to the relief that I won't have to tell her now, but then she picks up.

"Hello," my sister's voice comes through the line, and the familiarity of it has me starting to crumble.

"Cath," I push out.

"What's wrong?" she asks, that one word already giving me away.

"Where are you?"

"Home. Why?"

"I have to, um …"

Jameson squeezes my leg.

"I have to tell you something. Johnny he's … um … he's …" I can't get the word out. I haven't actually said it out loud yet.

I feel tears streaming down my face when she says, "Sam," the word drenched in fear. "Johnny's what?"

"Dead," I say on a sob. "Johnny's dead."

She sucks in a breath, and I hear the phone drop. Seconds pass before she picks it up again.

"Cath," I say quietly. "Are you—"

"How?" She chokes out. "How did he …?" Her question fades away as tears take its place.

"A car accident."

"Oh my God." She swallows. "What …? What happened?"

"He was being chased by the cops and hit a tree," I answer, trying my best to separate myself from the words coming out of my mouth.

"*The cops*? Why was he being chased by the cops?"

"He was trying to steal a car."

"What're you …? A car?" Her words come out in a rush. "I don't understand. Why would he be stealing a car?"

I clear my throat, forcing my own tears back. "He was on a job."

"A job?"

She doesn't know. Of course he didn't tell her.

"Sam," my sister pushes, "what job?"

I dart my eyes to Jameson. "He was working for Levi Baxston."

"What? Are you fucking kidding me?"

I go silent.

"Why would he do that? Why didn't he ask me for help?" she whispers. "I could have—"

"You know how he is," I say, my mind catching on the last word.

Is.

I guess it's *was* now.

"When did …?"

"Last night," I tell her. "Around one in the morning."

"And nobody called me until now?"

"I was ..." I look over at Jameson. "I was really messed up, and I just ... I'm sorry ... I couldn't ..."

"I didn't mean ..." She blows out a breath. "Fuck ... I didn't mean to make you feel bad. I know the two of you were ... well, you were always his favorite."

Jameson wipes the tears from my face.

"I'm sorry I wasn't there with you," she says, choking back her own tears. "I should have checked in with him more. I should have known—"

"It's okay," I try to reassure her. "I'm okay, Cath. This isn't your fault. It's—"

"You're alone in that house now," she cuts me off in a whisper, like she's not supposed to confess the way Carson and our father act. How even with them both still here, I might as well be all alone.

"I left you and now ... and now ..." A guttural sob tears from her, and I squeeze the phone. "He's gone. How is he ...?" She sucks in a breath. "This doesn't seem real."

"I know," I whisper. Not sure what else to say. How to make her feel better.

Because there is no feeling better with something like this.

"Is Adam home?" I ask, not wanting her to be all alone.

"Yeah," she answers, her voice dazed. "He's, um ... he's in the shower."

"Okay, good," I say, relieved that she has someone there with her.

"I think I just ... Do you mind if I go now? Would that be all right?"

"Yeah," I tell her. "Yeah, of course."

"I love you," she says before the call ends.

Jameson rubs small circles against my back until I've stopped crying. I wipe away the lingering tears with the palm of my hand, turning to look over at him.

"Baby, I'm—"

Billy walks back into the room, his expression cutting off Jameson's words. I watch as he tries to mask the worry on his face, but it's too late.

The bed dips as Jameson pushes off of it, moving to stand. "What is it?"

Billy shakes his head. "Nothing."

"Don't bullshit me." Jameson takes a step forward. "Not now."

"She's, ah ..." Billy rubs the back of his neck. "She's being difficult."

Jameson's jaw works before he nods, like he knows exactly what Billy means when he says *difficult*.

"But my dad's got it handled," Billy pushes. "You don't need to—"

"Yeah," Jameson sighs, "I do."

He shifts to me. "Are you gonna be all right if I go home for a bit?"

"I'll be fine," I tell him. "I should probably go check in downstairs, anyway."

He lowers himself in front of the bed so he's eye level with me. "Are you sure?"

I nod. "I'm sure. Go do what you need to do."

"I'll have my phone on me, so if you need me, call. All right?"

"I can stay with you," Billy says. "So you have someone here."

I turn to him. "I'm okay, really. You should go with Jameson."

A look of understanding flickers across his face as Billy acknowledges what I'm really saying—*Look out for him*.

"Okay," Billy agrees. "But same thing, you need us, you call."

"I will," I assure them.

They both seem satisfied with my answer and start moving around the room, pulling on their shoes and collecting their things. Jameson drags the blue duffle bag out from underneath the bed.

"Can I get another one of those pills?" I ask, twisting my ring nervously. "Just in case I need it today."

He watches me for a minute, like he's unsure, before he unzips the duffle and sorts through it, pulling out a small baggie. Taking a step forward, he drops a little blue pill into my open palm.

I pocket it, and he swings the duffle over his shoulder then asks, "Door or window?"

"They already know you're here," I answer. "Unless you don't want to deal with running into them."

"It's up to you, baby. I have no problem going down there."

I don't tell him that I'm scared to go downstairs alone. I have no idea what I'm going to be met with, but the idea that Billy and Jameson will be with me when I find out calms my nerves.

"Okay," I say. "Then the door."

We move out into the hall, Jameson right at my back and Billy following behind him. I strain to listen for any noise, but all I hear is the sound of the TV drifting up the stairs.

I peer over the railing and see Carson sitting on the couch. I then look over to our father's favorite recliner and find it empty.

I thought he would be home by now. He usually turns up by morning.

We descend the stairs, and Carson moves his gaze over us. I wait for him to start questioning me, but he just drags his attention back to the TV.

As I walk farther into the room, I notice how exhausted he appears. His eyes look heavy, hollow even, and I wonder if he slept at all last night.

I think about asking if he's all right, but I don't want to possibly start something with him, especially when he seems to be leaving me alone. Instead, I quietly lead us through the living room and out to Jameson's car.

Billy comes up in front of me and pulls me into a hug. "Hang in there," he mutters before rounding the car and dropping into the passenger seat.

Jameson starts for his door, but before getting in, he turns to face me. We don't say anything, just watch each other for a moment. I step forward until I'm just inches from him, and he leans down, taking my face in his hands and brings his lips to mine.

The kiss is short, but the meaning in it's clear. It tastes like the three words we haven't said to each other yet.

He moves back, and I move forward. Stepping up onto my toes, I take his face in my hands and silently tell him those three words back as I press my lips against his.

Chapter 29

Jameson

The whole ride home, I prepare myself for what I'm about to walk into.

My imagination is far better than reality.

I push open the front door and am immediately met with the sounds of my mother yelling, *pleading* actually. It sounds like she's being held hostage.

I quickly cut a glance at Billy, who looks just as concerned as me.

Luke's truck is in the driveway, but maybe someone got to him? A million scenarios play through my head.

Has word about my old man already gotten out?

Did he have someone after him that I don't know about?

Have they come to collect when they think we're weak?

My steps move faster as I quickly pull my gun from the duffle bag, keeping it tucked at my side.

I stop short in the kitchen, taking in the scene. The floor is covered with broken dishes, chairs tipped over, the space utterly destroyed. My mother is in a chair, with her arms tied behind her with a dish towel, her back to me.

My hand on the gun twitches, but I keep it lowered until I know what I'm dealing with.

I look around the room, searching for Luke, and find him leaning against the counter, his arms crossed over his chest, a bruise blooming above his right eye.

"What the fuck is going on?" I spit.

"Jameson," my mother forces out. "Oh God, Jameson, you've gotta help me."

Luke moves toward me, broken glass crunching under his boots.

I swing my attention back to him. "I need you to explain this real fucking quick."

My mother rocks her chair, trying to turn in my direction.

"Jesus Christ," I mutter. "I've only been gone since last night."

"Let's go into the living room to talk," Luke says, lowering his eyes to the gun in my hand. If he's surprised to see it, he doesn't show it.

He says my name, but I can barely hear him over my mother's ranting. Her words are blurring together, and I only catch pieces of what she's saying.

"... Levi would kill you if he saw what you're ..."

"... he never liked you, anyway, you fucking ..."

"... Jameson, I swear to God, if you don't ..."

My eyes are locked on her hands, and I take a step forward. Everything inside me is screaming to untie her. She shouldn't be ...

"Let me talk to you where it's quiet," Luke pushes gently.

My gaze stays fixed on my mother, his words slipping past me.

"Watch her, will you?" he tells Billy before placing a hand on my shoulder. "Jameson?"

I shrug off his touch. "Yeah, okay," I answer, my voice taut.

"You can't just leave me in here!" my mother screams.

Luke takes a tentative step back, dropping his eyes to the gun at my side. "Why don't you put that down, huh?"

"I'm your mother, Jameson; don't you fucking forget that!" she continues, her words pressurizing around me. "I don't have to listen to you," she says, her tone turning hysterical. "You have to listen to me!"

My hand flexes against the gun, the weight of it comforting.

My mother continues to rant, her words a jumbled mess of threats and pleas.

"Jameson," Luke says, his tone stern in a way I rarely ever hear it. "Give me the gun. You're not ..." He shakes his head. "Just give me the gun."

I blink, the fog around me clearing. "I'm fine," I tell him. "Let's go."

Without waiting for a response, I turn and head for the living room, Luke following behind me.

He watches as I place the gun in a drawer before shoving it closed.

"All right," I say. "What happened?"

He hesitates for a moment, as if trying to gauge my state of mind.

Fucked. My state of mind is fucked.

But I don't have time to deal with that right now. Not when my mother is the way she is, her cries carrying into the living room.

"I thought she was asleep," he starts. "She was inconsolable after you left. Barely knew what was going on, just kept repeating his name over and over again." He pauses, shifting. "I coaxed her to the bedroom and got her to lie down. She cried herself to sleep not long after."

I watch as he begins to pace in front of me. "I thought she'd be out for a while after she wore herself out like that, so I came back out here to the living room." He wrings his hands. "I wasn't gonna sleep in case ... just watch some TV." He glances at me. "I'm really sorry, Jameson."

"For what?" I straighten. "You do something to—"

He slows his step. "No, no, of course not. It's just ... I ..." Guilt washes over his features, and he's really starting to freak me out. "I told you I'd watch her, and then you come home to this."

"It's fine," I tell him with a sigh. "I know how she can be." I drag my hands down my face, hoping it'll help the steady pounding in my head.

I'm so fucking tired.

"I know, but—"

"We don't have time for this," I snap, my exhaustion making the words come out harsher than I intended. "Sorry," I mutter when I see the dejected look on his face. "It's just ... I can't ... I can't leave her tied up in there. You've gotta tell me what happened so I can go deal with it."

He swallows. "No, yeah, you're right. Sorry." He looks toward the kitchen then down to the floor.

As I watch him, it occurs to me how different he is than my father. Than me.

He folds under pressure.

He can't handle his shit.

And as much as my old man's methods were crazy, he really did prepare me for what he left me with.

"How'd she get where she is now?" I question, forcing my voice to be calm for his sake.

"I, uh ... I ended up falling asleep," he confesses. "The sound of her smashing things woke me up. She was ... belligerent."

"Drunk?" I ask.

He nods. "Not sure if she took something, too. She wouldn't tell me."

"So, why's she tied up?"

Luke motions to his face. "I couldn't get her to calm down. She came at me, and ... I didn't know what else to do. I was afraid she was gonna hurt herself."

"How long has she been like that?"

"Not long," he answers. "Maybe twenty minutes."

"All right." I nod. "I've got it from here."

"What?" He pulls his head back. "No, I'm not leaving you to deal with this alone."

"It's not your problem—"

"And it's yours?" he cuts in roughly.

"It is now."

"No, this is all too much." He takes a step toward me. "Now's not the time for you to push people away. You don't have to carry this all yourself."

"And how's anyone supposed to help me, huh? I mean, really?"

I don't mean to sound as harsh as I do, but he's starting to piss me off. I get that he means well, but nobody can help. Nothing can make this better. It's delusional to think otherwise. *He's* delusional to think otherwise. And his words are just a reminder of how fucked up things really are.

I blow out a breath when his face twists, his expression so pained I look away.

"It's just ... there's no fixing this, not really. It is what it is." I glance back up at him. "Thank you for wanting to help, but I honestly don't know how you even could."

His gaze goes unfocused, like he's caught up in the past. "I promised your dad that if anything happened to him, I'd be here for you and your mom." His eyes go glassy. "Let me keep that promise."

"There's stuff I need to handle—"

Luke holds up a hand. "I know you're more than capable of taking care of things yourself, but that doesn't mean you should have to." He watches me carefully. "Just promise me that if things get bad, you'll come to me. Can you give me that?"

"Yeah." I nod, trying to shove down the emotion his words make me feel, to bury it deep with everything else. "Yeah, I can do that."

He pulls me into a hug. "You're gonna get through this. You're a tough kid," he mutters.

"Thanks," I say quietly, stepping back. "For everything." I turn, glancing over my shoulder, toward the kitchen. "I should really ..."

"I'll come with you," he says, following behind me.

Billy looks up from his phone as we enter the room. He's sitting on the counter, facing my mother, who's slumped in her seat. "She fell asleep a couple minutes ago," he explains.

I push away the evidence of her outburst with my boot, clearing a path over to her chair. I crouch down in front of her and tap her leg. "Ma."

Nothing.

I grip her shoulders and gently shake her, speaking louder this time. "Come on, Ma."

Her eyes flick open. "Jameson?"

"Yeah, it's me."

She darts her gaze around, taking in the space, and panic flashes across her face at the position she's in. "What's going on?" she questions. "What'd you do to me? Why am I tied up?"

"You got upset," I tell her. "Destroyed the room."

She looks around and sucks in a sharp breath. "H-he's gone, isn't he?"

I clear my throat. "Yeah, Ma, he's gone."

She blinks slowly, a tear falling down her face, as she says more to herself, "I'm nothing now. He said that if he wasn't …" Her words fade, the sound of them all wrong.

The sight of her like this makes me want to crawl into myself. Disappear. I'd rather deal with her angry than completely shattered.

"I'm going to untie you now," I tell her. "Okay?"

She doesn't say anything, so I move behind her and unknot the dish towel around her wrists.

Once she's free, she moves her hands into her lap, clasping them in front of her.

I don't know what I expect her to do, but she just sits silently, her gaze locked on her folded hands.

I start to stand when she whispers, "My head is so ..."

Crouching back down, I ask, "It's what?"

She licks her lips. "I'm tired."

"Okay," I say softly. "Let's get you up."

I hold out a hand, and she takes it, stumbling as she stands. "Wrap your arms around my neck," I tell her. "I'll carry you."

She doesn't argue, and I scoop her up, her body too light in my arms. I move past Billy and Luke as I exit the room and start down the hall.

I set her on the bed, making sure she's on her side, and within a couple minutes, she's out again.

When I step back into the kitchen, Billy and Luke each have a trash bag and are clearing things off the floor. I move to help them, but Luke stops me.

"Why don't you go shower or something? Give yourself a minute. We've got this."

I glance over at Billy, and he nods.

After muttering, "Thanks," I make my way to the bathroom and for the first time since it all happened, I'm alone.

The door shuts with a *click* behind me as I lock it, and for several seconds, I do nothing. Just stand here. Then, as if all at once, everything I carefully pushed away crashes into me.

Pain.

Sadness.

Grief.

Every emotion swirls around in my head.

And it's too much.

Too much to feel.

Too much to deal with.

So, I grab onto the thing I'm used to. The emotion I know how to handle.

Anger.

It courses through me, burning everything in its path.

Until there's nothing but a white hot rage.

How could my father leave me like this?

How could he do this to me?

He picked his pride over me, and because of it, he's gone.

And Sam. He fucked her up, too. He took her brother away.

He took *everything* away.

All my fucking life, he's taken everything.

He took my mother away. Made her a shell of herself.

He took my childhood and forced me to become something—someone—I don't want to be.

And now he's gone, and I don't know how the fuck I'm supposed to feel.

Because I hated him.

Wanted him to die more times than I can count.

But he was my father, and for some fucked-up reason, I still loved him.

And now he's gone.

I pace back and forth, the walls of the small bathroom closing in on me.

I rake my hands through my hair, pulling at the strands, the pain quieting the noise in my head.

And I want more.

I don't just want it quiet.

I want it *silent*.

I don't want to think.

With that as the goal, I whirl, smashing my fist into the wall. It breaks through, my arm buried in the drywall. I pull my hand out and do it again, and again, until my knuckles crack and pain slices through my thoughts.

Silent.

My mind is finally silent.

The door handle jiggles, and then a loud knock sounds.

"Jameson!" Luke's voice is panicked. "Jameson, open the door."

I stand there frozen, the sound of him pounding against the wood growing louder.

Just a few more seconds.

I close my eyes.

I just need a few more seconds.

My hand begins to throb as I count to three in my head. Moving slowly from one number to next, searching for more time in the silence.

One.

Two.

Three.

I open my eyes, and the noise slips back in.

The pounding of Luke's fist suddenly seems deafening. A reminder that my fucked-up life is waiting for me on the other side of that door.

Mindlessly, I step forward and pull it open. Luke's wild eyes meet mine before he drops his gaze to my hand, to the blood that's dripping down my cracked knuckles. He then looks past me, his eyes roaming over the three holes that now decorate the wall.

I wait for him to say something, to admonish me, but he just moves back and waits until I step out of the room.

Billy lingers behind him, and once I'm in the hall, he shifts to the side, giving me space. I keep my gaze trained on the floor, not wanting to look at either of them.

"First-aid kit?" Luke asks.

"Under the sink."

He grabs it and starts for the kitchen, me and Billy following behind him. The floor has been cleared and the furniture reset.

I move stiffly over to the table and drop into a chair.

"Let me see," Luke says, sitting to my right.

I lay my hand out on the table in front of me and suck in a breath as I set my palm down flat against the wood.

Luke quickly glances away, like he can't stomach to see what I've done to myself, and pops open the first-aid kit. "Get some ice," he says to Billy.

Silently, he begins working on my hand. I'm glad he doesn't push for a conversation.

Billy comes back with the ice and moves to my other side.

Minutes tick by as I sit between the two of them, trying not to let my mind wander. Trying not to think about how I'm going to get through this. All that's waiting for me on the other side of today.

"You feel any better?" Luke asks once he's finished wrapping my hand.

"Guess so," I lie.

"It'll get easier," he says. "Time heals and all that shit."

"Yeah." I nod, trying to give him something, that sense of delusional hope he tried to feed me earlier. "I know."

He looks relieved at my acceptance, but all I can think about is: how much time does it take to heal from a lifetime of pain?

And when do you begin to heal if you're still in the trenches? Does the clock keep resetting each time another fucked-up thing happens? Because, if that's the case ...

I don't think I'll ever outrun the clock.

Chapter 30

Sam

It's been just over three months without my brother.

My world is emptier.

My house is missing the person who made it a home.

And even my good days are never as good as they once were.

But the world keeps turning.

It's weird how that works. How, when your world seems to end, the world around you still carries on all the same.

I've been doing better, at least on the outside, but a lot has changed in these last few months. I went back to school a week after it happened. It helped to have Jameson and Billy there with me. The funerals went by in a blur. Cathleen came and stayed with us for a few days before she had to go back home for work. While she was with us, she dropped the bomb that she's pregnant.

Luke had to let me go from the garage. Without the money coming in from Levi's dealings, he couldn't afford to pay me anymore. I got a job as a waitress, working all the hours I can get. Without the money Johnny brought home, we desperately need the check.

My father fell on a construction job a couple months ago, so at least his disability will be steady for a bit. I knew where Johnny kept his money and found a few thousand dollars hidden in his secret spot. Still, things have been tight.

Carson isn't working, even though we're barely getting by. He just committed to play quarterback at Auburn. Most of the top schools want him, but he wants a chance to start as a freshman. Him and my father think that if he plays well his first year and gets the attention that comes with it, he'll have NIL money rolling in.

So, I'm the only one in the house who works. And yes, it pisses me off, but there's nothing I can do about it.

Jameson has been working any chance he can get, too. Luke couldn't pay him anymore either, so he's been taking odd jobs, mostly construction. He also found some money in a safe, so he's had that to lean on.

Marcus has been trying to pressure him to get back to the work his father had him doing, but I've begged him not to go down that road.

He told me he won't. I think he's scared of what could happen if he does, too. But, honestly, I don't know how long it'll stick.

His mother has been a mess. She barely leaves her room, and when she does, she's not much of a help. He's the only one providing for them, and I can see the pressure starting to take hold of him. More than once, he's come to my window bruised or bloodied. Sometimes, he doesn't come at all, and I just find him that way in the morning before school. He says he's fighting for the money, but I know it's more than that. It's his way of escaping the noise inside his head.

At first, I tried to stop him, worried that he wouldn't be the one who walks away on top one of these times, that he'll be left with more than some cuts and bruises. But I can't really judge him for having a destructive habit, a fucked-up coping mechanism that keeps him sane. Not when I'm doing the same thing.

He fights when he can't shut off the noise. And I numb myself with alcohol until the world goes quiet.

"Sam, you've got table seven," Maria, another server, says, her voice cutting through my thoughts.

I refocus and realize the sugar container I'm filling has started to overflow, little white crystals falling onto the counter.

Quickly, I set down the large bag in my hand and wipe the excess sugar away. Then I move over to my table—a young couple—and take their order.

It's Sunday, and I've been here all day. Patsy's is a twenty-four hour diner, but I usually don't get scheduled for too many late nights. It's just turned eight now, and I'm grateful the dinner rush has started to slow. I'm off at nine, so not too much longer. My feet are aching, and all I want is to go home and rest. But I know when I get there, I'll only be met with more chores to do.

A couple more tables come in, and the rest of my shift passes by quickly. Still, I'm relieved when Patsy gives me the go-ahead to clock out.

I grab my things from the back room, pulling out my phone and finding a text from Jameson that he's running fifteen minutes late.

He usually picks me up most nights I work, not wanting me to have to take the bus this late. If he can't, Billy often swings by instead. He finally finished fixing up an old motorcycle he was working on and will take any excuse to bring it out for a ride.

I shoot Jameson back a text, telling him I'll wait out front, then pull on my jacket and swing my bag over my shoulder.

Icy air hits my face the moment I step outside. There's still remnants of snowfall on the ground from the storm we had earlier this week, but I've never minded the cold.

I love it, actually.

Digging through my bag, I pull out a cigarette and light it, watching the smoke mix with the fog of my breath as I exhale. I drop down on the bench that's in front of the diner and grab my new book from my purse. I run my hand along the shiny cover, a smile tugging at my lips.

It was my sixteenth birthday a few weeks ago, and this was my gift from Jameson, a brand new copy of *The Picture of Dorian Grey*. My favorite.

I was shocked he had remembered from that first conversation we had the day we met.

When I opened it, he told me, "To replace the copy you lost, because you should always have your favorite."

I never told him that I didn't actually lose the book, although I think he might have guessed. One day, Carson "accidentally" knocked over his cup of coffee, and it spilled all over my prized copy. When I accused him of doing it on purpose, he acted like I was being ridiculous. Told me I was crazy, actually. My father was the only other one at the table and, no surprise, he sided with Carson.

That was over a year ago, and I haven't had another copy until now.

I flip open the book and start reading, getting lost in a story I've read dozens of times.

I've just finished my cigarette when I hear my name being called over the sound of passing cars. Looking up, I see Jameson through the rolled down passenger window.

Shoving my book back into my bag, I jog over to the car, sliding into the seat.

"Hey," he says, his voice a low rumble. "How was work?"

"Fine," I answer, setting my things down by my feet.

He leans forward, slinging an arm behind my neck and pulling me into him. "I missed you," he breathes against me before bringing his lips to mine.

I deepen the kiss, grabbing his hair and pushing into him.

He laughs, hot air tickling my skin. "Looks like you did, too."

I begin to trail my hand down, sliding it over his chest, when the sound of a phone ringing breaks through the quiet.

"Shit," he mutters against my mouth. "I've been waiting on a call."

I move back, allowing him to pull his cell out from his pocket and listen as he curtly answers, "Yeah." He's quiet for a minute while he listens then replies, "Got it. I'll be there."

"Who was that?" I ask as he hangs up and tosses his phone into the center console.

"Just details for a construction job tomorrow." He pulls away from the curb and starts down the road. "I need to be there real early, so you'll have to get a ride to school with Billy."

My stomach sinks. "You're cutting again?" It's been happening more and more lately.

His body tightens, the action subtle enough that if I didn't know him so well, I would have missed it.

We pull up to a light, the hum of the car's engine filling the space between us. He glances over at me, and I see his face is just as tense as his body.

I tilt my head as I look back at him nervously. "What?"

"I have to tell you something."

The car jolts forward as the light turns, and he shifts his attention back to the road.

"Okay, then tell me."

He hesitates. "I don't want you to get upset."

"You're freaking me out, Jamie. Just tell me."

"I'm dropping out," he says in a rush, briefly flicking his eyes over to me.

I had a feeling this was coming, but his words still hit me like a truck.

"When?" I force out.

"Now."

"What?" My voice is pitched high, the question coming out like an accusation. "You're not coming back at all?"

He flinches at the tone.

My surprise is quickly replaced with anger. "How long?"

His eyes flit to me. "How long what?"

"How long have you known you were gonna drop out?"

"Sam," he rasps.

"No," I push, my voice growing louder. "How long have you known? You weren't even going to talk to me about this?"

I thought he saw me as someone he could come to. Someone he could talk to about things. Someone he trusted.

He throws up a hand, bringing it down hard on the steering wheel. "What's there to talk about?" he shouts. "How fucked I am? Is that what you wanna talk about?"

"That's not—"

"I need to make money," he cuts in. "And I can't do that while I'm at school all day. I can't ..." His grip on the wheel tightens. "It's too fucking much, and I'm just so tired all the time. I can't ..." He trails off, and I sag at how defeated he sounds. "I just can't do it anymore," he says quietly.

We slow to a stop outside my house, and I turn to face him.

"It's okay," I whisper.

Cutting the engine, he drops back in his seat and lets out a long breath. "I tried," he mutters. "I really fucking tried." He sounds so lost, so broken.

"I know you did."

"I'm sorry," he says, his eyes meeting mine. "I didn't want to spring it on you like this. Really, I didn't. I thought I could make it all work, balance it all, but I ..." He runs a hand through his hair. "I'm sorry."

"I get it," I tell him. If it weren't for my promise to Johnny to graduate, I'd probably be doing the same thing. "It's gonna suck without you, though," I murmur.

"You'll still have Billy."

I shift in my seat. "Not the same."

"You know I wouldn't do it if I didn't think I had to."

"I know," I reassure him. "I just wish everything was easier for you ... that I could somehow make it easier."

"You do." He reaches over, grasping my hand. "You have no idea how much you do, baby."

I thread my fingers through his. "So, what are you gonna do now?" I ask. "I mean, after you drop out?"

"I don't know yet," he confesses. "I'll try to stay with this construction thing, but there's not always steady work, and the money is shit compared to ..."

His other option hangs in the air.

He drops his eyes like he's guilty of something. "Marcus has been calling."

I already know he has; this is just the first time Jameson has actually acknowledged it.

A wave of anxiety rushes through me as I ask, "And?"

"And a lot of options are open." He pulls his eyes back up to meet mine, gauging my reaction.

"Am I the reason you haven't said yes to them?"

"Yeah," he answers before shaking his head. "No. I mean ... I don't know."

"I can't ..." I swallow, the memories of that night flashing through my mind. "I can't lose you, too."

He squeezes my hand. "You won't."

"That's what he said." I pull my hand from his, dropping my eyes to the floor. "He promised." My voice cracks. "So, don't try to tell me 'you won't' because you don't know."

How can he even think about going back after …

"I'm not gonna do anything like that," he tries to reason. "I'm not messing with cars."

"That whole life is dangerous!" I shout, turning back to him.

"I know," he says, his gentle tone turning sharp, defensive. "You think I don't know that? That's why I told you to stay away from me, but you didn't, did you?"

I pull my head back as his words hit me. "That was before."

"This is who I am," he says, not sounding like himself. Not how he is with me. "I told you from the very beginning."

"It's not who you have to be, not anymore."

"Yeah, right," he scoffs. "I'm just as trapped as I was when my old man was alive. This is all I know. All I'm good for." He says it with such certainty. Like he's heard it before. Like he's been *told* it before.

And I realize why he doesn't sound like himself—because his words aren't his own. They're his father's.

"That's not true. You could be—"

"What?" He lets out a hollow laugh. "More? Better?"

"Yes!" I shoot back. "Why not?"

"This is the hand I've been dealt. This is my life. Take it or leave it."

Take it or leave it?

"What's that supposed to mean?"

He looks right at me, his face blank, devoid of any emotion. "Just what I said."

This isn't him. He's put up the barrier his father taught him how to build.

"You're doing it again."

"What?" he barks. "I'm doing what?"

"Pushing me away," I answer. "You're trying to push me away."

"Well, maybe you should listen this time," he says, doubling down.

And that does it. His words tip me over the edge.

"Fuck you," I spit.

"Yeah, sure," he mutters. "Fuck me, 'cause this is all my fault, isn't it?"

"You think it's mine?"

"I warned you. I told you exactly what you'd get with me."

My heart sinks. "I know, but ..."

"But nothing," he tells me, his voice flat. "You said if it got to be too much, you'd leave." He shifts forward, his eyes locked on mine. "So leave."

"I can't!" I yell, the words slipping out on their own. "Don't you get it? I can't!"

"Why not?"

"Because I fucking love you," I confess. "I love you so much it hurts, and the idea of losing you—"

He grabs my face so fast I don't even know what's happening. Then he crashes his lips to mine.

My hands are already fisting his shirt, my movements frantic, trying to hold on to him, to get even closer.

He grips my hips, shifting me so I'm straddling his waist, our kiss never breaking. His hand moves to my hair, pulling my head back lightly. "You love me?" he questions, his eyes disbelieving as they search mine.

"Don't you?" I ask. "Don't you love me, too?"

"Yeah," he breathes, answering without thought. "Yeah, more than anyone."

Relief courses through me at his response, at how easily the words came. How much he sounds like he meant them. How much he sounds like himself.

"I can't leave," I tell him. "So, please don't make me."

"I don't want you to." He lets go of my hair and slides his hands down the back of my shirt, resting them on my hips. "But I don't know if I can be who you need me to be. I can't promise you that ..." His hands flex against me. "I'm doing the best I can with what I have."

"I know you are," I whisper.

"I'm probably gonna go back to it, dealing at least." When I lean away from him, he rambles on, "That's as far as it'll go, though. I'm not gonna get into anything more than that."

"Just dealing?" I ask slowly, playing it out in my head.

He nods. "You gonna be okay with that?"

I pull my bottom lip between my teeth, and he watches me think it through. "You promise?" I ask. "That's all. Just dealing?"

He dips his chin. "I promise."

"And you'll tell me if it becomes anything more? You can't lie to me."

"I trust you," he says simply, easily. "I'll tell you if anything changes. But baby?"

"Yeah?" I murmur, trying to process his words.

"You have to trust me, too."

"I do," I answer instantly.

He shakes his head. "With this. You have to trust me with this."

"I—"

"Can you do that?"

"No cars?"

"No cars," he confirms. "I promise. Never that."

"Okay." I let go of a breath. "Okay, yeah, I trust you."

He brushes his thumb against my hip, leaning in and bringing his lips to mine, as if sealing the promise.

Our vow to each other.

I deepen the kiss, silently telling him that I'm all in, that I trust him.

He pulls back, drawing his gaze up my body until he finds my eyes. "You really love me," he says, like he's trying to make himself believe the words.

I lean into him, pressing my lips against his in response. "More than anyone."

Chapter 31

Jameson

Heavy rain bounces off my windshield as I idle in front of the school, waiting for Sam and Billy.

It's been a few weeks since I dropped out, and if I'm not working, I always drive Sam in the morning and pick her up in the afternoon. Normally, Billy takes his motorcycle, but I offered to drop him off at the garage so he could avoid the rain.

Things have been a bit easier now that I don't have to worry about school. But, in a way, I've just traded one issue for another.

I'm still working all the construction jobs I can get, but not nearly enough have been coming my way. I've also kept up with my training, taking fights whenever Ryan calls. But the bills have been stacking up. It's not enough. Not when my mother is a shell of herself and leaves it all to me.

So, I've filled in the gaps the only way I know how—working with Marcus again.

He's my connection to the distributor, but he keeps trying to reel me into other jobs.

I always say no.

Between that, the money I make fighting, and any construction jobs I can pull, we're getting by.

I've gotten my mother to leave her room a bit more, and she seems to be starting to slowly come back to herself. Although, I don't think she knows exactly who she is now that she doesn't have my old man telling her who to be.

Things with Sam have been better, too. After that night in my car, any remaining distance between us is gone. I ended up climbing in through her bedroom window and didn't leave until morning. I didn't know you could feel for another person the things I feel for her. Love someone the way I love her. And the fact that she loves me back … despite everything, it's the only thing saving me right now. The only thing getting me through.

The passenger door opens, snapping me out of my thoughts. I turn as Billy climbs into the back seat, Sam sliding in after him.

Her hair is even darker than usual, weighed down and wet. Black streaks run down her face, and I move to wipe it clean, my eyes following the dripping water that drops from her chin.

"What?" she asks, looking up at me through her wet lashes.

I lower my hand. "Nothing."

"You're looking at me weird."

"Just missed you today," I say quietly.

She smiles. "Missed you, too."

"Can you swing by my house?" Billy asks, oblivious to the moment we're having. "I wanna change before going over to the garage."

"Sure," I answer, shrugging off my flannel and handing it to Sam. I wait until she slides it on before pulling away from the curb.

Reaching into her bag, she grabs a cigarette and cracks the window. After she takes a drag, I hold out my hand, and she passes it to me. I bring it to my lips, inhaling, before I pass it back.

"How'd that presentation go?"

She shrugs. "Good, I think." Leaning forward, she changes the radio station. "Everything go all right today?"

"Fine," I respond. "Ryan called."

She drops back in her seat.

I know she doesn't like it when I fight, but she only asks, "What time?"

"Nine."

"That early?"

"I just go when he tells me."

She turns to Billy. "You'll be working?"

"Yeah," he answers. "Gonna be late."

Sometimes, she'll go to my fights to watch, but only if Billy goes with her. I can't focus when nobody's looking out for her.

I glance back at him in the rearview mirror. His body is hunched, his expression hard.

"What's up with you?" I ask. "You've barely said anything."

"Just shit at home," he mutters.

Ever since everything with my old man, stuff has been tense with his parents. It was rough before, but it's only gotten worse.

My father used to pay half the rent on the garage, maybe even more than half. After he died, Luke became the sole owner, and without my father's money, he had to let two other mechanics go. He's at the shop seven days a week, trying to keep up. Then Billy quit the band and started helping out as much as Luke will let him. They're keeping it afloat, but just barely.

I tried to step in, but Luke wasn't having it. He said he should be the one helping me. He wasn't happy when I told him I was dropping out and even more unhappy when he found out I was working with Marcus again, but there's really nothing he can do.

I think that's what upsets him the most—that he has nothing left to give. He's still there for me, the closest thing to a real parent I've ever had, but he can't bail me out of a life he's trapped in, too.

Instead of supporting her husband, who's stretching himself thinner than anyone should, Billy's mother has only become more resentful. I've heard her say things around Billy, *to Billy*, that nobody should ever have to hear.

I don't understand what Luke sees in her. She's clearly not happy with her life. I mean, she's so careless about the fact that she's cheating on him that it's like she *wants* to get caught.

Luke must know. He has to.

Pulling up in front of Billy's house, I turn to face him. "It's not any better?"

"Worse."

"Fuck, man." I shake my head. "I'm sorry."

"It is what it is," he answers, tapping Sam's seat. She moves, dropping it down so Billy can climb out.

He runs inside, emerging a few minutes later in new clothes and an umbrella in hand.

It's a quick drive to the garage, the car quiet without Billy's incessant chatter. After dropping him off, I start for Sam's house.

"We still going to the movies?" I ask.

We planned on a whole day tomorrow, bouncing between theaters. It's the first Saturday we've both had off in I can't remember how long.

"Course." She nods. "You sure Billy can't come, too?" she questions. "Maybe we should ask again or talk to Luke. He's not ..." She hesitates. "I think he could use a break."

I drop my hand to her knee. "I'll ask."

"I hate seeing him like this," she says quietly.

I trace slow circles against her skin. "Me, too."

"You think his parents will split up?"

"Don't know. They haven't yet, so ..."

I pull into her driveway, and she moves to take off my flannel. I hold out a hand. "Keep it."

She smiles, and I lean forward, tracing her bottom lip with my thumb.

"Come over after the fight," she breathes.

I lower my hand, tilting her head back and bringing my lips to hers, dragging her bottom lip between my teeth. "It might be late."

"Doesn't matter," she murmurs. "I'll be up."

I shift in my seat, clearing my throat. She smiles at me again, but this time it's fucking devious.

"I'm obsessed with you," I tell her without thought.

She laughs, and it only makes me want her more. "I know," she says then slides out of the car.

Chapter 32

Sam

I push the front door open, even more drenched than I was when I got into Jameson's car. I wrap his flannel around myself tightly as a shiver rakes through my body.

My father, unsurprisingly, is on the couch, his foot propped up in a boot from when he fucked up his ankle on a construction job. The only positive has been the steady disability check. Otherwise, it's only given me more to do around the house.

He got off his crutches last week, so it's been a little easier, but he still can't drive.

"There you are," he says as I walk into the room. "I need you to run to the store for me."

I look down at myself. "It's pouring out."

He glances over at me. "Ever heard of an umbrella?"

If he wasn't already enough of an asshole, the pain has only made him worse.

"What about Carson?"

"He's at practice."

"Can't he go on the way home? What do you even need?"

"Watch that tone of yours," he sneers. "If I tell you I need you to go to the store for me, then you go. Doesn't matter what I need you to get."

"Let me see if Jameson can drive me," I say, just wanting to get away from him.

"Samantha," he grinds out, and I snap my head up from where I was digging through my purse to look at him. "You can't rely on people to drive you around forever."

Ever since Johnny ... I haven't been able to get behind the wheel. For some reason, I'm fine being in a car, even on the back of Billy's bike, as long as it's not me who's driving.

I should have my license by now, but I can't do it. I'll get it at some point, just not now.

"I know," I say quietly before dialing Jameson's number.

He picks up on the first ring. "You all right?"

"Yeah, I'm good."

"You don't sound good," he says. "You sound pissed."

I ignore his comment, aware that my father is watching me. "Can you come back? I need to run to the store."

"Why didn't you ask when we were out?"

"I didn't know we needed anything."

"Mmhmm," he hums. "*You* need something from the store?"

I sigh. "Jamie."

"He was gonna make you walk, wasn't he?" My silence is confirmation enough because he mutters, "Piece of shit."

I glance over at my father, even though I know he can't hear the other line.

"I'll be there in five."

"Thanks," I respond, ending the call.

I run upstairs, quickly change out of my wet clothes, then search for an umbrella but come up empty.

Fuck.

Guess I'm getting soaked again.

My father shifts his eyes from the TV to me once I'm back in the room.

"What do you need?" I ask.

He rattles off a short list: beer, chips, milk, cigarettes.

"Got it," I answer, starting for the front door.

Jameson's waiting in the driveway when I step outside. I run toward the car and into the door he's already pushed open for me.

"Thanks for coming back," I say, out of breath.

"Where's Golden Boy?" he asks, using his nickname for Carson.

"Practice."

"He couldn't go after?"

"Guess not."

"You do way too fucking much around that house. I don't like it."

"It's fine."

He shakes his head. "All the shifts at the diner. And keeping up the way you do with school. It's—"

"Can you just drop it, please?"

He looks over at my house. "I should go in there."

"And do what? You'll just make things worse." I wrap my arms around myself, fighting off the chill in the air. "We're lucky he lets me out with you as much as he does. He didn't used to …"

"What?" The word is barely restrained. "He didn't used to what?"

"Nothing …" I twist the ring on my finger, and he notices. He always notices. "I just don't want to give him any reason to trap me in that house, okay?"

He runs his hand through his hair, saying nothing.

"Jamie?"

"Fuck." He blows out a breath. "Yeah, okay."

Jameson dropped me back home a couple hours ago. I wished him luck on his fight tonight and made him promise to text me the minute it was over.

Since then, the night has been uneventful. I've used the rare night off to catch up on chores and studying for a unit test I have next week.

Jameson wasn't wrong when he said I do too much, that I carry way more weight than I should around this house, but bitching about it in the past hasn't gotten me anywhere but worse off.

The last thing I have to do tonight is put away the load of laundry that's in the dryer, and then I'm done. I can lock myself in my room with a book and wait for Jameson to sneak through my window.

Carson and my father are reviewing tape when I step into the living room. I quickly move past the TV and mutter, "Goodnight."

"Night," my father answers distractedly.

"Those mine?" Carson asks, nodding toward the basket in my hand. "I'm out of T-shirts."

You could always do your own fucking laundry, I think but bite back the response and answer, "Most of them."

I asked him one time to wash his own clothes. He looked at me dead serious and said, "Do you see a pair of tits on me?"

Johnny smacked him on the side of the head. My father just laughed.

I trudge up the stairs and stop in front of Carson's room. *Johnny's room.*

I give myself a few seconds before pushing open the door, and my eyes automatically drift over to Johnny's side. It looks the same as it always has—all his things still in their place, as if waiting for him.

We never talked about what we'd do with his things. I guess it just seemed natural to leave them be.

After a few weeks passed, I expected Carson to start taking over the room, but he's left Johnny's side completely untouched.

It's still hard for me to come in here. Each time I push through the door, it's like I expect I'll magically find him waiting inside. There are those few seconds of misplaced hope before I realize the room is empty.

Because, of course it is.

I let out a breath and step through the door, walking over to set the basket of clothes down on Carson's bed. I'm halfway there when my foot catches on something and I stumble forward, dropping my hands down in front of me to catch my fall.

The carpeted floor cushions my hands and knees, but the folded basket of clothes is now dumped all over the ground.

Great.

I start collecting everything, refolding them and putting them back in the basket, but when I grab for a pair of socks that rolled under Johnny's bed, my hand brushes over something hard.

I pull it out, and my heart drops when I see a small box wrapped in shiny silver paper. There's an envelope taped to the top with "*Bug*" scrawled across it in Johnny's handwriting.

I fall back on my heels, the box gripped tightly in my hand.

It takes me a second before my mind clears and I realize he must have gotten me this for my birthday.

I scramble up to my feet and quickly throw any remaining clothes on the floor into the laundry basket. I set it on Carson's bed then rush into my room, locking the door behind me.

I gently set the box down on my desk, my eyes fixed on it like if I look away, it'll disappear.

Should I open it?

I start to pace.

What am I thinking? Of course I'm going to open it.

I move to grab it, but stop short. Maybe I should wait for Jameson. I don't know if I can do this alone.

My brother's handwriting stares back at me.

No, I decide. I can't wait. It could be hours until Jameson gets here. There's no way I can knowingly have something from my brother and wait hours to open it.

I snatch the box from its place on the desk and drop down onto my bed. Carefully, I peel the envelope from the box. I drag my finger over the front of it, over the name only Johnny ever called me. My throat tightens, tears threatening to fall. *I can't do this.*

I set the envelope down and eye the box in front of me, grabbing that first.

I tear the paper open before I can overthink it. Inside is a deep green velvet box. Snapping it open, my breath catches.

Cushioned inside is the most *me* ring I've ever seen—a silver vintage style band with an onyx stone.

It's perfect.

I pull it from the box and slide it onto my finger, holding my hand back to look at it. I've always worn a bunch of rings, usually cheap ones I find at the thrift store, but I've never had one as nice as this.

I remove the card, and as I start to open the envelope, a tear drops down, hitting the paper.

The card is simple, a black background with "*Happy Birthday*" written in silver. It matches the ring.

Hesitantly, I open the card and read the last words I'll ever get from my brother.

> *Happy 16th Birthday*
> *I don't know when you got so old. But you'll still always be my baby sister.*
> *Love you Bug*
> *- Johnny*

I can almost hear his voice, like he's still here saying the words to me.

God, I miss him so fucking much.

I choke out a sob, the card falling from my hands.

This is too much. I should have waited for Jameson.

Glancing down at the card, I see spots where my tears have fallen. I keep reading the last line over and over again.

Love you Bug
Love you Bug
Love you Bug

Suddenly, the room feels too small, too stuffy.

I push up from the bed and open the window, sticking my head out and taking in unsteady gulps of air. Then I reach for my cigarettes, grabbing one and tucking it between my lips with trembling fingers. My hands are shaking so badly I can't get the damn lighter to spark.

Fuck.

I throw the lighter onto the desk, jamming the unlit cigarette back into the pack.

I've gotta get out of here.

I reach for my phone and dial Jameson's number. It rings several times before I remember he's probably still at his fight. I disconnect the call and start to dial Billy's number, but stop myself. I don't want to bother him while he's at work.

All you are to everyone is a burden.

Johnny wouldn't be dead if he didn't have to take care of you.

I scream in my head, begging the thoughts to stop, but they won't stop coming.

Jameson will only be able to take so much.

You're too broken. You know you are.

Alone.

You're going to be all alone.

I squeeze my eyes shut, trying to silence the noise. When did the thoughts get so fucking loud?

I suck in a breath and open my eyes. Dropping to my knees, I wiggle open the bottom drawer of my desk. After pushing aside a pile of papers, I pull out a nearly empty bottle of vodka. Twisting off the cap, I down it in one swallow. Then I stand up, grab a jacket and my purse, and start for the window, climbing out into the night.

Luckily, the rain has stopped, but the roof is still slick. My foot slips, and I let out a low curse as I struggle to find my balance.

I make my way down the side of the house and start walking. I haven't made it far when I hear loud music drifting into the street. I know where it's coming from before I even find myself in front of the house.

The Donaldson brothers throw a party every week. Usually multiple times a week, actually.

They've been on their own for years, the oldest brother, Jackson, practically raising the younger two.

I've been to their parties with Jameson and Billy before, but I mostly know them through Johnny. Him and Jackson grew up together.

I stare up at the house, my eyes catching on the people milling around out front. Most of them, I don't recognize, which is exactly what I want.

This place reminds me of Johnny, having tagged along with him countless times when he came to play gin or hang out. But on nights like this, when there's so many people that the party is spilling out from the house onto the lawn, I can get lost in the crowd.

I can escape.

Moving forward, I weave my way through couples pressed against each other and overly loud conversations, trying to make my way to the kitchen.

The house is packed, the air inside stale. Music pulses through the room, the sound of deep bass filling my head and chasing away my thoughts. Bodies brush up against mine as I shoulder my way through the space with one goal in mind.

Finding a drink.

Well, more like a bottle.

Finally, I slip into the kitchen, going right for the counter. I reach for a red Solo cup when I hear a familiar voice.

"Little Barlowe."

Shit.

So much for getting lost in the crowd.

I turn and see Jackson leaning against the wall, his arms crossed over his chest, a drink in hand. I've seen him a couple of times since the funeral, but he still eyes me wearily, his attention moving from me to the bottle in my hand.

"You here alone?" he asks.

I wave a hand toward him. "Not alone."

He sighs. "You know what I mean, kid."

I fill my cup with vodka—or is it tequila? I never actually looked—and shoot it back before pouring another.

"Aw ..." I say, peering up at him. "You looking out for me, Jackson?"

Instead of answering, he asks, "Where's Jameson tonight?"

I down my drink. "I don't need a babysitter."

He brings his hand out to stop me as I reach for the bottle again. "Slow down, huh?"

I bat his hand away, grabbing the bottle. "What's up with you? You used to be fun."

His expression turns hard, reminding me so much of the one Johnny used to give me. "You're not here to have fun," he states. "He would have wanted me—"

"Well"—I tip the bottle—"he's not here, so you're off the hook."

"Sam ..."

I slam the cup down harder than I intended, the contents sloshing around inside. "Can you just give me a break? A fucking second to ..." I sigh, and he takes a tentative step toward me. "I just need a night, okay?"

He watches me for a second before he nods. "Yeah, okay. But you come find me if you need anything, all right?"

I let out a breath. "Thank you," I whisper, my eyes on the table. "You know, for caring."

He sets his hand on my shoulder, squeezing once. "Anytime, kid."

"Jackson," someone calls from the other room, pulling his attention.

He points at me. "Pace yourself at least, yeah?"

I tip my cup in a mock salute, and he shakes his head at my non-answer before following the voice that's calling for him.

Once he's gone, I start for the backyard, settling on a spot at the far corner of the deck. I take in a long breath, the cool air filling my lungs.

"You got a light?" someone with a deep voice asks as I feel them move in beside me.

I'm about to tell them to fuck off when I turn and see a guy I don't recognize holding up an unlit joint.

"Depends," I tell him.

"On what?"

"If you're gonna share."

He looks me over, a smile coming to his lips. "Yeah, I'll share."

I empty my cup, set it down on the railing, and search through my purse before handing him my lighter.

He takes a hit before passing the joint to me.

Inhaling, my shoulders drop as the smoke hits the back of my throat. I hold it there for a moment before letting it go. When I turn to hand it back to the guy, I find him watching me.

"What?" I ask.

"You're just ... um ..."

My head is turning foggy, the drinks starting to curl around my mind.

He holds the joint back out for me to take.

"I'm what?"

"You're the hottest girl I've ever seen."

I exhale a cloud of smoke, settling into the feeling of numbness that's beginning to wash over me.

"You must get that a lot," he rushes on when I don't respond.

"All the time," I mutter, and he laughs.

I laugh, too, but I don't know why. I don't think anything was actually funny.

He takes it as an invitation to step forward.

"I have a boyfriend," I tell him.

"Course you do." He takes another step, and I take one back. He looks around. "I don't see him anywhere, though."

"He's not here," I answer before realizing that might have been the wrong thing to say.

"Why not?"

"Fight," I mumble.

"Hmm?"

"He had a fight."

"A fight?" His head tilts to the side. "Who's your boyfriend?"

"Jameson."

"Jameson who?"

"Huh?" I ask, my head beginning to swim.

"Baxston?" He steps back. "Is your boyfriend Jameson Baxston?"

"You know him?"

"Yeah," he answers, putting more space between us. "Everybody knows him." His face shifts, and he looks serious, or mad, or I don't really know. Different, though. He looks different now.

He grinds out the last of the joint into the railing, and I frown.

"What's wrong?"

"Are you here by yourself?" he questions. "Did you come with friends?"

I laugh. "Friends?"

"Jesus," he hisses. "You're Sam, right?"

"How do you know my name?" I back away from him. "Who are you?" Stumbling, I fall back, hitting my shoulder against the railing. "Ow," I whine.

"Shit," the guy says, leaning forward to help me up. "How much have you had to drink?"

"I'm fine," I slur, trying to move away from him, but it feels like the space around me is spinning.

"I'm just gonna lay down," I tell him, starting to lower myself to the ground.

"Whoa, whoa, whoa." He steps forward. "You're gonna fall."

I push his hands away. "I can do it myself."

"Just let me help you," he grits out, guiding me until I'm sitting with my back against the railing. Once I'm in place, he hovers over me and takes out his phone. I try to listen to what he's saying, but the words are muffled and I can only make out little pieces.

"... your girl ..."

"... the Donaldson house ..."

"... I swear I didn't know ..."

He hangs up and begins to pace in front of me.

"You're making me dizzy."

He slows his movements, standing over me like a guard or something.

"Why are you being so weird?"

"I'm not."

I lick my lips. "Yeah huh."

My head lulls, and I blink, the space around me growing blurry. My body feels heavy as I lean my head back and rub my palms against my eyes, hoping that'll make the pressure building behind them stop.

The sounds around me fade, and I let the darkness wash over me. Everything floats away, and it feels good to turn it all off.

I sink deeper into the oblivion until a voice pulls me out of it.

The voice.

His voice.

My eyes flit open, and I find Jameson staring back at me.

CHAPTER 33

JAMESON

I CLOSE THE DISTANCE between us, crouching down in front of Sam. She looks so fucking small, her body curled in on itself.

"Jamie?"

Reaching out, I take her hand. "Yeah, baby," I murmur, trying to keep the worry from my voice. "I'm here. You're all right."

When my fight ended, I had a missed call from Sam. I tried to call her back, but she didn't answer. I tried a second time, but still nothing.

I was on my way to her house when Ben called. Right when I heard his voice, I knew something was wrong.

After he told me about Sam, I sped over here, barely knowing the details. All I knew was that she was drunk. He told me he hadn't known who she was, didn't know she had so much to drink, and that he wouldn't have shared a joint with her if he had.

When I stormed through the back door, his eyes widened, but I didn't give a shit about him. Not now, anyway.

All I care about is the girl who's staring back at me. The girl I love who's watching me like I'll somehow save her.

I wish I fucking could.

"Jamie," she murmurs again. "What happened? How'd you get here?"

"Shh," I hush her. "Let's just get you home, okay?"

"No." She shakes her head. "No, I can't."

"Why not? What happened?"

"The ring," she mutters. "And the room."

"What room?"

"It was too small. I couldn't breathe again." She reaches for me. "Please don't ... Please don't make me go back there."

I lean forward, brushing away the hair that's fallen into her face, "I won't. I'll take you to my house."

She doesn't say anything, but she doesn't argue either.

"Can you stand up for me?"

I help steady her as she struggles to her feet then wrap an arm around her.

"Don't let me go," she mumbles.

"I won't let you go, baby. Just hold onto me, okay?"

She wraps her arm around my waist as I pull her into me.

Before we start for the car, I turn to Ben. "Thanks for calling."

He nods. "No, yeah, of course. And again, I didn't mean—"

"It's all good," I say, silencing him.

I shift my attention to Sam. "You ready?"

"Mmhmm."

Slowly, I start for the side of the deck, figuring it'll be easier to lead her around the house rather than making our way through the crowd inside

But when we get to the stairs, she stumbles. "I don't know where my feet are supposed to go anymore."

"I've got you," I tell her, scooping her up into my arms. She buries her face into my chest as I carry her toward the car.

We're almost to the front of the lawn when she smacks my arm. "Put me down. I'm gonna—"

I lower her to her feet right before she hunches over and pukes. I grab her hair, pulling it away from her face as she heaves again and again.

She straightens and groans when she notices the mess she's made of her jacket and shirt. Dropping her eyes, she whispers, "I'm so sorry I ... This is so—"

"Stop," I say softly. "You're fine."

I start leading her back to the car, and she shrinks as she realizes people are staring.

Turning, I shoot them a look that has them suddenly minding their own fucking business then wrap my arm around her and walk the rest of the way to my car.

Opening the passenger door, I position her so the door is covering one side of her body and I'm covering the other. I quickly glance around to make sure nobody can see us then strip off her ruined jacket and shirt. After balling them up, I toss them into the back seat and pull my gray hoodie over my head before sliding it over hers.

"All better," I say, looking her over.

She peers up at me, and I step forward, pulling her into my arms. Gently, I settle her into the passenger seat and buckle her in. Then I round the car, dropping into my seat.

"You sure you're good to come to my house?"

"Locked my bedroom door," she answers. So nobody will know she was gone if I have her back by morning. Good. At least there's that.

I nod, starting up the car. I want to ask what happened, but then I look over at her and any questions fade from my mind.

She's slumped in her seat, her knees pulled up to her chest, her eyes fixed on the window, staring at something that isn't there.

I pull away from the curb and save my questions for later, knowing that, right now, she just needs someone to take care of her.

I push the front door open, Sam balanced in my arms. Tucking her body into mine with one hand, I use the other to switch on a light. She curls into me, pressing her face into my chest.

Moving down the hall, I glance into my mother's room and see that she's asleep. Quietly, I shut the door then continue down the hall until we've reached my room. There, I shoulder the door open and set Sam down on my bed.

Hovering over her, I wait for her to look up at me, but her eyes stay trained on the floor. She has her arms wrapped around her middle, her shoulders curled forward.

I start to lower myself in front of her when she blurts out, "Jamie, I'm gonna—"

She lunges from the bed, stumbling forward.

I shoot up, wrapping my arm around her and rush us to the bathroom across the hall. She drops to her knees in front of the toilet and heaves.

Leaning forward, I gather her hair and pull it back, rubbing slow circles on her back with my other hand. "That's it," I breathe. "You're okay. Just get it all out."

We stay like this until she drops onto her heels and scooches away from me.

"You should go," she says, attempting to cover herself. "I don't want you to see me like this. I'll just—"

"I'm not going anywhere."

She lets out a breath, still failing to meet my eyes. "I'm disgusting."

"You're beautiful."

"I'm covered in puke. You just watched me throw up all over myself. I'm ... This is ... I'm a mess."

"So let me help you get cleaned up."

She shakes her head, muttering more to herself than me, "I'm a mess on the inside. You can't just wipe that away and make it better."

I inch forward. "I can try."

Finally, she looks up at me. "Why?"

"Because I love you."

She fidgets, pulling at the sleeves of my hoodie she's swimming in. "Still?"

"Always."

A tear falls down her face, and I move to brush it away.

"Jamie?"

"What, baby?"

Another tear falls. "I don't know how to stop being sad."

I try to keep my face neutral as my heart fucking breaks.

Before I can say anything, she mumbles, "Can I get clean now?"

I clear my throat. "Yeah, let me help you." Moving forward slowly, I give her time to tell me to stop or pull away, but her arms drop from her body, the wall between us falling.

After closing the lid to the toilet, I pull her up and settle her into a seated position. Grabbing the bottom of the hoodie, I say, "Lift your arms for me."

I strip the hoodie off and turn, finding a washcloth and wetting it with warm water.

Crouching in front of her, I gently drag the cloth over her face and chest. I check her hair, but it's clean, so I turn to look for a toothbrush.

I find a spare under the sink and hold it out to her. "Do you wanna try to brush your teeth?"

She nods, moving to stand.

I help her over to the sink and squeeze some toothpaste onto the brush before handing it to her. She brushes clumsily, and I hold her hair back again as she spits.

Once she's done, I lead her to my bedroom and walk her over to the bed. She sits on the edge as I go to my dresser and pull out a T-shirt.

She takes it, and I kneel, unlacing her Converse. "There," I breathe, looking up at her.

Her eyes are dazed as she peers down at me. "I love you," she whispers.

I stand, pulling back the blankets, and motion for her to lay down. She shuffles under the covers, and I lean in, tucking them around her, then kiss the top of her forehead. "Love you, too, baby."

Chapter 34

Sam

The sound of an alarm seems to split my head in two. I groan and hear a muttered, "Sorry," before the noise stops.

I drag my palms down my face, but it does nothing to stop the thumping in my head.

Turning onto my side, I'm met with Jameson's bare chest, and his heavy arm that's draped over me pulls me in closer. Instinctively, I curl into him, the heat of his body wrapping around me.

He moves his hand up to the back of my head, and I feel his fingers lightly run through my hair.

"How are you?" he whispers.

The question breaks through the fog, and memories of last night start to play through my mind.

The party.

Getting wasted.

Jameson coming to get me.

Throwing up.

Oh God.

"It's all right," he says, and I realize I must have said that last part out loud.

The fog continues to lift, and I wish it wouldn't.

I don't want to remember, but I'm stuck in a place where I can't forget.

Jameson's fingers are still threaded in my hair, his arm still wrapped around me like an anchor. I move in even closer to his chest, trying to block out the rest of the world.

Carefully, he asks, "What happened? Why'd you ...?"

I reach down, feeling for the ring Johnny got me.

Jameson pulls away from me, trailing his eyes over my body until they lock on the place where all my attention has gone.

"It was supposed to be for my birthday," I explain quietly.

"The ring?"

I nod.

"From Johnny?"

I nod again.

He takes my hand, sliding his finger over the ring. "How?"

I blink up at him, feeling tears prick at the back of my eyes. "I was putting away laundry. I tripped, and when I was cleaning up, I found it hidden under his bed. There was ..." My voice breaks as I feel a tear fall down my face. "There was a card, too."

Jameson stares back at me silently, giving me the space I need to continue.

"When I read it, I realized it was the last thing that he'll ever get to say to me and that he's really gone. I just ..." I clear my throat. "I just really fucking miss him, and I lost it. I wanted to forget ... so I ... I'm sorry."

Jameson brings my hand up to his mouth and kisses it. Then he leans forward and kisses where the tears are trailing down my cheeks.

"I'm trying," I tell him as he smooths my hair back out of my face.

"I know you are," he says softly. "This was just one day."

The alarm sounds again, and I flinch. "God, my fucking head."

He twists, smacking the alarm clock, and I watch the new tattoo spanning his rib cage stretch with the movement, a snake that goes down the side of his body, coiled around a knife.

"Wanted to make sure you were home in time," he says, explaining the alarm.

This isn't the first time we've done this. I've spent more nights than I probably should sneaking out and sleeping over in his bed.

If I'm not here, he often sneaks into my room. We lock my bedroom door and make sure I'm home or he's gone by morning. It's worked so far, but it's like we're playing a dangerous game, just waiting to get caught. Although, at this point, it feels like it's worth the risk. I can't sleep now unless I'm next to him.

He pushes up from the bed. "I'll go get you some Advil."

A minute later, he's back, and I sit up, stretching my arms over my head. He drops two pills into my open palm and hands me a tall glass of water.

I swallow the pills and drain the whole glass before handing it back to him.

Jameson moves around the room, getting ready, and I slide on my shoes.

"You still up for the movies?" he asks, passing me a flannel to pull on over his T-shirt I'm still wearing.

"Yeah," I answer. "I've been waiting all week."

I never used to go to the movies, but he's gotten me hooked. What used to be his thing has become *our* thing.

He smiles. "Me, too."

It's rare that we both have a whole day off, and even after yesterday, there's no way I'm wasting it.

"Did you ask Billy if he can go?"

Nodding, he answers, "Told him I'd pick him up."

"Good," I say. "He needs a day."

I grab my purse, and we start for the door.

Walking out behind me, Jameson mutters, "We could all use a fucking day."

LOYALTY

Jameson drops me off down the street from my house, and I walk the rest of the way home, climbing in through my bedroom window.

He told me he'd swing around to pick up Billy before coming back for me, so I have a few minutes to take a quick shower and change.

I pull on a pair of low-rise sweatpants and a cropped zip-up hoodie, run some eyeliner, then mascara over my eyes, and call it a day.

My father is sitting at the kitchen table when I make it downstairs, Carson behind him, mixing up a protein shake.

"Morning," I mutter, brushing past him.

"What happened to my laundry?" he asks, screwing the cap onto the bottle in his hand and shaking it vigorously. "It was all just thrown in the basket. Only half of it was folded."

"I tripped on something on the floor. The basket fell."

"And?"

"And," I bite out, "I hurt my leg. Had to go lie down."

His gaze moves to my legs. "Don't look hurt."

"Yeah, well, it's better now."

He grunts then turns back to what he's doing.

I fill up a cup of water in the sink, down it, then search the cupboards until I find a pack of crackers.

"I'm going to the movies. I won't be back until tonight."

My father turns in his seat. "With who?"

"Jameson and Billy."

"Don't you have any friends?" Carson asks, dropping into a seat at the table. "You know, who are girls?"

I don't respond. Instead, I turn my attention to my father. "Is that all right?"

"No work today?"

I shake my head. "I have the day off."

"We could have used the check."

Biting the inside of my cheek, I stop myself from snapping that maybe if I wasn't the only one in this house who worked, we wouldn't be so hard up.

"Sorry. Couldn't get scheduled."

That's a lie, but he doesn't need to know that.

"So," I push, "can I go?"

He takes a sip of his coffee and nods.

"Thanks," I say while texting Jameson to let him know I'm good to go. He responds back a minute later, telling me that he's around the corner.

Carson and my father are deep in conversation, so I shrug on a jacket and head for the door.

Jameson's pulling up when I make it to the end of the driveway, Billy in the seat beside him. He jumps out of the car, moving to the back and giving me his spot.

Once we're all situated, Jameson turns to me. "How's your head?"

"Still feels like shit," I say. "But better than when I woke up."

He drops his hand to my thigh as he starts to drive. "A dark theater will help."

"You doing all right?" Billy asks. "Jameson didn't tell me much, just that you were really fucking hungover."

"It was a rough night," I answer, not wanting to lie. Not to him.

Other than Jameson, Billy's the only person I really trust. Well, and maybe my sister. But she's barely around anymore. She offered to move back home after Johnny, but I convinced her not to; told her I was fine, that I have Jameson and Billy. When she calls, I only tell her half-truths, not wanting her to worry. She got out, built a life for herself, and I'm not gonna be the one who takes that from her.

I spend the rest of the ride to the theater telling Billy what happened, the emotion stripped from my voice. If I don't lock the feelings away, they'll consume me.

They still might, anyway.

He keeps quiet as I talk, listening intently, as Jameson runs his hand up and down my leg in a silent show of support.

"And," I finish, "that's why I have this killer hangover."

Billy leans forward, squeezing my shoulder. "I'm really sorry." I nod, and he smiles at me sadly. "Today will be better, though." He tips his chin toward Jameson. "We'll make it better."

"I just want to"—I blow out a breath—"have fun. You know? Have shit not feel so heavy for once."

"There's a party—"

"I don't know if a party is a good idea tonight," Jameson cuts Billy off, looking over at me then back at Billy in the rearview mirror.

"She said she wanted to have fun."

Jameson's hand on my leg stills when I say, "I wanna go."

"Baby ..."

"I'm good, really." I put my hand over his. "I'll go easy, promise."

He watches me for a minute before he nods then asks Billy, "Whose party?"

"Dougie's."

Jameson grunts, pulling into a parking spot. I know he's not really into parties, but he goes for me and Billy.

"We should head in," he says. "First movie is about to start."

I push out of the car, lowering my seat for Billy. Jameson comes around and takes my hand, threading his fingers through mine. He leads us inside, nodding at the guy he knows who lets us in for free before heading for the concession stand.

While Billy and Jameson get snacks, I run to the bathroom and come out to find them waiting for me. Jameson holds out my favorite kind of chocolate and a soda. I take them, smiling up at him, and he slings his arm over me, directing us to the theater.

We find our usual seats in the back just as the previews start to play. I look over at the two of them, the bright screen lighting their faces, and I can't help but feel lucky.

Even with everything.

Even with last night.

Because no matter how heavy things get or how hard life seems to feel, at least I have them.

And for that, I'm lucky.

Chapter 35

Sam

It's dark when we step out of the theater, the marathon of movies having stolen the day. We hopped from one to the next, getting through three before deciding we'd finally call it quits and head to the party.

With each movie, the tension Jameson always carries seemed to slip away. Sometimes, I wonder what he'd be like without the burdens he has to carry. What all of us would be like.

I guess all we can really ask for are these little glimpses. The moments we can carve out of our lives, where we can forget. Let go. Where we can just be.

We all file into the car, and I switch on the radio, turning up the volume and cranking down my window.

Jameson glances over at me. "Better?"

My head bobs to the song that's drifting around us. "Better."

His face softens before he turns, bringing his arm to the headrest behind me and backing out into the street.

I light a cigarette, handing the pack to Billy after he taps my shoulder. Jameson holds out his hand, and after taking a drag, I pass mine to him.

"Welcome to the Jungle" by Guns N' Roses filters through the speakers, and I lean forward, turning it up until they rattle.

Billy's drumming on the back of my seat speeds up, and I laugh when he belts the lyrics. Jameson's hand brushes mine as he slips the cigarette from my fingers again and tucks it between his lips. He hands it back as we slow in front of Dougie's house, the song just coming to an end.

I take one last drag then step out of the car and grind the cherry out under my shoe. A cool wind whips around me, blowing my hair into my face. Jameson comes up behind me, and I feel his rough hands smooth it back into place.

The gate to the backyard is open, voices and a steady thump of bass spilling into the street.

"Let's go," Billy says, following the sound of the party.

A tall bonfire lights the space, the flames flickering as people dance and move around it. The heat cuts through the chill as we walk over to the foldable table lined with liquor bottles.

Billy goes for the tequila, as Jameson lingers at my side. He passes me a cup then hands one to Jameson when a brunette comes up to the table.

She looks between the three of us, her eyes going to Jameson's hand that's wrapped around my middle, his thumb hooked into the top of my sweatpants. A blush colors her cheeks as she quickly looks away, focusing on Billy. It's not until he says her name that I realize it's the girl from the front office that changed Jameson's schedule on the first day of school.

"How've you been?" Billy asks, rounding the table.

She bites her lip, fumbling with the cup she just grabbed. "Good," she breathes as he stills her hand and takes over pouring her a drink.

He pushes further into her space, leaning down and talking quietly against her ear. She nods, and he smirks before glancing back at me and Jameson.

"Gonna go dance. Catch you later, yeah?" He doesn't wait for an answer before he follows her over to the crowd around the fire.

"That might be a new record," Jameson mutters.

"Do you think—"

"Jameson," a low voice cuts in.

A guy I don't recognize is standing in front of us, his attention drifting to me and lingering a bit too long.

"Stop looking at her like that," Jameson barks as he moves around me, blocking me from the guy's view. "What do you want, Evan?"

"I was just wondering if you had any—"

Jameson holds out a hand, cutting him off.

Evan immediately snaps his mouth shut.

Pointing, Jameson says, "Go wait for me over there."

Evan slinks off, and Jameson turns to me. "Sorry, baby, just give me a minute to go deal with him, okay?"

I know the drill by now. This isn't the first time this has happened at a party.

"I'll wait here," I tell him.

He dips down, brushing his lips over mine, and then I watch as he walks over to Evan. Once he's in front of him, he jerks his chin toward the front of the house, and Evan follows behind him.

I turn back to the table, taking a slow sip of my drink. I want to down it, but I'm trying to pace myself, remembering my promise to Jameson.

A couple people wander over to the table, grabbing a drink without a word. After a few minutes, I start to get bored and fish a cigarette out from my purse.

"Those things will kill you, ya know?"

I exhale, looking over my shoulder, and am met with dark eyes and a flirtatious smile.

"Hadn't heard," I deadpan.

The guy moves around the table until he's next to me. "Not very friendly."

I take a step back. "Not interested."

Instead of being deterred, he takes my words as a challenge, closing the space between us. "Bet I can make you interested. Hot girl like—"

"Fuck off," Jameson demands. "Now."

The guy startles, turning to face him. "We were just—"

Jameson crosses his arms over his chest, a hard look on his face, and the guy inches back.

"Sorry," he stammers before looking over at me. "Sorry," he repeats. "I didn't—"

"Stop talking," Jameson says dryly.

"Yeah." The guy shakes his head. "Yeah, sure. I'm just gonna ..." He trails off, quickly turning to leave.

Jameson comes up beside me as I drop my finished cigarette into an abandoned cup of beer. "You okay?" he asks.

I nod, glancing up at him, rolling my lips.

"What?"

"Nothing."

"No, what?"

"Just ..." I smile into my cup. "That was satisfying."

He tilts his head.

"Watching you make him run away like that," I clarify.

He laughs. "He did run away, didn't he?"

I snort before taking a sip of my drink.

Jameson nudges my arm. "You still taking it slow?"

"This is only my second," I answer. When he keeps quiet, I add, "And my last."

He stares down at me for a minute then nods.

Reaching out, he takes my hand and leads us over to the fire pit. He sinks into one of the empty lawn chairs, and I go to sit in the one next to him, but his grip on my hand tightens.

"Where're you going?"

I flick my eyes up to meet his and watch as they drop to his lap.

Slowly, I move toward him, holding his gaze. He leans back into the chair, spreading his long legs out in front of him. I lower myself down so I'm balanced on his thigh, and he wraps an arm around me, pulling my back into his chest.

I tilt my head, my lips nearly brushing his ear. "I wanna go dance."

He groans, shifting beneath me. "Now?"

"Mmhmm."

"But we just sat down."

"No, *you* just sat down. *I* was practically pulled into your lap."

"I like you in my lap."

"I know you do."

"So, why don't you stay in it, hmm?"

"I already told you." I skate my fingers across his arm that's draped around my waist. "You gonna dance with me this time?"

He shakes his head. "I'd rather watch."

I tap his arm, and he loosens it, letting me shift so I'm facing him.

"Really?" he says, the word teasing. "You're pouting now?"

"Is it working?"

"I told you, I don't dance."

"But you're not just dancing," I say, leaning forward. "You're dancing with *me*."

His gaze heats, and I know I've almost got him.

I brush my lips against his. "Come on, Jamie; don't you wanna dance with me?"

He lets out a breath. "You fuck me up. You know that?"

I tilt my head innocently.

"I'd probably jump off a building if you asked me to."

"That a yes, then?"

"Yeah, baby," he says with a low laugh, "that's a yes."

I pull my bottom lip between my teeth, hiding a smile, and slide off his lap.

He stands behind me, letting me lead us into the crowd of people dancing, where everyone seems to part for us, surprise flashing across their faces when they see Jameson.

Finding a spot in the center, I throw back the rest of my drink and drop my Solo cup, crushing it beneath my shoe. The low bass of the music pulses around us as I start to move.

At first, Jameson is stiff, rigid even, but soon he starts to mirror my movements, his body melting against mine. His hands come to my waist, pulling me in closer. Everything else fades away, one song blurring into the next.

His touch fuels me, and I flip my position so my back is to his front, loving the fact that he's only here for me. That he's never danced with another girl. Never had his hands on anyone else. That he's mine. That he's only *ever* been mine.

Chapter 36

Jameson

A breeze drifts through the window as Sam shifts beside me in bed. It's a warm night for April, the heat of summer beginning to creep in.

I watch as her chest gently rises and falls, the stress she carries gone as she sleeps.

In the six months that Johnny's been gone, she hasn't gotten much better. It's been hard to see her in so much pain. To not be able to take it away.

I try to give her as much good as I can, hoping that if I fill enough space, it'll push away all the bad.

Most nights, I sleep next to her, knowing that if I don't, she won't sleep at all. At least that's something I can give her. A moment to rest. A moment of actual peace.

Pulling her into my chest, I let my eyes drift closed, the rhythm of her breathing guiding me toward sleep.

Just as my body begins to grow heavy and my mind starts to slow, a loud ring echoes through the room.

I snap my eyes open as Sam stirs beside me, reach over her, and grab my phone, ready to berate whoever is on the other line for waking us. But when Billy's name pops up, the anger is quickly replaced with worry.

When I answer the call, the other line is silent, and I somehow know what he's going to say before he even says it.

"She's gone," he chokes out.

I sit up. "You sure? Maybe she just—"

"She left a note."

"What's going on?" Sam asks, her voice groggy.

I hold up a finger, keeping my focus on Billy as he says, "He lost it. You should've heard him. I don't know …"

"Where is he?" I question, knowing he's talking about Luke.

"Asleep," he sighs. "Passed out on the floor of their bedroom."

"I'm—"

"How could she just leave? I mean a *note*," he snaps. "A fucking note, Jameson."

"We'll come get you, okay?"

"No, you don't—"

"Not asking," I say, already moving to get out of bed. "You're not gonna be alone through this."

Sam follows behind me. "*His mom?*" she mouths.

I nod as I tell Billy, "We'll be there in ten. All right?"

"Thank you," he pushes out. "I know you've already got enough of your own shit to deal with."

"Your shit *is* my shit." I grab my keys. "You need me, I'm there. It's that simple. Always has been."

"Thank you," he repeats, and I can tell by his tone that he's out of it.

I reach for the door. "We're heading out. Want me to stay on the phone?"

"Nah, man, I'm good. I'll see you when you get here." His answer doesn't sound even remotely convincing.

"Why don't I put Sam on, yeah?"

"You really don't have to—"

Sam holds out her hand, and I pass her the phone.

"Hey," she says, the greeting coming out tender, careful, like she knows what it's like to be the person on the other end of the line.

I guess she does.

I guess we both do.

"You wanna talk about it?" she asks as we step outside and I lock up. "That's fine. We don't have to. Just stay on the line with me, okay?"

We settle into the car, and she keeps the phone pressed against her ear the whole way over to his house, not saying anything but giving Billy the constant reminder that he has people who are here for him. People who aren't going anywhere.

"We're here," she says softly as I pull into the driveway. "Okay, yeah, see you in a minute."

She hangs up and passes the phone to me. "He went to check on Luke."

"He say anything else?"

She shakes her head. "Nothing. The only thing he said was that he didn't want to talk about it."

"She left him a note," I mutter.

"Fuck."

"Yeah. He didn't tell me what it said, but ..."

"You think she's gone for good?"

The words die on my lips when I see Billy step out of the house. His shoulders are slumped, his head bowed. He looks completely fucking defeated.

He looks like a kid whose mother just abandoned him.

Sam pushes her door open as he walks toward us. He keeps his eyes on the ground, his body rigid. She takes a step forward, closing the remaining distance between them, and throws her arms around him. His body is stiff, his arms pinned to his sides, but after a few seconds, I watch as he lets go. As he lets himself break. He wraps himself around her like she's a lifeline. Like even though he's twice her size, she's the only thing keeping him standing.

My grip on the steering wheel tightens as his body begins to shake. I stay in the car, giving him the space he needs as he sobs, grieving something he never should have had to lose.

Minutes pass before he finally pulls away from her. She says something to him, and he nods, following her to the car.

I step out as they approach, rounding the car to meet them. Sam's eyes are glassy as she glances over at me, and I wonder if this is all too much for her. If Billy's pain is hitting too close to home.

She must read it on my face because she raises her chin and gives me a sad smile. The words clear—*I'm okay*. She tips her head toward Billy—*I can do this for him*.

I nod, grateful to have her here. Grateful that Billy has someone like her by his side.

Shifting my attention to him, I take in his bloodshot eyes, the heaviness in them illuminated by my glowing headlights.

I sling an arm around his shoulders. "You're gonna get through this," I say quietly.

He jerks his chin into a nod. "Yeah, I know." He steps away from me and clears his throat, trying to straighten, as if he's fine. "I just needed a minute."

"You can have more than a minute," Sam says.

"She doesn't deserve it," he mutters.

"Yeah," Sam whispers. "But you do."

He pulls his head back.

"You're allowed to be upset," she tells him.

"I know." He kicks a rock at his feet, crossing his arms over his chest. "But I don't want to be upset anymore. It's too much. I just want a distraction."

"We can give you that." I nod. "What do you wanna—"

"I just need to get away from this house," he cuts in.

"All right," I answer, knowing exactly how he feels. "Get in."

He slides into the back seat, and Sam takes her place up front.

We drive around in silence until Billy says, "I wanna go to the park and get drunk."

I raise an eyebrow, looking back at him in the rearview mirror. Billy drinks at parties, but he's never really been someone who drinks to get drunk. Although, I guess if there was gonna be a time to do it, it would be now.

I swing into the nearest gas station, willing to give him whatever he needs to get through this. "Be back in a minute," I tell them, throwing the car into park.

It doesn't take me long to secure a twelve-pack. I've had a fake ID since I was fifteen, but it's been a while since I've been carded. I either know the person working, or they take one look at me and assume I'm not worth the trouble.

The engine roars to life as I start for the park. Billy cracks open a beer in the back seat, but other than that, it remains quiet.

It's a short drive, and after a few minutes, we're pulling into an empty lot. Darkness covers the abandoned park, only a few dim streetlamps lighting the space.

We spread out along a picnic table, me and Sam on a bench and Billy taking a spot on top. He stretches out his legs in front of him as he opens another beer.

Sam grabs one, handing it to me and then takes one for herself.

I bring the can to my lips as Billy leans back on the table, his eyes fixed on the sky. It's eerily quiet, the swings on the playground creaking with the wind.

A lighter sparks behind me, and I turn. "Can I get one of those?"

Instead of handing me the pack, Sam passes me her own then lights herself another. I inhale, needing to give myself something other than Billy to focus on.

It doesn't work like I hoped it would. I still can't stop glancing his way. I don't know what I'm looking for, but I can't seem to stop searching for it, anyway.

"I'm fine," he finally says, looking over at me. "What're you waiting for? Me to disappear or something ...?" He trails off on the last word before he laughs, the sound all wrong. "Never mind. Guess you can never be too sure, right?"

I shake my head. "That's not—"

"We're just looking out," Sam finishes for me.

"I know you are, but can you ...?" He blows out a breath. "Fuck. I don't know. Can you just not?" He pushes himself up, sliding off the table. "You tiptoeing around me and acting all weird is ... I just need to ..." He pauses. "Separate from it, you know? I can't do that if you're acting like I'm about to lose it."

"Are you?" Sam whispers.

"Am I what?"

"About to lose it?"

He's quiet for a minute. "I just need to move on. Shit is what it is."

"That only works for so long," she says on an exhale.

"Then I'll start with tonight; worry about tomorrow when the sun comes up."

"That'd be a good tattoo," I mutter.

Billy snaps his fingers. "Now *that's* a fucking idea."

"What is?"

"Tattoos," he says. "We should all go get tattoos."

"Didn't know you wanted one."

He shrugs. "Why not?"

Sam stands, grinding out her cigarette. "Like matching ones?"

"I never thought about getting one 'cause I never had a reason." He looks between us. "Something for the three of us is a reason. Has meaning, you know?"

"You'd really want that?" Sam asks, dragging her attention from Billy to me. "Something that permanent? I understand you guys, but me ... I'm not ..."

"You're not what?" Billy asks.

She wraps her arms around herself. "You know ..."

"You two are my best friends," he says. "My family. And it's got shit to do with blood. It's loyalty." He shifts, glancing between us. "Tonight, always ... you're both always there."

Sam glances over at me, her eyes searching.

I nod. "Like he said, it's always gonna be the three of us. There for each other, no matter what. I have no problem getting that loyalty inked."

She's quiet for a minute before she says, "That's what we should get." She looks between us. "*Loyalty.*"

The door chimes as we walk into Big Jim's studio. I called him right after we all decided on the tattoo, and he was more than happy to stay open for us.

"Kid," he calls from his place behind the front desk, pushing back his chair and rounding the counter. I've been in here a few times since my old man died, but still, he approaches me carefully, his expression weary. "You doin' all right?"

"You know," I answer.

"Yeah," he grunts then clears his throat, bringing his attention to Sam at my side. He smiles, the movement distorting the tattoo that runs down the side of his face. "You must be Sam."

She nods. "Hey."

"Heard a lot about you," he says. When her eyes flash to me, he chuckles, the sound gravelly from years of smoking. "All good things, darlin'."

Finally, he turns to Billy, glancing at the remaining beers in his hand. "One of those nights, huh?"

"Worse," Billy answers.

"Let's head back then," Big Jim says, never one to pry.

We follow behind him, and I watch as Sam and Billy take in the space for the first time, their gazes lingering on the frames that cover every inch of the walls.

"So," Big Jim says, "you all want the word *loyalty*?"

Billy looks over his shoulder. "Yeah."

"Just the lettering?" he asks.

My eyes catch on one of the frames—angel wings drawn in black. I think about the word we're all getting inked, not only what it means to the three of us but also for those we each lost. That we rose above it, because of each other.

"What about that?" I point to the frame. "Loyalty above angel wings."

Sam and Billy step closer, both of them agreeing, the look on their faces making it clear they get my meaning.

Big Jim sketches up the design while the three of us decide on placement.

Sam picks her ribs. Billy over his heart. And me, a piece that spans my chest.

Big Jim comes back with the design, holding it up for us to see. "You're all sure?" He looks between us. "Don't gotta tell you this is for life." His gaze moves over each of us as we all nod.

"Yeah," I answer. "We're sure."

Part 3: The Aftermath
One Year Later...

Chapter 37

Sam

I press my pillow over my head, trying to drown out the sound of Jace's crying.

Cathleen moved in a few months ago after her boyfriend split. She came home one day to all his stuff gone and hasn't heard from him since. She had no money, no job, and a four-month-old son. So, the only option she was left with was to move back home.

Now, the space that was once mine, my escape when things at home got rough, has become overrun. All sense of privacy stripped away.

Jace's crying turns into a high-pitched wail, and with his crib being right beside me, the pillow I have pressed over my head is laughably ineffective.

"Cath," I groan.

"Can you?" she pleads, her voice strained. "I didn't get home till three last night."

I push myself up, not mentioning that I barely slept either. That I haven't since she moved in. It's not just Jace who still wakes up during the night sometimes. It's that Jameson rarely sleeps beside me anymore.

I trust Cathleen enough that I told her how, before she moved in, I'd been sneaking out. How, for months, I was either in Jameson's bed or he was in mine.

But now, things have become complicated. Cathleen works nights as a dancer, and she wants me here with Jace while she's gone.

I get it, so I don't argue.

But with her coming home in the middle of the night or even early morning, I can't lock the bedroom door. Which means I can't risk Jameson being inside. So, for the last few months, I've spent almost every night alone. And I've spent almost every night desperate to fall asleep.

I hover over Jace's crib, shushing him. He reaches his little arms up, grabbing for me. "Let's let your mama sleep, huh?" I pull him into my chest, and he nuzzles his head against me.

"Thank you," Cathleen says, rolling onto her side and pulling the blanket around her. "I'll make it up to you."

I take her in, how small she looks, how tired. She's lost too much weight in the last few months. Something she dismissed when I brought it up.

Weaving my way through the mess of my room, I dodge Cathleen's discarded heels, Jace's toys, and an overflowing hamper.

I go through all his morning steps, changing and feeding him, then setting him up in front of the TV so I can get some homework done before my shift at the diner.

My father is asleep on the couch and, like always, he barely stirs. Even when he's not passed out, he still sleeps on the couch. I can't remember a time he's ever slept in his actual bedroom. The room has been completely untouched since our mother left.

It doesn't go unnoticed that me and Cathleen are cramped in a room with Jace, while we have a perfectly good one sitting empty. But neither of us are brave enough to broach that topic.

Eventually, the house starts to wake up, which is the time I usually try to make myself scarce.

Cathleen takes Jace, and I head upstairs to start getting ready for my shift. "You think you can drive me to work?" I ask when she walks into our room.

She sets Jace down on the bed. "No Jameson?"

"He's working," I tell her.

She purses her lips, and I busy myself with my makeup. She wasn't happy when she found out what Jameson does, especially when she learned who his father was and his connection to Johnny. But she's come around over time, especially after I told her how much Jameson was there for me after everything happened. And now, in the last few months, she's seen it for herself.

"Yeah," she answers. "I can drive you."

I turn from the mirror, setting down my eyeliner. "Cath?" I start tentatively.

"What?"

"You know how you said you'd make it up to me."

"You mean, when my brain was barely functioning?"

I snort. "Yeah."

"Mmhmm," she hums. "I remember."

"Since you're not working tonight. I was hoping you could cover for me. You might not even need to, but—"

"I've got you," she cuts in.

"And in the morning, too, so I don't have to rush home ..."

Jace babbles next to her, and she scoops him up into her arms. "Yeah, all right."

I move around the room, shoving things into my purse. "I've gotta get to work," I tell her.

She stands, sliding Jace onto her hip. "You wanna go in the car," she coos. "You wanna go bye-bye."

He claps his hands, and I smile over at him.

"I'll go get him buckled in," Cathleen says.

"Thanks," I answer, searching for my lighter. "Meet you down there."

LOYALTY

The day goes by in a blur, the Saturday rush never slowing.

By seven o'clock, I'm desperate to get off my feet and see Jameson.

I find my purse in the back room and pull my phone from it, my shoulders dropping when I see a text from him saying he's running late, and then another that he's sending Billy to come get me.

It's not that I don't want to see Billy; it's just that I'm *exhausted*. Between the lack of sleep, homework, school, and long hours at the diner, I feel like I'm fucking drowning.

All I want to do is get to Jameson's house, shower off the smell of fry oil, crawl into his bed, and watch a movie until I fall asleep.

I step out into the night and move to my usual bench in front of the diner. Nights like this make me wish I didn't have to rely on someone to drive me around. But not enough to actually make me want to get behind the wheel.

I pull my now battered copy of *The Picture of Dorian Grey* from my bag and read until I hear the familiar rumble of Billy's bike.

Grabbing my stuff, I walk over to him, take the black helmet he's holding out for me, then swing my leg over the seat and settle in behind him. I tighten my arms around his waist as he speeds away from the curb, the wind whipping past us.

It's not long until we pull up to Jameson's house. Billy cuts the engine before I slide off the back and hand him my helmet.

"Want me to come in and wait with you till he gets here?"

I shake my head. "I'm fine. Thanks for the ride."

"You all right?" he asks.

"Just tired."

He nods, and I know he gets it. "Get some rest, yeah?"

"You, too," I answer before turning and starting up the lawn.

I let myself inside, and as I close the door behind me, I hear Billy take off.

The house is as dark and lifeless as it always is. Ever since Levi died, it's like this place is haunted by his memory.

Jameson's mother still barely leaves her room. I don't think she knows who she is without Levi. Who she is without being tied to a man.

Moving past her room, I peer inside. The space is dim, only illuminated by the glow of a TV. She's propped up against the headboard, a red silk robe falling off her shoulder.

"Jameson?" she calls out.

I step into the doorway. "It's me."

She smooths down her hair, straightening. "Oh, hi, honey."

A soap opera plays in the background, the sound filling the space between us.

"Where is he?" she asks.

"Working."

She pulls the fallen robe up her shoulder.

"Did you need something?"

"I ... ah ..." She shakes her head. "No, no, I don't need anything."

I nod, turning to leave, but she calls out my name.

"Will you let Jameson know I need to talk to him when he gets home?" There's a sort of desperation in her tone.

"Sure," I answer, the word clipped.

I know Jameson gives her pills, that he hates himself every time he does. He keeps trying to cut her off, but she keeps reeling him back in.

I drop my stuff in his room before showering, the hot water washing away the day. By the time I step out of the bathroom, I can hear heavy footsteps moving around the kitchen.

After throwing on one of Jameson's T-shirts, I find him hunched over the sink, scrubbing dishes. His jeans are low on his waist, his flannel hanging over one of the kitchen chairs, leaving him only in a white undershirt.

I walk up behind him, snaking my arms around his waist, and press my forehead against his back. "Hey," I breathe.

He shuts off the water, turning to face me. "Hey."

"Everything all right?"

"Yeah." He clears his throat. "Sorry I couldn't pick you up."

He doesn't offer an explanation, and I'm too tired to ask for one.

I look up at him as he tucks a strand of hair behind my ear.

"Did you eat?" he asks.

I shake my head.

He drops his hands to my sides, sliding them down and toying with the hem of my shirt. "Go get in bed. I'll bring you something."

"You don't have to—"

"You're tired," he says, gently stroking my hip. "You've been on your feet all day." He tips his chin toward the hall. "Go."

I step up on my toes and give him a quick kiss. "Oh," I mutter. "Your mother was looking for you. She said she needed to talk."

His body tenses against mine. "I'll handle it."

"Jamie..."

He turns toward the fridge. "Not now, okay? Please."

I swallow. "Okay."

"Why don't you go cue up a movie? I'll be right in."

"Sure," I say to his back before turning to go.

LOYALTY

Low voices filter down the hall as Jameson speaks to his mother, their conversation dragging on. I can't tell what they're saying, but by the time he walks into the room, he looks worn out, defeated.

He's got two plates balanced in his hands, and two cans of Coke tucked under his arms.

I move up to my knees from my place on the bed and grab the plates, freeing his hands. There's a turkey sandwich and chips on each plate, mine cut in half with an added few pieces of chocolate.

"Thanks," I murmur as he slides in beside me.

"Course," he answers, and I position the DVD player between us, hitting *play*.

He relaxes next to me as we eat, his eyes fixed on the movie.

Once we're finished, I stack the plates on the table next to us and curl into him, resting my head on his chest. He traces his fingers down my arm, and I eye his newly tattooed knuckles—the word *"live"* on this hand and *"fast"* on the other.

It seems like every few weeks, he's getting a new piece, his body quickly becoming covered in them. Big Jim does them for free, and Jameson just keeps going back for more.

I've only added one since the loyalty tattoo, a piece for my brother. I got *"Love you Bug,"* in his handwriting down my arm, taken from the card he left me. Whenever I see the words, I think of him. How lucky I was to have him in my life.

Jameson shifts beside me. "You done watching?" he asks, motioning to the movie. "Ready to go to bed?"

"Yeah," I answer, and he pushes the DVD player aside, folding his body around mine.

"Cathleen said she'd cover for me in the morning," I tell him quietly. "So we can sleep in."

He pulls me into him and lets out a long breath. "One day, I'll have you next to me every night, and there'll be no more of this sneaking around." His warmth envelopes me, my back flush against his chest.

"I'd give anything for that," I whisper.

CHAPTER 38

JAMESON

I've just dropped Sam off at the diner when my phone buzzes. I pull it from my back pocket and answer Marcus's incoming call.

His voice crackles over the line, the connection weak. "I don't like waiting."

Glancing at the clock, I confirm that I'm already ten minutes late. "I'm almost there."

He grunts, and I know I've pissed him off. I wait for him to lay into me, but the line just goes dead.

Since my old man's been gone, Marcus has taken over most of what he's built. The guys who were loyal to my father shifted that loyalty to him.

I resisted getting back into it for as long as I could but, eventually, the need for cash won out. I called Marcus up, and he was more than happy to put me to work.

Still, I have my limits. Lines that I won't cross.

Or, at least, I hope I won't.

I know how much this life chips away at your moral compass. How it can turn you into a person you never thought you'd be. But it's not just me I'm thinking about. It's Sam. I can't be another person she loses.

Gravel crunches under my tires as I pull around the back of an abandoned warehouse. Half the windows are smashed, the other half boarded up, and graffiti litters the stained brick walls.

Luke refused to let Marcus operate out of the garage, so this is our new spot.

I cut the engine and reach into the glove box, retrieving the envelope of cash I stashed there this morning, then step out of the car, sliding it into my back pocket.

Walking up to the warehouse, I check for my gun, reassuring myself that it's tucked in place.

If my old man taught me one thing, it's that you never know what kind of shit you're walking into. Just because you think something is going to go one way, doesn't mean it can't go south fast.

I stop at the old wood door, knocking in a pattern of threes before it's pulled open. A gun is pointed at my head before it's lowered.

I'm used to the greeting because, just like my old man, Marcus doesn't fuck around with *what ifs*.

Adrian steps away from the door, tucking his piece away and letting me pass.

I scan the room, clocking all the exits out of habit before striding over to Marcus. He's sitting at a foldable card table, positioned in the middle of the room, cleaning a gun. He snaps his eyes up when the door slams closed behind me, the sound echoing through the cavernous space.

On my way to the table, I move past Jonah stripping a BMW and Marcus's girl, Naomi, bagging pills. Their presence doesn't make me any less on edge. I'm more than familiar with how power structures like these work.

Marcus is in charge, so if he wants to fuck with me, nobody's gonna step in.

I stop in front of him, grabbing the envelope from my back pocket. "Sorry, I'm—"

"Sit," he commands, nodding to the chair opposite him.

I lower into the seat, sliding the envelope toward him. He sets down the gun and reaches for it, tucking it away without checking its contents.

"I give you a lot of free passes 'cause of who you are, but this is the second time you've made me wait on you." When I don't say anything, he asks, "Things at home all right?"

"Fine," I answer. I'm not about to tell him shit. It's none of his business.

"Your mother?"

My jaw ticks. "Her husband's dead, but other than that ..."

"Lucky she has you."

"You got the product?" I ask. "I'm here to pick up, not for a therapy session."

I wait for him to lose it, maybe pistol whip me or something for giving him lip, but he just tilts his head back and starts laughing.

When he looks back at me, I notice his dilated pupils. "You're one cold motherfucker, you know that?"

"Just here to work," I tell him.

He watches me for a minute before he shakes his head. "He really did a number on you, didn't he, kid?" Before I can respond, he drums his hands on the table and shouts, "Naomi!"

She looks up from where she's working and quickly starts toward us.

When Marcus started bringing her around, it was clear the only reason she was with him was drugs and money. Well, and maybe the ego boost of being with a man in power. She's at least fifteen years younger than him and the type of pretty he would never be able to pull if he wasn't who he is.

Her hips sway as she saunters toward us, her skimpy outfit leaving little to the imagination. As she approaches, she runs her eyes over me appreciatively.

I look away, not wanting her to get any ideas.

When she reaches the table, Marcus yanks her toward him, and I shift, about to step in, but he drops his hand.

"What do you think you're doing?" he questions, his voice low.

"What do you mean? I—"

"You were practically eye-fucking him the whole way over here," Marcus spits.

She turns toward him, running her hand down his chest. "I wasn't looking at him any kind of way."

"You sayin' I'm lying?"

"No." She shakes her head. "No, that's not what I—"

"Do you want to fuck him?"

"W-what?"

"I *said*, do you want to fuck him?" he asks, drawing out each word.

Her eyes widen. "No, of course not, no. I only want you. You know that?"

"You gonna show me just how much you want me then, hmm?"

She leans into him and nods as he trails his hand up her leg and grips her ass. He slaps it then tilts his head toward me. "Give him the bag, and then go wait for me."

I stand and she passes me a duffle bag, barely making eye contact this time, before making a show of kissing Marcus then scampering off.

I grip the handle of the bag, the fabric digging into my palm. This whole situation makes my fucking skin crawl.

"Same time next week," Marcus says, pushing his chair back. "And you better not make me wait." He holds up two fingers. "You're already at two strikes. Don't make me show you what happens if you get to three."

I fight to hold back a response, dying to put him in his place. Wanting to remind him that he used to be someone's bitch, too. That I still remember the hold my father had over him, the way he followed my old man around like a dog begging for scraps.

He stands. "You hear me, kid?"

I stare him down, not playing into his bullshit, satisfied when it's him who finally drops my gaze. Then I sling the duffle bag over my shoulder and turn without a word.

"Jameson?" he says to my back.

"Yeah, Marcus," I call out, not bothering to look at him, "I hear you."

LOYALTY

I swing into the driveway, stopping home after some drop-offs and a few hours at my usual spots. I'm done for the day and have a couple hours to kill before Sam needs to be picked up.

The house is quiet when I step inside. I know I shouldn't be surprised, but each time I come home, there's a part of me that hopes she'll be up. That the mother I used to know will be back.

I picture walking into the house and it smelling like the roast chicken dinner she used to make because she knew it was my favorite. That she'd be in the kitchen, looking way too done up to just be cooking, humming some song the way she used to.

Instead, it smells like stale cigarettes, and the only sound is my boots hitting the floor.

I pass through the kitchen, noting the dirty dishes piling up in the sink. I ignore them for now, heading to my room so I can stash the duffle bag.

"Jameson?" my mother's voice rings out as I start down the hall.

I take in a breath, slowing in front of her room. "Yeah," I answer, lingering in the doorway.

Her room looks like a cave, the window covered with a sheet, blocking out any natural light. Her clothes are strewn around the room, an overflowing ashtray balanced on her nightstand.

"You've gotta clean this place up," I tell her. "Seriously, Ma. This is getting to be too much."

I move for the window, stepping over the mess on the floor.

She groans when I pull the sheet away and light floods the room.

"Get up," I tell her. "This has gotta stop."

This isn't the first time we've gone through this routine.

Or even the second.

Or third.

I've been trying for months.

I click off the TV and turn to face her, tensing when my eyes land on her frail body.

She's so fucking thin. Her knees are pulled to her chest. The satin robe she always wears pooling around her.

"You eat anything today?"

She shrugs, and I know that means she didn't.

"We talked about this," I say, moving around the room and picking things up. "It's the middle of the day. You can't just not eat."

"I'm not hungry," she mutters.

I sigh, facing her. "How much longer are you gonna do this? It's been over a year."

She looks up at me, her eyes hollow. "If I just had something to …"

"I'm not giving you more coke. The pills are bad enough."

"I want to get better," she pushes. "I do, really. I just need some help getting started. Something to help me get out of bed, you know?"

"That's what you said last time."

"I messed up last time. This time, it'll be different."

"No."

"Jameson," she pleads. "Come on; don't you want me to be better. *I* want to be better."

"Of course I do, but—"

"I just need a jumpstart." She shifts forward. "That's it."

I sit on the edge of the bed. "You can do it without the coke."

She shakes her head.

"Just take it one thing at a time."

"You don't fucking get it," she snaps.

"Oh, I don't get it." I scoff. "You think this shit is easy for me? That I don't wish I had the privilege of locking myself in my room and forgetting that this is my life."

"It's not the same."

"You know how long I had to get it together after that night? About five fucking minutes. And do you know where you were when I was losing it?"

She stares back at me.

"Passed out drunk in this bed."

She flinches.

"I tried to coddle you. Give you time. But I'm not gonna just sit back and watch you kill yourself. Watch you fucking disappear."

"I'm not—"

"So, here's what you're gonna do. You're gonna get up and shower. Then you're gonna come sit in the kitchen, *not in this bed*, and eat something."

She pulls her robe tightly around herself. "Who do you think you are giving me orders like that?"

I stand. "I tried to be your son, but you didn't respond to that. So now I'll be the one thing you actually will respond to."

"And what's that?"

"Your drug dealer, Ma. That's what you want, isn't it? What I'm good for?"

"That's not ... Jameson—"

"You do what I say, you get your pills. Got it?" My voice is flat, completely void of emotion.

She blinks up at me. "Why are you doing this?"

"Because you need me to."

She stares back at me, resigned. Then, dipping her chin, she stands, brushing past me without a word.

I wait until I hear the water start then move for my room, slamming the door shut behind me. My fist cracks against it, splitting the wood.

"Fuck!" I shout, shaking out my hand.

I start to pace, the built-up energy inside me having nowhere to go.

My mind keeps playing the last few minutes over and over again in my head, trying to rationalize that I did the right thing.

That what I did was for my mother's own good. That it was the only way. That I'm not turning into my fucking father.

Pacing isn't enough. *Nothing* is enough.

I need ...

I pull my phone from my back pocket and dial Sam's number. It rings several times before she picks up.

"Hello?" she says, the end of the word tilting up in confusion.

I almost never call her when she's at work.

"Baby," I push out. "I—"

She must hear it in my voice. "Hold on. Let me get on break."

I continue to pace as I wait, listening to the muffled sounds coming from the other line.

"Okay," she says. "I'm back. What's going on?"

"I don't want to be him," I whisper.

"You're not," she's quick to respond, her tone certain. "You know you're not."

I shake my head even though she can't see me. "I'm not a good person."

"Where is this coming from?"

"My mother ... I ..."

She gives me time, letting the silence sit between us.

"The way my life is ... the way it's been ... it's made me ..."

"It's made you what?"

"Broken," I tell her. "Violent. Numb."

"No," she says. "No, you're not broken."

I blow out a disbelieving breath.

"You're the strongest person I know, Jamie. You're just trying to protect yourself."

"What kind of person gives their mother drugs, huh?" I fight to keep my voice even, to not take my anger out on her. "What kind of person bribes their mother with them? Talks to her like she's a stranger?"

"Listen to me," Sam says. "None of this is your fault. I've watched you with her. I've seen all the ways you've tried to help her. You're a *good* person, Jamie."

I grip the phone so hard that it feels like the thing's about to shatter.

"Whatever just happened, whatever you just think you did, I know you feel like it had to be done. And even though it was hard for you, you did it for her."

"You don't even know what happened."

"Yeah," she answers. "But I *know you*."

"I don't know how you see the good in me. How you have such blind faith."

"That's 'cause it's not blind. You've shown me over and over again who you are."

I drop down to sit on the bed.

"And not once did I see your father. Not once did I think you were broken. And not once did I think you were anything but good."

I'm quiet, her words sinking in.

"Do you believe me?"

I open my mouth to answer, but nothing comes out.

"I'll keep telling you then," she says, "until you do."

Chapter 39

Sam

It's been a week since Jameson called me upset. We talked again that night, and he told me the whole story, everything that's been going on with his mother. I'd picked up pieces from being around, but I hadn't realized how bad things had actually gotten.

Today when we got to his house, after he picked me up from school, we found his mother sitting at the kitchen table. She looked brighter than I've seen her since everything happened. A bit of life to her that wasn't there before. Just the fact that she was out of her room, dressed, and eating is a huge step. One that I know Jameson will never take credit for.

Every time he gives her pills, it breaks another little piece of him. I know his mother sees it, but she keeps asking. Keeps taking.

Still, things are getting better. They're not good, but they're also not as bad as they were a week ago.

And that's something, I guess.

"Baby?"

"Hmm?" I ask, looking up from my calculus book.

Jameson hovers over where I'm sitting on his bed. "I said, do you want a burger? I'm gonna run by Matty's."

"Oh." I smile. "Yeah, thanks."

He leans down and quickly kisses me before starting for the door.

"Don't forget—"

"No tomato," he finishes. "I know."

"Thank you," I tell him as he steps into the hallway.

I focus back on the worksheet in front of me, trying to cram for a test on Monday. There are about a million other ways I'd rather be spending my Friday night, but since I'll be working all weekend, this is the only time I have to study.

It's nights like these, when the numbers in front of me start to blur together, that I think about dropping out. My promise to Johnny, sometimes it's the only thing that keeps me going.

My eyes automatically snap up when I hear a laugh from the doorway, startling when I see Jameson.

Has it been that long already?

He motions to the book in front of me. "You look like you wanna murder the thing." He drops his gaze, lingering on the pencil I'm biting.

"You would be, too, if you were trying to solve this shit," I whine. "I've been on the same problem since you left."

"Good thing you'll never use calculus a day in your life," he says, leaning against the doorframe.

"Tell that to Newton," I mutter.

"Huh?"

I shake my head. "Issac Newton, he invented calculus. Well, him and this other guy, Leibniz."

He snorts. "Why the fuck do you know that?"

I shrug. "I don't know."

"You're such a nerd."

"I am not," I say, standing.

"Just 'cause you don't look like one"—he drags his eyes up my body, slowing on the cleavage my crossed arms are pushing up—"doesn't mean you aren't one. You're the smartest person I've ever met." He takes a step forward. "Only makes you hotter."

I tilt my head as he closes the distance between us. "You like me for my brain then, huh?"

He drops his voice as he slides his hands up under my shirt, causing my arms to fall, then drags his fingers along the band of my bra. "Among other things."

"Hmm," I breathe. "And what other things do you like about me?"

His hands continue to explore as he presses his body closer to mine. "I'll show you later," he answers before stepping back.

I sag forward, instantly missing his touch. "Later?"

He motions to the door. "Food's gonna get cold."

"Are you kidding me?"

"What? You can be patient, can't you?"

"You're such a fucking tease."

"Gotta pay you back for all the times you've done it to me."

"I'm not a tease," I shoot back.

He raises an eyebrow.

"What?"

"You ever seen yourself?"

I stare back at him.

"Everything you do is … Let's just say I've already had a lot of practice being patient."

I pull my bottom lip between my teeth, making his eyes drop to my mouth again.

He jerks his chin in my direction. "Case in fucking point."

"Well," I murmur, stepping toward him, "you better make it worth the wait."

"You know I always do."

"That's a lot of big talk," I say, inching forward.

He smirks. "Not like I can't back it up."

"We'll see," I breathe.

He pulls away from me again, starting for the door. "Let's go," he says, his voice even, as if the last five minutes didn't even happen.

I scowl, pushing past him. "You're gonna pay for this."

He comes up behind me, shutting his door with a *click*. "Can't wait."

LOYALTY

Jameson's mother is already at the table when we walk into the kitchen, three plates laid out and the bag from Matty's in front of her.

I slide into a chair, Jameson taking the one next to me. He looks over at his mother's empty plate.

"You didn't have to wait for us."

She tucks a strand of hair behind her ear. "I wanted to."

He watches her for a moment then nods, a spark of hope in his eyes before he blinks and it's gone.

I take the burger he passes me, offering a quiet thanks, and unwrap it as he hands out the rest of the food. He eyes the fries I've dumped onto my plate and mutters, "Almost forgot."

He stands, and a minute later, he's back, placing a chocolate milkshake in front me.

I grin over at him, popping off the lid and dipping a fry inside. "You're the best."

He smiles back at me. "Gotta keep you sweet."

I lean into him, dropping my voice. "Thought you liked me mean."

He lets out a low laugh, and I pull away from him, grabbing another fry.

I look up and find his mother watching us, eyeing Jameson curiously. She picks at her burger, only taking a bite when she realizes he noticed she's barely touched her plate.

She sets the burger down, clearing her throat. "I was wondering if maybe ..." She shakes her head, picking it back up and taking a bite as if to silence herself.

"Wondering what?" Jameson asks.

"Never mind. It's stupid."

"Wondering what?" he repeats, his voice gentler this time.

"If I could ... get my hair done. Maybe my nails." She drops her eyes to the table. "I want to go out ..." She looks back up. "Like we talked about ... but I don't want anyone to see me when I look like this."

"Like what?"

She motions to herself as if it's obvious. "Ugly. Old."

"You're thirty-six, Ma," Jameson answers. "And you're not—"

"Please," she says quietly. "I need this to feel ..." She lets out a breath. "I just need this."

He watches her silently.

"And I've been doing good, right?" she presses. "A lot better."

He nods.

"Maybe I can even get a job. Help out, you know? I heard what you said about this all being on you—"

A phone ringing cuts her off, all of us looking around until we realize it's mine.

It's rare that anyone other than Jameson calls me, so when I pick up, my answer is nervous. "Hello?"

"Where are you?" my sister asks, her tone frantic. I can hear Jace crying in the background.

"Jameson's. Why?"

"Carson went down during the game."

"Went down?"

"They rushed him to the hospital. I don't have all the details, but it's ..." She trails off. "I'm heading there now."

"Fuck," I breathe, meeting Jameson's eyes. "Is he gonna be okay?"

"I don't know," she responds. "Can you get here? I might need help with Jace. I don't know how Dad's gonna be."

"Yeah," I tell her. "Yeah, I'll leave now."

Jace's cries turn to high-pitched screams as she says, "I gotta go."

The second I hang up, Jameson asks, "What happened?"

"I need you to drive me to the hospital." I push back my chair. "Carson went down during the game tonight. That's all I know ... but Cathleen sounded ..."

In an instant, he's standing. "I'll grab my keys."

He's back a minute later, and his face pinches when he sees me standing in the same place he left me.

"Hey," he says softly. "I'm sure he'll be fine."

As guilty as it makes me feel, I shake my head. "That's not what I'm ..."

He steps closer to me.

"My dad's gonna lose it. You don't understand. If he can't play ..."

He takes my hand. "I'll stay with you, okay?"

I nod.

He turns to his mother. "You good here?"

She waves him off. "Go, I'm fine."

Then she turns her focus to me. "I hope everything's okay."

"Thank you," I respond before Jameson leads me to the car.

The hospital doors slide open, a sterile smell and cold air hitting my skin.

We turn into the waiting room, and I tense when I hear my father yelling, "Don't you fucking tell me to calm down!"

He's pacing in front of where Cathleen sits, bouncing a crying Jace on her lap.

"Jesus," he shouts. "Does that kid ever shut up?"

A woman wearing scrubs stands across from him. "Sir," she says sternly. "You need to sit down or step outside."

He turns to face her, muttering something I can't make out before he storms off, walking past me like I'm not even here.

Jameson's grip on my hand tightens as we walk up to Cathleen.

When Jace sees me, he squirms in her lap, holding out his arms to me. I step forward, dropping Jameson's hand and reaching for him. "Hi, baby," I murmur as he tucks his head into the crook of my neck.

Cathleen stands, rolling out her shoulders. "They took him back into surgery a few minutes ago."

"That quick?" I ask.

"I didn't understand a lot of what they were saying. I hate when they use all those fancy words, you know?"

I nod.

"But they were saying stuff like trauma and other things that ..." She shifts nervously. "I think it might be really bad."

I look over my shoulder, toward the door our father just exited. "Dad?"

"You saw him," she says.

"Maybe we should—"

"I'll go," she cuts in, dropping her gaze to Jace. "You stay with him."

"Are you sure? 'Cause I can—"

"I'm sure," she answers firmly. "I'll deal with him." She nods to the chair she was just in. "Sit. I'll be back." She looks over at Jameson. "You staying with her?"

He nods.

She watches him for a minute, noting his protective stance beside me. "Good," she says before starting after our father.

Chapter 40

Sam

"Sam!" Carson yells from his place on the recliner.

Standing in front of the stove, I roll my eyes. This is the *third* time he's called me over since I woke up this morning.

I quickly turn off the burner underneath the eggs I'm cooking and step into the living room, taking in his slumped form, his braced knee stretched out in front of him.

He ended up tearing his ACL and dislocating his knee. So, like Cathleen suspected ... it was bad. Possibly the *career-ending* kind of bad. Now his dream to play quarterback in college is fully dependent on how his recovery goes.

The first few weeks after the surgery were rough, his and my father's anger spiraling out of control. Now they both seem to have slipped into denial, their anger morphing into depression.

My father's drinking has reached an all-time high. He's been back at work, a new job after he lost the last one, but I'm not sure how long he'll manage to keep it. I'm honestly surprised they've kept him on this long.

I stop in front of Carson, ignoring our father sleeping on the couch.

"Can you get me more water?" he asks, holding out his glass to me.

He's twisting the cap off his prescription of Oxy when I come back into the room, a full glass of water in hand. "Thought you were supposed to be done with that," I say, handing him the glass.

"Why don't you mind your own business, huh?" He glares up at me. "Do you know how much fucking pain I'm in?"

"Sorry," I mutter as he snatches the glass from me, water sloshing over the top.

He turns back to the TV, and I head for the kitchen.

If I thought he was a nightmare to live with before, it's nothing compared to how he is now.

Since school got out a month ago, I've spent as much time away from the house as I can. But between Jace and Carson, someone always has to be home. If I'm not working, I'm usually trapped here. The walls of this house are starting to feel more and more like a prison than a home. But, thankfully, I have today off. It's my first break in weeks, and Cathleen promised to cover for me so I can get some time away. She got in late from work, so I'm handling the morning, but once she gets up, I'm out of here.

We're all going down to the lake. Me, Jameson, Billy, and the rest of our group. I can't fucking wait.

Jace hits his hands against the top of his high chair, smashing pieces of cut-up banana into it.

"It's coming," I tell him, moving back to the stove.

I get through breakfast, clean the kitchen, and give him a bath by the time Cathleen's getting up for the day. I let her have some time to get herself together before texting Jameson that I'm ready.

His response comes back a minute later, telling me he's on his way.

I quickly change and pack a bag before excitedly bounding down the stairs. Keeping my gaze lowered, I move through the living room, trying to avoid my father and Carson's attention, relieved when I make it to the front door without incident.

Hot summer air wraps around me, and I drop to sit on the steps while I wait for Jameson. My eyes drift closed as I let my head fall back, the sun warming my face.

The low rumble of an engine tells me Jameson's here before his car even slows in front of my house. I blink my eyes open, sliding my sunglasses over them.

Billy hops out of the car as I start toward them, moving to the back.

"Hey, baby," Jameson greets me after I drop into the passenger seat, his voice just loud enough to hear over the music blaring from the speakers.

I smile over at him. "Hey."

His hand comes down to rest on my bare thigh as he peels away from the curb.

By the time we get to the lake, sweat is trailing down my back, my hair is wild from the wind, and the tension in my body is slowly starting to slip away.

I step out of the car, the sound of laughter carrying from down by the water as Billy climbs out of the back. Leaning over, he grabs a few cases of beer, balancing them precariously until I reach out to help.

"I've got it," Jameson says, cutting in front of me. "Can you get the towels from the trunk? I threw a blanket in there, too."

I nod, rounding the car to grab them then follow the two of them down to where our friends have set up.

As we get closer, their laughter and the music flowing from the speaker they brought grows louder.

"There they are," Mason shouts, jumping up from his spot and jogging over to Billy, taking a case of beer. "We were wondering if you were ever gonna get here."

I glance around, noticing that we're the last ones to show up.

Billy breaks off from us, him and Mason moving over to where Dylan and Rowan are standing. They all greet each other in that way guys do—grabbing hands and smacking each other on the back. Even though Billy's not in the band anymore, they're all still close.

There are a few other kids here who we hang around with, but at things like this, me and Jameson tend to keep mostly to ourselves.

We drop off the beers we brought into the big cooler, and Jameson grabs us a couple before we set up our blanket among the others.

I look over toward the water as a girl shrieks, watching as Billy splashes her. Laughing, I crack open my beer.

"Cards?" I ask Jameson.

He nods, and I pull out a deck.

Two games of gin later, Billy saunters over, dropping down next to us. "Deal me in," he says, shaking out his wet hair and leaning back.

I pass Jameson my cigarette then shuffle the cards. "How's the water?" I ask.

"Feels like a bathtub." He sorts his cards. "You gonna go in?"

"Yeah," I answer, taking my cigarette back from Jameson. "I'm baking."

"Well, you can go in real soon, right after I beat you."

"Like how you beat me the last time we played." I pause, tilting my head. "Oh, wait, that's right; I beat you both three times in a row."

"That was luck."

I snort. "Then I guess you're pretty fucking unlucky 'cause I beat you all the time."

He picks up a card, turning to Jameson. "Help me out here."

Jameson shrugs. "She's not lying."

"Whatever." Billy grins. "This is gonna be my time, you'll see."

What's supposed to be one game turns into three because when I win the first, Billy wants a rematch. Then, when he wins the second, he wants a tiebreaker.

Setting down my cards, I call out *gin*, and Billy throws back his head. "Come on. Seriously?"

"Guess I'm still lucky," I taunt.

"Whatever," he grumbles, but I know he's only teasing. He stands, starting for the cooler. "I'm gonna go grab another beer."

Glancing over at Jameson, I raise a brow. "What? No whining from you?"

"I like it when you win," he answers simply. "You get this look."

"What look? What do you—"

"When you win"—he leans forward—"right before you set down your cards, your face gets all"—he shakes his head—"I don't know … excited."

I stare back at him. "Do you even like playing?"

"Sure, it's all right."

"Jamie!" I throw out a hand. "We play all the time ... or we used to, at least, before things went to shit."

"I know."

"So, you're saying that you've been playing all this time just 'cause you like the look on my face when I win?"

"I mean, that's not the only reason," he answers. "But yeah, mostly."

"That makes no sense."

"It makes total sense."

I tilt my head.

"You're happy when you play," he says. "And I like to see you happy. So, I play, too. Simple."

"You're ..."

"Obsessed with you?" He nods. "Yeah, baby, I think we've already established that."

Billy comes up beside us. "I thought you were dying to get in the water," he says.

"I ... um ..." I pull my eyes away from Jameson. "I am."

"Well then, let's go," he shouts before shotgunning his beer.

Jameson stands, offering me a hand, and I take it, allowing him to pull me up beside him. I watch as he strips off his shirt, giving me a full view of his latest tattoo. It goes across the top of his back—one side, an angel, and the other, a devil, both of them reaching out toward each other.

He turns toward me, his eyes slowing on my black bikini top and dropping down to the jean shorts I'm shimmying off.

"Baby," he groans under his breath, stepping into me. "You're killing me in that thing."

"Billy," a girl yells from the water. "You coming in or what?"

"You guys done staring like you wanna rip each other's clothes off yet?" Billy laughs. "I was gonna wait for you, but … if you need a minute …"

"Fuck off," Jameson mutters, throwing an arm around me. "We're coming."

Chapter 41

Sam

By the time night falls, the small hangout has turned into a full-blown party.

I take the joint Dylan hands me, bringing it to my lips, before passing it on.

I've been taking it slow, feeling Jameson's watchful eyes on me with each drink I pour. At this point, I'm only two shots deep and plan on keeping it that way.

I know it bothers him when I get out of hand, but sometimes it feels like I can't help it. When the thoughts get too loud, it's the only way to make them stop. I've been trying to be better, though. To not let myself drown when that's all I want to do. But some days, the thoughts win and I'm not strong enough to silence them on my own.

"You good?" Jameson asks against my ear, his chest pressed to my back.

I turn, looking over at him. "Yeah."

"You almost ready to get out of here?"

"We can go now if you want."

"I'm not trying to rush you, baby. If you wanna stay—"

"No, really, it's fine," I tell him. "Can we go back to your house for a little bit, though? I don't want to go home yet."

"Course," he answers, glancing around. "You see where Billy went?"

I shake my head, searching the crowd for him. Finally, I spot him wrapped around some girl and point him out. "Over there."

Jameson starts in their direction, and I follow closely behind.

"We're heading out," he tells him. "You with us or staying here?"

Billy pulls his attention from the girl. "You go ahead. I'll find a ride."

I take the girl in. She's a pretty brunette, her eyes wide like a doll's. She blinks them up at Billy, her gaze fixed on him.

"All right, man," Jameson says, his tone resigned. "Catch you later then."

Billy tips up his chin in a silent goodbye before turning back to the girl.

Jameson wraps his hand in mine and leads me back to his car.

"I fucking hate that," he mutters, sliding into his seat. "The way he uses them. Lets them use him."

"He ever talk about it?"

"Billy talk about how he's feeling? Yeah, no." He starts up the car. "Everyone thinks I'm the one who's closed off, but he's just as bad."

"Maybe you should try—"

My words are cut off when Jameson's phone rings.

"Hold on, baby. Sorry," he says, grabbing it.

I sit back as he answers.

"Yeah?" he snaps, clearly growing irritated by what's being said on the other line. "Now? I thought we said tomorrow morning." He sighs. "No, yeah. No, it's fine. I'll be there."

Hanging up, he tosses his phone into the center console. "I've gotta go pick up." He looks over at me. "It'll be quick. That okay?"

"Yeah, that's fine."

"Sorry," he murmurs. "It was supposed to be tomorrow. You know I don't like to take you there."

"I'll just wait in the car like always. It's all right."

He nods, the movement tense.

Fifteen minutes later, we're pulling into the back parking lot of a familiar worn-down warehouse. I've been here with Jameson a few times. Each of them, he's refused to let me come in with him.

He cuts the engine and, just like all the other times, pulls out his gun and holds it out to me, muttering, "Just in case."

The first time he handed me the gun, he asked if I knew how to use it. When I said yes, he gave me a questioning look and asked, "Johnny?"

I nodded, explaining how my brother had taught me the basics with the reasoning that he always wanted me to be able to defend myself if I needed to. He'd said the same words actually, "*Just in case.*"

Now the gun sits heavily in my lap as I watch Jameson walk up to the warehouse door. It swings open, and the same huge guy who always guards it fills the doorway, pointing another gun at Jameson.

He looks maybe ten years older than us, and his massive frame, along with his ever-present gun, make him plenty intimidating. Jameson warned me the first time to expect this, but I still suck in a breath, holding it until the man lowers the weapon.

Minutes pass, and I keep my eyes trained on the door, waiting for it to open and for Jameson to walk back out. With each minute that ticks by, the gun grows heavier in my lap, reminding me that Jameson gave me his only real means of protection.

Another car pulls into the parking lot, and I sink back into my seat, watching as a man exits and stalks up to the door. He gets the same tense greeting Jameson did before he slips past the guy and into the warehouse.

My knee starts to bob, my energy restless as I continue to wait. Fishing through my purse, I grab a cigarette, cranking down the window before lighting it.

I inhale, closing my eyes, trying to calm myself.

He's fine. I'm sure he's fine.

My body tightens thinking about the time I thought that same thing and things *weren't fine*. I bring the cigarette back to my lips and realize my hands are shaking. I snap my eyes back to the door, willing it to open. It's never taken this long before.

I grab my phone and shoot off a quick text, asking Jameson if everything's okay.

Minutes go by without an answer, and I'm starting to wonder if I should go in there.

Two minutes. I'll give him two more—

The sound of a gunshot splitting through the air cuts through my thoughts.

I jump, dropping my cigarette, and hiss as the cherry burns my thigh.

I'm out of the car before I can even think about it, running for the door. I pull down the handle, cursing when I find it locked, and start pounding my fist against it.

This can't be fucking happening.

I can't lose him, too.

Not him.

Finally, the door flies open, and I stumble, losing my balance.

"Who the fuck are you?" the huge man asks, his gun trained on my face.

"Jameson," I breathe. "Where's Jameson?"

He lowers his eyes to the gun I have clutched in my hand. "Drop that," he says. "And back the fuck up."

I shake my head. "Where's Jameson?"

"He's fine," the man grits out. "Now step back."

"I want to see him."

The man takes a step forward. "He'll be right out."

"No," I push. "Now."

"I'm not going to tell you again. Drop the gun and back up."

When I stay rooted in place, the gun still firmly in my hand, he sighs, muttering, "I tried." In the next second, he's got me disarmed and my wrists securely locked behind my back. "You should have just listened," he says, kicking the door shut behind us.

"Let me go!" I scream. "I need to—"

"Quiet," he hisses as his hold on my wrists turns bruising. "Now here's what's gonna—"

The door flies open, cutting off his words, and my knees weaken when I see Jameson fill the space.

"Jamie," I choke out, my voice breaking, frantically trailing my eyes over him, searching for a wound, for blood. I let out a strangled sob when I find nothing.

He's okay, I try to convince myself. *He's okay.*

"Get your fucking hands off her," he snaps, his gaze locked on where the man has my wrists pinned.

"She yours?" he asks.

"Yeah, she's fucking mine," Jameson seethes. "So get your hands off of her—now."

"She came storming—"

"Stop talking!" Jameson all but shouts.

The man pulls his head back. "What'd you—"

"I'm not listening to shit you have to say until you step away from her." He moves toward us. "I don't care what she did."

The man drops his hold on me, and Jameson is at my side in an instant.

"You okay, baby?"

"Yeah," I tell him. "You? When I heard the …" I shake my head. "I thought …"

"I know," he whispers. "I know. I'm sorry."

He wraps his arm around me, and I press into his side as he turns his attention to the man.

"We good here?"

The man stares him down, flitting his eyes to me before drifting back to Jameson. "You better lock this shit down," he mutters. "The way she came storming in here ..." He shakes his head. "She was lucky."

Jameson steps forward, his body moving in front of mine. "That a threat?"

"Just letting you know she might not be as lucky next time."

"Go wait in the car," Jameson forces out.

"No," I say, reaching for him. "Come on; let's just go." When he doesn't move, I tighten my hold on his hand. "Please."

My plea seems to snap him out of his rage, because he jerks his chin into a nod and begins to turn.

The man barks out a laugh. "Damn, never thought I'd see the day."

Jameson stills, looking over his shoulder. "What was that?"

"Bitch has got you leashed, doesn't she?" Assessing me, he drawls, "But with a body like—"

"Don't finish that fucking sentence," Jameson cuts in, dropping his eyes to the gun in the man's hand and pushing me behind him. "You wanna say that shit to me without hiding behind a gun, huh?"

"He took yours, too," I whisper shakily. "He has your gun."

"You think I'm scared of you?" the man scoffs. "You're just some punk kid who thinks he's tough 'cause of who your old man was. Everyone walks on fucking eggshells around you. I'm fucking sick of it. You haven't earned shit."

Jameson lets out a low laugh, the sound menacing. "Oh, I haven't earned shit? And you have?" He motions to the outstretched gun. "You gonna drop that or keep hiding behind it?"

The man lets go of the gun, his face smug. "Happy?"

"Kick it away."

He does.

"And my gun you took off her."

The man grabs Jameson's gun from the back of his jeans, discarding it. "There," he says. "Even."

"You know," Jameson mutters, moving toward the man. "I never liked you. Well"—he cocks his head—"actually, you never really crossed my mind when you were in my old man's crew. I barely knew your name." He takes another step forward. "But you knew mine, didn't you?"

The man charges for Jameson, who shifts his attention to me for just long enough to ensure I've moved out of the way. Then he sidesteps a punch the man throws, laughing as the man swings his fist again through the air. Each attempt to land a hit on Jameson is futile, and it's only making the man angrier.

Not once has Jameson returned the effort, and I realize that rather than giving a fight, he's planning on delivering utter humiliation.

The man's breathing is becoming heavy, and I see the satisfaction light in Jameson's eyes. He lets out a condescending laugh.

"Shut your fucking mouth," the man bellows, "and fight me!" He throws another punch that Jameson dodges, bouncing on his feet. "Come on."

"Why would I?" Jameson asks.

"What?"

"Fight you," he clarifies. "Why would I fight you? It'd be a waste of my fucking time."

The man's movements slow, confusion etched into his face. "But we—"

Jameson throws out a hand. "I've already proved my point." He looks back at the man like he's bored.

"What do you—"

"You think I haven't earned shit." Jameson steps forward. "You can't get a hit in, and I haven't even swung at you once." He tips his chin toward the door. "You're supposed to be the muscle, and that's what you've got? It's fucking pathetic."

The man shrinks back, staring at Jameson.

"And what's worse," he continues, "is that you're stupid. That you clearly don't know when to shut your fucking mouth. Isn't that right?"

Again, the man stares back at him, silent.

"Adrian," he prompts, stepping forward, and the man's eyes flash at Jameson addressing him by name. "Isn't that right?"

Slowly, Adrian nods.

"I could have let it go," Jameson says, "but then you went and called my girl a bitch." He tsks. "Like I said, stupid."

Before Adrian can register what's happening, Jameson throws out his fist, connecting with his jaw. The man staggers back, spitting out blood.

Jameson grabs his gun, tucks it into the back of his jeans, then picks up a duffle bag he must have dropped when he came out here and walks back over to Adrian. "We still have a problem?"

"No." Adrian shakes his head, his eyes wide. "No problem."

"That all you gotta say?" Jameson asks, flicking his gaze over to me.

"Sorry," Adrian says in a rush. "I shouldn't have said that."

I dip my head.

Jameson pats Adrian's chest in a way that's completely fucking degrading. "Good," he mutters then nods toward the other gun. "Now get your shit and go back inside before I change my mind about leaving."

Adrian scrambles over to the gun, grabbing it before pushing back through the door. It swings shut behind him, closing with a loud *click*.

Jameson watches the space for a minute then turns to me. "Let's go."

There's anger still radiating off of him as I wearily follow him to the car.

Just after I drop into my seat, the engine roars to life and we speed out of the parking lot.

"Jamie."

His hands flex against the wheel.

"Talk to me."

He glances over at me before bringing his eyes back to the road. "I told you to wait in the car."

"Really?" I respond. "*That's* what you've got to say?"

"Things could have gone—"

"There was a gunshot, Jameson." I cross my arms over my chest. "I heard a fucking *gunshot*. What did you want me to do, huh?"

"I *wanted* you to wait in the car. Like I told you to. Like you said you would. Where you were fucking safe. That's what I wanted you to do."

"You think I was gonna just sit back and hope you were fine? When I heard …" My voice breaks, and he tenses. "I thought you might have been shot. That you could have been …"

"I'm fine," he says, his tone softer. "I was fine."

"Yeah, well, I didn't know that. All I was thinking was—"

"I'm sorry," he breathes. "I shouldn't have gotten upset with you. I know you were scared. It's just that you can't put yourself in those situations."

I throw out a hand. "*You* can't put yourself in those situations."

"It's different," he says. "You know it's different."

"What even happened?" I ask. "Why was a gun going off?"

"It had nothing to do with me. Like I said, I was fine."

"Maybe this time"—I fidget with my hands, twisting the ring Johnny gave me—"but what about next time? You just pissed off the guy who points a gun at your head every time you go to work."

"He's not gonna try anything."

"How do you know that? How do you know anything? You can't play Russian roulette with your fucking life, Jameson."

"Oh, like you're one talk," he shoots back defensively.

"What's that supposed to mean?"

"The drinking. The partying. Hell, even your fucking chain smoking. Don't start lecturing me about making safe choices when you get black-out drunk at random parties."

"Come on? Really? That's not the same thing, and you know it."

"How many times have I picked you up because you were too out of it to get home, hmm? How many parties have we been to where you barely knew where you were by the end of the night? You think that shit isn't dangerous? That it doesn't scare me when I see you that way? Hurt me to watch you do that to yourself?"

I curl in on myself, not knowing what to say, because it's true. Everything he's saying is true, and I hate myself for it.

"I—"

"But I get it," he says. "I get why you do it, and I'm there for you when you need me. I don't judge who you are."

My shoulders drop as his words hit me.

"I don't judge who you are either." I say, the fight gone from my voice.

"Yes, you do," he whispers. "Do you know how much it already kills me that this is what I do? That each day I do it, I feel like I'm slipping closer to becoming my father?" He lets out a breath. "Like tonight, how I acted, that's the exact kind of shit my old man would have done."

"I wasn't judging you tonight," I say gently. "I was *scared* for you. There's a big difference."

He pulls onto his street. "Yeah, well, I was scared for you, too." Cutting the engine, he turns to face me. "When I saw that fucker with his hands on you, a gun pulled ... I ..." He blinks his eyes closed. "You were in that situation because of me. You had a gun pointed at you *because of me*."

"Jamie." I lean forward, and he opens his eyes at the softness of my voice. "Don't do this to yourself."

"Why shouldn't I?" he answers. "I brought you there. You were scared because of me. And now I'm what ...?" He shakes his head. "I'm fucking yelling at you for it? Taking it out on you?"

"You're upset," I tell him.

He laughs, and it sounds so broken that I reach for him.

"Yeah, I'm upset. Look at my fucking life. Look at what I'm doing to you."

"You're not doing anything to me," I say quietly.

"Don't lie to me, baby. I know what it does to you ... how scared you get that one day I won't come home." He runs a hand through his hair. "I shouldn't have put that back on you."

"No," I tell him. "Everything you said ..." I clear my throat. "Everything about my drinking, it's true. And I know what seeing me like that does to you."

"But we both still do it."

I nod.

"And neither of us are gonna stop."

"Probably not."

"So what then?" he asks. "We just keep on hurting each other?"

"It only hurts because of how much I love you," I answer. "I'm only scared of losing you because if you were gone, you'd take me with you."

He nods like he understands, like that's exactly how he feels. "But that doesn't make it any better."

"Yeah," I say. "But you hurt me less than you love me," I tell him. "And when you hurt me, you never mean to. Do you?"

He shakes his head. "Never."

"And I never mean to hurt you." I pause, biting my lip. "So, yeah, I think we'll keep hurting each other, even though neither of us mean to." I look back at him. "But we'll keep loving each other more."

He stares over at me, his expression strained, his eyes vulnerable.

"We'll keep loving each other more than the fear," I murmur. "More than the thoughts that tell us we aren't worth it. That we don't deserve it. More than all of it."

"More than all of it," he repeats under his breath, the words sounding like hope. Like a chance.

"Do you think you can do that?" I ask. "That we can do that?"

He dips his chin with no hesitation. "Yeah, baby, I can do that." His eyes find mine. "You?"

Nodding, I whisper, "Yeah."

"All right," he says, leaning in until his lips are just inches from mine. He watches me carefully, reverently. "Then I'll always love you more."

"Always more," I echo before his lips brush over mine.

Chapter 42

Jameson

I keep Sam's hand firmly gripped in mine as we walk up the driveway, needing to remind myself that she's okay. That *we're okay*.

"Let me just drop this off before we head in," I tell her, holding up the duffle bag that's clutched in my other hand.

I push through the side door that leads into the garage and move for the safe. After typing in the code, I spin the handle, and my heart fucking drops at what stares back at me. Or more like what *doesn't*.

"No." I shake my head. "No, no, no."

"What?" Sam asks.

"It's gone." I step back. "It's fucking gone."

"What's gone?"

"I'm so—" I pull away from her and slam the door to the safe shut. "Fuck!"

"Jamie, what's going on?"

"I should have known." The door to the safe swings back open, and I kick it closed. My foot coming down on it over and over again. "Goddammit, I should have fucking known." I pull at my hair. "She took it. She took the money."

Understanding flashes across Sam's face. "Shit," she mutters.

"I was out when the landlord came to collect rent. She told me she'd take care of it, so I gave her the code ... I thought she was doing better ..."

I pace in front of the safe, the door drifting back open as if to mock me. "How could I be so fucking stupid?"

"She was doing better," Sam says, trying to reassure me. "She got that job. You couldn't have known she was gonna ..."

Her words begin to fade away as I move around her, heading for the door.

She chases after me, calling out my name.

I throw the door open, my boots echoing through the hall. "Ma!" I shout.

Her bedroom door is open, the room empty, so I keep moving, but my steps falter when I hear a deep voice coming from the kitchen.

I round the corner, my gaze falling on my mother and a man sitting across from her at the table.

"Who the fuck are you?" I yell before looking at my mother and pointing at the man. "Who the fuck is this?"

"Jameson," she says, her voice all wrong.

I can feel Sam at my back, and it calms me but just a fraction.

I snap my fingers in front of his face. "An answer. Now."

"Whoa, kid. Calm down." He laughs nervously.

"Who is he?"

"This is Calvin. I met him at work."

She looks up at me, and it's then that it clicks. Her pupils are blown wide, her eyes glassy.

I shake my head. "At work, huh?"

She fidgets in her seat, giving herself away.

I turn to Calvin. "Get out of my house."

"Jameson," my mother scolds. "You can't—"

I hold up a hand. "I'll deal with you in a minute."

"I'm not asking you again," I say to Calvin, my voice dangerously low. "I'm in a shit mood, and it's only getting worse, so do yourself a favor and get out."

He sizes me up. I must look as unhinged as I feel because he pushes his chair back. "Yeah, all right." He turns to my mother. "Another time, Aubrey."

She starts to stand. "I'll walk you—"

"Sit down," I grit out.

"You can't talk to me like that!" she shrieks. "I'm sick of you acting like …"

I block out her rant, following Calvin to the door and out onto the porch.

The minute it shuts behind us, I have him pressed up against the side of the house. "She get that shit from you?"

"You better step back," he grunts.

I fist his ratty T-shirt. "That's not an answer."

"Yeah," he chokes out.

"She pay?" I ask, easing up a bit.

He nods.

"You don't sell to her again, understand?"

"Look, kid, I'm sorry you mom's a junkie and all—"

I slam him back against the wall. "She's not a fucking junkie."

"Sure she isn't."

"Who do you work for?" I spit.

"What?"

"You in a crew?"

He stares back at me, a look of genuine confusion on his face. "What are you …? No." He shakes his head. "No, I just sell a bit on the side. Met your mother, we hit it off—"

"You're done with her," I cut in. "Got it?"

"Kid—"

"Stop calling me that," I growl. "You have no fucking clue who I am. What I'm capable of doing if I find out you're selling to her again."

"That's not what it was like. I …" He shifts. "I like her."

"No."

"No?"

"No," I repeat. "This is the last fucking thing she needs right now—believe me. She does not need another man like you in her life."

"Like me?" He lifts his chin. "Why don't you look in the mirror? Glass houses and all that shit."

"Get off my porch." I snarl, stepping back and shoving him toward the steps. "Don't let me catch you around her again."

He mutters something under his breath, and I'm fired up enough to go after him, but the screen door pushes open and Sam sticks her head out. "Everything good?"

I watch the guy reach his car parked across the street before turning back to her. "Fine."

"She's uh ..." Sam hovers in the doorway. "She's ..."

I blow out a breath. "I'm coming."

I move past Sam, heading back to the kitchen, trying to calm myself for what I'm about to be met with.

"What'd you do to him?" my mother demands.

I ignore her question, asking my own. "Where is it?"

"Where's what?"

I scoff. "Don't play dumb."

She stares back at me, her arms crossed over her chest, a defiant look on her face.

"The money!" I yell. "Where's the fucking money, Ma?"

"Gone," she says.

"No," I tell her. "I gave you the code yesterday. There's no way you …" I notice the robe she's wearing, realizing I've never seen it before. "Where'd you get that?"

She shrugs.

"There should've been over a grand in that safe. You spent a fucking grand in one day?"

I can't believe she did this, or maybe I can and that's what's worse.

Thank God I have another safe in my closet or we'd really be fucked.

Sam comes to my side. I barely register her touch when she sets a hand on my arm.

I break free of her hold, storming down the hall and into my mother's room. I throw open the closet door, finding shopping bags piled on the floor. "It's all going back."

I gather up the bags, toss them out into the hall, then move for her nightstand. I rip open the drawer, shifting through the contents.

My mother tears through the room, moving toward me frantically. "You can't just go through my things like this. I deserve privacy. I deserve—"

"You lost that right when you spent our money on a shopping spree and your next fucking high."

"Oh, stop being so dramatic."

"*Dramatic*?" I yell, my hand stilling.

"I make my own money. I should be able to buy—"

I turn, cutting her off, "You work part-time, Ma. The money you bring in barely covers the electric bill and groceries." I wave a hand around the room. "How do you think we pay for all of this?"

"Believe me," she says, "I know exactly how we pay for it. You never let me forget."

I shift back to the drawer and continue rummaging through it.

She closes the space between us, her words coming out too fast. "I never get anything. I have nothing for myself. No space. You can't just come in here and …"

I shake my head when I finally find the little bag of white powder I knew would be here. Grabbing it, I push the drawer shut.

"Give me that!" she screams.

"No."

She snatches my hand, trying to pry it open.

"Jesus, Ma. Stop!"

I pull my hand back, and she stumbles forward. I reach out to steady her, but she moves away from me.

"I hate you!" she throws at me. "I fucking hate you!"

I freeze, and Sam moves from her place in the doorway, stepping into the room.

She's high, I tell myself. *She's only saying this 'cause she's high. She doesn't actually hate you. She doesn't ...*

"Did you hear me?" she sneers.

"Yeah, Ma," I mutter, my voice hollow. "I heard you. You hate me."

"Give me back my things," she says, pacing. "I need my things."

"No."

She grabs the ashtray from the nightstand and hurls it across the room. "You can't just take my things!"

"You need to calm down," I tell her, moving for the door.

"Where are you going?"

I motion for Sam to step out into the hall.

"Jameson! Where are you—"

She rushes for the door, but I close it behind me before she can reach it, holding it closed as she yanks at the doorknob.

"Open this fucking door," she pleads.

Sam grabs my other hand as I listen to my mother rant and bang on the door, saying things I try to ignore.

"... I'm a prisoner in this house ..."

"... I have nothing ..."

"... you're nothing ..."

"... you're useless, Jameson ..."

"Block it out," Sam whispers beside me. "She doesn't mean it. Just block it out."

I try.

I really fucking try.

But as much as I attempt to rationalize it, tell myself that she isn't thinking straight right now, each insult, each accusation, hits like a blow to my gut. Another stab to my already shattered heart.

Sam brings her hand to my face, forcing me to look at her. "Focus on me," she murmurs. "Tune it out."

Something breaks on the other side of the door.

"... this is what you wanted ..."

"... I hope you're happy ..."

"... just open the fucking door ..."

Briefly, Sam's eyes flick to the doorknob at my whitening grip on the handle. "Let me take over," she says. "You should go somewhere else. You don't need to hear—"

"I'm fine," I tell her. "It's nothing I haven't ..." I clear my throat. "It's nothing I haven't heard before."

Anger flashes across her face, but instead of arguing with me, she just nods.

I'm not sure how long passes before my mother finally quiets down, her ranting turning into a low sob.

I blink my eyes closed and suck in a breath before I turn, pushing open the door.

My mother looks over at me from her spot curled up against the wall. Her eyes are filled with tears, her knees pulled into her chest. "Jameson," she cries, her voice cracking. "Jameson, I'm …"

Slowly, I step into the room, taking in the mess she's made of the space.

"I'm so sorry," she chokes out. "I'm horrible. I'm …"

"It's okay," I mutter, not sure if even I believe my words. "You just need to sleep it off."

She looks up at me, eyes wide. "I didn't mean—"

"I know," I cut her off. "You never do."

She flinches, pulling her knees in even tighter.

"Do you need help getting into bed?"

Her eyes drift past me as Sam walks into the room, a dustpan in hand. Shame colors my mother's face as she watches her begin to sweep up a shattered picture frame.

A silent tear falls down her face, and she bats it away as if she wasn't just hysterical a few minutes ago. "No," she says, answering my question. "No, I'm fine."

I nod, stepping back, giving her room to stand.

My eyes meet Sam's, and she tilts her head toward the door. I nod back before she walks out, giving us space.

My mother stands and shuffles over to the bed. She lets out a muttered curse, the springs creaking below her as she climbs in.

Moving around the room, I begin to put the space back together, if only just a little bit, as if erasing the evidence of what just happened will mean it never did.

Turning with a pile of clothes in my hands, I still when I find her passed out on top of the covers. Setting the clothes down, I move toward her slowly.

Her hair is fanned out in a tangled mess, her arms crossed awkwardly. I grab the throw blanket from the end of the bed, cover her, then click off the lamp on the nightstand.

Moving into the hall, I eye the shopping bags scattered on the floor, clothes spilling out of them. Tucking the items back inside, I gather the bags, bringing them into the kitchen.

Sam turns when she hears me come in, shutting off the sink and placing a clean bowl on the counter to dry. Her gaze drops to the bags before she drags it back up to meet mine. "She out?"

I nod.

She watches me wearily, trying to gauge what state I'm in.

"I talked to Cathleen," she says as I drop into a chair at the kitchen table. "She's not working tonight, so if you want me to stay—"

"Yes," I say, looking up at her. "Please."

She comes up behind me, draping her arms over my shoulders and down to my chest. "What do you need right now?"

"You," I answer immediately. "Just you."

Pulling back, she walks around the chair and drops into my lap. "I'm here. Whatever you need." Her eyes flick up to meet mine. "Always."

Chapter 43

Sam

I watch the leaves fall, the trees becoming shades of orange and brown. The parking lot is nearly empty now as I sit on the curb outside of school and wait for Jameson to pick me up.

The first few weeks of school have dragged by now that I'm all on my own. It was bad enough without Jameson, but now I'm missing Billy, too. Even all of my friends were their friends, and with everyone already graduated, it's back to the way things were before.

But I won't drop out.

I won't give up.

Not after I promised Johnny.

The rumble of an engine pulls my attention, and I stand as Jameson slows in front of me. I slide into the passenger seat, dropping my bag. Before I can even turn to him, his hand is on the back of my neck, guiding my face to his.

"Sorry I'm late," he says before crashing his lips against mine.

It takes me a second to catch up, but once I do, I grip his shirt, fisting the fabric and deepening the kiss.

His hold on me tightens, the possessiveness of his touch fueling me. I pull his bottom lip between my teeth, biting it lightly, a low hum spilling from my lips as he groans. When I lean back, he drops his hand, his eyes roaming over me.

"I have a surprise for you," he says, a slight nervousness in his voice.

"You do?" I ask excitedly. "Can I have it now?"

He shakes his head. "Not here."

"What is it?"

We pull away from the curb, and he looks over at me. "Wouldn't be much of a surprise if I told you, now would it?"

"Am I gonna like it?"

He laughs. "I really fucking hope so. It's not exactly something I can return."

"What does that—"

"Baby."

"Yeah?"

He lowers his hand down on my thigh. "It's a surprise, remember?" He squeezes once. "So stop asking questions."

I let out a huff. "Fine."

"How was your day? How'd that physics test go?"

"My day was okay," I tell him, fidgeting with my ring. "And the test was pretty good. Only one question I wasn't sure about."

"I'm bet you aced it," he says.

"How about you?"

He turns onto his street. "Things were slow today. Pretty easy."

"Good," I respond. "You need a break." Pulling into his driveway, I look up at the house. "And here?"

He clears his throat, running a hand through his hair. "She's at work now, but she was fine this morning."

"Was she—"

"I really don't want to talk about it," he says softly. "I just wanna be with you."

I glance over at him, seeing that the burdens he carries are so obvious in the way he holds himself. It's been a few weeks since the whole money incident, and he's been even more on edge.

"I wish I could make it easier," I whisper.

"You do," he says. "Sometimes, I just can't ..."

"I get it," I tell him. "Trust me; I really do."

"Let's go in," he says, forcing lightness into his voice. "Don't you want your surprise?"

I nod eagerly, pushing my door open and following him inside.

He leads me to his bedroom where I look around for anything that's different.

"Sit," he tells me, motioning to the bed.

I drop down, and he stands over me, running a hand through his hair.

"You look nervous," I murmur.

He stares back at me as if he might say something, but then he just strips off his shirt.

Confused, I let my eyes rake over him, pulling my head back when I see plastic wrap taped to his chest. "You get a new tattoo?"

He nods.

I inch forward, realizing it's a word, but I can't make out what it says.

He keeps his eyes on me as he slowly peels off the wrap.

I suck in a breath. "Jamie ... that's ..." I look up at him. "Jamie, that's my name."

"Yeah, baby," he murmurs. "I know."

He steps forward, and I move up to my knees, bringing me eye level with my name written in script over his heart. It's right above the *Loyalty* piece that spans his chest.

"Do you like it?" he asks, his voice achingly vulnerable.

I trace my fingers up his bare chest, circling the tattoo, careful not to touch it. "I love it," I whisper.

His shoulders drop, stepping into me even closer, and I gasp when he pushes me back onto the bed. I watch as he slowly climbs over me, moving until his hips are straddling mine, his arms caging me in.

"I can't believe you ..." Reaching out for him, I study the tattoo. "This is permanent."

He snorts.

I smack his chest playfully. "I'm serious. Jamie, this is ..."

"It's what?" he asks, leaning in so close that I can feel his breath tickle my skin.

"Forever."

"Yeah," he says. "Well, so are we."

"Then I want one, too."

He pulls back. "You want my name on you?"

Biting my lip, I nod, watching his eyes heat.

"I think I'd lose it if I saw that," he mutters. "Saw my name marked on your skin."

"I better get it done soon then," I rasp, my gaze locked on his. "I love when you lose it."

"Keep talking that way," he says against me. "And I'll show you right now."

I drag my hands up his chest, my eyes fixed on my name scrawled over his heart. "I still can't believe you got my name tattooed on you." I feel his fingers flex on my hips. I shake my head and laugh. "You're fucking crazy."

"For you," he nods. "Yeah."

Chapter 44

Sam

I twist my key into the front door as Jameson watches from his car in the driveway. Shutting it behind me, I hear the rumble of his engine when he pulls away.

We reluctantly dragged ourselves from bed, having to get back to reality. He has to go meet Marcus, and I have to take over watching Jace while Cathleen goes to work.

Deep laughter fills the space, and I tense when I step into the living room, the sound quieting as Carson and his friends' attention shifts to me.

"Oh, good," Carson says loudly, pitching his voice over the noise of the TV. "You're here."

"Where's Cath—"

"Can you make us something to eat? I'm fucking starving."

I drop my purse. "I just walked through the door."

"Yeah, man," the stocky brunette to his left cuts in. I think his name's Brian. "She just got home. Needs to relax a minute." He pats the open seat next to him on the couch.

"Knock that shit off," Carson says, glaring at him.

"Just bein' nice."

Carson scoffs. "No, you aren't." Shifting his focus back to me, he asks, "So, food?"

The stairs creak, and I turn as Cathleen walks down them, her work bag and Jace balanced in her arms.

She's all done up, her hair big and teased, a full face of makeup. But her body's completely hidden, swallowed up in an oversized pair of sweatpants and a baggy T-shirt.

A whistle sounds from the living room, and I realize it's coming from Miles.

I fucking hate that kid, which is why it was so satisfying when Jameson put him in his place that day at school.

"Lookin' good, Cath."

She ignores him, handing me Jace.

He leans forward. "Gonna have to swing by Sugar's sometime to see what's—"

"Jesus, dude, shut up," Carson growls. "You know what? Let's get out of here."

"What about the food?" Brian whines.

"We'll swing by a drive-thru."

They all push up from the couch, arguing about where they're gonna go eat.

Relieved they're leaving, I move through the room, taking Jace into the kitchen and setting him up in his high chair, hiding out until I hear the front door slam shut.

"You all right?" Cathleen asks, going over to Jace and dropping a kiss on the top of his head when he calls out to her.

"Fine," I answer.

"You've just gotta ignore them," she says. "They're idiots."

"Sometimes, I don't wanna just ignore them."

She snorts. "Yeah, I know. I was the one who got the calls home from school, remember?"

"They all deserved it."

"Not saying they didn't."

"Then what are you saying?"

"You've gotta be smart, that's all."

I turn to her. "And what's that supposed to mean?"

She sighs. "Fuck, I don't know. Maybe I'm just used to it."

"Yeah, well, that doesn't make it any better. Any less shitty."

Looking over at me, she blows out a breath.

"Probably actually makes it worse," I add.

"I just worry about you."

"I can take care of myself."

She fidgets. "I know."

"Then what?"

She shakes her head. "I don't know. Maybe it's just being your older sister. Can't help but worry. It's like it's my job or something."

"I don't think it's that," I tell her. "'Cause I worry about you, too. Worried about …" I don't say his name, but she knows who I'm talking about. "It's nice," I say, clearing my throat. "It's nice that you worry, Cath."

She drops her eyes and swallows hard. I know it fucks her up that she couldn't protect him.

"I've gotta get to work," she mutters, stepping forward.

I nod before she pulls me into a hug.

"Love you," she whispers.

"Love you, too," I whisper back.

LOYALTY

A few hours later, I've just gotten Jace down to sleep when the house phone rings, its shrill sound reverberating through the quiet house.

I slip down the stairs as my father stands from his place on the couch to answer it.

"Hello," he mumbles.

I look from him to the coffee table, noting the scattered beer bottles. He got home from work just after Cathleen left, so he hasn't been at it too long.

"You what?" he questions in a voice I rarely hear him use, but the few times he has …

I inch up the stairs, hiding myself from view.

"Do you have any idea what this means?" he shouts. "You've really fucking done it now, you know that?"

Who's he talking to?

"Everything we've worked for, pissed away. Gone! You think they're gonna let you keep your scholarship now, huh? Let you play? You were already on thin fucking ice."

Carson, I realize. He must be talking to Carson.

"Driving drunk and hopped up on that shit." He shakes his head. "And to get caught, too. How stupid can you be?"

I freeze. That's not good. That's really fucking not good.

"Oh, you think I'm gonna bail you out?" He laughs. "You good for nothing little shit. You got yourself into this mess, now you fucking clean it up."

I jump as he slams the phone back onto the receiver. Then I watch as he pulls it back and slams it down again and again until it's falling apart.

"Goddammit!" he bellows. "Fuck!"

He paces the living room, moving in front of the coffee table and flipping it. Beer bottles shatter and wood cracks as he kicks the table. Then, taking a broken leg, he goes for the TV.

I hear Jace begin to cry and inch up the stairs, trying to go unnoticed. Once I reach the top, I quickly move down the hall, slipping into my room. I lock the door and slide our dresser in front of it before going to Jace.

After managing to soothe him back to sleep, I text Cathleen, letting her know what happened.

Finally, it all hits me.

Carson going pro was the only thing he and my father had. The only thing that seemed to keep them from fully slipping into the worst versions of themselves.

His injury was one thing, but there was still hope.

Now …

The familiar creep of anxiety begins to consume me.

Now, they've got nothing.

They've both been worse these last few months. It's not just the substances they drown themselves in 'cause, let's face it, it's not like I'm one to judge. They've been meaner, demanding more, inching closer to a line neither of them have fully crossed before.

What happened tonight, coupled with the fact that Johnny's not here anymore, it's getting harder for me to deny that

I'm not scared to live in this house. I mean, I've got a dresser pushed in front of my door right now, for fuck's sake.

I know I could tell Jameson. Tell him about the few times I've been shoved a little too hard out of the way or had my arm grabbed a bit too tightly to get my attention. But I'm stuck here and afraid that if I tell Jameson, he'll only make it worse.

I've already lied to him once about a small bruise on my shoulder that I got when Carson shoved me into a wall. There's no way I'd be able to hold Jameson back if he knew Carson hurt me. He'd go ballistic, and I just ... can't have that happen.

I don't want Jameson constantly worrying.

I don't want things to get even more tense at home.

I don't want my father keeping me locked up here if he thinks I'm bringing trouble.

I don't want any of it.

And it's not like I can't handle myself. I've been doing it all my life.

But ... I always had Johnny.

And now ...

I begin to pace, thinking for the hundredth time about leaving, all the possible scenarios playing out in my head. And just like always, I come to one conclusion ...

I'm fucked.

First of all, I'm broke. Almost every dollar I make gets spent on taking care of this house.

I know Jameson would let me move in with him, but I'm too scared of how my father would react, especially now. With everything that's already going on ... I just can't.

There are no real options. No realistic way I'm leaving this house.

My steps falter. I need to get out of this room. To do something other than sit with my fucked-up thoughts.

Peering out the window, I let go of a breath when I see my father's car is gone.

Quietly, I drag the dresser back and slip out of the room. I tiptoe down the stairs, even though nobody but Jace is home, and pause when I see the destroyed living room.

I'm careful to avoid the broken glass on the floor as I move to get a broom. Then I spend the next hour cleaning, trying to pick up the pieces of my shattered life and put them back together again.

When I finish, I step back, taking in the space, and imagine what it would be like to live anywhere but here.

Chapter 45

Jameson

I pull my hood up as a gust of cold air hits my face, the crunch of fresh snow sounding under my boots. Sliding my sleeves down, I try to cover as much of my hands as I can, wishing I'd been able to find my gloves.

A light dusting of snow continues to fall as I shovel the driveway, making me think I'll only be back at it later tonight.

We've gotten off easy this year so far. It's only the first snowfall, and it's already past Thanksgiving.

My mother has been doing better since we had that big blow out a few months ago. I'm still on edge, though, still not letting myself get my hopes up that it'll stick, but it's been good.

She's kept her job, even picking up some more shifts, and although she's still hooked on the pills, I think she's been clean from everything else.

Either that or she's getting extremely good at hiding it.

Sam, on the other hand, hasn't been as great. She's trying to fake it, make it seem like she's all right, but I see right through it. I know her too well.

Ever since Carson's arrest, she's been on edge, more so than usual. She's quicker to anger, quicker to slip into that need for an escape.

I try to get her to talk to me, and she gives me pieces, but I know she's holding back.

From what she's told me about Carson and her old man, I can't imagine either of them are taking all this well. Carson's scholarship officially got pulled, meaning his chances at a pro career—at any career—are over. All the hope they had to get out of this life was tied to that reality. A reality that no longer exists.

I can see how that'd fuck you up. Of course I can. But based on how Sam's been acting, I'm only becoming more worried that they're taking it out on her. I've asked her about it enough times that we've gotten in a fight about it twice. She swears she's fine, but she's evasive when she answers, like she's trying to dodge the truth so she doesn't have to outright lie. She says she can handle herself, but that's what fucking worries me. People don't say that shit unless there's something going on that they need to handle.

If anyone knows that, it's me.

But there's really nothing I can do to help unless she lets me. Unless I find evidence that something is actually going on.

Maybe I'm only being paranoid. It's just … being around her … it feels like she's about to snap.

I'm pulled from my thoughts when I realize I've made it to the end of the driveway. Sweat is dripping down my back, and my hands have gone a bit numb.

Leaning forward, I rest my weight on the shovel, catching my breath.

I let my eyes drift from our house to the one next door before I start making my way over there. The driveway is covered in a thick layer of snow, my boots sinking so deep that my jeans are turning wet.

Finally, I make it to the porch, knocking before I step back to wait. A couple of minutes pass before the door creaks open and I'm greeted by a familiar face.

"Jameson," Mrs. Richardson beams, tipping her head back so her gaze can meet mine.

The Richardsons have been our neighbors for my whole life. But, for most of it, it's just been her. Mr. Richardson died years ago, and they never had any kids. So, I've always helped her out—fixed the things that needed fixing, mowed her lawn, things like that.

Mrs. Richardson is the kind of person who doesn't seem to belong in a neighborhood like this one. She must be nearly eighty now and is one of the only people I've ever met who seems to be all the way good. She's also one of the only people who doesn't seem to see me as *me*. She doesn't look at me like I'm no good, even though she's fully aware of where I come from. *Who* I come from.

"You look like you're freezing," she says, waving me inside.

I shake my head. "I'm fine. I was just coming to tell you I can shovel your driveway."

She purses her lips. "Absolutely not."

"But I—"

Stepping to the side and opening the door wider, she cuts me off. "Not until you come inside and get warmed up."

I dip my chin, knowing she won't take no for an answer.

"Good." She smiles, leading me into the kitchen.

I tower over her small frame as I follow her inside, my stomach growling when I smell the soup bubbling on the stove.

"Sit," she says, motioning to the table.

I do as she asks, sliding into the worn wooden chair, and watch as she moves around the kitchen. She's slower now than she was when I was younger, and her hands shake as she sets down a bowl of soup in front of me.

"Thank you," I tell her as she places a plate piled with fresh bread next to the bowl then brings over a butter dish.

My lips tip up as I remove the top, the handle made of a painted ceramic bee sitting on a hive.

Mrs. Richardson's kitchen is bright yellow and covered in bumble bee knick-knacks. It matches the rest of her house that's overflowing with the kind of decorations you'd find at a yard sale.

She lowers herself into the seat next to me and watches until I dip my bread in the soup and take a bite.

"So," she starts, "how've you been?"

I nod. "Good."

"Jameson," she prompts, not buying my easy answer.

I've never talked to her about my life before. Not really, anyway. Although, I'm sure she knows enough from living in this town and from the things she's heard over the years, being next door. She's never brought it up outright but has always made it clear that she's here for me if I should ever need her.

After my old man died, she showed up at my house with a plate of cookies, pulled me into a hug, and reminded me that she's always just a knock away.

I take another bite of my bread. "I'm good, really."

Her brows furrow, but she doesn't push me. "And your mother?"

"Better," I tell her.

"You know you can talk to me," she says, placing her hand on my arm, and I fight the urge to flinch. "You've had to take on quite a lot for a boy your age. There's no shame in needing a little help."

I attempt to brighten my face, to make my voice reassuring. "Thank you, Mrs. Richardson, really. But we're managing fine."

"Well," she says, "you remember what I always tell you?"

I nod. "Just a knock away."

"All right then." She leans back. "Tell me about this girl I've seen you around with. She your girlfriend?"

"Yeah," I answer, caught off guard by her question. "Her name is Sam."

"I thought so." Mrs. Richardson smiles. "What's she like?"

I think about it for a minute, not sure how to answer. "She's ..." I shake my head. "I don't know ... She's ... Well, she's really smart. Like, kind of brilliant actually. She reads all the time, too. And she's in all of these hard classes at school, knows all these random facts."

She nods, her face bright. "What else?"

I take a bite of my soup, thinking. "She's fucking fearless—"

"Language," Mrs. Richardson cuts in.

"Sorry," I mutter. "She's fearless, though. Which is sometimes a bad thing. Gets her into trouble." I snort. "But mostly, it's just ..." I fidget with the spoon in my hand. "She's really strong. Doesn't let anything stop her from what she wants. And she isn't scared of me. Never was. Calls me out on my shit—" I glance up. "Fuck, sorry." I shake my head, cringing. "Sorry."

"It's okay." She laughs. "What else?"

"I don't know." I shrug. "She just ..."

"She what?"

"She gets me. You know? We just click. It's easy ..." I pause. "Well, not easy. She can be ... Sometimes, she struggles. But I don't mind 'cause I know I can help her, make her feel better. And she gives it back. She's seen me at my worst, too, and she doesn't care. She doesn't leave or make me feel bad. She makes me feel better, good even."

"You love her," Mrs. Richardson says.

"How do you—"

"Your whole face lights up when you talk about her." She gives me a teasing look. "And I think this is the most I've ever heard you talk at once."

I stare back at her silently.

"I'm happy for you, Jameson." I watch her gaze drift over to a picture of her and Mr. Richardson. "Not everyone is as lucky as us." She turns back to me. "Did you know I met Frank when I was your age, younger even?"

I shake my head.

"He's the only man I've ever loved." She smiles. "Fifty-two years I spent with him, and it only got better."

"That's a long time."

"Didn't feel like it," she murmurs.

"I'm sorry you lost him."

"I miss him every day," she answers. "You know we both had a hard time growing up, too. Things weren't always easy."

I shift in my seat. "You never told me that."

She nods. "The way you talked about your girl, about being there for each other ..." She flits her eyes back over to the picture. "If you have that, you have everything. You understand what I mean?"

"Yeah," I tell her, thinking about all the shit me and Sam have already been through together. How each and every time we've helped each other get through it. "Yeah, I understand."

Chapter 46

Sam

The bell rings, and I push up from my desk, shoving my notebook into my bag.

It's the first day back since winter break, and it's actually been nice to be in school again. It feels like a vacation after the long shifts I pulled at the diner. If anything, at least I get some time off my feet.

I move along with the shuffle of other kids, making my way into the cafeteria. I didn't have time for breakfast this morning or time last night to pack a lunch, so I'm starving.

Taking a tray, I start down the line, grabbing anything that looks close to edible. I swear the shit they serve barely resembles food, but my lips tip up when I see a bowl of chocolate pudding. At least I know that'll be good.

Leaning forward I reach for it, just before another hand snatches it.

Turning, I look over at the girl who took it, glaring when I see her smirking at me.

"That's mine," I snap.

Slowly, she drags her gaze down to her tray, baiting me. "No, actually, I think it's mine."

"Juliette," the girl behind her whisper-hisses, nudging her with a shoulder. "What are you doing?"

Juliette shrugs, feigning innocence. "Nothing. Just getting my lunch."

"Yeah, well"—I reach for her tray—"that's my fucking pudding."

She scoffs. "What? You think you're just entitled to everything because of who you are?"

I raise a brow. What does she mean *because of who I am*?

"You know"—she leans into me, dropping her voice—"your loser brother used to steal from my dad's store."

"What?"

"He wasn't even that subtle about it."

"What Carson does has nothing to do—"

"No." She shakes her head. "I'm not talking about him. I'm talking about the dead one."

"Keep moving," the lunch lady hollers, but I don't listen. I barely even hear her.

"The fuck did you just say?"

"Johnny was his name, right?"

I go utterly still. "Don't say his fucking name."

"Juliette," her friend warns.

"Can't say I was surprised when I heard what happened, though. I mean, he was a thug; not like his life was going anywhere. We're all probably better off—"

All I see is red.

The next thing I know, I'm on top of her, smashing my tray into her face. The crunch her nose makes as it breaks gives me a sickening sense of satisfaction.

She's shoving at me to get off of her, blood dripping down her face. People around us are shouting, their voices a blur as her words play through my head.

The dead one.

Johnny was his name, right?

Life was going nowhere.

Probably better off.

My mind is spinning, the voices too loud, too many. I feel arms around my waist, pulling me back, and my body sags, my legs nearly giving out.

"Help her up," the person behind me shouts, and I watch as two boys help Juliette to her feet. "And somebody go get the nurse."

People start rushing around us, and I spot Mr. Garcia, the SRO, pushing through the cafeteria doors.

Fuck.

He stops in front of us, his gaze moving past me. "I've got it from here."

"Are you going to stay calm if I let you go?" the person behind me questions.

I nod.

He shifts, and I suddenly find my history teacher, Mr. Martin, standing in front of me, a look of disappointment on his face. I don't know why it bothers me so much, but it does. He's one of the only teachers in this school I actually like.

I look from him to Juliette. She's covering her face with her hands, her friends fussing around her.

Mr. Garcia moves in front of me just as the nurse flies into the room, going right for Juliette.

"Sam," he says, dragging my attention back to him. He stares down at me, a scowl on his face. "You gonna make this difficult?"

I shake my head, and he motions to the door. Grabbing my bag, I start moving, my body tense as he follows closely behind me.

Once we're out in the hall, the fog of what just happened begins to clear, and I realize fully what I've done.

My steps falter, and Garcia's voice sounds from behind me to keep moving.

The closer we get to the principal's office, the more I begin to panic, worried that I've finally pushed it too far this time.

"I've gotta pee," I blurt out, turning to face him.

Garcia's lips thin, like he doesn't believe me, but he nods toward the closest bathroom and mutters, "I'll be right outside. You've got two minutes."

Quickly, I push into the bathroom, grateful to find it empty. I move over to the sink and fish through my bag, grabbing my phone and dialing Jameson's number.

"Come on, come on. Pick up," I breathe as it continues to ring. When I get his voicemail, I slam my hand down on the sink. "Shit!"

I step back, pacing, when the phone begins to ring.

"Jamie," I say, my voice frantic.

"What happened?" he answers immediately. "You okay?"

"I fucked up, Jamie. I really fucked up this time. And I don't know what—"

"Slow down," he cuts in. "Just tell me what happened, all right? And we'll fix it."

I blow out a breath, trying to calm myself. "Yeah, all right."

When I still don't say anything, he pushes, "You're freaking me out, baby. You've gotta tell me what happened."

"I ..." I swallow. "I smashed this girl's face with my lunch tray, and I'm pretty sure I broke her nose."

"What'd she do?"

"Huh?"

"To make you smash her in the face?" he asks, his voice lethal.

"She took my pudding and—"

"Baby?"

"Yeah?"

"You broke a girl's nose 'cause she took your pudding?"

"What—no! Do you think I'm insane?"

"I mean, you're not exactly known to be chill about things."

"Jesus, Jamie, no, I didn't break a girl's nose for taking my pudding."

"Then what?"

"She was talking shit about Johnny."

"Who is this girl?" he growls.

"I don't know. Her name's Juliette. Said Johnny used to steal from her father's store. Told me he was a thug and that—"

"That what?"

I clear my throat. "That everyone was probably better off that he—"

"Oh, fuck no," Jameson mutters. "What'd she think was gonna happen to her, saying something like that?"

"It's not like I regret it."

"You shouldn't."

"I don't. It's just that it happened in the middle of the cafeteria. A teacher had to pull me off of her, and there was a lot of blood. Everybody saw, and I'm—"

A fist pounding on the door cuts me off.

"Time's up," Garcia shouts.

I walk over to the sink and turn on the water before yelling back, "Be right out."

"Who was that?" Jameson asks.

"Garcia. He was taking me to the office, but I told him I had to go to the bathroom. He's waiting outside."

"If her nose is broken …"

"I know," I tell him. "That's why I'm freaking out. What if they press charges? And you know they're gonna call my dad." My words are coming out a mile a minute. "He's gonna be so pissed. I don't even know—"

"It's all gonna be okay."

"You don't know that. What if—"

"Listen to me. Whatever happens, we'll deal with it. Okay?"

I don't answer.

"Baby?"

More pounding sounds from the door. "Sam!" Garcia calls out. "You have thirty seconds, or I'm coming in."

"I've really gotta go."

"Tell me you hear what I'm saying," Jameson presses.

"Yeah," I mutter. "I hear you."

I hang up, sliding the phone into my back pocket just before the bathroom door pushes open.

"I'm coming," I call out.

Garcia narrows his eyes at me when I slip past him, following behind me as I start toward the office.

I pull the door open, and he motions toward the chairs in the reception area. "Sit."

Scowling at him, I bite back my response, trying to play this smart.

He greets the secretary, Mrs. Jacobson, with a smile, and she nods back at him dismissively before going back to typing.

"So," I start to ask, pulling his attention back to me from where he's leaning against the wall, his arms crossed over his chest, "what am I looking at?"

"Well, it's not just going to be some slap on this wrist this time, if that's what you were hoping for."

I fidget in my seat.

"You brought yourself into a whole other league with that stunt you just pulled."

"Bitch deserved it," I mutter under my breath.

He leans forward. "What was that?"

"Nothing," I mumble.

Several minutes pass in silence before I motion to Principal Hansley's office. "So, what are we waiting for?"

"A report from the nurse."

I nod.

"And your father."

"My father?"

"He's on his way."

I knew he'd likely be called, but my hands still curl in on themselves until my nails dig into my palms.

"And if her nose is broken?"

"Depends."

I wait for him to explain, and when he doesn't, I take the bait.

"Depends on what?"

"If they press charges."

"You think they'd—"

"Yup," he answers before I can even finish.

His chin is tilted forward, a smug fucking look on his face, like the idea of me finally messing up this badly satisfies him.

Well, fuck him.

I rip my gaze away from his, turning so I'm facing forward.

"You'll be lucky if you're not expelled." He clicks his tongue. "It would be such a shame if you made it this far only—"

The door pushes open, and I snap my eyes up, locking with my father's as he storms into the room.

Garcia steps forward. "Mr. Barlowe—"

"What were you thinking?" my father seethes, moving until he's right in front of me.

"I—"

"No," he cuts in. "You weren't thinking, were you? You never do. I had to leave work for this, Samantha. Do you get that? The foreman was up my ass—"

"Mr. Barlowe ..." Garcia tries again, but it's like my father doesn't even hear him.

"Have I not got enough shit to deal with, huh? Now you've gotta go and do this. It's like you're just asking for it. Just asking for me—"

Garcia drops a hand down on my father's shoulder. "Let's just calm down and—"

"*Calm down*?" My father laughs. "Yeah, okay, buddy. You try having her as a daughter and then tell me to calm down. It's one thing after another with this one." He turns back, pointing at me. "And you've really done it this time, haven't you? What a set of kids I have, huh? All fuck-ups, the lot of you."

"Mr. Barlowe," someone else calls, and I see Principal Hansley standing in his open doorway. "If you could please step inside so we can discuss the situation at hand."

My father nods. "Yeah, all right," he mutters, starting toward the door. "Let's hear it then."

Principal Hansley's eyes meet mine. "We'll be just a few minutes. Mrs. Jacobson will be here watching you, so don't try anything."

"Oh, she won't," my father chimes in, looking over his shoulder at me. "Isn't that right?"

I duck my chin before the door shuts behind them.

I sag forward as I exhale a breath and reach for my phone, pulling it from my back pocket. I start texting Jameson, telling him what's happening when I hear Mrs. Jacobson say my name.

"No phones on school grounds," she states.

"I'm just—"

"Getting written up is the last thing you need right now, don't you think?"

I tilt my head, taking her in. Her blonde hair that's clearly dyed is pulled back into a tight bun, her pink cardigan buttoned up to the top. For a second, I think about asking her what it feels like to have a stick wedged that far up her ass. Instead, I swallow the remark, making a show of tucking the phone into my purse.

She gives me a satisfied smile, as if she's tamed some sort of beast.

I roll my eyes, shifting my attention to Principal Hansley's door, waiting for it to open. The minutes drag on and with each that passes, my anxiety only worsens. I would kill for a cigarette right now. Or a drink.

As time continues to drag by, I think about asking to go to the bathroom and slipping outside for a smoke. Just as

I'm about to ask, the door pushes open and Garcia steps out, crooking a finger for me to come join them.

I walk in behind him, my eyes finding my father's, and when I see the fury in them, I dart my gaze back to the door.

I don't want to be in this room.

"Please, take a seat," Principal Hansley says, waving his hand to the empty chair beside my father.

I hesitate, feeling Garcia move in behind me.

"Sit down, Samantha," my father barks.

Forcing myself to move forward, I drop into the chair.

"Let's get right to it," Principal Hansley starts. "Juliette's nose is broken, and her parents have decided to press charges."

I suck in a breath.

"What this means," he continues, "is that, in addition to the legal ramifications, you will be given a ten-day suspension, during which time the possibility of your expulsion will be discussed." He leans forward, steepling his hands on the desk. "Do you understand what I've just shared with you?"

"Yes," I answer, the word clipped.

He sits back. "Good. Now, I'd like to give you the opportunity to share your side of the story. To explain why you acted out this way."

I want to ask him why it even matters. It's not like it's helped any of the other times I've sat in this chair. I know he's already written me off, and each time I let my anger win, I'm only confirming who he already thinks I am.

"What'd this girl do?" my father asks, surprising me. "She say somethin' to you?"

"Johnny," I push out.

"Huh?"

"She talked shit about Johnny."

My father pulls his head back. "What'd she say?"

"I don't—"

"No," he cuts in, his voice edged with anger. "You tell them what this girl said to you."

I turn to Principal Hansley, looking him right in the eye. "She told me my brother was a thug. That she wasn't surprised when she found out he died. That she thought we were all *better off*."

I watch as his gaze drifts past me, briefly looking at Garcia, who's still standing behind me.

"You got nothing to say to that?" my father snaps.

"Something like that shouldn't have been said—"

"You fuckin' think?"

"I know that this is obviously a difficult subject, and I'm sorry for your loss," he adds, looking between us. "But that is not an acceptable reason to act the way your daughter did. In fact, there is no acceptable reason."

"I don't know," my father leans forward. "Seems like a pretty damn good reason to me."

My head unconsciously whips in his direction. Did he just *defend* me?

"Mr. Barlowe—"

"Are we done here?" he interrupts.

"Excuse me?"

"Are. We. Done. Here."

"Well, yes, I guess so," Principal Hansley sputters.

"Your suspension is effective immediately," he says, shifting to me. "And there will be a hearing about your possible expulsion within the next few days."

My father pushes his chair back. "Let's go," he says to me, standing.

I move to follow him out the door, but he turns back to Principal Hansley. "You ever lose someone you love?" he asks. "A child? A brother?"

His face pinches before he clears his throat. "My wife."

"Think about how you would have reacted if someone said that shit to you. Said that shit about your wife."

Before Principal Hansley can answer, my father guides me out the door.

"Thank you," I mutter, my eyes on the floor. "For saying all that."

He grunts a non-response as we step outside, heading for his car.

I slide into the passenger seat as my father takes his spot behind the wheel and starts up the car.

We drive in silence, and it's not until we pull in front of the house that he turns to me. "He was wrong. What you did"—he shakes his head—"after what that girl said, was perfectly fucking acceptable."

I stare back at him.

"There's gonna be consequences," he tells me.

"I know."

"But you'll deal with it."

I nod. "Yeah."

For Johnny, I'll deal with it.

Because nobody talks about my brother like that and walks away untouched.

Chapter 47

Jameson

I pull up to the park just outside of town and watch as Sam strips off a bright yellow vest before bounding over to the car, a smile breaking across her face when she sees me.

She got eighty hours of community service and a six-week course of anger management classes after the whole "lunch tray incident." Luckily, she wasn't expelled. Her grades and the fact that she's only months away from graduating must have made them lenient. Still, adding on the classes and this community service was the last thing she needed in her already hectic schedule.

Over the last few months, since it happened, I've tried to do all I can to support her—driving her around, bringing her take-out, anything I can to make it a bit easier.

I lean over, pushing open her door.

"God, I'm sweating like a whore in church," she groans, wrapping her hair up and lifting it off her neck.

A laugh springs from my lips as I grab the Coke I got her. "Extra ice," I say, holding it out.

Her head falls back. "I fucking love you."

"You're easy to please."

She grabs the cup, humming in satisfaction as she drinks it.

"What time does the show start again?" she asks as I pull onto the street. "I desperately need a shower."

"They're on at seven."

The band Billy used to play in is opening for a local group tonight down at Red's. It's all the same guys from high school, so we're going to show support.

I asked Billy if he was okay going, not sure if it would upset him to see what he had to leave behind, but he just waved me off in his usual fashion.

Sam leans back in her seat, lighting a cigarette. "I can't believe they're playing at a real venue."

"I know," I agree. "It's gonna be weird."

"I haven't heard them play in so long."

"Billy says they're really good. Like 'they could be famous kind of good.'"

Sam exhales, turning to me. "Could you imagine?"

I shake my head. "It'd be wild. Someone famous from around here?"

We turn onto my street.

"Cathleen still covering for you tonight?" I ask. "There's a party after."

"Yeah," Sam answers. "I'm good."

"How're things at home with—"

"Fine," she cuts in.

"Baby ..."

"Can we just not talk about heavy shit tonight?"

I kill the engine and face her.

"I was at the diner since six this morning," she continues. "And then at the park, picking up trash all afternoon. I don't want to spend my night thinking about my fucked-up home life. I just wanna forget, you know? Just for a little bit."

I nod, though I must look wary because she leans forward and grabs my hand.

"Not forget like that," she clarifies. "I just need a night to let go. To be with you and not think."

"I get it," I tell her, leaning in and brushing my lips over hers.

She deepens the kiss for only a second, like she can't help herself, before pushing me back. "I'm all sweaty," she breathes, turning to open her door.

I follow her into the house, and she slows when I stop in the kitchen.

"What're you doing?"

Opening the fridge, I pull out some cold cuts. "You never eat when you're busy."

She stares back at me.

I tip my chin toward the hall. "Go shower. I'll have this ready when you're done."

"You don't have to—"

"Baby"—I step forward, silencing her—"we talked about this."

She tips her head back as she looks up at me.

"What's my job?"

She bites her lip.

"Hmm?"

"To take care of me," she whispers.

"And why do I take care of you?"

"Because I'm yours."

"And?"

She smiles. "Because you love me."

"That's right," I tell her, stepping back. "Now, go."

LOYALTY

"You're late," Billy shouts over the noise of the crowd.

I look toward the empty stage. "Looks like we're fine."

"We were all hanging out backstage before, remember?"

"I thought that was after?"

"It was both."

"Shit, sorry," I mutter, glancing down at Sam. "Something came up."

Billy snorts. "Yeah, I'm sure it did."

Sam laughs from beside me.

I shake my head. "You guys are like a pair of twelve-year-old boys."

"Looks like a good crowd," Sam says, taking in the space. "We could barely find you."

Billy nods. "Yeah, the guys are freaking out."

"And you?" I ask.

"Told you, I'm fine." He runs his hand through his hair. "I'm happy for them."

"Yeah," I say, keeping myself from pushing. "This is legit."

"I just hope they—"

Billy's words are cut off when the lights dim and Rowan walks onto the stage, followed by the rest of the band. They go right into the first song. It has this real heavy rock sound, and it's good. Really fucking good.

I lean into Billy. "Who sings this?"

"They do."

"No, I mean, who's song is it?"

"It's theirs."

Well, damn.

The crowd is into it, moving to the beat, catching onto the chorus.

They go right into the next one, and it's just as good.

By the time their set is over, they've got the crowd eating out of the palm of their fucking hands.

Billy wasn't lying. Maybe they really are gonna make it out of here.

I turn to look at him, expecting to see, I don't know ... jealousy? But he's just watching them with a big smile on his face, yelling with the crowd as Rowan leans into the mic and says, "Thank you. We're Lights Out."

The lights raise as they all walk off stage, the crowd restlessly waiting for the main act.

"You wanna stay and watch or head back?" Billy asks.

"Up to you," I tell him.

"I wanna see the guys," he says. "That was fucking awesome!"

I grab Sam's hand and follow him backstage, the room larger than I expected. The guys are buzzing around the space, their energy contagious.

Rowan notices us first, moving away from the group scattered around him. "Did you hear them?"

"Fuck yeah I did!" Billy beams. "They loved it."

"What'd you guys think?" Rowan asks, turning to me and Sam.

"It was amazing." Sam smiles. "Really."

I nod. "Didn't know you were that good."

Someone calls his name, and he looks over his shoulder. "You guys staying?"

"Course," Billy answers.

Rowan slaps his back, leading him over to where the others are standing, Sam and I trailing behind them.

Loud music sounds from the stage as the main act goes on, and by the time they've wrapped, the hangout backstage has turned into a party.

Sam is balanced on my lap, a cigarette perched between her fingers, happily buzzed. Billy is off talking to some girl, a redhead who said she loves drummers. And I'm sitting back, watching it all unfold around me.

"Jameson," Dylan calls out, stopping in front of me.

I peer around Sam. "What's up?"

"You mind meeting someone?"

I press my lips against Sam's ear. "Let me go take care of this real quick, okay?"

She hums, sliding off of me, and I stand, trailing behind him.

"This is Graham," Dylan says, motioning to some preppy-looking kid who's waiting for us. "The one I told you about."

I size him up, taking in his collared shirt and fucking loafers. "The producer's kid?"

He nods. "Wanted an introduction."

"All right," I answer, and Dylan takes it as his cue to leave.

I nod toward the hallway, and Graham follows me into a quiet corner. "What're you looking for?" I ask.

"Just some weed."

"No pills or anything?"

He shakes his head.

"I don't have anything on me right now, but we can set something up."

"Yeah, man, that's cool," he answers. "No problem."

I give him a price, happy when he accepts it with no question since it's three times what I usually charge. I always up my price for the rich kids—none of them seem to know any better. Or maybe they just don't care.

When he stays rooted in front of me, I cross my arms over my chest. "There a reason you're still standing here?"

He takes a step back, a crease forming between his brows. "Uh, no," he mutters. "No, I'm good."

"I'll be in touch then," I tell him before going back to the party.

Sam's eyes lock with mine as I stride into the room, and she stands once I'm in front of her.

"I know that look," I murmur.

She steps up on her toes, her arms coming around my neck. "I'm ready to go home."

"Are you now?"

She nods, pressing against me, trailing her hand up my chest.

"Greedy," I whisper against her skin.

"For you," she says, "always."

And that does it.

I pull back, gazing down at her. "Let's get out of here then."

Chapter 48

Sam

The window above the kitchen sink is open, a soft breeze filtering into the room, and I hum to myself as I stir the pot of spaghetti on the stove. I'm distracted, lost in the moment, so I don't hear the movement coming from the other room.

"Where are they?"

I startle, nearly dropping the wooden spoon in my hand, when Carson barrels into the kitchen.

"What?"

He shakes his head. "Don't play with me."

I sigh, not wanting to deal his shit right now. "I don't know what you're talking about, Carson."

"My pills," he snaps. "Where're my fucking pills?"

"I don't—"

"They were on the coffee table earlier." He moves toward me. "I know you took 'em."

I step away from him, my back hitting the counter. "I didn't take them. Maybe you put them somewhere—"

"I know you've just been dying to get a taste. Don't think I haven't see you eyeing them."

"I don't know what you're talking about. I don't want your fucking Oxy. I don't even take pills."

"You think I'm a fucking idiot."

I inch back as he closes the distance between us.

"You think you're better than me?"

My breathing turns heavy as he cages me in, the hot stove dangerously close to my back. I subtly reach behind me, flicking off the burner.

He stares down at me, eyes wild, and I rack my brain, trying to figure out what to do. How to get him away from me.

"I'll help you look," I offer.

He grabs my arm, yanking me forward and pulling me into the living room. I wince as his grip on me turns painful. Shoving me forward, he waves out a hand. "Then look."

I stumble, catching myself against the wall.

"You're not gonna find shit," he says, pacing in front of me.

"Are you sure you left them down here?" I ask cautiously.

The worse his dependence has gotten, the more forgetful he's become. That on top of the mood swings, paranoia, and his worse-than-usual fucking personality, I have to play this safe.

I don't know why he's gotten it into his head that I took his pills, but with the way he's glaring at me, I know there's no reasoning with him right now.

I wasn't lying when I said I don't take pills. Other than those few times Jameson gave me Xanax after ... well, other than those few times ... I've never touched them. I've seen what getting hooked on them does to people. Not that my other vices aren't a problem—I know they are—but at least I've stayed away from anything hard. Plus, I couldn't do that to Jameson. Not after his mother.

I scan the room, quickly moving past our father passed out on the couch. He's a whole other issue that I don't even want to think about right now.

I move forward, sidestepping Carson, and start to sift through the cluttered coffee table, but all I find are an empty bottle of gin, an overflowing ashtray, dirty dishes, and baby toys.

No pills.

My father snores loudly behind me, his arm draped across his bare stomach, smelling of stale alcohol and sweat.

"What'd I tell you?" Carson says, his voice close. "Maybe we should check underneath, huh? Just to be fucking sure." He gives me a condescending look before stepping forward and flipping the table, making the contents tumble to the floor. Glass shatters, but he just steps around it.

I suck in a sharp breath, darting my eyes to our father, but he doesn't even stir.

Carson moves for the recliner and flips it. "Nope," he says, looking back over his shoulder at me. "What do you know? Not under here either."

He goes for the side table next, knocking it over. The lamp shatters, and I jump.

"Stop," I whisper. "You've made your point. I—"

"You gonna give 'em to me now." He turns to face me. "Or do you want me to keep looking?"

I back up, slowly inching toward the stairs. "I didn't take them. I don't know what to tell you." I grab onto the railing. "I don't know where they—"

He rounds the tipped recliner as I take the first step up the stairs. "Where do you think you're going?"

As fast as I can, I turn, flying up the stairs. I can hear him shuffling behind me, glass crunching underneath his shoes.

Only a few more steps, and I'll be—

He grabs a hold of my ankle, pulling my feet out from under me. I fall, throwing my hands out and clawing at the stairs, kicking my foot back behind me. Pain sears through my knee as it hits the hard wood.

"Get the fuck off me!" I kick out again and feel his hand slip away.

Without hesitation, I scramble up, running to my room.

"Sam," Cathleen calls, sticking her head out of the bathroom. "What's going on?"

Carson chases behind me, and I hear Jace start wailing.

"What the fuck are you—"

Cathleen's words are cut off as I slam my bedroom door closed behind me and lock it. Heavy fists immediately come down against it.

I scan my room frantically, my heart pounding.

"Open this fucking door!" Carson shouts. "I know you fucking took 'em!"

Panicked, I slide the dresser in front of the door, barricading it, and call Jameson.

"Hey," he answers. "You at work?"

I told him earlier that Cathleen could drive me, but Jace woke up from his nap sick. I planned to ask Jameson for a ride after I finished making dinner, but then all hell broke loose.

"N-no," I stutter. "Jamie … I need you …" My voice cracks as the door rattles, the knob twisting. "I need help. Carson, he's … I'm in my room, but he's at the door. I don't know if he's gonna—"

"Are you hurt?" he cuts in, his rage barely contained beneath the question.

I look down at my skinned knee. "I'm fine," I tell him. "But I've never seen him like this before … I …" I trail off as Carson screams through the door. "I don't know what he's gonna do."

"He's not gonna do anything, okay? I'll be there in five minutes. I'm not gonna let anything happen."

"Okay," I choke out.

"Who else is in the house?"

"My father's passed out downstairs."

"Cathleen and the baby?"

"Jace … he's … he's sick, so she was giving him a bath." I swallow. "I don't want him to go after them if he can't get to me. What if he—"

"He won't," Jameson jumps in. "Stay in your room. I'll be there soon."

I tense as something slams against the door.

"Sam?"

"Yeah," I push out.

I hear an engine roar to life as he says, "I'm gonna hang up now so I can get there quicker."

"Okay."

"It's all gonna be fine."

"Thank you," I manage before the line goes dead.

In rapid succession, three kicks land against the door. "Goddammit, Samantha, open this fucking door. I'm done playing games."

Jace's crying is a constant background to the threats Carson is spewing. My instincts are screaming at me to go to him, to open the door and let Carson in, if only to calm Jace down.

The fear that if I don't give in to what he wants, he'll only turn his anger on them. But I hold myself back, forcing myself to think clearly.

Jameson's coming.

It'll all be okay.

He'll make this all okay.

I pace in front of the door, my eyes catching on the window.

I could just climb out.

Escape.

Why didn't I think of that before now?

I rush over to the window, seeing Jameson and Billy running up the lawn. Just as I push it open, they disappear out of view.

"I know you fucking took 'em!" Carson continues to rant. He just keeps repeating the same thing over and over again, like he's completely losing it.

I stand still in the space between the door and the window, not knowing what to do.

Suddenly, Carson goes quiet. I move closer to the door, hearing shuffling on the other side.

Something hits the wall before Carson starts back up again, but this time he's not talking to me.

"Who do you think you are coming into my house?" he spits. "This is none of your fucking business."

Jameson. I sag forward. *He's talking to Jameson.*

"Baby." I hear his voice against the door. "Open up."

I shove the dresser aside, letting him in and slipping my gaze into the hall to find Billy standing over Carson's slumped body.

Jameson crowds me, pushing the door shut behind him, his hands coming to either side of my face. "You okay?"

I nod.

"What happened?"

"His pills ..." I answer. "He ... he thinks I took his pills. But I didn't. Jamie, I didn't take them."

"I know, baby. I believe you."

"He wanted me to help him look for them, and I tried, but he ..." I shake my head. "I don't know ... He ... he just lost it."

I don't mention the fact that he chased after me or the bruise that's surely forming on my knee. I can tell Jameson is barely holding it together as it is, and I just need to get out of here.

I need to get Cathleen and Jace out of here.

"My sister"—I swallow—"and the baby. They ... they should still be in the bathroom."

Jameson nods. "We'll get 'em out."

He steps back, grabbing my hand, watching me with a question in his eyes, asking if I'm ready to go out there.

I dip my chin, which is all he needs before he pulls open the door and moves into the hall.

Cathleen is standing in the bathroom doorway with Jace, who's wrapped in a towel, in her arms. He's quieted down, but he's still fussing, his face buried against her chest.

Her eyes catch mine for just a second before they shift to Carson. She inches back into the bathroom. I follow her gaze and see him pushing up onto his feet.

He flails his finger in front of him, pointing it in my direction. "This is all your fault." He shakes. "If you didn't take my fucking pills ..." He steps forward, and Billy moves with him. "Look at what you did to Jace." He raises a hand to his face. "And this. You called your fucking dogs and had me jumped. Just give them back! I know you—"

"She didn't take your goddam pills," Jameson mutters. "She isn't like you."

I drop my eyes to the floor, embarrassed by the situation. Embarrassed by my fucking life.

Carson laughs, pulling my attention back to him.

He locks gazes with Jameson, a cruel smile pulling at his lips as he motions to me. "Bet you'll be right at home with her, won't you? All you have to do to see her future is look at your mess of a mother?"

How does he ...?

Before I can begin to piece together how Carson even knows about Jameson's mother, he's slammed up against the wall, a knife pressed against his throat.

"You know nothing about her," Jameson grits out. "And nothing about my fucking mother."

I watch, wide-eyed, as he forces the switchblade against Carson's neck until he draws blood.

Carson's gaze is wild, his fists curled at his side, before he shifts, kneeing Jameson between the legs. I stagger forward when Jameson lets out a hiss, dropping the knife away from Carson's neck.

Billy throws himself into the fight, pulling Jameson out of the way and standing in his place. Carson swings at him, missing the first time but connecting with Billy's stomach on the second attempt. Billy wheezes out a strained breath, but the hit only seems to fuel him.

Jameson joins in, and they both start throwing hit after hit until Carson's legs give out and he drops to the ground.

I inch closer as Billy backs away, our eyes briefly meeting before we both turn back to Jameson.

He looks lost, his gaze hollow, vacant.

Carson has his arms curled around himself, but Jameson doesn't stop.

"Jamie!" I call out, but he just keeps going at him.

I try again, yelling his name, but it's like he can't hear me.

Carson groans beneath him, his body starting to unfurl.

"Jamie, stop!" I scream. "You're gonna kill him!"

Nothing.

Billy shoots me a look before stepping forward and dragging Jameson away. He fights at first, trying to shove Billy off of him.

"Jamie," I breathe, and his gaze finally meets mine. He goes lax in Billy's arms, the fight leaving him.

He blinks his eyes shut for a moment, and when they open, he's back. He looks me over, zeroing in on the bruise that's coloring my leg.

Anger flashes across his face, and he yanks free of Billy's hold, moving to crouch down beside Carson, staring at him in a way that makes my gut churn.

Pure fucking hatred.

I hold my breath as he leans in, his voice menacing. "If you ever pull something like this again," he growls, "I'll kill you."

Carson doesn't answer, doesn't move.

I'm not sure he could even if he wanted to.

His eyes are fixed on the ceiling as Jameson closes the space between them.

"Do you understand?"

It takes Carson a second, but he eventually nods.

I wrap my arms around myself as Jameson clicks his tongue, grabbing Carson's face. "Look at me when I'm talking to you," he demands, digging his fingers into the bruise that's already forming on Carson's cheek. "And answer me properly."

"I understand," Carson struggles.

Jameson lets go roughly, shoving his head back. "Don't make me regret walking away with you still breathing," he says, pushing up to stand. Then he comes right to me, taking my hand.

I stare up at him, opening my mouth to say something, though I'm not sure what.

"Get the baby dressed and meet us downstairs," he orders.

I turn, finding Cathleen standing behind us.

"Let's go," he says, squeezing my hand.

I follow him, Billy moving to stand behind me. And it hits me, just how safe I feel in the space between them.

The stairs creak beneath our feet as we move down them, stepping into the destroyed living room. I immediately look at my father, relieved when I see he's still knocked out, completely unaware of what just happened.

It briefly occurs to me how fucked up it is that I'm happy he was out of it for all of that. How sad it is that I'm not sure if I could have counted on him to protect me. He's never once stepped in when Carson's acted out against me. Would this time have been any different? What would Carson have to do, how far would he have to go, before my father would finally interfere?

"Baby?" I feel Jameson's arm come around my waist.

I shake my head, shifting my attention away from my father. "Huh?"

"You just completely zoned out."

I notice Billy watching me carefully.

Cathleen comes down the stairs with Jace on her hip, and I sag in relief at seeing them both fine.

She stops in front of me, wrapping an arm around me. "You okay?"

I relax against her. "Yeah. You?"

"Fine," she says, but her tone is hard, bitter.

She pulls away, looking past me. "Thank you," she offers. "I ... um ... well ... just thank you."

"Course," Jameson says simply. "What do you wanna do?" He glances between us, settling on my sister. "Is there somewhere you want us to take you? You can come to my house if—"

"We're okay," she answers, readjusting Jace. "He's sick and ..." She glances toward the stairs. "I can't just leave ..." She pauses like she's warring with herself. "I need to stay here."

Jameson raises a brow. "You sure?"

"Yeah, I'm sure."

"Cath—"

"He can barely stand. I'll be fine."

"I didn't take his pills," I blurt out, because it somehow feels important that she believes me. That I know she doesn't think this is all my fault.

I drag my nails against my palm as she watches me. She's not saying anything. *She doesn't believe me.*

"Cath," I whisper. "I didn't—"

"I know," she cuts in. "No, I know."

"He's gone too far this time. I don't know—"

"I'll deal with it," she interrupts again. "Just maybe …" She tilts her head toward the door. "Maybe just get out of here for a bit."

Jameson moves forward, his chest brushing against my back. "I've got her."

"Yeah," Cathleen says, "I know you do." She looks behind me, eyeing our father. "He'll probably be out for the night. Come back in the morning and—"

Jameson wraps an arm around me. "Come back? No, she's not—"

"I can't do this right now," I say quietly, silencing them both.

It feels like I'm crashing after what I just went through, the adrenaline quickly wearing off.

"All right," Jameson says, his voice low. "Let's just get you out of here, okay? We'll figure this all out later." His face darkens as he moves around the tipped-over coffee table, the room a clear depiction of what went on before he got here.

We drive back to his house in near silence, Jameson's hand on my thigh the whole way there, like he needs to touch me. Needs to know I'm okay.

We bypass his mother, who gives us all a questioning look from her place at the kitchen table, before settling in Jameson's room. I drop down on his bed, and Billy sits on the floor, his back against the wall, but Jameson stays standing, moving around restlessly.

"I didn't mean to scare you," he finally says, his eyes on the floor.

"You didn't."

He glances up at me. "You were screaming and I ..." He runs a hand through his hair. "I ..."

"You protected me."

"I just ..." He scrubs at his jaw. "When he said all that ..." He continues to pace. "I don't know what happened. I just ... I couldn't stop. And then, when I saw your knee ..."

"You would've," Billy says.

"I don't know ..." Jameson drops his eyes to my leg. "You told me he didn't hurt you."

"Because I'm fine."

"He's hurt you before, hasn't he?"

Billy's head jerks up at the question.

"And you haven't told me."

I play with the hem of my shirt. "Not really."

Jameson's jaw ticks. "*Not really?*"

"Just little things," I mutter. "It's not a big deal."

"What little things?" Billy asks, pushing to his feet.

I shake my head.

"You're not gonna tell us?" Jameson steps forward.

"You're both already on edge," I answer. "It's nothing, really."

Jameson juts his chin toward my knee. "How'd that happen?"

"Jamie …"

"I already gave him a beating for it. You might as well tell me."

"Yeah, and you nearly killed him." I look between the two of them. "You got the message across. He's not gonna try anything again."

Jameson shakes his head. "You don't know that."

"I'll tell you if something else happens, okay?"

They both stare back at me, neither of them looking satisfied with that answer.

"I promise," I add.

"I don't want you going back to that house."

"I can't just—"

"You can come stay with me."

"I don't know …"

He watches me carefully. "You don't have to be scared of them."

"That's not ..." I chew my bottom lip. "I'm not scared of them."

He sits down on the bed beside me. "You've got me now." He motions to Billy. "Both of us. We're not gonna let them get to you."

I know they'll protect me, but that's what I'm scared of. I saw how Jameson reacted to a fucking scrapped knee; what would he do if they really came after me? How far would he go? And what would happen to him if he crossed a line he couldn't come back from?

I paste what I hope looks like a reassuring smile on my face. "I'll think about it, okay?"

"Baby ..."

"I don't want to talk about this anymore," I say, my voice coming out harsher than I intended. I shift, twisting my ring. "Sorry ... I'm just ... I'm kind of done with today."

"Okay," he says, taking my hand. "We can be done with it for today."

I nod.

"But Sam?"

"Yeah."

"I meant what I said. He's never gonna hurt you again."

Chapter 49

Sam

"I should go in with you," Jameson mutters as we idle in front of my house.

"We both should," Billy adds.

"No." I shake my head. "That'll only ... I just need to see what I'm dealing with."

Jameson reaches for me. "Baby ..."

"Maybe it won't even be that bad. I mean, my dad's not oblivious to the way Carson's been acting." I let my eyes drift over to the front door. "He could side with me. He did after the fight at school." My voice sounds hopeful, almost desperate.

When I turn back to Jameson, he's watching me wearily. "I'll call you if anything happens, and you can come and get—"

"I'm not leaving," he cuts in.

"Jamie ..."

"I'll stay out here," he relents. "But I'm not leaving this driveway until you give me the okay."

"All right," I say softly, realizing arguing with him is futile. "Thank you," I add before looking over my shoulder at Billy. "Both of you."

"You know we've got you," he answers. "No matter what."

"I know," I breathe out. "This is just ... a lot."

Jameson brushes his thumb against the back of my hand, an unspoken promise. A reminder that he's got me. That I'm not a burden. That I can count on him.

I give him a tired smile, one that I hope will soften the look on his face. The fear he's holding for me. Then I start to pull away and reach for the door, but he grabs my wrist.

"Anything," he says. "And I mean anything, you call."

Nodding, I step out of the car and head up the driveway, each step closer to the house adding to my mounting anxiety.

When I reach the door, I turn back, finding both Billy and Jameson watching me.

You're gonna be okay, I chant in my head.

You're gonna be okay.

I push open the door.

You're gonna be okay.

"Look who finally decided to come home!" my father shouts, standing from the couch, his face twisted in fury.

I stumble back, glancing behind me at the door I've just closed.

I should leave.

This isn't—

"Stop standing in the fucking doorway and get in here."

Shaking my head, I take a step back.

"Do not test my patience right now, Samantha." He snaps his fingers, pointing at the place in front of him. "Now."

I move forward, taking in the room, searching for Cathleen, but the couch is empty.

My father's large form is blocking the recliner, but once I'm in front of him, he steps aside, throwing out a hand. "Take a good look."

I drag my gaze over Carson—his busted lip, his bruised face, the way his body's awkwardly angled on the chair.

"You did this," my father spits.

"I didn't—"

"Bringing an outsider into our house!" he yells. "Into our business!"

I motion to Carson. "He was chasing me! Threatening me." I turn to my father, my voice pleading. "You know what he's been like since—"

"Your brother has been through a lot. He's been in pain. You have no idea what it's been like for him. And what did you do?" he bites out. "You took his pills and then lied about—"

"I didn't take his fucking pills."

"You've got that boy"—his eyes darken—"that good-for-nothing criminal, wrapped around your little finger, don't you? Think you can go around doing whatever you want now and he'll come clean it up for you."

"What are you—"

"But that's done," he says. "I already have one whore for a daughter; I won't have another."

My head rears back. Who the fuck does he think he is?

"You can't say shit like that," I snap.

He steps forward. "Why not? It's true, isn't it? How else did you get him wrapped around your finger, huh?"

"I called him because I was scared, because I felt unsafe in my own fucking house!"

"Oh, come on," he scoffs. "Quit with the goddamn dramatics."

"Carson chased me up the stairs! *Chased* me, Dad."

He quickly flicks his eyes to Carson before returning them to me. "That wasn't something he should have ..." He rubs at the back of his neck. "He shouldn't have done that, but you put him in a position that made him act that way."

"Are you kidding me?"

"And then you went and ran to that scum—"

"Don't call him that."

"That boy's father already got Johnny killed."

I flinch, taking a step back.

"And still you're with him. Still you bring him into our house."

I glare at him. "Jameson's nothing like his father."

He laughs, the sound nearly pushing me over the edge. "Why don't you take a good fucking look, sweetheart," he chides, pointing at Carson. "That boy's exactly like his piece of shit father."

"He was protecting me," I counter. "God knows I needed *someone* to."

"What's that supposed to mean?"

"You were blacked out. Dead to the world. I needed someone to protect me from your precious golden boy," I sneer. "And I knew it wasn't gonna be you."

"Watch that fucking mouth of yours."

"Or what?"

He raises an eyebrow. "What? Are you tough now, is that it?"

My response dies on my lips as he steps forward. I grab my phone, but he rips it out of my hand, tossing it aside.

"You can't just—"

"I can't what, hmm? I've had enough of this attitude. I'm your father—you need to show me some goddamn respect."

"I don't need to show you shit," I tell him before I can think better of it.

His eyes flare, and I shuffle back, starting for the door, but I don't make it far before his large hand circles my wrist. I let out yelp as he throws me onto the couch. "Sit down."

Panic courses through me as I take in my position.

I'm trapped.

Alone.

"He'll come after me," I force out. "He's waiting outside."

"No, he won't."

"You don't know how he—"

My father bends down, handing me my phone. "Because you're gonna tell him you're fine, that this is a family matter."

I start to shake my head.

"He almost killed me," Carson says, drawing our father's attention.

The statement sets him back on his mission, and he nods. "You're done with that boy. I don't want you seeing him again."

"No." I lean forward. "No, you can't tell me to do that. I'm eighteen; you can't make me stop seeing him."

"I can when you live under my roof."

"Fine, then I'll leave."

"And where are you gonna go? To him? No fucking way."

"Why do you even care?"

"Because you're my daughter!" he bellows.

There's no love behind his words. It comes out as a statement. A claim of control. And it only fuels my rage.

He's given me nothing. Never cared for me. Never put my needs before his own. He's been a pathetic excuse for a father my whole fucking life.

"Oh, don't try to act like that's ever meant anything to you before," I scoff.

He closes the space between us, his eyes blazing, and my rage is quickly replaced with fear.

"You go to him, and I'll show up at his house and drag you back by your hair. I'm not scared of that little punk."

"Why are you doing this?" I ask, my voice cracking. "Why can't you just leave me alone?"

"Because"—he motions to Carson—"your actions have consequences, and this time, you really fucked up."

"I didn't do—"

"I don't want to hear it," he barks. "And if I ever see that boy of yours in my house again, you're not gonna like what happens. You can fucking trust me on that."

I'm not even sure what to say. I just stare back at him, wide-eyed.

He points to the phone in my hand. "Now you call him back and tell him you're fine. None of this crybaby drama shit. I don't need him storming in here from your fucking theatrics."

I move to stand when Carson says, "You got nothing to say to me."

I tilt my head. "What do you—"

"An apology."

"*An apology?*"

He looks over at our father, and I trace his gaze, finding him watching me expectantly.

I swallow down my rage, my fucking fury. But I'm stuck, literally and metaphorically backed into a corner.

"Samantha?" my father presses.

"I'm sorry," I force out.

"Doesn't sound like it," Carson shoots back.

I grit my teeth, meeting his eyes. "I'm sorry, Carson," I tell him, my voice barely sounding like my own.

He nods, and our father backs up, finally giving me room to stand.

"School, work, and community service, that's it for you. You hear me?"

"Yeah," I answer, feeling myself shrink as he looms over me. "I hear you."

"I catch you sneaking out to see him and you're done."

I don't know what me being *done* means, but I don't want to find out.

Before I can answer, my phone rings, and my father tips his chin, telling me to answer it. "Don't do anything stupid," he mutters.

"Hello," I breathe, careful to keep my tone neutral, but it doesn't fool Jameson.

"What's taking so long?" he asks. "You all right?"

"I'm fine," I tell him, my eyes meeting my father's. "We're just talking."

"You don't sound fine. Are you being watched or something? You sound weird."

"Everything's good," I press, but again, he doesn't buy it.

"I'm coming in."

My father keeps his gaze pinned on me, a silent threat.

"No, no. Seriously, Jamie, I'm fine."

"Sam."

"I'll call you later, okay?"

Please just hang up.

"Are you bullshitting me? You've gotta tell me, baby, if you are."

"No," I answer, "I'm not."

He's quiet for a minute before he blows out a breath. "You'll call me if anything changes?"

"Yeah."

"All right," he gives in, and before he can push for more, I hang up.

My father steps out of my path, giving me permission to leave. "I'm doing this for your own good," he says as I move for the stairs. "Things have gone too far. He's no good for you."

I don't know how to tell him that Jameson is the *only* good thing for me. That he's sometimes the only reason I get up in the morning. The only good part of my day.

So, I say nothing and walk up the stairs I was dragged down just yesterday.

Into the room I had to lock myself in.

And I break.

Wondering how much longer it'll be until there are no more pieces of me left to put back together.

Chapter 50

Jameson

"Jameson!" my mother hollers from the kitchen. "Have you seen my keys? I thought they were—"

"Here," I say, holding them out for her as she breezes into the living room. "You left 'em on the coffee table."

Her shoulders drop as she takes them from me. "Thanks," she murmurs, brushing her hand across my arm. "What would I do without you?"

When I don't respond, her face falls before she quickly forces a smile.

She's been trying lately—I'll give her that—but things are still strained between us. It's almost harder for me when she's doing well than it is when she's spiraling. At least then I know what to expect. When she's like this, I'm just waiting for the rug to be pulled out from under me.

Each time I try to grip onto hope, I hate myself for being so naïve.

"You gonna be home for dinner?" she asks.

I shrug. "Not sure yet."

"Are you, um ...?" She swallows, tucking a strand of hair behind her ear nervously. "Are you doin' okay?"

I'm not sure how to even respond to that, so I don't. Instead, I say, "You're gonna be late for work."

She watches me for a moment, her mouth opening as if to say something before she thinks better of it and nods, turning for the door. It slams shut behind her, the sound rattling through the house.

My mind starts to spin about how I handled that, if I was too harsh, too cold. If I should have just thrown her a fucking line.

She's trying, I remind myself.

But then I remember how many times she's tried before.

How many chances do you give someone before you become the idiot who keeps handing them out?

I push the thoughts of my mother away, bringing my focus back to Sam and the shit we just went through.

It took everything in me to drop her off at that house this morning, to leave her with her father and Carson.

On the phone, I knew she wasn't telling me the full story, and I've been waiting ever since for her to call me back.

I just got home about fifteen minutes ago, but with each minute that passes, I'm only becoming more worried.

I shouldn't have left.

Pacing throughout the living room, I grip my phone, waiting for it to ring.

"Fuck it," I mutter to myself after another five minutes passes then dial her number.

I let out a breath when she picks up on the second ring, but the tension I just let go of quickly comes back when I hear her voice break. "Hey," she croaks.

"Are you crying?"

She clears her throat. "No."

"Baby," I press, "why are you crying? What happened? Do I need to—"

"Stop," she cuts me off. "You've gotta stop."

I still. "Stop? What do you mean, *stop*?"

"We need to be careful," she says.

I start pacing again. "You're not making any sense."

"He's mad," she whispers. "*Really* fucking mad."

"Your old man?"

"Yeah," she answers so quietly I barely hear her.

"He made you cry?" I grit out, my anger barely restrained.

"He'll cool down," she reasons, but the words come out shaky. "But, for now, we need to be careful, like I said."

"What do you mean, *careful*?"

"He … uh …" She hesitates, and it pushes past my limit, past the restraint I was trying to hold on to.

"What?" I spit. "He what?"

"He doesn't want me to see you anymore," she says in a rush. "But—"

I stop in place, going rigid. "That's not happening."

"I know," she says. "Obviously."

The fear that's gripping me eases a bit.

"You can't come by, and I'll have to give excuses when I leave. It shouldn't be hard to tell him that I'm doing community service or working. It's not like he'll check, and he'll forget about this soon," she says like she's trying to convince herself. "People in town talk, but Carson's not really friends with any of the people we hang out with, and my dad barely talks to anybody, so we should be fine," she rambles on. "And you'll have to—"

"Baby," I cut in. "Breathe. All right? Just breathe."

She sucks in a breath, but it doesn't do much to calm her. I hear a lighter spark as she says, "I just feel like my life is a fucking cage, y-you know," she stutters. "Like I'm always being watched, and I'll never get out. Never be free of this bullshit."

"You will," I tell her, my voice firm. "This isn't gonna be forever."

I won't let it be.

"I don't know how it's ever gonna change."

"You're eighteen—you can leave."

She lets out a sad laugh like the idea is ridiculous, a delusion. "You know it's not that easy."

"Why not? I told you that you can come stay with me."

"I don't want them coming after me," she pushes out. "You didn't hear him today, Jamie. He's … I can't …"

I should have been in that fucking room with her.

I shouldn't have let her convince me to drive away.

"I wouldn't let them get to you," I say, the words coming out as a threat.

"It's not me I'm worried about," she responds.

"They can't do shit to me."

"Yeah," she says, "but *you* can do shit to them."

"Baby, I—"

"We just need to lay low for a bit—that's all," she cuts in. "It's just like Carson's DUI. My dad lost it, and he's fine now. Acts like he walks on water again."

I run a hand through my hair. "I don't know."

"The one benefit of him not actually giving a shit about me is that he doesn't care," she says simply, as if that's not fucking heartbreaking. "Not really. He just has to feel like he's in control."

"So, what? We're just supposed to wait out his tantrum?"

She exhales. "Pretty much."

"I don't like this idea," I mutter. "I don't like you in that house."

"It's the best option," she reasons.

"Are you—"

"I don't want to make things worse," she interrupts.

As much as I hate it, what she's saying makes sense. At least for now, given the options. Or the fucking *lack* of options.

But still, I don't like it. I don't want her there where I can't protect her.

"Jamie?" she whispers.

"If this is what we do," I respond, "you've gotta make me a promise."

"Okay," she offers hesitantly.

"From now on, if someone hurts you, makes you feel uncomfortable, scared, you tell me."

"Jamie, I—"

"I know you've kept some of it from me. That you say you've got a handle on it." I let out a breath. "But, baby, I'm gonna go out of my fucking mind wondering if you're okay if I think you won't tell me when something's wrong."

She's quiet.

"Can you do that?"

I need her to say yes.

I need her to promise.

"Yeah," she finally says. "Yeah, I can do that." Clearing her throat, she adds, "You've gotta make me a promise, too, then."

"What is it?" I ask, not liking the idea of promising anything around this.

"Unless you really need to"—she pauses—"unless things are really bad, I need you to stay away from my house."

"Sam ..."

"I mean it. And I need you to make sure I don't fuck this all up, that I don't get myself into more trouble."

"What do you mean?"

"My drinking," she explains. "If I'm not ... If I can't think straight ... I need you to tell me no if I want to go back to your house or if I want you to come to mine. I just can't risk ..."

"I've got it," I tell her. "I won't come in, and I won't let you stay the night at my house."

"Thank you," she breathes.

"Unless I have to," I clarify. "I'm not risking you getting hurt."

"Okay," she murmurs, although she doesn't sound okay.

I drop down on the couch as silence settles between us, minutes passing before she finally speaks.

"Do you think it'll ever not be like this?"

"Like what?"

She sighs. "So fucking hard all the time. It just feels like it's one thing after another. Like we can't ever catch a break."

"I don't know," I answer honestly. "Sometimes, it doesn't feel like it."

"It scares me," she confesses. "That this life will destroy me, eat at me until there's nothing left."

"That's not gonna happen."

A lighter sparks again. "How do you know?"

"'Cause you've got me. You've got Billy. And there's no way either of us would let you lose yourself like that."

"You never know what'll happen, though."

"Doesn't matter," I say. "'Cause for there to be nothing left of you, there'd have to be nothing left of me."

"Jamie ..."

"And trust me, baby; I'd give you fucking everything."

She sucks in a breath.

"And you'd give me everything, too, wouldn't you?"

"Yes," she whispers.

"So that's how I know," I tell her. "Why I'm not scared. Because life can't leave us with nothing when we're both willing to give each other everything."

Chapter 51

Sam

"Don't forget, I start at the food bank today," I say as we pull into the parking lot of the diner.

The project at the park wrapped up a couple of days ago, so I'm finishing the last few weeks of my community service at the local food bank.

"I know," Jameson answers, turning to face me. "I'll be there to pick you up."

"Thanks," I murmur, leaning in to kiss him.

We've been sneaking around the last few weeks, trying our best to avoid my father and Carson. Whenever Jameson picks me up, he parks down the street and if we go out, I tell my father I'm working late.

Him and Carson seem to be losing interest in keeping tabs on me, but we're still careful.

Jameson threads his fingers through my hair, pulling me in closer.

"I'm gonna be late. I'm supposed to help open."

"So be late."

"You know I can't ..."

He lets out a low groan, nipping at my bottom lip, before reluctantly pulling back. "I hate leaving you."

"You'll see me tonight."

He shakes his head. "Too far away."

"Well, you'll just have to wait," I tell him, biting back a smile. "You're gonna get me fired."

"Oh, come on; they'd never fire you. And you know it'll only be Patsy this early in the morning."

"You're a bad influence."

He nods, grabbing my thighs and yanking me toward him. "The worst."

I squeal, a laugh pouring out of me, but it's quickly silenced when his lips crash against mine. He grips my hips, pulling me to straddle him.

I quickly gaze around the parking lot, but it's empty since we don't open for another hour. The sun hasn't fully risen yet, the sky barely even light.

The skirt of my uniform is bunched up, leaving my thighs bare, and I shiver as Jameson brushes his knuckles up and down my skin.

His kisses turn more languid as he wraps his arms around my middle, anchoring me to him.

I pull away, our eyes briefly meeting, before I drop my forehead to his chest.

"I never thought I'd want to be around someone as much as I want to be around you," he says softly. "But whenever you're away from me, it's like …" He brushes his lips against my hair. "I don't know … I just … I fucking hate it."

I breathe him in, burrowing deeper against his chest. "I feel the same way."

"It's like I'm a fucking addict," he muses. "Don't even want you to go to work."

I lean away from him, my back hitting the steering wheel. "I'll see you tonight, though," I tell him, and his eyes heat at the promise in my voice. "We're still going to Dougie's party, right?"

He nods.

"Well, then you should be able to get your fill of me there."

His grip on my hips tightens, and I grab his hands, sliding them away from me before I start to move back into my seat.

"But I've really gotta get to work now."

"Fine," he sighs.

I grab my purse and reach for the door.

"What time am I picking you up?"

"Don't know," I answer, looking back at him. "I'll text you."

The door clicks shut behind me, and I hear him call out my name. Turning, I duck down into the open window.

He grabs my chin, pulling me into a kiss. "Love you, baby."

"Love you," I answer before breaking the kiss and rushing toward the diner.

I push in through the side entrance, the familiar smell of fry oil hitting me as I walk in.

"You're late," Patsy says when I step into the kitchen.

"Sorry," I respond, not offering any explanation.

"I can't keep letting this slide," she continues.

I nod, even though I know she's all talk. As the owner, she acts like she runs a tight ship when, really, she lets just about anything go. I don't even know how many times we've had the *I can't keep letting this slide* talk, yet I'm still here.

"Won't happen again," I offer for good measure.

"All right," she says, turning back to the fruit she's prepping. "Well, get to it."

I spend the next forty-five minutes racing around the space, making up for the time I missed. When I flip the sign on the front door to "*open*," I'm already ready for the shift to be over.

LOYALTY

We've been slammed all morning, the Saturday rush keeping us busy. It's just me and another waitress, Maria, so we've been scrambling to keep up with tables.

I'm refilling coffees when the door chimes and a group of kids my age walks in. They glance around the space like they've never stepped foot in a diner before.

When they seat themselves in one of Maria's booths, I'm grateful they aren't one of my tables. I'm not in the mood to deal with a bunch of snobby rich kids right now. Although, I might have gotten a good tip out of it.

I move over to a couple of my regulars—two older men who come in every morning and order the same thing. I give them a small smile as I fill up their cups, their conversation quieting as I do.

In the short lull, I hear a whistle come from one of the rich kids, followed by, "Damn, she's hot."

I keep my eyes fixed on the task in front of me, not wanting to catch his attention. He might not even be talking about me.

I turn to start for the kitchen when one of the girls at his table says, "If you want to slum it."

Assholes.

The door chimes again, and a worn-looking man walks through, settling into one of my booths at the back.

Quickly, I drop off an order before starting for his table, pasting a smile on my face. "I'm Sam, and I'll be your server. Can I get you started with something to drink?"

He looks up from the menu, his weathered face twisting with surprise, and I watch as his entire demeanor shifts. The hunched posture I walked up to disappears as he rolls his shoulders back and straightens.

"Well, hello. Aren't you a pretty little thing?"

Great. I hold back a sigh. *One of these guys.*

"Can I get you something to drink?" I repeat, attempting to keep my voice light.

"Coffee. Get me some cream and sugar, too," he answers before he winks—fucking *winks*—and adds, "I bet you know how to give some good sugar, don't you?"

My skin crawls from his words, itching to snap back at him. But he isn't worth it and, anyway, that never seems to work. Instead, I drop my eyes and head back to the kitchen, determined to ignore him.

A few minutes later, I bring him his coffee, walking past the booth of rich kids, and notice one of the blonde girls who's with them eyeing me curiously. Her friends are talking around her about prom, but she's tuned out, distracted. Somehow, she looks completely out of place sitting with them.

I reach the asshole's table, set down his coffee, then ask for his order, trying to keep the interaction as short as possible. I just want to get him his food and get him out of here.

He drops his menu in front of him instead of handing it to me, and as I reach forward to grab it, I feel his rough fingers move up my leg and under my skirt.

My heart starts to race as I step to the side and slap his hand away. "Don't even think about it."

"Oh, come on," he says. "I saw how you shook that ass when you walked away. You were practically beggin' me to watch."

I scoff. "Yeah, not a chance."

He narrows his eyes.

I reach for the menu again, desperately wanting to get away from him. But before I can grab it, he snatches my wrist, and I freeze, panic coursing through me.

"Why don't you watch that tone of yours, huh? You sound like a bitch."

I pull my hand back. "Then you clearly don't know what I sound like when I'm being a bitch. Don't fucking touch me again, or you won't like what happens."

He laughs, and the sound only puts me more on edge. "You've got a mouth on you, don't you? I kind of like that. Makes me want to find out what else you can do with it."

His words hit me like a blow, and I stare back at him like the fucking lowlife he is before walking away without a response.

I don't know what to do.

What to feel.

I'm angry, I know that. Really fucking angry that men like him think they can talk to me like that. That they think the way I look gives them some sort of right.

But there's also a feeling of shame, of embarrassment. I know none of this is my fault, but words like his have followed me around ever since I can remember. The continual accusations of stealing other girls' boyfriends, being called a slut, the crude things boys say to me.

My breathing begins to quicken the farther I get from the table, my mind starting to spiral. I pass by the kitchen, ducking my head in.

Patsy looks up, her gaze finding mine. "You all right?"

I nod, biting my lip.

"You sure?"

"I just ... uh ... I need a quick break. I'm gonna step outside for a minute; is that all right?"

She watches me carefully. "Sure, honey, go ahead."

I mutter a thanks before pushing out the back door, bending forward and gulping in unsteady breaths.

It's not that big of a deal, I tell myself. *You're overreacting.*

But the panic won't stop. The voices in my head won't stop screaming at me to listen.

I pull my phone from my back pocket and dial Jameson's number.

He doesn't pick up, and I mumble a curse, trying again. On the final ring, the call goes through.

"You all right?" he asks, out of breath.

"Were you in the middle of something?"

"Doesn't matter," he says. "Why are you calling?"

"I'm just …"

"Baby?"

"There was this guy and …" I swallow back the panic in my voice.

"What guy?"

"A customer."

A heavy door slams before he says, "He do somethin' to you?" When I don't respond, he pushes, "You promised."

"He said some things …"

"*Some things*? What things?" he forces out, his voice dangerously low.

"It doesn't matter."

"Oh, it fucking matters."

"He … um … he said he wanted cream and sugar and that he bet I gave good sugar … and then my mouth …"

"*Your mouth*?" he asks slowly. "What'd he say about your mouth?"

"I snapped back at him—"

"Good," Jameon cuts in.

"And then he said I have a mouth on me and he liked that." I clear my throat. "That it made him want to find out what else I could do with it."

"I'll be there in ten minutes."

"Jamie …"

"Is that everything?"

"What?"

"Is that all he did? All he said?"

I debate not telling him, worried about how he'll react. But I promised I'd tell him if anyone hurt me.

"You can't freak out."

"What'd he do?"

I hear the car engine start.

"Baby," he pushes. "Someone fucked with you, so I'm gonna fuck with them. Now tell me."

"He ... he tried to put his hand up my skirt."

"I'm gonna kill him."

"No. No, Jamie, you can't kill him."

"He *touched* you. Put his hand up—"

"I know," I snap. "Fuck, I know, but you can't—"

"Then I'm gonna beat the shit out of him."

This isn't the first time Jameson has stopped by the diner because of an incident like this, but it's never been this bad. Nobody has ever gone this far. Said things yes, but never touched me.

"That's the least he deserves," Jameson adds.

I don't respond.

Seconds pass before he asks, "Are you okay?"

"I'll be fine," I breathe. "But I should get back inside. I just kinda ran out on my shift."

"You can wait till I get there."

"No, I'm ... I'm okay."

"Shit like this shouldn't happen," he mutters.

"Yeah," I answer. "But it does."

I hear the door crash open, and then Jameson's deep voice.

"Where is she?"

Setting down the plate in my hand, I round the corner, and the instant he sees me, he's moving toward me.

"Which one?"

I point. "The guy in the back booth, sitting—"

Before I can even finish, he's striding over to the man, stopping in front of his table.

I stay where I am, watching as Jameson grabs the guy by the back of neck and slams his head against the table. Then he motions me over, not letting up on his hold, and demands that the man apologize.

I can't help but feel satisfied when his eyes meet mine and I see they're blown wide with shock.

Yeah, fucker, how do you like that?

Jameson slams the man's head against the table again when he hesitates to apologize.

Finally, after some coaxing, the guy finally spits out, "I'm sorry, okay?"

"What are you sorry for?" Jameson sneers, his tone making it clear that he's not gonna let this guy off easy.

But the man's too stupid to hear it.

Too self-assured.

"What?" the guy asks.

"What. Are. You. Sorry. For," Jameson repeats slowly, his words full of condescension.

"You've got to be kidding me."

Jameson leans in. "Do I look like I'm fucking kidding?"

"I don't know what you want me to say, man."

I see Patsy rush into the room just as Jameson starts to pick up the guy's head again. She briefly moves her gaze to me before she hollers at Jameson to stop.

He lets go of the guy's head, and the man scrambles back into the booth as Jameson reasons with Patsy, telling her what he did to me.

She looks over the man, who's running his hand across his head, checking for damage.

"You've clearly handled it," she tells Jameson. "People are trying to eat here."

I glance around the room and notice everyone with their heads down, purposely minding their own business. Nobody here likes to put their nose where it doesn't belong, and this is clearly a personal issue.

"Yeah, all right," Jameson tells her. "I'll leave when he does."

"I'm not leaving," the man says. "My food hasn't come yet."

I pull my head back. This guy is an even bigger idiot than I thought. Why wouldn't you just leave when you have the chance?

As expected, that answer doesn't go over well with Jameson, and they get into it again, their words quickly escalating into a fist fight.

The man doesn't get a hit in, but Jameson does. He cracks him right across the face before he grabs the man by his hair and says something into his ear too low for me to hear.

The next thing I know, the man is being shoved in front of me, his eyes glued to the floor, the fight completely beaten out of him.

"I'm—"

"Look her in the eye when you're talking to her," Jameson interrupts him.

He corrects himself immediately, meeting my gaze. "I'm sorry for how I talked to you."

Jameson closes the space between them.

"And that I ... that I touched you like that."

I nod, and the man darts his eyes to Jameson before moving toward the door.

Before he can get far, Jameson calls out, "Where are you going?"

The man turns. "W-what? You told me to leave."

"You didn't leave a tip."

I stare back at Jameson, raising an eyebrow, and he smirks.

"A tip?" the man asks. "I didn't even get my food."

"And whose fault is that?" Jameson bites back, motioning to me. "It sure as shit isn't hers."

The man deflates, his shoulders sagging, but he walks back to the table and sets down a five-dollar bill.

"Since you enjoyed the service so much," Jameson mutters, "I think she deserves a little more than that, don't you?"

I stand by and watch as he squeezes another thirty-five dollars out of the man before he barks, "Good. Now get out of my fucking sight."

The man scrambles away, heading for the door.

The second he's gone, Jameson moves for me. "You okay?"

"I'm fine," I tell him.

He stares down at me for a moment before he looks over his shoulder at Patsy and says, "She's taking her break."

Patsy doesn't argue, even though I technically just took one. My shift is about to end, anyway.

Jameson grabs my hand, leading me to the door.

We pass by the table of rich kids, and I notice the blonde girl watching me again, the look on her face catching me off guard.

She looks angry. Pissed, even.

I briefly wonder if it's me who she's angry for, but I shake the thought away, focusing on keeping up with Jameson's quick pace.

He pulls me around the corner, finally slowing when we're tucked away in the alley next to the diner.

I take him in as he shifts restlessly in front of me, his body teeming with energy. My eyes drop to our interlocked hands, noticing his cracked knuckles.

"I feel like all you're ever doing is saving me," I whisper.

He blinks, his gaze softening, his breathing beginning to slow.

"It feels like, lately, it's been …"

"What?" he asks, his voice a low rasp.

I shrug. "A lot." I drop my eyes. "Too much."

He tips my chin up. "It's not."

"You say that, but …"

"Even if it's a lot," he tells me, "it's never too much."

I shake my head.

"I'd give you everything, remember?"

"I just feel bad that I …"

He takes my hand, sliding it up the side of his body, over where the tattoo he got for us lies.

Always Love You More

It's a silent reassurance. A promise forever marked in ink.

"None of this shit matters," he breathes. "The drama. Your family. Fuck, even the stuff I deal with. 'Cause we love each other more."

I stare up at him.

"You said that. It took a long time, but"—he leans in—"you finally made me believe it."

I feel a tear fall down my face, and he lightly brushes it away.

"We're more than this shit. More than the fucked-up lives we were born into. You and me"—he motions between us—"we're more."

I pull my bottom lip between my teeth, fighting back the emotion lodged in my throat. "We're more," I whisper, telling myself that the words are true.

Making myself believe them.

He closes the distance between us, bringing his lips to mine. The kiss is soft, slow, a reminder of what I already know.

That nothing can be too much when we love each other more.

THANK YOU FOR READING!

Want more? Read *A Yes or No Question*, which picks up right where this story leaves off. See what happens to Sam and Jameson next and watch Billy's romance unfold.

If you enjoyed the book, please consider leaving a review. They're like gold, especially to indie authors. Your review can help other readers find the book and, hopefully, connect to these characters.

Acknowledgements

I can't believe I'm at the point again where I'm writing another acknowledgements page!

This book was never intended to be written, but when writing *A Yes or No Question*, I grew to love these characters so much that I knew I had to share their story.

I've lived with a version of these characters and their stories for over a decade. I remember, at this point nearly fifteen years ago, in my childhood bedroom, tacking up pictures on a corkboard as inspiration for *A Yes or No Question*. Back then, knowing that these books would one day be on shelves and people would actually be reading them would have blown my mind.

I want to first thank these characters, Susan, Billy, Sam, and Jameson, for truly changing my life. They made me an author. They allowed me to find a community of writers who have brought me incredible joy and creative inspiration. But, most of all, they've been the catalyst to finding a passion that lights me up every day. I can't wait to continue sharing stories and meeting new characters. But I know that these four will always hold a special place in my heart for all they've given me.

To my mom, thank you for your unwavering support through all of this. I can't express how much it means to me to have someone like you cheering so loudly in my corner. And thank you for all the phone calls discussing plotlines, for being my first and last reader, and for loving these characters as much as I do.

To Auntie Donna, thank you again for beta reading, for your sharp eyes and your continual support. I'm so grateful!

To Tasha, thank you for being the best friend anyone could ask for and standing by my side for over twenty years. I'm honored that the only book you finished last year was mine.

To Dave & Ashely, thank you for being a constant show of support and joy in my life.

To Jess & Julia, thank you both for being the funniest beta readers out there! Not only did you help me shape this story into its best version, but you also made me laugh out loud with your comments and reactions. I'm so lucky to not only have found great betas, but friends like you.

To SWAG, thank you all for welcoming me into your writing group. It has been so great to find a community like ours to help keep me accountable and inspired. I look forward to our meetings every month.

To Kate, thank you again for illustrating another beautiful cover. Your art helped bring the story to life.

To Angelee, thank you once again for designing such a gorgeous cover. I'm absolutely obsessed!

To Kristin, thank you for your wonderful edits. All of your tweaks and suggestions helped this book be the best it can be.

And finally, thank you to my readers! You have all blown me away with your love and support. I can't express how happy it makes me to see you connecting with these characters. I'm so excited to continue sharing stories with you!

Until next time,
Lauren

ALSO BY LAUREN MONICA

A Yes or No Question
What I Would Have Told You – A Poetry Collection

About the Author

Lauren Monica is an author and poet who lives in Austin, Texas. When not writing or getting lost in her ever-growing TBR, she loves to spend time with family, cuddle her two kitties, cheer on the Texas Longhorns (Hook 'Em), and go to concerts.

Website: laurenmonicawrites.com
Instagram: @laurenmonicawrites
TikTok: @laurenmonicawrites

www.ingramcontent.com/pod-product-compliance
Lightning Source LLC
LaVergne TN
LVHW091651070526
838199LV00050B/2147